Twenty Years After
Pink I

By S. N. Maan

Epilogue

It is a truth universally acknowledged that everybody in the world is made from stardust. Well, it might not quite be universally acknowledged, but it is a truth. And it is one that is acknowledged by the Universe, if not quite everybody in it. It is widely accepted that the Universe started because of a Big Bang. The story goes that, once upon a time, the entirety of space was compacted into an infinitely small space. Some might argue that it couldn't have been 'once upon a time', as time only started to exist after the Big Bang and is intertwined with the very fabric of the Universe. You could say 'Once upon no time', and there is a case for saying 'Once upon all time' if you wanted to be more accurate, but, to be honest, that isn't a very nice way to start a story. Most people telling the story of the origin of the Universe are willing to sacrifice a little bit of accuracy for the sake of style.

Once upon a time, everything that exists now, has ever existed, or will ever exist was compressed into a small ball of infinitely hot energy in an infinitely small space with infinite density. As soon as no time at all had passed, the dimensionless point of energy rapidly inflated. Some of this energy turned into particles – quarks, electrons, muons and neutrinos – which would later be used to build the Universe. Some of the energy turned into anti-particles – antiquarks, positrons, antimuons and antineutrinos. One would be forgiven for thinking of these particles and anti-particles as being distinct from the fabric of the Universe. Clearly they were something separate. But they also were not. They were created from the energy of the Universe and therefore were one and the same. Even in this incredibly early stage of the Universe, the very few things in existence were drawn to something bigger. Most of the particles found their anti-particles and, as if by magic, together they annihilated into pure energy. They merged again with the

5

rest of the Universe as if, together, they became a single drop of rain rejoining the ocean from which they had evaporated.

As chance, or fate, would have it, the Universe created more particles than anti-particles. This meant that, after all the annihilation occurred, there were still some particles left over. Everything that is a part of the Universe has a natural tendency to join with something similar and, together, form something greater than the sum of its parts. Quarks very quickly joined together to form protons and neutrons. The protons and neutrons began to join with each other in different combinations, forming basic nuclei. Barely a minute had passed since the beginning of the Universe and, already, particles that could not rejoin the Ocean were joining together to form the nuclei that would build the physical Universe that we inhabit today.

Unfortunately, nothing of overwhelming interest happened for the next million years or so. A lot of the particles had resigned themselves to the fact that they would remain in this form for the foreseeable future, and so continued to combine to form atoms. They could do nothing but float about, slowly drifting apart in the abyss. However, after the first million years passed, something a little bit more exciting happened. As fate, or chance, would have it, hydrogen atoms in the very centre of the Universe were drawn to each other. Like I said, everything that is a part of the Universe has a natural tendency to join with something similar. As they were drawn closer and closer to each other, they got faster and faster. No longer were they to float around without meaning, but they were to fuse together. They got closer, and faster, and closer, and faster. All of a sudden, there was an almighty burst of light. The very first star came into existence. The very first starlight emanated outwards into the abyss.

Within the core of this very special star, hydrogen atoms were joining together to form larger and larger elements. Every time any two atoms join together, they send out a tiny little signal that can be detected by anybody lucky enough to be paying attention. The Universe knew that something special was happening at its core. Billions of tiny little signals were being sent out to all its corners as these tiny, seemingly insignificant, particles were joining together to form things greater than the sum of their parts. Nitrogen and oxygen were formed, some of which is in the Earth's atmosphere right now. Carbon and other heavier elements were formed. As the products formed were getting larger and larger, the Universe could feel more and more strongly that this was the dawn of a new age. Throughout the Universe, billions upon billions of stars started to do the exact same thing, each with their own story, unfortunately none of which fall into the remit of this one.

The first star continued in this manner for a mere one million years. Once it had sent out all the light it had to send, it burst. All of the matter that it had formed within it was sent hurtling out into the Universe. Just as significantly, or perhaps more so, the energy that dwelled within the star was torn into fragments and thrown in all directions. Had you been watching carefully, you might have seen it. Clouds of light in all different colours were thrown every which way. One with a slightly reddish hue hurtled in the opposite direction to one that seemed somehow to be a combination of blue and gold. One with a colour that human eyes cannot detect was thrown in the exact opposite direction to one that was the richest shade of pink you would ever see (which was curious, considering that pink exists solely within our own minds). A cloud that somehow managed to be a combination of purple and silver and green all at the same time was thrown violently from the centre of the explosion, spinning so frenetically that it seemed that only sheer willpower prevented it from tearing into two pieces itself. This was the largest, most violent, explosion that the Universe will ever know. Each of these pieces of matter and clouds of energy spread out into the Universe ready to begin their own separate stories, leaving behind a tiny, empty space in the middle of the Universe.

It is a truth Universally acknowledged that you are made from stardust. Every piece of matter inside your body was formed in the very heart of a star. However, you are still much more than this. Within every living being resides a piece of energy torn from the fabric of the Universe, bringing life to it. The energy knows that it is nothing but a drop of rain to a vast Ocean.

That is the story of how you are made from stardust and how you are more intertwined with the fabric of the Universe than you could possibly imagine. Not only are you made from the Universe, but the Universe resides within you.

Chapter 1 - Laith

It was a mild night in April as Laith sat outside in the field that his family had been tending to for the past four years. There was a small clearing by the well that they had dug and built when they arrived, and a small shelter that they had built out of wood with a simple tin roof – the type that would amplify the sound of mild rain into a thunderous cacophony that never failed to comfort Laith. Tonight, however, Laith sat in the open air and the silence of the night and watched the wheat, illuminated only by the strange yellow light of the Moon, flutter gently in occasional gusts of light wind. It was as though even the wind did not wish to ruin such a temperate evening, but felt an obligation to blow by virtue of its nature and so did so half-heartedly. Laith felt the light wind blow his shoulder-length dark hair across his face, where it would get caught in his thick beard. After releasing it for the third time, he decided to tie it up. He knew that he wanted to stay out in the field for a while longer, where he could be alone with his thoughts, and so he made himself comfortable.

Laith liked to sit outside in his deckchair when he was feeling particularly pensive, as he was this evening. He knew that tomorrow was a significant day, and it had been playing on his mind for the last few days despite his concerted efforts to ignore it. He would have to be up early tomorrow for the harvest festival, which he was grateful for – the community spirit and the sounds of the drums and children playing were always a welcome source of happiness for him. However, this particular celebration would be tinged with sadness – it would be the twentieth anniversary of the fateful day that tore his family, as well as the community, apart. He was only three years old when the Massacre occurred. His father had managed to save him and his sister, who was only a baby at the time. His mother had not been so lucky.

Laith's father had never left him nor his sister wanting for anything. The community had always been a close-knit one, according to his father, and became even more so since the Massacre. Aunts and uncles became second mothers and fathers. Relationships between adults and their friends' children strengthened as everybody rallied around to help each other. With nearly two thousand members of the community having been murdered in cold-blood, this became necessary to survive. Laith's father always made it a point of emphasis to him and his sister growing up how much their aunt loved and cared for them, and how lucky they all were to have such a close community where every single person cared for every other. Laith knew that his father was well respected in the community and, although he took the responsibility to act as a father figure to many other children who had lost their own, he always made it known to them that Laith and his sister were his priority. Laith knew that, in this respect, he was lucky. But it never quite stopped the feeling that something was missing. Whenever it came to the forefront of his mind, he would tell himself that it must be the feeling of growing up without a mother. However, a part of him suspected that it was something more than this.

As he looked up at the Moon, his thoughts turned to the events that happened nearly twenty years ago to this day. Whenever he looked up at the Moon in the type of mood he was in tonight, he would think about how this was the same Moon that his mother used to look at. It had been a constant for thousands of millions of years, and must have been the same source of awe and wonder to millions before him. As he looked past the Moon and deeper into the stars, he felt his wistful feeling of wonder deepen. Some of these stars might have been around since the beginning of time. Some of the stars he was looking at might have already died, but their magic was still being gladly received by the wheat in the field in which he was sitting.

He was too young to remember the night of the Massacre in very much detail but, during some of the nights that he would think about it, some of the details would come back to him in a blur. He could remember his father giving him a glass of sugarcane juice as he was standing and talking with the man who was pressing it out of the freshly harvested sugarcanes. It was traditional that everybody would have a glass of this during the Pink Moon Harvest celebrations. He didn't know this at the time, but he did remember holding the cup of sugarcane juice in both hands and sipping it. As far as he could remember, this was the first time that he had ever tried it. He could not remember now whether his father had built it up to him as something special before he gave it to him, or if he got that impression from the way he smiled as he gave it to him, or even if he had just made that up in retrospect, but he did know that, when he took the first sip, he had thought it was the most wonderful drink ever. Over time, the quality of the raas had diminished, but this was due to the problems with the land that had been affecting the whole community for a long time now. It never tasted as magical now as it did in those days. He could remember the loud sound of the drums when he had tried it for the first time, and he could remember large crowds in the community garden. There was a huge bonfire – it must have been seven or eight feet tall – much taller than the ones that they have at the festivals now. The garden was full of families gathered everywhere, and Laith followed his parents around as they were greeting everybody. He vaguely remembered playing with his sister, who was only a baby at the time – he was sure that he had some sort of a toy or a rattle, possibly a colourful caterpillar that he was waving over her as she watched it, laughing, and tried to reach it. He vaguely remembered seeing his friend, Esmy, there. He had always been close with Esmy. Their families were friends and they happened to be born on exactly the same day, so their mothers had been through pregnancy together. They had always played together when they were younger, and were still close friends to this day. He did not remember much about their meeting on this day, but he did have a vague feeling that he saw her too.

Laith, although he sometimes struggled hard to try, could not remember much about his escape that day. It must have happened so quickly, before the three-year-old him had even realised anything was happening. All he could remember after the raas, the bonfire, the colourful toy of some sort and, possibly, Esmy, was being on top of a ten-foot wall. Try as he might, he could never remember how he got there, but he did remember that his father had been holding him in one hand and his sister in the other. There had been a lot of noise and shouting. In this part of his memory, he was sure the sky looked a deep grey. His father jumped off the wall and, to Laith, it felt like they were falling for an eternity. His father landed on his feet and ran away from the ambush, firmly holding both Laith and his sister. His father had run all the way home, and that was the last thing that Laith could remember about that day. Lying awake at night, he would sometimes remember a black-haired woman being just behind them when running. Sometimes he would also have a brief memory of a faceless man standing on top of the wall. He did not know who either of these people were. He sometimes wondered if the woman was a false memory of his mother – he had seen pictures of her, and she did have long, black hair. He thought that maybe his brain was trying to provide him with a scenario in which the whole family had escaped. He knew, in reality, that these people were likely to have been two of the other people who were lucky enough to escape the onslaught of arrows with their lives in tact. Well, as in tact as their lives could be after such an atrocity.

Laith had once asked his father about escaping over the ten-foot wall. Once. His father had told him that he could not remember much about how they escaped that day, and that he was just acting on instinct. Laith did tentatively ask his father about the faceless man and the black haired woman. Well, he didn't really *directly* ask his father about them – he had once tentatively brought them up as being one of the many people there, and hoped that his father would correct him and reveal some special information about them. He had been disappointed when his father had confirmed what he himself had suspected – that those memories would have been any of the thousands of people trying to escape. His father confirmed that he had only been able to save him and his sister on the day and did not remember any details about anybody else who was there. He had been focused only on Laith and his sister. Laith had been confused by his own disappointment at this news – he already knew that his mother had not escaped. At the time, he wasn't sure whether his father had replied in an angry tone or an upset one. Laith came to realise over time that his father's heartbreak from the day must have manifested as a sense of anger, possibly towards the people responsible or even maybe at his own helplessness at the time. Laith's father was not the type who would take feeling helpless in his stride. Either way, Laith learnt that it was not really a subject he should encroach again. He had nothing to gain from it, other than the knowledge of what happened. Knowing what happened was not really a great benefit to him, and the cost was far too high. Besides, he already knew the only important detail – that his mother had not made it.

As Laith and his sister got older, their father, seemingly of his own accord, had told them exactly what had happened to their mother that night. Laith remembered the moment that they had found out. It was late at night, and completely out of the blue. Laith was sat with his sister. He was in his late teens, and his sister was fourteen or fifteen. They were sat together in their dining room and their father had come in and stood near them. He remembered how the atmosphere had suddenly changed from being incredibly relaxed to unbearably tense the moment his father had walked in – a premonition of what was to come. His father must have been deciding whether to stand or sit, because he had paused for a brief moment before sitting opposite the two of them. Without any warning, he had told them that their mother had died immediately upon being hit by a poison-tipped arrow. Laith remembered feeling sick as soon as those words hit him. He did not know why – he knew that his mother had died, and he knew that she had died in the attack. Hearing his father say it like that must have made it real for him. It was no longer merely a vague event that had happened in the past - it turned quickly into a tangible loss that had made his heart suddenly drop. Laith's father went on to explain that the reason he had brought it up was that he could tell that they wanted to know. Their father was right in this respect - Laith and his sister had always wondered exactly what had happened to their mother, but neither of them had ever had the heart to ask. Laith's sister had asked him once what he remembered, but he was unable to say much other than escaping over a ten-foot wall. They did not know how their father would react if they did ask him, but they knew that it would upset him, and they did not want to bring back any of his bad memories. He went on to tell them that, once he knew their mother could not be saved, his first priority was to save both of their lives. He made sure that they knew that, no matter what happened, he would always put the two of them first. As Laith grew up, he could see that this was a philosophy that his father strived to live by. They were clearly not just meaningless words to him.

As Laith continued to stare deep into the stars, more of them revealed themselves to him. He liked the feeling of looking at stars anyway but he liked it most of all when he would get lost in them and started to see the ones that others might miss. It made him feel as though they were appearing just for him.

The wind started to blow with a little bit more desire. Though it was not particularly cold, it did become apparent to Laith that he was only wearing a thin shirt. He thought about going back inside, but he suspected that his father would still be awake. Although Laith was not avoiding his father as such, he felt that he would rather stay out for a little while longer and go back home when he knew that his father would have gone to bed. As he came to this decision, he heard somebody start walking towards him.

He didn't need to turn around to look - he could tell by the speed and strength of the footsteps that it was one of the only two people he would actually like to sit by at this moment in time. His sister put down her own deckchair as close to his as possible and then pulled her long, dark, wavy hair out of her face. She exaggerated a spitting sound as she pulled some out of her mouth, making sure that Laith was fully aware of the mild inconvenience the gentle wind had inflicted upon her. She then took off her bow and quiver, and put down her shield - it was part of their culture to always carry a weapon and a shield with them - Laith's shield was by his side, and his sword was safely in its sheath. Laith's sister sat down, pulling a blanket over herself. She rested her head on her brother and they both sat in silence.

Laith's father was probably the best swordsman that Laith knew – he was highly respected for it. Laith's sister was definitely the most skilled archer that he knew and, annoyingly, she was incredibly humble about it. All three family members would practice with both weapons, but Laith and his father would both generally carry a sword. Strangely, the right-handed Laith would carry his sword in his left hand - a habit that he had since he was small. He was always taught to carry it in his right hand, being right-handed, but would naturally switch to his left. His father and other teachers eventually came to accept this quirk of his and, if anything, it allowed him to be reasonably skilled with a sword in both hands. He favoured carrying his shield in his right hand instead. Maybe, he thought, it was because he was in some ways more skilled with his shield than with his sword and so he would have it in his stronger hand. He had never needed to fight for real, but always sparred defensively. He would frustrate his opponents by somehow managing to block every attempted blow and kept his energy to attack once they had tired. This was never a conscious tactic for him, but it was effective. He actually enjoyed archery more than sword fighting, but his father had always encouraged him to favour the sword. He knew that it was partly because his father wanted him to follow in his footsteps, but he also knew that it was a sensible decision because his strength and speed were a lot better than his aim and precision. Maybe it was his strength and speed that made him favour a defensive form of fighting – he was able to block multiple quick and heavy blows, but did not have the best technique to get through his opponents defences.

Laith started to feel grateful for the warmth coming from his sister, and her blanket brushing against his bare arm felt tempting. Without feeling the need to ask, he pulled some of the blanket up over himself as his sister lifted her head off his shoulder.

"Oh, we're sharing my blanket, are we?" she demanded with faux-gravitas.

"Brothers and sisters love sharing", Laith replied.

"Oh, fine", she huffed, as she gave him more. "What's wrong?' she asked.

"Nothing. I just like to sit."

"You're frowning. But you're always frowning, I suppose. Grumpy."

Laith tutted. He knew that they were both aware why he was in a solemn mood – well, more so than usual. He also knew that she was waiting to bring it up because she was having the same feelings.

"Well, anyway," she said, "Dad's being annoying. He keeps looking at me. So I thought I'd come here and annoy you."

"Oh, joy", Laith said, sarcastically. In reality, he appreciated the company and he knew that his sister did too.

"What time are you waking up tomorrow?" he asked her. He knew the answer, but they were both trying to avoid talking about how they were feeling for a little while longer.

"Probably around six-ish", she replied "What about you?"

"Five fifty-nine", he said. "We aren't all lazy, like you".

She pushed her head deeper into his shoulder and grunted. He knew this to be a headbutt in response to his insult.

"Are you sad about tomorrow?" he asked her.

"I don't really know", she said, after taking a moment to think about it. "Are you?"

"I don't know".

"Yeah."

They sat in silence. Laith watched the stars as his sister closed her eyes and continued to rest on his shoulder.

Chapter 2 - Esmeralda

The night was deathly quiet as Esmeralda sat directly outside her bedroom window staring up at the waxing Moon. Looking closely, as she often did, she noticed a sliver of the left hand side of the Moon in shadow – it would not be full until tomorrow. Despite this, it seemed brighter and larger than usual. Although she was sure that anybody who took the time to look would also be captivated by its beauty, particularly tonight as she noticed its unusually yellow tint, she felt that they did not appreciate it in quite the same way that she did. For as long as she could remember, she felt a strange affinity with the Moon that she could not put into words.

She wondered why the Moon looked yellow tonight. She could not recall ever seeing it as deep a shade as this before. She wondered if it was something to do with the atmosphere. Maybe it was the fact that the night was warmer than usual, and this had some kind of effect on the air. Both of these suggestions seemed reasonable to her, and so she accepted them and gave no further thought as to the reason for its colour. Instead, she simply stared up at it, lost in its beauty. She felt that she had a responsibility, both to herself and to the Moon, to not avert her gaze until she had absorbed its every last detail tonight – the shadows of the craters complimenting the vivid brightness of the hills, even brighter tonight than usual. For a fleeting moment, she wondered if anybody else was also staring up at the same Moon at this exact moment and felt its presence the way that she did. With this thought, a slight tinge of sadness crept upon her that she was unable to explain. She wondered if it was a feeling of loneliness – a feeling that, maybe, she was hoping that somebody else would feel the same kind of celestial connection that she did - although she was quite certain that they did not. It was strange, but she had always felt a kind of wistful longing for the Moon – a vague melancholic feeling that she either missed it, or wanted to be there, or wanted to be a part of it. She did not quite know which, if any, of these she felt, or if it was a combination of all of them. And she did know that none of her feelings really made any sense. After all, how could she miss somewhere she had never been? Or feel at home in a place she knew to be cold and isolated? Or be a part of something that was clearly a completely separate and lifeless entity? But she did know that thinking about it for too long deepened her longing. Perhaps the most frustrating thing about it was the feeling that she was yearning for something that she was unable to even conceptualise.

Esmeralda had lived with her maternal grandfather ever since her parents and two older siblings had died at the Massacre of the Pink Moon. He was the one who had saved her from the stampeding crowds and the onslaught of poison-tipped arrows on the day, and he had cared for her ever since. Esmeralda had always been special to her grandad. He was the one who named her the moment he first laid eyes on her, and he had played a big part in her life even while her parents were still around. The memories of playing with her grandad were some of Esmeralda's strongest memories from the happier times. In fact, even though she did not remember much about the fateful evening of the Massacre, she did remember that she spent it playing with him – some kind of game with a red ball. She knew that the rest of her family were there, but did not remember anything about them on the day. Nights when she had strained hard to remember what happened, all she could remember was holding a red ball and laughing and running with her grandad before the sudden onset of a sense of panic when he picked her up and started running. She remembered that the sky somehow turned grey as soon as the panic set in, stealing the beautiful golden evening light before it. And there was something about a brick wall and an alleyway with a crowd of people. She had known that she was safe with her grandfather, but remembered being scared of the noise from the crowds and confused with what was happening – she was only three when it happened, and had never asked her grandfather for the details.

Throughout her childhood, she had received a lot of passing, lighthearted comments made about her name from members of the community. It was rare, but not unheard of, for people of her heritage to have green eyes and she had come to learn that, when the community heard the news that her grandad had insisted on the name Esmeralda, most expected that the new little baby had been blessed with vibrant, green eyes. However, instead, they were met with a chestnut-haired, hazel-eyed little girl, staring up at them. This was a story that she had heard from a number of people, a number of times. Each time, she smiled along politely at their faux-horror without ever offering an explanation that, it seemed to her, some people felt that they were owed. In reality, she never knew the reason behind her name and neither had she ever questioned it. Having grown up with the name, she had never considered it odd for a brown-eyed girl to have the name Esmeralda. It was certainly no more odd, she felt, than girls called 'Ruby' not having red eyes. There were girls called 'Rose' who were distinctively thorn-less. She had heard of the name 'Fern', and was quite certain that these girls were not, nor had they ever been, a type of non-flowering plant. In reality, she knew that the comments and questions from her parents' and grandparents' friends were good-natured at heart, and so she always kept these thoughts to herself and offered an awkward smile as a response instead. She quite liked her name, and she liked that fact that her grandad gave it to her. It made her feel as though they had a special connection, which was important, considering he was the only family that she had left.

Esmeralda felt that, maybe, it was time to go back inside, and so she opened the front door to her cabin. She lived, as did everybody in the community, in a small log cabin. They were always intended to be temporary, although she had lived in this one for nearly eight years now. She was, in a way, more settled than she had been for a while. She was also, in another way, perhaps more unsettled than she had ever been. Eight years was the longest that she had ever lived in one place. This brought her some sense of being at home, but it was at the expense of a sense of purpose. When they would move around, she always had a feeling that she was heading towards something – they had always had to make the new settlement habitable and then work to live off the land. Now that she was settled here, she lost this sense of purpose. Being settled was quite unsettling.

Every few years for most of her life, the community had been forced to move further south to try and make use of fertile land. Sometimes they could just move fields whilst remaining in their same cabin but, after rotating the fields for around six years, there was no way of squeezing more life out of them and so they had to move on. In the old age, the land was incredibly fertile. Her tribe was able to make use of the red flower in order to make and provide mixtures and potions to the farmers who used this to ensure their crops grew in abundance. The farmers could, in turn, provide enough food for everybody with ease. When the North took control of the land, they also controlled access to the red flower. They said that it was in the best interests of the community to have a central reserve of the flower to prevent the danger of it inadvertently taking over the land and seeping into the rivers. They said that this could end up destroying everything. Esmeralda's grandad had told her that, although some members of their community were concerned with the North taking over, the North had given an air of power to people in the land that they felt were key. This, in conjunction with the fact that the land did seem to prosper under the leadership of the North, assuaged many peoples concerns so that they did not question the restricted access to the red flower. They could see that the land was more prosperous than ever and, at a glance, the logic of their visitors made enough sense for it not to be worth the hassle to go against it. The introduction of the

North had benefitted the natives as well as their uninvited guests, and there simply were not enough people with strong enough convictions to resist the small and subtle changes. Collectively, they accepted the comfortable lie. However, after the Massacre, once the land was split in two, the new Southland had no access to the red flower. The entire reserves were in the Northland. Esmeralda's community lived just south of the border once it was formed, and the land there remained fertile for only a couple of years. The community moved further south and made a new settlement – they chose to build cabins that were temporary and easy to move, knowing that the land would not remain fertile for too long. Esmeralda's grandad had told her that, as they moved further and further south, their cabins got smaller and smaller as they chose to transport less of the materials. Although the farmers were able to grow enough crops to feed the entire community, fewer horses were bred as they knew that, soon, it would become more difficult to feed them. It became more difficult to transport the building materials and so their cabins got smaller. This did not bother Esmeralda. Firstly, she had grown up in this age and so it was all she ever knew. Secondly, the community spirit and the love she and her grandad shared never made her feel that she needed any more material possessions than she already had.

Esmeralda opened the door to her cabin directly into a small room that was a combination of a kitchen and a dining area. From the dancing light of the lone flickering candle sat on the dinner table, she could see that the room was empty. Her grandad must have gone to bed already. She walked over to the table to and saw that he had left her a biscuit on a small plate. He knew that she liked these small biscuits that he made – he must have baked them earlier. She smiled as she put it all in her mouth at once, blew out the candle and crept quietly to bed, so as not to wake him. Tomorrow was going to be a significant day but, as she tasted the biscuit her grandad had made her, she knew that she would be able to get through it.

Chapter 3 - Cahya

Cahya woke up when he was certain that it was 5.15am on the dot. He always liked to rise before the Sun so that he could watch with a cup of tea as it appeared above the horizon. Today was no exception. Most often, he would watch it from just outside his own cabin, allowing its energy to soak into him every morning. On very rare occasions, and only if it was far too cold, he would watch through the window from the dining table. Today was a special day. He knew that the tall stalks of wheat would be felled in the harvest today, and so he wanted to make the trip over to his friend's field to watch them soak up the last bit of the Sun's energy that they would. The light from the sunrise today would be particularly special, and so he was not going to waste this opportunity.

Cahya sat up in his bed and swung his legs over the side, searching for his slippers. His bun had come loose in the night, and so he untied his hair completely and let his long silver hair fall to his side. He estimated that he had just over half an hour before he should head out, which was plenty of time to brush his teeth and make tea. He went to the bathroom and looked at himself in the small, round mirror. It was an old mirror, with a crack in the top left and a few small chips on the side. The imperfections brought him comfort. The small wrinkles around the brown eyes in the reflection looking back at him certainly belonged to a man much older than he felt. Nevertheless, he retied his straight silver hair back into a neat bun on the top of his head and brushed his teeth. He washed his face to wake himself up fully, smoothed out his short, white beard and headed to the kitchen to make tea.

Cahya navigated his way to the kitchen table where he saw a small plate that was completely empty but for a few crumbs. This put a little bit of joy into his heart. He lit the candle that was sat on the table. He did not want to turn on the electricity. He told himself that this was because he did not want to disturb his granddaughter, who would still be sleeping, with the sound of the generator, but really it was because he found the gentle light from the candle more comforting. He lit the gas stove, which gave him more than enough light to work with, and the bonus of some warmth, and filled his favourite small pan a quarter of the way up with water. He placed it on the stove and reached for some tea leaves from the jar in the cupboard above his head. He added these to the water that was still gently warming, and watched as a bit of the colour slowly leaked out from the leaves and swirled slightly in the water. He liked to take his time when he was making tea – it was the start of his day, and it was important to start it well. He pretended to himself that he was thinking about what mix of spices he would use, but really he had already decided on this long before he had fallen asleep last night. He put in a bit more cardamom today than usual – he quite fancied its dull warmth, and a bit less ginger than he did yesterday. He already felt a sharpness to his energy today, probably due to the date, and so he did not need much more. He only put in two cloves so they would not overpower the feeling he was aiming for in today's cup. He added three beams of winter sunrise, complimenting the warmth of the cardamom and more panela than he knew was good for him – it was a special day after all, and he told himself that he needed to sweeten his mouth to get the day off to the perfect start.

Panela was one of the small differences between the culture of Cahya's tribe and the rest of the community. Essentially, all it was was sugarcane juice that was evaporated and set into solids. The other tribes would traditionally add small amounts of spices to it when they made it, but Cahya learned from his grandparents to keep it pure. Sugarcane was one of the most important manifestations of energy, they would tell him, and it was important to not dilute this when preparing it. He remembered the fun he would have, many many years ago as a child, extracting the juice from the sugarcane with his grandfather. They would then give it to his grandmother, who would use the remaining dried pulp as fuel to light the fire on which she would evaporate the juice while a young Cahya carefully stirred it. She would show him how to tell when it was just the right thickness to pour into trays and let it set. Cahya loved every aspect of its preparation, from start to finish. He did not want to miss out the harvesting and pressing with his grandfather, or the evaporating and setting with his grandmother. Although his grandparents were now long gone, they lived on in the traditions that they taught him. Whenever Cahya prepared it now, he would always make sure that his granddaughter was with him, in the hope that he could recreate the feeling that he had when he learnt from his grandparents. He hoped that these moments were as special to her as they were to him.

Cahya was born in this land, of course before it was partitioned twenty years ago, but it was his great-grandparents who had come over from the west as children with their parents to build a new life here. They were persecuted in their home. Their unrivalled willingness to see and harness parts of the Universe's energy saw them labeled as demons. People feared what they did not understand, Cahya's grandparents had always told him, but this did not mean that they should change their ways. They were welcomed with open arms into the new community when his ancestors had sailed over from the west and settled over a hundred years ago now. His tribe had fully assimilated into the community. Over the years, they embraced the culture of the natives and shared parts of their culture too. They would work together with the farmers to ensure crops grew in abundance – his tribe was the best at harnessing the energy of the red flower. They were the first people that anybody would come to when they had any illnesses or ailments for recommendations on what they should eat or drink. Their unrivalled willingness to see and harness parts of the Universe's energy made them the perfect people to know what crops needed to thrive, and what people needed to heal. Although some people remained skeptical of the healers' special abilities, their culture was embraced and respected in this land.

Cahya poured in just enough milk until the tea turned the perfect colour, and waited for it to come to the boil. Once he could smell the perfect combination of brown and gold, he poured some in a flask for himself and the rest in a mug for his granddaughter to enjoy once she woke up. He placed a plate over the mug he made for his granddaughter to keep it warm for as long as possible, picked up his flask, three small empty glass bottles and a cloak, and headed out to the field.

Cahya felt a reasonable chill as he stepped outside – it was slightly colder than he expected it to be although, when he thought about it, he didn't actually have any real reason to expect it should have been warmer than it was – the significance of the day had fooled him. He was glad of his cloak and his warm flask of tea. He tackled the three-minute walk to the field at a reasonably brisk pace, hearing the glass bottles clinking in the pockets of his cloak as he walked, and arrived at a small clearing by a well. This morning, he noticed that there were two deckchairs sitting next to the well. One had been folded and lay peacefully on the floor, but the other was perched open as though it itself was waiting for the sunrise. He sat cross-legged on the floor next to the deckchair. This made him the most relaxed – he could connect with the Earth. He poured himself some tea and waited peacefully - he still had a few minutes before the Sun began to rise.

Cahya heard some footsteps coming up behind him. He turned around to see a shadowy figure coming towards him. He had a sword by his side and his dark, wavy hair was blowing in the wind.

"Hello, Laith", said Cahya, "I thought you were your dad".

"No, he's still in bed. Lazy, ain't he?" replied Laith, as he stood behind the open deckchair with his hands resting on top of it.

"Normally you're the lazy one", chuckled Cahya in good

humour, "How come you're here so early, for once?"

"What do you mean 'for once'?" demanded Laith, jokingly. "I'm here every day".

"Yeah, right", said Cahya, rolling his eyes. He enjoyed Laith's company. He had an energy that was similar to that of his own granddaughter – the kind that, when he was at ease, would resonate within other people too. Cahya knew that he was one of the very few people that Laith felt at ease with.

"I wanted to wake up early to see the Sun rise today, but I couldn't really sleep anyway. I wasn't that tired," said Laith. "Sarama said that she was gonna come as well, but she's still asleep, so I just came by myself". Laith took his shield off his back and put it on the floor, resting upright against his leg. Cahya knew the reason that Laith was still standing was because he himself was sat on the floor. He knew that Laith, like his whole family, could not sit comfortably on the floor. He also knew that Laith would not sit on the chair while he was on the floor, even if he told him to.

"Pass me that other chair, Laith", asked Cahya, "I'm getting tired of sitting on the floor. Getting too old for sitting down here for too long, now", he lied. He would much rather connect with Laith than with the Earth.

"Have this one, Uncle", said Laith, gesturing to the one he was leaning on. "I'll open the other one".

"Good job you two were too lazy to take them back yesterday," said Cahya

"Lazy? It's called 'good forward planning'", Laith argued. "We knew that you would be coming today, so we thought we'd better leave both chairs here – one for you to sit on, and the other to put your feet up."

Cahya rolled his eyes and smiled. "Yeah, because you know how much I love to do that." He could feel that Laith's heart was smiling, even though his face wasn't showing it.

Cahya finished his tea, got up off the ground and sat on the deckchair as Laith joined him on his right. Cahya poured some more tea into the lid of the flask and offered it to Laith.

"No, thanks. I'm gonna have some later".

Cahya knew that Laith was joking – he never drank tea. Even though he knew this, he would always offer some to him, as he would with everybody. He might want to try it one day.

"It has panela in it," he said "and you know what day it is today. Have a little bit, at least. You need to sweeten your mouth."

"No, thanks, Uncle".

Cahya knew that it was important that Laith sweeten his mouth today – for the sake of tradition, of course, but more importantly for the sake of enriching his soul. He offered Laith some panela from this pouch.

"Here. Have this instead".

Laith gratefully accepted the chunk and broke a little piece off, putting it in his mouth.

"This is really nice", he said

"Of course it is" laughed Cahya. "I made it".

"Thanks", said Laith. "That was really nice".

"Have some more",

"No, thanks. My mouth is already sweet now".

Cahya poured some more tea for himself as the sky began to lighten. The two of them sat in silence and watched as the Sun began to appear over the horizon and bestow its magic upon the wheat in the field, which gladly received it. They watched gratefully as the sky became a deeper shade of red. Cahya waited until he knew that the flavour of the sunlight was exactly as he wanted it, and then uncorked one of the glass bottles that he put in his cloak and pointed it towards the Sun.

"Do you want some help, Uncle?" asked Laith.

Cahya got the remaining two glass bottles out of his cloak. He handed one to Laith and put one on the ground in between their two chairs. Laith uncorked the bottle he was given and pointed it unsurely towards the Sun. Cahya knew that Laith was unable to see the energy in the way that he could, but he also knew that it didn't really matter. He appreciated Laith's sentiment, and knew that he couldn't really do it wrong anyway. Cahya looked carefully inside his own bottle and saw the red-ish, yellowy gold energy faintly glittering inside it. He put the cork on the bottle and looked towards Laith's. Laith held his up to his own eye and strained to look inside. Cahya could tell that he was waiting for some instruction from him. "That's good, Laith", he said. He could tell that Laith corked the bottle with some relief and so Cahya took the last bottle for himself – there was no need to put any undue pressure on Laith. "I'll quickly do this one", he said. "We don't really need that many – it's the moonbeams that are more important today, but I thought I might as well get a few from the Sun anyway".

The two sat in the field and watched the red slowly dilute itself in the blue of the morning sky, preparing for this most significant of days.

Chapter 4 - Sarama

Sarama was lying in bed when she felt the sunlight beaming through her window, penetrating her eyelids. She had planned to wake up early today to see the sunrise but, by the time she got to sleep late the night before, she had all but come to terms with the fact that this would not be a reality. She justified this by telling herself that it was going to be a big day – there was a lot of work to be done and a lot of joy to be shared, and so she needed to be well rested. Really, she knew that she was waking up late because, despite how she was told she should feel about this day (which was still a day of celebration – and now it was also about celebrating the lives of those who lost theirs so it was even more important to be joyful), she actually did not want to make the day last longer than it needed to. The longer she stayed in bed, the quicker the day would pass.

Sarama had never really known her mother – she had been killed when Sarama was only a baby – and so she thought that she could not really be missing her. But still, it kept her up last night, even after she had come home from the field with her brother. Maybe she missed the idea of her – she was unsure. One thing that did bring her some comfort was that she had her brother. She did not really speak about it much with him – not because either of them didn't want to, but because she was unsure of how she actually felt, and she knew that he was too. She had always been told that this day in particular should be a celebration, and she therefore felt an obligation to be happy. But she also felt that she should, in some way, be mourning for her mother – a woman she never really knew. These conflicting thoughts were what made her seek out her brother yesterday night – she knew that he would be having the same confused feelings. Even though neither could really articulate what they were feeling, it brought her some comfort to be with him, knowing that he was the only person who was going through the exact same thing.

Sarama turned over in bed, groaning as she turned, and pushed her face deep into her pillow, cursing the inconsiderate sunlight streaming in through the window. She knew that she could only really do this for a few more minutes before she would have to get up and get out of bed. She had planned to watch the sunrise with her brother and wondered if he had gone to the field himself when she didn't wake up. She suspected that he would have done – she knew that he wouldn't have woken her while she slept. He had tried that once before when they had planned to wake up early together and she hadn't, and that was enough for him to never try again. She hoped that he had woken up early and gone by himself, because she knew that he found it calming when he was out there. He always seemed to prefer it at either sunrise or in the dead of the night. She also, somewhat selfishly, hoped that he had not gone. She hoped a little bit that he would be in the kitchen waiting for her, for the same reason that she sought him out the night before. She knew that, in the hustle and bustle of the day, she would be fine and happy while her mind was distracted, but she did not really want to be alone for too long. Well, not completely alone, as her thoughts would be there too.

She heard a noise coming from the kitchen, which prompted her to get out of bed. From the clumsy sound of careless clattering, she knew it to be her brother as oppsed to her father. She rolled out of bed and walked out of her bedroom. From the small corridor, she could see the open kitchen and dining area, and waved at her brother in the kitchen.

"I'm making you some porridge," he said from across the room. "I'm glad that you've finally woken up so that you can have some. Some of us have been out in the fields collecting the sunrise with Uncle"

"Ooh, thanks, I love porridge", Sarama replied. She wasn't actually too fussed about the porridge. She was happier about the fact that her brother was awake and would be waiting in the dining area by the time she had brushed her teeth and got dressed.

She crossed the hallway into the bathroom and splashed some water on her face. She had to pay special attention to the area around her eyes as she was washing her face, making sure that everything was perfectly clean, so as not to worry her brother with an unintended disclosure of her full feelings. Once she had done this, she felt more awake and as though the day had actually started. She pulled her long, black hair out of the way of her face so that it hung all the way down her back and allowed her to brush her teeth properly. Once she had done this, she went back into her bedroom to get dressed. She could hear her brother fiddling about with pots, pans and bowls in the kitchen, making unnecessary noise as well as porridge. She came out into the dining area and took her bowl of porridge as her brother just sat down to start eating his.

"Did you put panela in it?" she asked

"No, I didn't really fancy it"

"No, neither do I. But you're supposed to today"

"You can put some in yours, if you want. I had some with Uncle earlier anyway so I'm sorted", said Laith. "Not all of us have been in bed all our lives". Even though Laith and Sarama only had one living uncle – their dad's sister's husband – Sarama knew that Laith was referring to their family friend, Cahya. Although not technically their uncle, he had always treated both Sarama and her brother as his own family, and they had always considered him to be as such. Neither of them could ever dream of calling him anything other than 'Uncle' and, furthermore, referring to an uncle without qualification automatically meant him over their real uncle.

"No, I don't want any. It's bad for you anyway", Sarama decided. "I'll just have some raas later when they are pressing it in the field"

"Yeah, that'll be nice. I like it."

"And me," Sarama agreed. "And it doesn't count as being bad for you today, either, so it's even better. Nice porridge, by the way. Well done"

"Thanks".

Their relaxed tone and their conversation would have been the same on any other day, but today it felt different. Although the same words would normally flow naturally, they felt forced for now. They were both avoiding the elephant in the room by way of their usual conversation that was a parody of itself.

"Has Dad gone already?" asked Sarama.

"Yeah, he got there a few minutes before I left", replied Laith. "Him and Uncle are still there. People will probably start getting there in an hour or so". Sarama tilted her bowl and quickly finished the last few spoons of her porridge. She waited until her brother had finished his and then took his bowl and spoon off him. "I take it I'm washing these?" she said.

"Well, seeing as you've done bugger all so far, you might as well. Some of us are exhausted from all the sunbeams we've been collecting with Uncle, and all the porridge we've been making for everybody", replied her brother.

"Everybody?" Sarama asked. "Two bowls of bloody porridge, and you're acting like you're the saviour of the community".

Sarama felt better. The conversation was exactly the same, but now it was flowing freely from the heart unhindered by the mind.

"Everybody in this room, I meant", her brother replied.

"And you probably didn't even collect any sunbeams. Probably just watched Uncle do all the hard work while you just sat there, not knowing what's going on."

"Actually, I did collect a bottle. And I did know what was going on. Kind of. Well, I knew when to close it, anyway. When he told me. Anyway, shut up – you've been in bed all bloody day."

"All day?", Sarama tutted. "It's like seven in the morning".

"Exactly – the day's half gone. Anyway, hurry up and wash them and then we can go", said Laith. "I'll go and get some sickles. Dad already took the scythe. I said that he looked like Death when he turned up with it. I don't think he found it very funny", he said.

"Well, what did you expect, you idiot?" Sarama laughed. "He wouldn't even find that funny on a normal day. Did he say anything?"

"No, but you could probably cut the tension with a scythe. I probably shouldn't have said anything. I don't know why I did. Good job I was going anyway".

Sarama did the washing up as her brother went to collect the sickles from the small shed behind the house. She suspected that she knew the reason that her brother felt the need to make that joke, despite the day. And the reason was because of the day. She knew this for the same reason that she found the image funny herself – it acted as a sort of distraction. Not a distraction from the day, but a distraction from how they felt about it. It was a way to ensure that they didn't have to think about how they were actually feeling. It was easier to adhere to the obligation of having fun despite the dark cloud hanging over them if they had fun at the expense of the dark cloud hanging over them. Still, she thought, she would have had the sense to keep her bloody mouth shut.

She finished the washing up and dried her hands. She could hear her brother in his room, probably picking up his sword and shield. She decided that she would take her sword today, too, rather than her bow and arrows. It would be more comfortable for her as she helped to harvest the wheat. She went to her room and picked it up in its sheath. She tied it around her waist and put her small shield on her back. "Hurry up," she shouted to her brother. He came out of his room ready, holding five sickles.

"Let's go", he said. She took two sickles off him, and they headed out of the door.

She wondered who would be there already. Their father's was only one of a few fields – she knew that everybody in the community would be spread out over different fields today. Normally her and her brother would stay and help in their field for most of the day, but take some trips to other fields to symbolically exchange some of their harvest with other people. In reality, the whole of the harvest was always for the whole community, and everybody would gather in the communal area in the evening anyway. She expected that her dad's sister would be there for most of the day too, with her husband and their two young children. Uncle Cahya would be there, with his granddaughter. And then lots of people would come and go. It really was a community event.

They got to the field in just a minute or two. Sarama saw that her dad was alone in the field at the moment. Her uncle must have gone home, she thought, and her dad had already started with the scythe. He was stood with his back to them, sweeping the scythe effortlessly to bring down the wheat. He had his bronze shield on his back, which was larger than the one either she or her brother carried. It had a simple pattern – one slightly raised circle in the middle and then three smaller evenly spaced circles around the outside. His sword was in its royal blue sheath hanging on his left hand side. She could see its elegant silver handle. He had left his hair open, as he normally did. It was slightly longer than her brother's, with the same wavy and slightly tangled nature, but it contained some small streaks of grey. She noticed that there were already a few sheaves that he must have bundled together himself. He was nothing if not a hard worker, and it did not surprise her that he had started without them.

"Hi, Dad", she said loud enough for her voice to carry to him. He turned around.

"Hi, Sarama", he replied. "Do you want to start collecting those sheaves over there?' he asked, pointing towards them. Noting the rhetorical nature of the question, she started stacking them underneath the shelter with the simple tin roof. Her dad had taught her in the past how to properly stack them so that they can dry out and last longer. She had noticed that, year after year, these bundles had been getting smaller. She had never had to be told to tie smaller bundles whenever she had done so – she noticed that it was something her dad had started doing without explicitly stating or giving a reason. The reason was obvious.

"Here, Dad, I can take over with that scythe", she heard Laith offer.

"Nah, don't worry about it, I'm alright for now", their dad replied. "You can help your sister stack those...oh she's done it...ok you can carry on with the cutting and I'll start tying some more of these up". He passed Laith the scythe and he carried on where their dad had left off. Sarama saw that her brother was nowhere near as fluent with the scythe as her dad, but he was getting it done slowly. Sometimes he would have to come back to hack at the pieces he missed, unlike her dad who would fell the wheat in one fluid motion. She joined her dad tying the wheat into sheaves and then they both stacked them under the shelter together. "Are you doing it like this?", he asked her, gesturing towards his own. He rearranged her stack in a way that, as far as she was concerned, made it materially no different to the way that it was before. She didn't say anything.

"Here, Laith", he projected, "I'll carry on with that. You have a break, now". Laith handed over the scythe. He didn't seem particularly pleased nor disappointed to be off scythe-duty, but he picked up a sickle to continue instead. Sarama joined him, and the three of them worked silently in the field until Uncle Cahya turned up with his granddaughter.

"Hi, Uncle. Hi, Esmy", Sarama shouted over to them as they were walking towards them.

"Hi", her uncle shouted back, as his granddaughter waved at them all. "Decided to wake up, then?" he asked her.

"I needed to rest to make sure that I have enough energy to last the whole day", Sarama replied

"Yeah, I'm sure", laughed Uncle Cahya, as he picked up a sickle and also started cutting some wheat. Sarama noticed that Esmy had gone over to help Laith by tying up his wheat into bundles. Sarama knew that Esmy had always been close with her brother. Sarama was very fond of Esmy too, and it was probably for this reason. She liked how her brother was when he was around Esmy. It seemed to her that her brother just seemed a lot lighter when he was around her, as though he was carrying around a large rock on his back that he would put it down when he was around Esmy. This made Sarama happy, as she knew that she herself was the only other person that had a positive effect on him possibly with the exception, to a lesser extent, of Uncle Cahya. And the twins, actually. But Esmy was different. Sarama got the feeling that her dad did not feel the same about the relationship her brother had with Esmy. He was happy that they were friends, and Sarama knew that he did like her a lot, but she always sensed an undertone of worry from him that there was something more between her brother and Esmy. This was something that would have been a huge problem, with them being from different tribes. It was good to be friends but, when choosing a life partner, you have to stick with your own tribe. Sarama did not have this same worry – partly because she knew that her brother and Esmy were nothing more than friends, and partly because she wouldn't care even if there was something more between them. There wasn't, though – it was just her dad's paranoia. Sarama was watching her dad talking to Uncle Cahya. He had a smile on his face, but she noticed that he kept glancing over at Laith and Esmy.

The four of them continued to work in the field as different members of the community came and went, some bringing small amounts of the harvest from their own fields. They were only small amounts at the moment, as the gesture was symbolic. Later, the harvest would be truly shared out between all members of the community. Although technically it was work, today it did not seem as such. Sarama enjoyed the community coming together, and really enjoyed the feeling of lots of different people coming to pitch in. At any one time, there would be between twenty and thirty people in the field. They would take it in turns to cut, bundle, stack and rest. When more and more people came, everybody's rest breaks seemed to get longer and longer and the laughter got louder and louder. Sarama noticed that her dad was the one person who did not stop other than to have a quick glass of water. He was like this every year. When he finally wanted to have a longer break, he insisted that everybody else took a break as well.

"Come on", he said loudly, with a smile, "It's about time we all had a bit of a rest". He put down his scythe and walked towards anybody who was still working. "Come on," he said, patting people on the back as he walked past them, "Put it down. We can carry on later. Come on, let's have a bit of fun too, it's supposed to be a fun day". Sarama knew that this was because her dad could not truly relax if other people were still working. It might have been because he felt responsibility as one of the senior members of the community, or maybe because it was technically his field – he had responsibility for it, even though the harvest from it really belonged to everybody. It may even just have been because he had a strong work ethic – this was something that she felt her and her brother had inherited from him too, but it was nowhere near as strong as his.

As soon as her brother put down his sickle, she saw her two young cousins stop their game of sword-fighting and run over to him excitedly. They were both only five years old – twins – and were the children of her dad's sister. They were both very fond of Laith, as well as her, but she knew that today they had been waiting patiently for Laith to fight against them. As members of their tribe, they had their own shields and swords that they had brought with them. At the moment, these were only made out of wood. They would be given blunt aluminium ones when they were a bit older, and then steel when they were actually old enough for battle.

"Laith, Laith", shouted Tamzin, the older one by seven minutes, as she ran towards him, "Will you teach us how to fight properly?"

"Yeah, will you teach us how to fight properly?", shouted Tamsyn, her younger brother.

"He doesn't even know how to fight properly himself," interjected Ayan, their older brother. He was about the same age as Laith and had the same style of long hair, although his was slightly shorter and slightly lighter, as was his beard. "All he does is defend. I can tell you what he's gonna teach you right now – 'block everything, don't go for any shots yourself, and just wait for your opponent to die of old age'. " Ayan rolled his eyes and smiled at Laith as he said this, surely anticipating a retort.

"Laith, is that what you were really going to say?", asked Tamsyn, looking up at him.

"No, Ayan is just jealous because he can never beat me", said Laith rolling his eyes back at his cousin.

"I could beat you in a real fight. When we do spar, you just bore me to death – that's why you win those ones. In a real one, I'd definitely win."

"I'm so sorry", Laith replied sarcastically. "I didn't realise that you go to battle to entertain the opposition. Maybe you should take some juggling balls instead of a sword. I would rather win so, if fighting defensively works, then that's what I'd do".

"Yeah, Ayan, that's what Laith does", said Tamzin to her brother, holding onto Laith's leg. Sarama knew that Tamzin was just taking any opportunity to side against her own brother, as she was hoping to do herself, but Sarama also knew that Laith actually had a good point and so she just kept quiet.

Sarama silently watched on as her brother played with her two little cousins. He would let them attack him and block their blows, before countering very slowly so that they could block his.

"You have to work as a team", she heard him say. "One of you need to come and get me from this side", he said, gesturing to his right. "Make me bring my shield over there and then one of you can get me from the other side". Sarama watched on as her two little cousins huddled together to devise a plan. Tamzin cupped her mouth and pointed it towards her brother's ear as he listened intently. She was talking too quietly for Sarama to hear, but she suspected that her cousin was whispering to her brother the exact same instructions that Laith had just given them both. As Sarama expected, Tamsyn ran over to Laith's right hand side and tried to hit him with his sword. Laith brought his shield over to his right to block the shot and then waited for Tamzin to hit him in his left.

"Argh!" exclaimed Laith. "You've both beat me. Well done, Tammi. Well done Tamsyn". Everybody tended to abbreviate Tamzin's name to Tammi, to save the obvious confusion over their similar names. Tamsyn always remained Tamsyn.

"Let me try and beat you by myself, now," Tammi demanded sweetly of Laith.

"Then me, afterwards. I want to try by myself too", said Tamsyn, hopping up and down excitedly. Laith agreed, and Sarama watched on as her brother defended a few blows from Tammi before purposely letting his shield drop to his right hand side and giving Tammi an open shot. He collapsed dramatically on the floor as Tammi took her chance and then leapt up and shrieked in delight at the prospect of murdering her own cousin. Once Laith had allowed Tamsyn to do the same, and collapsed on the floor in equally dramatic fashion, he told them to go and fight their brother.

"Ayan, will you fight us now?", asked Tammi.

"I do want to, but Laith wants to fight you again", replied Ayan. Sarama heard this and, grateful for the opportunity to side against her brother, agreed.

"He does want to fight you again", she told her two little cousins. "He told me earlier, before you all came. He said 'I'm gonna tell them to fight Ayan, but secretly I want to keep on fighting them'".

"Did you really say that?', Tamsyn asked Laith, with an excited smile on his face.

"Not with words but, yeah, I did. I said it with my heart and Sarama heard it", Laith told him.

"Okay, let's fight", Tamsyn said. "Can me and Tammi both fight you at the same time? Actually, I don't want to fight. Will you throw me in the air?"

"Oh yeah and me", agreed Tammi, throwing her sword down.

Sarama watched on as they both ran towards Laith again, and he threw them both in the air in turn until Uncle Cahya came over to them.

"Come on, you two, let's go and get some raas from your uncle's field, and you can give Laith a rest", he said to them both.   They both excitedly ran towards Uncle Cahya. These were the moments that Sarama was most grateful for, especially today.   The day always came with mixed feelings but keeping busy and sharing these moments of joy with children unburdened by the sadness were really something to look forward to.

Chapter 5 - Cahya

Cahya loved seeing the positive energy from the twins as they ran towards him excitedly. There was something special about the pure light emanating from the innocence of children that seemed to fade for most people as they got older. Being around the twins recharged Cahya – he always felt that his soul was lifted after being around Tammi and Tamsyn, and he could see that it had had this effect on Laith too. Laith was a lot brighter now than he had been in the morning, partly because of the effect the twins had on him. Despite this, Cahya still thought it was time that he took the twins to get some raas – partly to give Laith a rest, partly because he wanted to spend time with the twins, and partly because he wanted some raas. He also, if he was being honest with himself, wanted a bit of a break from the field and needed a bit of a walk to recharge his energy. Tamsyn got to Cahya first and gestured that he wanted to be picked up. Cahya smiled. He was more than happy to oblige. As he picked up Tamsyn, he realised that maybe neither of them were as young as they used to be but he did not mind. He rubbed the top of Tammi's head as she reached him, and the three of them headed out of the field.

"Make sure their mum and dad know I've got them", Cahya shouted towards his granddaughter and her friends. Although Cahya had no blood relation to the twins, he knew that they considered him their uncle.

"Okay, Grandad, don't worry" Esmeralda shouted back.

The three of them headed down the path towards another field where Cahya knew sugarcane would be being pressed.

"Uncle, we just beat Laith in a battle", said Tamsyn, smiling and pulling slightly backwards in Cahya's arms so that he could get a good view of his reaction as he told him.

"I saw. You both did very well to beat him. Not many

people I know would be able to beat Laith – you two will be very good fighters when you're older", smiled Cahya, as he bent down to put Tamsyn down.

"Come around onto my back", he suggested. Tamsyn was heavier than he had anticipated. As Tamsyn climbed excitedly onto Cahya's back, Tammi elaborated on their victory.

"We used a plan," she explained, before going onto to give a detailed account of their epic battle. Cahya exclaimed in all the right places as both twins talked over each other.

As they reached the right field, Cahya bent down so that Tamsyn could clamber down. He watched on, tired in body but energised in soul, as Tamsyn joined his sister running in circles just in front of him.

"Come on, you two", he said to them as he turned right into the field. There were another twenty to thirty people in this field, most of them standing around and not doing much at this stage, other than probably mentally preparing themselves for the gathering at the community area later on. The day was not long gone, but the harvest was getting smaller and smaller by the year. Nobody really wanted to outwardly acknowledge this fact, especially today, but Cahya, like everybody else, knew that it was true. He walked towards the man extracting the sugarcane juice in the press, a man who was around his age and he had known all his life, and greeted him.

"Hi, Reyhan", said Cahya. Reyhan looked up and smiled.

"Hi, Cahya. Oh and you've brought little Tammi and Tamsyn along too. Come here, you two," he said, as he got two steel cups from beside him. He picked up the steel jug that Cahya knew to contain raas, and poured a small amount in each cup for the twins. They both reached out with both hands to take them from him.

"Thanks, Uncle", they said in unison. Reyhan got another cup for Cahya and poured some more raas. Cahya accepted with thanks and then listened on as the twins recounted their earlier victory over Laith for their new audience of Reyhan. Cahya found it mildly amusing that

Reyhan gasped in slightly different places than he did, not that it made any difference to the twins' frenetic method of storytelling.

As Cahya bid his friend farewell, Reyhan stopped him as he poured some raas into another jug. "You'll be going back to Kabili's now, won't you?", asked Reyhan. "Here, take this for everybody there", he said, handing Cahya the jug before he had a chance to respond.

"Yeah, we are going back there now", Cahya said, accepting the jug. "Thank you. We will see you all later at the park". He knew that it was no longer really a park – not in this settlement. But the sentiment remained the same as it always had, regardless of where they were. Reyhan placed a small steel bowl over the top of the jug that fit inside it perfectly as a lid, and wished them all well.

"Go and beat Laith, again", he said to the twins, "and then beat your brother too". The twins said that they would, and the three of them headed back out, with Cahya waving goodbye to the rest of the people in the field.

He allowed the twins to run around in front of him and in circles around him. He was grateful that, this time, he was carrying only a jug of raas, not that he would ever let on to the twins that it was possible for him to tire. He watched on as people were walking between fields, some exchanging harvest and some carrying equipment. Some just seemed to be enjoying the day as best as they could. Most of the work would have been done by now and Cahya knew that people would spend maybe another hour or so in the fields before getting ready to go to the gathering. The three of them passed Laith and Esmeralda on their way back to Kabili's field. Laith was carrying a sheaf of wheat.

"Are you going to your Uncle Reyhan's?", Cahya asked them both.

"Yeah, we are. Laith's dad told him to bring this", replied his granddaughter, gesturing towards the wheat in Laith's hand as Laith nodded. "and I wanted to come for a walk too."

"Okay", replied Cahya. "I'm going back to your uncle's

now, so I'll see you both there when you come back".

Just as being around the twins lightened Cahya, he had always seen that being around each other seemed to lighten both Esmeralda and Laith. They both glowed with slightly more intensity when they were around each other. With both of them having suffered losses in their childhood, nothing made Cahya happier than to see them both happy. Cahya was there to pick up the pieces when Esmeralda had lost both parents and her siblings, so he knew first hand how badly she had been affected. He also knew that Laith had lost his mother in the worst circumstances possible – he could barely believe it himself. Thinking about it caused his heart to drop, even after all this time. However, his granddaughter and Laith always seemed to find an excuse to be around each other, and Cahya had no ambition to stop them from enjoying whatever happiness they could find.

As Cahya approached Kabili's field, he noticed that most of the harvest had been collected already. The last few people were finishing off and packing up and would soon be heading home to get ready for the gathering later. Cahya could not help but be drawn towards how small the harvest was under the tin roof of the shelter. Some had already been stacked on the trailer ready to be taken to the gathering and distributed further. He remembered the days before the Massacre, when the land was fertile and when the harvest would truly be a hard day's work for a much larger population. Times had changed now, and he knew that they were only getting worse. He said goodbye to the last few people on their way out of the field, and walked towards Kabili and his sister and brother-in-law – the twins' parents. Tamsyn ran towards his father, and gestured to be picked up. His father obliged, as Tammi went and pulled on his trouser leg.

"Dad," she said, excitedly, looking up at him, "we beat Laith in a battle".

"Yeah, Dad, we did", agreed her brother.

"Excellent," said their father. "Now you need to go home

and beat your lazy brother, and get ready for the celebration later. Come on."

The twins and their parents said goodbye as they left Cahya and Kabili alone in the field. Cahya noticed Kabili looking intently at the harvest shelter and knew that his friend was having the same thought that he had been having.

"Doesn't take as long these days, does it?", said Cahya, stating something that they both knew to be true.

"The land is getting less and less fertile", reciprocated Kabili.

Both men stood in pensive silence for a moment.

"We can't last much longer without the flower," said Kabili. Again, this was something both men knew to be true. It seemed to Cahya that he, as well as the rest of the community had been avoiding thinking about this difficult truth for a while now. It might have been down to unrealistic optimism that things would pick up by themselves, or the hope that somebody else would come to a solution. It might have even been simply because the community as a whole had been through enough hardship and wanted to avoid thinking about the prospect of things getting worse. But Cahya was forced to agree with his friend's assessment – this was the clear reality, however much he wished it was not. Cahya was one of the many people that were unhappy when access to the Red Flower had been restricted by the North, but nobody had done anything about it at the time. Everybody had accepted the dubious explanation given, simply because they still had access to the flower and it was easier to live in harmony and accept the explanation than rise up and fight. Once the land was split in two and their access to the flower was stopped, the community was finding that survival was becoming more and more difficult. Another reason for avoiding thinking about the problem had been dawning on Cahya for a while now – guilt. Taking the easy option went against everything that the community stood for and, especially in retrospect, this is exactly what they had done. They had known deep down that it was wrong, and they

46

had allowed it to happen. They should never have allowed it to happen.

Kabili looked over at Cahya. Cahya knew what Kabili was thinking. He also knew that Kabili was testing the waters with his comment. Kabili was revered in the community, but Cahya knew that he was the one person that Kabili most respected.

"No, we can't", agreed Cahya.

Chapter 6 - Kabili

With these three small words, everything that had been on Kabili's mind seemed to manifest itself into reality. He had known for a long time that something needed to be done, but he was always reluctant to bring it up. He often told himself that this was because he was unsure that he would get the support from the community, or that it might cause more problems than it would solve, or that he needed to keep his children as his priority. These justifications of interchangeable priority kept him reasonably satisfied and stopped him from admitting the real reason to himself. However, as his children grew up and times got harder, he knew that he needed to take responsibility as the pillar of the community and take action. It was *his* responsibility. Hearing Cahya say those three words filled him with a mixture of relief and fear.

"So, what are we going to do?", asked Kabili. He saw that Cahya looked over at him with no intention to reply verbally. "We need to bring the flower back", Kabili continued, "which will mean going into the Northlands. As long as we get one or two, we should be ok. We know how quickly they can multiply and how easy they are to grow. We might need a few more just to be safe but really getting in will be the hard part. It will take a few days to get to the border, and then we know where they keep the reserves from before the partition. They won't have moved them". Kabili had had this on his mind for a long time, and had formulated these thoughts over the course of many nights and many showers over the last few years. He finally had the opportunity to share them with the person whose opinion held the most weight with him. "The only trouble might be with getting into the compound where they grow the flower, but we should be able to get to the gate quite easily", Kabili continued. "I will go with Sarama and Laith.

The three of us will be able to do it ourselves." He paused here, hoping that Cahya would take the opportunity to interject.

"I will come too", came the words as music to Kabili's grateful ears.

"No, it will be too dangerous. Us three will be able to do it", Kabili half-heartedly argued. He didn't want to pressure his friend into going, but he knew that he would really need him there. He didn't want to argue so hard that Cahya actually changed his mind.

"The three of you will be better at clearing the way and keeping us safe from the people who want to do us harm, but there are other dangerous things on the way too", Cahya responded. "I have no doubt that the three of you are the best fighters, but you will need the protection of my knowledge to keep you safe. I can see what you can't. You know how dangerous it will be".

"Yeah, it will be dangerous", agreed Kabili. "It will be too dangerous for you. You can give us your potions before we go and tell us which ones we will need for different circumstances. You teach me before we go". Kabili said this knowing that it was not a viable option. Anything Cahya ever gave to anybody was brewed specifically for that person at that particular time. There was no way that he would be able to quickly teach somebody over the course of a few hours – it took Cahya a lifetime of devotion and Kabili knew it. There were very few people in the community who even came close to Cahya's knowledge, and they were all people from Cahya's tribe. This was the reason that Cahya never trusted anybody with his potions. As expected, Cahya responded with an insistence that he would come, and a reiteration that he could see what Kabili could not. Kabili was grateful for Cahya's insistence, as he knew his arguments to be true. He communicated his gratitude by protesting no further. The thought of arguing that Cahya needs to stay back to take care of his granddaughter did cross Kabili's mind, but he was worried that this argument was too strong and so he kept his mouth shut.

Both men stood in silence in the field. Kabili knew that this was going to be a turning point. He had been able to somewhat enjoy the peace since the partition. Of course there had been difficulties, and he had to lead the community to different settlements, but this was something that he was accustomed to. The fact that he was so respected made it easy for him – the community trusted his judgement and followed his lead in going to and developing new settlements without question. He knew that the prospect of doing something so dangerous and drastic would truly be a test of his leadership and his other skills, but he also knew that he would be the best man for the job. Kabili looked at Cahya out of the side of his eye. He knew he would have been lost in his own thoughts, looking out over the fields. Looking at his friend, Kabili's fears were slightly eased again. He was happy that he would have Cahya there to help his mission, but he still needed to break the news to his two children. He had no doubt that either would go. He had instilled their sense of duty into them, and he knew that they took it seriously. He still, however, needed to tell them about their impending trip. Both were vital to his mission.

It was a great sense of pride for him that his two children were the most skilled fighters in the community, particularly because of the part he played in it. His daughter picked up the bow and arrow from watching him practise, as did his son with the sword. The strong work-ethic that he instilled in them had helped them both surpass his own skills in their respective weapons – particularly his daughter with the bow and arrow. This was Kabili's secondary weapon of choice, but his daughter practiced relentlessly and Kabili was confident that she was able to hit targets that even he was unable to. Similarly, Kabili felt that Laith's strength and speed with the sword was probably better than his ever was, and certainly better than his was now that he was getting older. Something that Kabili particularly liked about Laith's style of fighting was how calm and composed he always remained. Again, Kabili felt that this was something that he had inherited from him. Kabili had always put an emphasis on fighting with your brain – 'we need to have the brains and the brawn', he used to tell his son. Kabili did feel that there was something different in how his son seemed while fighting as opposed to how he himself fought. Whereas Kabili used his brain to identify his opponents' weaknesses and attack them quickly, he had noticed that Laith could maintain concentration for long periods and just seemed to be naturally relaxed when fighting. He never seemed to be flustered. Kabili had considered that this was due to his quiet confidence in his superior skill. In any case, Kabili knew that it was an asset that he needed for his mission, and it was one that he needed to go home and secure, even if only as a formality. He knew that his daughter would be more enthusiastic about his mission than Laith, who was more likely to just take it in his stride. He thought about telling his daughter first, and then them telling Laith together so that her enthusiasm might rub off on him. This seemed the sensible thing to do, he decided.

A cold breeze blew across the field and alerted Kabili that it was time to awaken from his thoughts.

"I'd better go and get ready for the gathering. Hopefully Esmeralda is home getting ready now", said Cahya gently. The breeze had obviously jolted him out of his thoughts too.

"Yeah, I need to do the same", said Kabili. "I need to go and tell Sarama and Laith, too, actually. Maybe I will wait until after the gathering..." Kabili trailed off as he was speaking. Really he was thinking out loud. He exchanged a short goodbye with Cahya whilst his mind was on how and when he would tell his children about his mission – well, it was their mission now. He had already decided that it would be a good idea to tell his daughter first, but he wasn't sure if he should wait until after the gathering. Thinking about it, it did seem like a sensible idea to him – it would give his children the chance to enjoy this gathering as much as they could and then they could prepare together afterwards. Kabili picked up his scythe and a couple of sickles that he saw near the shelter with the tin roof and started the short walk towards his cabin, where he knew his children would be getting ready.

Kabili approached the front door of his cabin but did not go inside. Instead, he walked around the back to the store where he kept his tools. In there, he placed his scythe and the couple of sickles that he picked up. He would find out to whom they belonged soon enough. In any case, his store was always left open so whoever had left them in his field would know where to find them, should they need them. With the harvest having been collected for now, it was unlikely that anybody would need them in the immediate future. Kabili walked into his house through the back door. He heard the shower running, and the pump whirring around the back. He walked down the corridor to find the living room and kitchen empty, so went back up the corridor to take a quick look in his son's and daughter's bedrooms respectively. Both were empty, so he wasn't sure which one of them was in the shower. He suspected it was probably his daughter and that Laith was out somewhere with Esmy, as usual. He poured himself a small glass of fermented raas, placed down his sword and shield, and sat down for the first time today. Only upon sitting down did he realise how tired he was, and he sank down deeper into the sofa. He had better not get too comfortable – he had to go to the gathering soon. He heard the shower turn off and, from the strength and pattern of footsteps coming from the bathroom, realised that it must be his daughter. This could be the perfect time to break the news to her about their mission, as he had planned. It should make no difference if he told her before or after the gathering.

His daughter emerged from the bathroom.

"Hi, Dad", she said, smiling cheerfully.

"Hi, little one", he replied. He spoke lightly only to his daughter. "Where's Laith?", he asked her, as she came and sat down on the armchair next to him.

"He's still with Esmy in Uncle Reyhan's field, I think", she replied. "He'll probably be back soon, I don't know", she continued. Having been sat down for approximately seven seconds, she got up again. "I fancy some raas as well now

– it is the Pink Moon after all. Have we got any fresh one?"

"This is fermented", Kabili replied.

"Yeah, I fancy a bit of fresh", she said as she headed towards the kitchen area of the room. "There's some here. Do you want some?"

"No, I have this".

His daughter poured herself a small glass of raas – it only needed to be small as it was so sweet – and sat back down next to him. This would be the perfect opportunity to tell her about the mission, he thought to himself. As he was deciding on his opening sentence, he realised that it would actually be easier to have this conversation when both his children were together. It would also be fairer this way.

"Have you had fun today?", he asked his daughter, smiling.

"Yeah, I did, it was nice", she replied. "Did you?"

"Yeah."

There was a moment of silence.

"Me and your Uncle Cahya have just been talking", Kabili continued. He looked over at his daughter, waiting for a response.

"Have you?", she asked, after a small pause. "About what?".

"Well you already know about why we have to keep moving settlements and what is happening with the land. The harvest is getting smaller and smaller and there is hardly enough food to go around already. It's only going to get worse now. By the time you have children, there will be no food for them at all. We need to do something now to save their lives." As Kabili was putting forward his argument, he found himself getting more impassioned by it. Everything that he was saying was true, and he found that he roused even himself as he was putting his previously unspoken ideas into tangible arguments.

"What are we gonna do?"

"Well, that's the thing. Me and your uncle have decided that the only thing that we can do really is to go and get a Red Flower". He paused for a moment, trying to gauge his daughter's reaction. She gave nothing away. "That is the *only* way that we can get the land fertile again", he continued. "Without it, nothing will grow. Things will stop growing completely and your children won't have any food to eat." It was important to Kabili that his daughter understood the severity of the situation. "So that is what we are going to have to do". With the conclusion of this last sentence, the fire that he had ignited within himself died down and a different feeling began to creep over him. He felt a touch of nerves as he looked on towards his daughter for a response, and a small amount of doubt crept into his mind as to whether it was the right time to bring this up. Should he have waited for Laith? Was it even the right thing to do at all? Could there be another way for the survival of the community without doing something so drastic? These feelings extinguished themselves almost immediately after they began, when his daughter replied.

"Yeah, we will have to".

Kabili knew that he was doing the right thing. He had thought about it at length before today and, although difficult, he knew that he was the one person who could and would make the tough decisions for the greater good. He reminded himself that he had made tough decisions in the past that other people would not have had the strength to make. He knew he made the right decisions then, and he knew that he was making the right decision now. Decision-making was his strength – it was part of what made him a good leader, and it was why he was so well respected in the community. People trusted his judgement because he looked at things sensibly and logically, and always reached the conclusion with the best outcome for everybody, even if it was difficult for himself. It had been that way in the past and remained that way today. He was happy to sacrifice himself for the greater good. Despite this, he still needed to make sure that his daughter was happy to come along. If she wasn't, he would have to re-evaluate the likelihood of a successful outcome. He knew that he was handy with a bow and arrow, but he had to admit to himself that she was better. And he definitely needed her as an extra person there.

"Would you like to come with me and your uncle?", he asked. "Laith will be coming, too", he quickly added.

"Yeah, obviously", she replied, smiling. "I'm not gonna let you lot go by yourself. And Laith is rubbish, anyway, so you're all gonna need me".

"That's good," Kabili said. "It's going to be dangerous, though". He said this in a light-hearted tone, almost in a sing-song manner, somewhat undermining the actual danger that would be involved. The tone was partly to assuage any fears his daughter might have, but mainly to assuage his own of her backing out. The thing that he feared the most was any harm coming to his daughter, but he knew that he needed her in this mission. It was a tough choice that he wasn't afraid of making. "But I will make sure that nothing happens to you, anyway". You don't need to worry about anything when your dad is around". He said this in a more serious tone, so she would know that he was being genuine, and just in case his previous tone had seemed a bit too light-hearted.

"*I* will make sure that nothing happens to me, don't worry", his daughter replied with what seemed to him to be genuine relaxation. "Does Laith know?"

"About our mission?", he asked, knowing that this could really be the only thing that his daughter was referring to. "Not yet. I thought that we could tell him later". Again, he paused to try and gauge his daughter's reaction. Again, she gave nothing away. "Did you want to tell him with me?", he asked her.

"I don't mind. We can ask him together if you want", she replied. He smiled at her. A genuine smile. The type that he had only for his daughter.

"Okay. I'd better quickly get ready and then we can go in a bit. Is Laith coming with us or...? Well, he can meet us there, too, if he wants. It doesn't really make any difference".

"No, I don't know when he will be back. It will probably be soon", his daughter replied.

"Okay then, I'll go get ready".

"Okay".

Chapter 7 - Laith

Laith had been alone with Esmy in Uncle Reyhan's field for a while now. He had gone at his father's request to drop off some crops and had asked Esmy to come along too. He enjoyed being around her. He couldn't really explain it, but he felt different when he was around her. Happier. Or lighter. Brighter, maybe? He was unsure and, to be honest, he had never really thought about it in much depth. But he felt something inside him when she was near him, so hers was a friendship he truly appreciated.

Once they had got to the field, Uncle Reyhan had immediately greeted them with a smile and handed a glass of raas to Laith. As he was pouring a second, Esmy stopped him, saying that she would share Laith's. They stood speaking to Uncle Reyhan for a while, and it had soon become time for him to start packing up. They had helped him to pack away his tools and said goodbye to everybody as people slowly started going home to get ready. Soon, it was just the three of them left. Uncle Reyhan had offered them some more raas as the three of them sat down, but Laith and Esmy had both politely declined. Uncle Reyhan had jovially mumbled something about fermenting it instead and taken it away with him when he had left, saying that he would see the two of them at the gathering later.

Since Uncle Reyhan had left, Laith and Esmy had moved themselves to sit on the floor instead. Esmy found it more comfortable and Laith did not decline. Laith did have it in the back of his mind that it might have been time for them to both go and start getting ready for the gathering but, from Esmy's suggestion of sitting on the floor, it was clear to him that she did not mind staying for longer. He was glad. There was no real fixed time that they had to be there, and he would much rather spend his time alone in Esmy's company than in a noisy crowd of people.

Esmy's head was resting on Laith's shoulder as they sat in silence looking at nothing in particular. Laith had never felt much more comfortable than he was now. Internal comfort, mainly, considering he was sat on the floor. If anything, the only niggling bother he had was that he knew in the back of his mind that they would have to leave at some point. The temperature was dropping but there was still plenty of sunlight left to gently illuminate the newly-bare field in a slightly golden hue. The fields normally looked slightly strange to Laith immediately after the crops had been harvested – as though something was missing. He didn't feel that way today, though. He must be getting used to it, the twenty-third time of it happening. Today it felt magical.

Laith felt a breeze blow across him. This must have been what prompted Esmy to shuffle and then move a bit closer to him.

"It's been quite nice today, hasn't it?", Laith said to Esmy.

"Yeah, it's been really nice. This is my favourite part of the day, though", she replied. "Before it gets too busy later", she added, hastily.

"Mine too. Let's stay for a bit longer, before we have to go and get ready", suggested Laith. He hoped Esmy would not disagree.

"Okay", Esmy agreed, shuffling slightly closer again. "I wonder if Grandad is still at the field with your dad", she said. "Probably not by now. He's probably gone home".

"Yeah, maybe", said Laith. "That means Dad will have gone home too. And Sarama is probably getting ready".

The two sat in silence for a few more minutes. Laith wondered what Esmy was thinking about as she fiddled with the small bits of dried grass in between the two of them. He felt her shuffle again and realised that it was starting to get a bit late. Time, unfortunately, had a habit of passing when he would rather it didn't. He reluctantly moved his left shoulder, the one upon which she was resting her head, as a way to get her attention.

"Yeah, we should", she said to him, and picked her head up. Laith stood up and picked up his sword from beside him. He offered Esmy his hand, and she took it to hoist herself up. She did a little jump as she stood and brushed herself down before looking up at smiling at Laith. He took this to mean she was ready and the two of them set off slowly.

"I like Uncle Reyhan's field", Esmy told Laith as they were leaving.

"Yeah, so do I", said Laith. What he actually meant was he liked being with Esmy in Uncle Reyhan's field. He was yet to be convinced that the field itself was anything special. Although Laith and Esmy were together quite often, being together in Uncle Reyhan's field generally meant that they were away from his father and her grandad. For some reason, this made him slightly more relaxed. In a way, he felt more like he was himself when he could be there with her. He wondered if Esmy felt it too, and if this is what she actually meant with her statement. If pressed to think about it, he would have to admit that he hoped so.

Laith allowed Esmy to dictate the pace of the walk. She was walking slowly, something with which he was more than content. Every now and again, she playfully knocked into him. Laith knew that this meant that she was in a good mood. She always put him in a good mood too. Laith considered that some might find it strange that they were both relatively cheerful given what day it was, but that didn't seem to matter when he was with her. They slowly ambled towards the point in the path where they would normally split to go to their respective homes.

"I might as well come with you to the field", said Esmy. "I bet Grandad is still there".

"Yeah, him and Dad might still be there", said Laith, suspecting that they might not. He continued to walk with Esmy in the direction towards the field, close to his own house. They approached the field slowly and saw that neither his father nor her grandfather was there. They continued to the shelter regardless and stopped next to it, looking out towards the field. They had once been caught out in a heavy rainstorm in this field. Although the trip to his house was not very long at all, they had decided to instead take cover under the simple shelter with the tin roof. The metal had amplified the sound of the raindrops to nearly deafening proportions. It was the most terrible, thunderous, tumultuous tempest that Laith had ever experienced. He had hoped that it would never stop.

The sun was getting lower in the sky, casting long shadows in front of them. It felt like such a long time ago that Laith was there with Uncle Cahya collecting sunbeams – possibly because of the stark difference in the look of the field now that the wheat had been felled. It looked empty. A new era.

"I was collecting sunbeams with your grandad here earlier", he told Esmy.

"How did you manage that?", she replied, half-laughing. Laith knew that she was referring to the fact that he could not see them. He couldn't help but to smile back at her. When she laughed, he felt it too.

"Well, Uncle obviously told me what to do", he told her.

"Yours are probably crap", she teased him while laughing. "I'll go home and check them later. I'll be able to tell which ones are yours straight away".

"Oi, no you won't", he protested whilst giving her a playful shove. "I think that they'll all be equally wonderful." Laith smiled at Esmy, knowing that this would bring the matter to an end. "You can see them, can't you? What do they look like?"

"Grandad can see them more clearly, I think. He seems to find it really easy. I sometimes need to concentrate a bit harder to see it in detail but, yeah, I can."

"What do they look like?"

"I don't know. It's hard to explain. Like energy, I suppose. Like, do you know how you can tell when somebody is happy? Or angry? It looks like that. Kind of like…it looks brighter, or lighter. Or just a bit different.

Kinda like different colours, but not really colourful. You can tell the colours though, but they don't look physical. It's more that they have…a colourful…quality to them."

Laith was struggling to imagine what she meant.

"And the different ones look different too,", Esmy continued. "Sunrise is different to sunset, and you need them for different things. And then they are different at different times of the year as well, and just sometimes they are more intense if you are lucky".

Laith would have loved to have understood, but he was unable to relate to anything that she had just said.

"Oh".

"Grandad will probably be collecting the sunset ones soon too, because of what day it is. Maybe you should go and help him, now that you're an expert", she teased. Laith rolled his eyes at her.

"We had better go and get ready for the gathering", he said, somewhat reluctantly.

"Yeah, we do need to. Grandad will be wondering where I am. Actually, he'll probably be sat drinking tea. Oh, now that I've mentioned it, I hope he's made me some too. Okay, I'll see you later on – I don't want my tea to get cold. I hope it exists".

Laith touched her arm and then waved her goodbye as she walked across the field in the direction of her house. He paused for a moment and watched her long shadow bounce along the uneven ground in the golden hue of the hour. He paused a moment longer before turning and setting off in the direction of his own house. It just struck him that the temperature had actually dropped quite significantly since he had last given it any consideration, and he began walking more quickly. Also, he did actually need to get home and get ready for the gathering.

He soon got to his front door and opened the door into his living room, where his sister was sat on the sofa.

"Nice of you to finally join us", she quipped, as he removed his shoes to put them by the door. He knew how much she loved to argue with him.

"I've been busy doing deliveries", he responded. "I wish we all had time to sit around on sofas drinking raas all day". He loved to argue with his sister just as much.

"Maybe you would have time, if you didn't spend three hours doing a fifteen minute delivery"

"It's part of the customer service. Do you want a job done quickly, or a job done well?"

"I'm not sure how badly you could do a job of dropping off some wheat in a field that's about five minutes away"

"Ten. And, okay, next year I'll just run to the gate and throw it at people from there, shall I?"

"Yes, if you can get it done in good time. And, anyway, it doesn't take an extra three hours to walk from the gate to the person"

"The three hours is part of the service. I like to make sure that everybody is happy, and that requires me to stay behind and bring joy into their lives with my presence. That's why I'm the person who needs to go and not bloody you. I am joyous and you're a git".

"It's because Dad wants to get rid of you and not me. The only joy you bring into people's lives is when you leave".

"Dad sends me because I do a better job. Anyway, shut up, it wasn't even three hours – it was, like, one. Where's Dad?"

"He's gone early to help set the fire up. You know he hates sitting around. I thought I'd wait for you, though. Even though you take ages for no reason. You're welcome."

"Thanks. I'm gonna shower first, though. You can go if you want", Laith replied.

"No, I can't be bothered. Nobody will be there yet. By the way, Dad is gonna tell you about a mission that we're all doing".

Laith's immediate thought was that it was bound to be something relatively small and quite possibly unnecessary – building a fence or a store, or something along those lines. But then his sister surely wouldn't have used the word 'mission'? Unless that was the word that their Dad used when he told her, to make it seem more exciting, maybe.

"What is it?", he asked her

"We are going to go and get some Red Flower", she replied with an air of just popping to the field downriver. He knew that the only place of getting the Red Flower was from the compound in the Northlands, but thought that he had better clarify.

"From the Northlands?", he asked.

"No, I thought we could just pull it from my bloody arse", she replied. "Obviously from the Northlands. Will you come?"

"Yeah, obviously", Laith instinctively replied. "Well, I can't imagine I'll have a choice". As he said these words, his thoughts immediately went to Esmy. Although he knew that the mission should take only a few days – maybe a week – he already missed his friend. It seemed silly even to him that the mere thought of leaving was enough to make him miss her. It must be because they had never spent very much time apart from each other at all – not a day had gone by in their lives, he realised, that he hadn't spent time with her. His sister interrupted his thoughts.

"What's wrong?", she demanded.

"Nothing - just tired" he said.

"It won't be too dangerous. You know how good I am with the bow and arrow", she said. "And you're okay with the sword too". It seemed to Laith that she was trying her best to make it sound like she was saying this reluctantly. And she never complimented her own ability, either. She must really think that he was worried.

"I'm brilliant with the sword", he corrected her. Now that she mentioned it, he did realise that the mission would probably bring some danger with it. He couldn't imagine that the Northlands would give up a flower particularly willingly, and wondered how heavily it was guarded. Who would they be guarding it from? From what he knew, the people living in the Northlands had no reason to steal it, as they were just given as much as they needed to make their crops prosper. This would mean that, any guards, would be specifically guarding it from his own community. His own community did not consist of an overwhelming number of people, and so maybe this would mean that there was no need for the flower to be guarded particularly heavily. On the other hand, given that the vast majority of people were living in the Northlands, and their land was prosperous, surely they had guards to spare. They could easily afford to have hundreds of people guarding the compound, if they so wished. Rather unhelpfully, his train of thought had split and brought him to two completely opposite conclusions. Thankfully, however, the number of guards and the inherent danger in the mission was relatively low on his list of priorities.

Chapter 8 - Esmeralda

Esmeralda had been sat in her favourite seat at the dinner table alone for the last five minutes or so. As soon as she had parted ways with Laith at the field, she had hoped that there would be some tea waiting for her at her house. She got home and was grateful to see that her grandad had left some in a pan for her, which she duly heated up and was now grasping in both hands. The evening beams that were apparent in the tea comforted her. She had had it in the back of her mind when walking home that she hoped her grandfather used them in the tea, but she was worried about thinking about it too loudly as, actually, she'd have been grateful for any tea at all. Her hand was noticeably void of a biscuit, as there were none. She probably would have picked one up if there were some there, out of habit, but she was not particularly desperate for one this evening. She heard the shower turn off, which meant that her grandad would be joining her soon. In the meantime, she slowly sipped her tea and reminisced on the day's events.

Her grandad came out with his hair still open from the shower.

"Oh, you decided to come back, then?", he said with a smile, which she returned.

"Thanks for the tea", she said.

"Yeah, I thought that you would want it with evening beams today, after the day you've had", he said. Esmeralda was unsure how her grandfather would know that – she, herself, had only half-thought it once walking back towards the house. Her grandad must have prepared it before she even knew she wanted it. Impressive, she thought, although she did wonder what kind of day she had had that required the energy of evening beams. She thought better than to ask, in case she did not like the answer.

Her grandfather walked over to the soaking pan and started washing it.

"I was speaking to your Uncle Kabili earlier", he said to her. "We are going to go away for a few days". From his tone, Esmeralda inferred that this would not be for a holiday, not that her grandad or uncle were the holidaying type anyway.

"What for?", she asked. As she said it, the thought came across her mind that asking 'where to?' instead might have sounded slightly less indignant.

"We need to go to the Northlands", her grandfather replied. She noticed that he was trying too hard to sound relaxed. "You'll be okay here by yourself for a few days, won't you?"

Despite her grandad not actually answering her previous question satisfactorily, now that she found out that they were going to the Northlands, coupled with the fact that it was a plan devised with Uncle Kabili, brought a more pressing question to the forefront of her mind.

"Who's going?", she asked. She thought that maybe now it was her grandad's turn to notice her trying too hard to sound relaxed. She certainly heard it herself.

"Me, your uncle, Sarama and Laith". Esmeralda hoped that his emphasis on the last word was either unintentional or imaginary. However, in the short time since she asked the question, she had also made up her mind that she was going too. She communicated this to her grandfather, who let out a little chuckle. She personally did not see what was so amusing.

"It's going to be dangerous", he said. "You don't even know what we are going for."

"It doesn't matter", she replied. "If you are going, then I am going too. I'm not going to let you go by yourself".

"Yes", he replied, wryly. She decided to be unsure at what his tone meant and lean towards it being a light-hearted jibe at her stubborn nature.

"Why *are* you going, anyway?". It suddenly occurred to her that she would actually like to know this, too.

"We need the energy from the red flower", he replied, matter-of-factly. Thinking about it, this was true. She had lived nearly her whole life in this nomadic fashion, moving on when the soil no longer had enough life to provide them with sufficient crops, and she only ever very briefly wondered what it would be like if life was different. Maybe the red flower was not only what the community needed, but it was also what she needed in order to satisfy her vague feeling of loss and longing. It could be the anchor that she needed to keep her in one place, which might bring a feeling of contentment with it.

Her grandfather picked up her mug, which she realised was now empty, and washed it.

"Thanks", she said. "Anyway, yeah, we do need that energy. I'm coming with you – the others won't be very useful to you finding it, will they?" As she said this, she remembered that Laith had told her he collected some beams in the morning with her grandfather. Her eyes flicked towards the shelf where her grandfather kept them.

"Well, Laith might be quite useful", her grandfather replied. He seemed to have spotted where she was looking, as he reached up and pulled down a jar from the shelf and handed it to Esmeralda. She looked inside it carefully and saw what looked to be quite an impressive sunrise beam.

"This is one that Laith collected?", she asked, knowing the answer already. Her grandfather smiled silently in reply. "Well, I'm coming anyway".

"Are you ready to go to the gathering, or are you going to have a shower first?" her grandfather asked her.

"No, I will come with you now. I'll shower after – I don't like going to bed with fire on me".

"Come on then, let's go", said her grandad as he headed towards the door. The two of them headed outside and Esmeralda noticed the sun getting quite low in the sky.

"Are you going to go to Uncle's field first to collect the sunbeams, or are you going to get them from the park?"

"Your uncle will be at the park by now, I think. I am going to go straight there. Laith and Sarama probably won't be ready yet. Why don't you go to their house and then the three of you can come together? You'll probably be bored otherwise".

This sounded like a good idea to Esmeralda. She would much rather spend her time in the quiet environment of Laith's house than waiting for him at the community gathering. She told her grandad that she would see him later as they parted ways.

She realised that she suddenly felt lighter. It had not occurred to her before, but the thought of going on this expedition might have had her a bit worried, and now being alone gave her time to process it and think about it. Or maybe the fact that she was heading to see Laith and Sarama made her feel more at ease, as she knew that they were in the same position as her. She would have people to talk to about it honestly. They were around the same age – certainly the same generation – and they had all grown up together in this new age. She thought that maybe it was a bit more confusing for them, as they were used to living like this. They were not going on this expedition to get things back to normal, like her uncle and grandad were. For them, the reward for this mission would be to be cast into a completely new type of lifestyle. Still, she told herself, it would surely bring the feeling of home that she had always felt she was missing. For now, she knew that she was happy that she was heading towards Laith's house rather than to the loud and noisy gathering. She only ever really felt comfortable at those if he was there with her. Somehow, him being there made her feel less exposed to the noise and excitement. She continued to imagine what the expedition would be like as she walked towards Laith's house. She knew that they would be heading up north and surely this would mean that they would head past some of their old settlements. She wondered how many of them she would recognise. Certainly the last one, at least.

She got to Laith's house in a few minutes and stamped her shoes on the doormat. She took them off as she opened the door without knocking and stepped into the living room. It was empty, but the presence of Laith's shoes told her that he must be here. She heard the shower running and assumed that it must be him. She tried to make as much noise as she could to announce her presence whilst entering the house, in case Sarama was also here, and then sat down on the sofa to wait for Laith. She heard a door open and turned around to see who it was.

"Oh, hi, Esmy", said Sarama, heading out of her room. "Laith is in the shower, as usual", she said as she took a seat next to her. "I was just getting ready to go to the square. Well, I am ready. I'm just waiting for bloody Laith - story of my life. Do you fancy some tea? I'm gonna make some". She got back up and headed towards the kitchen without waiting for an answer.

"Umm, no thanks", replied Esmeralda.

"Are you sure? I can make it with beams. Your grandad always gives us some – we have some in the cupboard".

"No, honestly, I don't really fancy any". Esmeralda really only liked the way her grandad made tea – he seemed to be able to balance the ingredients properly. There always seemed to be some subtle variations in the taste from one day to the next, but it still somehow always tasted perfect in the moment. 'Felt', not 'tasted'. And 'tasted', actually. This was a skill that nobody else had. She could never get it quite right herself, and it seemed to her that Sarama would be in an even worse position.

"You sure? You'll be jealous when I'm having mine".

Esmeralda chuckled. "I'm sure, thanks".

She heard Sarama fiddling around with pots and pans behind her, and thought about starting a conversation about the expedition. She wondered if Sarama was aware of it yet. She must be, as her grandad had told her that Sarama and Laith were going. As much as she wanted to bring it up, she did not quite feel comfortable enough to do so just yet. She heard the shower turn off too, and footsteps in that room.

"Are you looking forward to the gathering?", she asked Sarama.

"Yeah, kind of. It should be ok. Are you?"

Esmeralda knew that this was the anniversary of the day that Sarama and Lath had lost their mother, as it was during the same massacre that she had lost her own family. She wondered if Sarama's lack of enthusiasm was down to this or, as with her own, just a vague feeling of detachment.

"Yeah". This was only half a lie. She wasn't *not* looking forward to it.

Esmeralda heard the bathroom door open and Laith came out, looking fresh. His hair was still quite wet – it looked as though it would still be dripping. He looked down the corridor towards the living room as he was heading towards his own bedroom. As soon as he made eye contact with Esmeralda, however, he smiled and changed direction towards the living room. She couldn't help but smile back. As he walked in, he looked towards his sister at the stove.

"Oh, you're making tea, as usual?", he asked her.

"None of your business seeing as you think you're too important to drink tea".

"You know that it's not the end of the world if some people just don't like tea", he said, as he sat down close to Esmeralda. She reached up and felt the hair that was hanging down his back.

"Your shirt is gonna get all wet. Aren't you going to dry your hair? You'll catch a cold", she said to him.

"Yeah, aren't you gonna go sit in your room for three hours and wait for it to dry like you normally do?", Esmeralda heard Sarama say from behind them.

"It'll dry, don't worry", said Laith. "Can you get me some water, please, seeing as you're in the kitchen?"

"Get it your bloody self, you lazy git", Sarama replied, pretending to be angry. Esmeralda always found it funny how Laith and his sister would argue about anything. "Do *you* want some water, Esmy?", Sarama asked, heightening the sweetness in her voice to unnatural levels, surely to annoy Laith. "I don't mind getting any for *you*", she smiled.

"No, thank you", Esmeralda laughed. Sarama came stomping from the kitchen and thrust a glass of water angrily towards her brother.

"Here", she said, before returning back to the kitchen area to pick up her own mug of tea. "I'm gonna go get ready", she said, as she took her mug and headed towards her room. Esmeralda heard the door close. She felt Laith's hair again.

"I can't believe you just sit like this", she said to him.

"I can squeeze all the water out onto you, if you like?", he said. She rolled her eyes at him.

"No, it's okay". She hesitated. "Grandad said that you were going with him and your dad to get the red flower?".

"Yeah. And Sarama".

"And me". As she said this, for some reason, she felt herself get happier. She saw in Laith's face that he was happy about it too. "Do you know what the plan is?', she asked him.

"No. I just found out that I am going. Dad will have a plan, I'm sure. I'm not really too fussed. I'm happy that you're coming, though".

"Do you think it'll be dangerous?"

"Nah, probably not. Well, maybe, actually. I don't know, I hadn't really thought too much about it. It might be, but it'll be fine anyway."

"Yeah, it will be. I'm quite excited for it now, actually". This was the truth. Far from what she was feeling just a few moments ago, now that she had seen and spoken about it with Laith, she was actually quite looking forward to doing this with him. They had always spent a lot of time together, but this felt different. It felt nice knowing that they would be working together to do something that could help to save their community. She wondered why she had not thought of this obvious positive before.

Chapter 9 - Laith

Laith was feeling decidedly more positive about the mission than he had been a few moments ago. In the shower, he had been trying hard to convince himself of the positives of the mission - it was both an honour and his duty to help the community; it shouldn't be too difficult; it was only a few days long. Now he actually believed them and, furthermore, couldn't even believe that he ever had any apprehension. If anything, he was quite looking forward to it now. Seeing that Esmy was excited about it made him feel the same. It would be nice to share this experience – it would be something nice to reminisce on when they were still friends in their eighties, with their children playing together in the permanent settlement that would not exist if it were not for the two of them. In this imaginary scenario, the faces of Laith's and Esmy's respective spouses were blurred out, but he knew for a fact that the four of them would be friends regardless. They would have to be, as there was no such thing as a future where he and Esmy were apart. In fact, he did have the vague knowledge of the existence of who he supposed would technically be Esmy's fiancé – Darma, his name was. He was somebody who was part of the same tribe as Esmy but the two of them did not often speak about it. She might have mentioned it once or twice in their whole lives. Laith just knew that it was part of the culture of Esmy's tribe - she had technically been engaged since she was very young, but she did not have much to do with the person she was expected to marry. Once she was older and feeling ready, the two of them would get to know each other and be married soon after. Whenever he would think about it, Laith would feel a little bit uneasy. His thought process always mapped out the same way - he always first decided that this was because he was worried that his friend might have to marry somebody that she did not want to. He would then realise that he actually knew that she did have the right to refuse, and the knowledge of this did not make him feel any less uneasy. He would tell himself that his feelings must simply be due to the fact that the notion of a marriage in this manner was different to how the other tribes did it, and the strange feeling he had must simply be unfamiliarity. Finally, he would always satisfy the feeling of unease the best he could - by telling himself that it was really none of his business and that she would be happy, therefore he would be happy, and stop thinking about it. This is what he did now, as he focused his mind back on the mission for which his positive feelings were now unforced.

Laith knew that they probably needed to leave soon, but he didn't really want to. He was enjoying where he was at the moment, and it seemed to him that Esmy was in no particular rush either. He sipped his water slowly.

"What do you think this mission will involve?", he asked Esmy

"I don't really know anything about it", she replied. "Grandad just told me that you were all going, so I said that I'm coming too".

"I'm glad you are", he told her. He wanted her to know.

"Yeah, and me", she replied. "I probably would have stayed if you did, but I think it'll be quite fun with both of us going". She reached up and grabbed his hair again. "As long as you don't spend the whole time dripping all over me".

"It'll dry, don't worry", Laith reiterated, pretending to be exasperated with the attention his wet hair was getting from Esmy. "Here", he said as he shook his head a little bit, flicking water all over her. "Are you dead? No."

"No, but I could have drowned just now. I'm not sure how happy I am with you being so reckless with my life like that".

"As if I ever would be", said Laith, earnestly. Even though Esmy was clearly making the comment in jest, it still made him feel a bit uneasy to hear it. He received a playful knock in his shoulder in return, and felt it in his heart.

"Oh my god are you still drinking your water?!", Laith

heard his sister demand, as she exaggerated a storm out of her room. "Come on, we haven't got all day. Dad is probably waiting for us".

"How do you know I'm still drinking it? How can you see it from there?"

"Well, have you finished it?"

"No, but that's not the point. You shouldn't assume. And anyway, if you assumed that I hadn't finished, that's because you know that it's not reasonable to expect a normal person to finish their water in such a short amount of time. Some of us like to enjoy it".

"No, it's because I know that *you* are not a normal person and you love to faff about when everybody is waiting for you".

"Some of us are tired from a hard day's work. You'd need to recover too, if you ever did anything."

"You walked to one field and then sat around all day. Hurry up and finish it", Sarama demanded.

Laith knew that she was probably right – he should finish it so that they could go. He tapped Esmy on the thigh twice gently with the back of his fingers to warn her of the fact that he would be getting up. She did not say anything but got up after he did and smiled at him. A non-conscious smile appeared on his face. He washed his cup as well as his sister's, which she helpfully put in the sink for him, and the three of them headed outside.

Laith noticed that the sun was beginning to creep below the horizon. This meant that the fire in the square would have been roaring for a while now – no doubt his father would have been one of the people in charge of setting it up. The three of them walked together in silence. Esmy was walking close to Laith's right, with his sister walking in front of the two of them, ensuring they kept to what she considered to be a reasonable pace. Thanks to this, the three of them got to the square in no time. They immediately headed towards the fire in the centre, where Laith knew his father and uncle would be.

"Alright", Laith greeted his father's back, as he approached him. His father turned around and saw him.

"Oh, alright", he replied. His eyes immediately flicked to Laith's right - Esmy and then Sarama. He smiled at them both.

"Do you need a hand?", asked Laith

"With what?", his father asked

"I dunno. Anything?"

"Nah, not really. I don't think there's anything to do", his father said, looking around as though in search of a tangible task.

"No, not now that we have done everything", laughed Uncle Cahya as he came from around the fire. "Trust you three to show up now".

"Hi, Uncle", said Laith. He heard his sister say the same. The sight of his uncle always put Laith in a good mood. "The sun is setting now. Are you going to collect some more beams?"

"Yes, of course", replied his uncle. "These are important ones today, although it's the moonbeams later that will be really special. I'm going to start now, actually. Do you want to help?"

"Yeah, okay. You might have to show me what to do again, though."

"No, it's easy. You did it perfectly this morning. Just do that again. Esmeralda will help you, anyway, I'm sure. Come on, let's go and find somewhere nice", said Uncle Cahya, as he handed Laith and Esmy some glass bottles.

The three of them walked away from the fire to find somewhere with fewer people. Although the square was not particularly big, Laith was glad to be moving away from the hubbub around the main attraction to some mild notion of peace and tranquility. Uncle Cahya stopped abruptly, which made Laith and Esmy do the same.

"This seems like a nice place", said Uncle Cahya. He looked at Laith, smiling. Taking this to be an invitation to share his opinion, though firm in the knowledge that his opinion in this matter would be based only on what his uncle thought anyway, Laith offered a non-committal smile and slight nod of the head. "Okay, good", Uncle Cahya laughed. Laith smiled more, feeling a combination of relief and happiness. He was relieved that he had picked a good place, and happy that his Uncle Cahya went to the effort of making him feel as though he had picked it when, in fact, it was obvious that he had done nothing. This was typical of Uncle Cahya, and was one of the reasons that Laith loved being around him so much. He had a knack for making people feel valued, or just positive in general. Laith watched as his uncle sat cross-legged on the floor and opened up his glass jar, pointing it at the intensifying sunset. Even Laith noticed that it was particularly intense this evening. He wondered how it would seem to his uncle.

"Do these ones taste different, Uncle?", Laith asked as he squatted down and uncorked his own glass bottle. "I don't think that I can tell the difference. Maybe I could if I had them side by side, but I don't think so. Do they taste different?"

"They feel different", his uncle replied. He stopped, and seemed to be thinking. "I'm not sure if I can taste the difference between them, but you can definitely feel the difference between them, even if you don't know you can. The differences may be subtle, but you would definitely be able to feel the difference. It's just about knowing which ones to use in which circumstances".

Laith thought about this. He thought that he might have understood, but wasn't sure he did.

"Sunrise and sunset look exactly the same, don't they?", asked Uncle Cahya. Laith nodded somewhat apprehensively. He was unsure himself, but he knew his uncle would be right. "The colour of the sky, the hue of the air, the light – everything – it looks the same at sunset and sunrise. You could look at a picture of one of them, and you wouldn't be confident in saying whether it was sunrise or sunset. I know that I wouldn't. You might take a guess but, if somebody told you it was the other one, you'd happily believe it wouldn't you?"

Laith nodded. He realised that this was true.

"But even if you were unsure of the time, and you were put in the middle of a field, you would be able to tell whether it was sunrise or sunset a lot more easily. You could feel the difference, even though you think you can't.

It's the same with the beams. The energy is different, and so they feel different when they are around you and inside you. They do different things. They do similar things", he acknowledged, "but definitely different. And we need both". Uncle Cahya corked his bottle and lifted it to his eye. Seemingly happy with it, he put it in his bag. Laith looked at his own bottle and then over at Esmy. She came over and sat down cross-legged on the floor by his side. She uncorked a bottle her grandad had given her earlier and rested it on the ground, holding and angling it so that the open end pointed towards the fiery sky.

"It is quite strong tonight, isn't it?", she said.

"It is", her grandfather agreed. "We got lucky that they are strong on this night".

Esmy tapped Laith on the hand that was still holding the cork, which he took as an indication that his bottle was full. He corked it and then stood up to go and hand it to his uncle.

"Thanks – that's good, Laith", said Uncle Cahya in a pleased tone of voice after holding the bottle up to his right eye. Laith smiled awkwardly, knowing that they were all aware that he didn't have much to do with the quality of the beams in the bottle he had just presented. On the inside, he felt included, though he suspected Uncle Cahya looking deeply into the bottle was solely for his benefit. He went back over to Esmy and sat down on the floor next to her, with his legs out in front of him. He looked at her and then back at the sunset, which was slowly beginning to fade. She corked her bottle and then grabbed Laith's hand and opened it. She placed the glass bottle inside it and closed it again tightly. As she did so, Laith realised that he could understand what his Uncle Cahya was telling him. The beams definitely had an effect on something inside him.

"Shall we leave the rest of the bottles for the Moon, Grandad?", she asked him.

"Yeah, that's a good idea. We can just enjoy the rest of the sunset", he replied.

Laith was glad of this. He had managed to get quite comfortable and did not want either himself or Esmy to have to shuffle to get another glass bottle out.

"I'm going to go and say hello to a few people", Uncle Cahya told the pair. "Come to the fire after the sunset, when you're ready. We will be around there, probably".

"Okay, Grandad", smiled Esmy.

"Oh, here you go, Uncle", said Laith, remembering that he still had the glass bottle that he needed to give to his Uncle Cahya. His uncle took it and thanked him, placing it carefully into his pouch. Although Laith had given the bottle, he still kept the feeling that it had given him. He was glad that he was beginning to have more of an understanding of the different energies around him. As he sat with Esmy watching the colours in the sky fade and the light disappear, nothing was going to dim his feeling of inner warmth.

Chapter 10 - Cahya

Cahya ambled back towards the bonfire with the beams from this significant sunset safely in his pouch. He was in no particular rush to get back. As much as he had enjoyed the day and being with everybody, he was grateful for a bit of time alone to recover – especially with the remnants of the Sun's magic still just about lingering in the air. He ensured that he consciously acknowledged the external energy recharging his own. This act of consciousness allowed the energy to resonate within him. There was nothing more satisfying to him than a hard day's work and the knowledge that he had fulfilled his duties as best as he could, but he certainly felt a lot older now than he did this morning and was grateful for this time to recuperate. Being around certain people did also recharge different aspects of his energy. He had just left two of them now, content in each other's company. He was grateful for the blessing of his granddaughter coming into his life, and Laith too. Although a lot had gone wrong for his family in the last twenty years, he knew that the correct pieces of energy of the Universe always found their way to where they needed to be. Right now, some of them were helping a not-quite-so-young man feel certainly a few hours younger.

Cahya arrived back at the bonfire where he saw Kabili, Sarama and the twins. Tamsyn immediately let go of Sarama's hand and ran towards Cahya, wrapping his arms around Cahya's legs in a tight hug. Tammi followed and gave him a hug too. Cahya crouched down so that he could hug both children properly. By the time he stood back up, he felt younger than ever. Cahya noticed Tamsyn eyeing his pouch. He chuckled and pulled out some panela for each of the twins, and then went and gave some to Sarama too. Having done so, he felt that maybe he and Kabili deserved a bit too. It was tradition, after all. He crouched back down and whispered to the twins

"I heard a secret that you two might need a little bit more."

This news evidently delighted both twins, as excitable little smiles appeared on both of their faces. Cahya broke a bit more off for each of them.

"Here you go," he said "there's a little bit of extra magic in there for you. It will make you extra happy".

The twins both accepted their extra pieces gratefully.

"Uncle Cahya?", asked Tamsyn, "Were you just with Laith? Sarama said that you had gone with Laith and Esmy to collect sunbeams".

"Yes, they are still there, they will be coming back soon – don't worry".

"Why don't you go and get them?", Kabili interjected. "They need to really come back now anyway. And you can show them your harvest presents, too. Have you opened them yet? I bet Laith will want to play with them with you, whatever you got". His tone was jovial, and Cahya noticed that he said the sentence in such a manner that would suggest he only had the twins in mind – it was no secret that they were fond of him, particularly Tamsyn. Despite this, Cahya couldn't help but feel that he had a different interpretation of the word 'need' to his friend, but he knew that it was not his place to say anything.

"Sarama, do you want to take the twins to go and find Laith?", Kabili asked his daughter.

"Come on", Sarama said, gesturing for the twins to take a hand each, "let's go and get Laith to do some bloody work for once".

"You've just been standing around too, watching your dad tend to the fire that me and him built", laughed Cahya.

"Yeah, but I was in the vicinity just to make sure that it carried on burning smoothly. It's a very important job", she replied, joking with a matter-of-fact pretence.

"Yeah, I'm sure it is", Cahya laughed back as Sarama smiled and walked off with the twins.

Cahya noticed that Kabili kept his eye on her as she walked off and then, when she was out of earshot, commented

"Those two spend a lot of time together".

Cahya knew this to be referring to Laith and Esmeralda. From Kabili's tone, he also interpreted it to mean more time than which Kabili was comfortable.

"They do". Cahya agreed with the verbal statement as opposed to the non-verbal one. "They are good for each other".

This was a statement of fact. Cahya had been able to see for a long time how each of their energies were enhanced by being around each other. It had been this way since they were children playing together. They needed to be around each other, just as Cahya needed some time to be alone. Cahya chuckled to himself - if Kabili knew what he was thinking, he would certainly agree that the two friends had a different interpretation of the word 'need'.

"Yeah, I suppose they are", Kabili agreed, though his tone lead Cahya to believe that he still remained somewhat unconvinced. "As long as they are careful".

The night began to get darker. The last remnants of the Sun's energy faded into nothing and allowed the moonbeams to saturate the air. Cahya knew that these were still due to get stronger, and so he did not collect them just yet. He did, however, make the most of the magic of the special night. Though nothing could diminish the strength of the magic of the night, the date itself was tainted. Thinking about the Massacre was one of the few things that made Cahya genuinely angry. For the North to indiscriminately slaughter hundreds of people was unforgiveable. To do it in such a manner – at a gathering where they knew people would be unarmed and defenceless – indicated to Cahya that these people had no sense of love or respect at all. Cahya always tried to see the best in people. It was something that he prided himself on – his ability to see deeper into people, which was something that he noticed that most people were unwilling to do. Looking into people and seeing their energy helped to remind him that all people were manifestations of the Universe, and thus reminded him to always look for the best in people. We are all the same. We are all part of the same entity. Cahya could think of examples of people committing other horrific acts, but being able to see deeper inside the person generally showed him that they thought they were doing the right thing and, even if they didn't, that he should judge people on the good things that they do as opposed to the bad. Even people who might have committed an act that Cahya found reprehensible are still good people, because they have love in their hearts for their children and their families. However, thinking about the Massacre caused a conflict in his mind. He could not come to terms with how anybody with any love in their heart at all could bring themselves to be part of such a horrific act on such a special day against defenceless people. No matter how many times he told himself that they also have love for their families, just as everybody who has done a bad thing, the manner in which this atrocity was carried out meant that Cahya was struggling to even convince himself. He felt guilt for the way that he could not forgive or see the best in the people behind the attack, and this was on top of the devastation he felt for his granddaughter who had lost everybody but him. He was thankful that she had Laith. And Laith's sister.

Cahya knew that he had to concentrate on the special aspects of the night. Just as before the Massacre, the Pink Moon still brought a special energy with it. The beams were getting brighter and more intense, and would soon be at the peak of their strength. Although he hated to admit it to himself, Cahya needed the feeling that they brought. He told Kabili that he was going to go somewhere away from the fire to collect the beams and that he would be back soon. He wanted to be able to see them more clearly away from the interference of the energy of the fire. He walked away from the fire, and also in the opposite direction to where he knew that Esmeralda and Laith would be. They woudn't want him disturbing them. He came to a place that was quiet and dark, and sat down cross-legged on the floor. He took a moment to himself to feel the energy around him and enjoy it as it soaked inside of him. He felt himself get brighter. He uncorked his first glass bottle and watched intently as the beams slowly started to pour in. Cahya thought of how Laith, as much as he wanted to, was unable to sense them. He imagined how he would describe them to him. He supposed that they would seem somewhere between a liquid and a gas – probably more gas, to be honest, but a heavy one. Although they were not silver in colour, their energy had a silver quality to it. This was something that he would find difficult to explain. But the silverness collected around the bottom of the glass first, where it got more intense and emanated throughout the rest of the bottle. The intensity got greater as more beams flowed into the bottle. Once the intensity inside the bottle matched the outside, Cahya corked it and put it beside him. He continued to collect the beams in one bottle at a time – he preferred it this way. He was in no rush – this was something he enjoyed doing, and each bottle deserved his full love and attention. Once all of the bottles were filled, Cahya remained cross-legged on the floor mindful of the moment. Over the last twenty years, the words Pink Moon had become synonymous with the Massacre. Cahya was using this time to concentrate on the two things remaining separate in his own mind. The Pink Moon was, always had been, and always would be a special time. Just as it was important not to forget the Massacre, it was equally important to remember the reasons why all of those innocent people were gathered in the first place.

Cahya felt that it was time that he should be getting back to everybody else. The main purpose of the gathering was to celebrate the harvest with the community, and he had been sat alone for quite some time today. He collected the bottles of moonbeam and placed them in his pouch. He buttoned it shut, but not before sneaking a quick piece of panela. He made his way back to the fire where he saw that Sarama and the twins had returned.

"No Laith and Esmeralda?", he asked Sarama.

"No, we couldn't find them, Uncle", she replied. It seemed to Cahya that she did not seem particularly displeased about this, or maybe this was just his own feeling that he was projecting onto her.

Chapter 11 ~ Esmeralda

The night tonight was a stark contrast to the last for Esmeralda. Less than twenty-four hours ago, she was sat alone staring at the same Moon outside her bedroom window. The background buzz of excitement being carried to her by the night air was a stark contrast to the pin-drop silence that chilled the air last night. More significantly, her feelings of longing and loss had been replaced with those of warmth and happiness. Her dull pain had disappeared. Just as the sliver missing from last night's Moon had been filled, so too had been the vague feelings of longing inside her. She thought more deeply about the strange affinity that she had always felt with the Moon. She had not been able to conceptualise the feelings she had last night, even though she often felt them when staring up at the Moon and stars. Tonight, however, she felt as complete as the night Moon. They did, after all, have an unfathomable connection.

She was resting her head on Laith's shoulder as they were both sat together on the floor. She turned her head slightly to look up at him. She wondered what he was thinking. The slight breeze was gently blowing his hair and he had a pensive look on his face. On feeling her head turn towards him, he broke his gaze on the Moon and turned to face her instead. His face was now expressionless, but soft. Esmeralda could feel that he was smiling on the inside. After a moment, a small smile appeared on his face and Esmeralda replied with the same. Neither said a word. The comfortable silence was one that Esmeralda wanted to keep and it appeared that Laith felt the same. She turned back to face the Moon. Just as the previous night, she wanted to absorb its every last detail. Tonight, however, she did not do so out of any notion of responsibility – it was simply because it was making her happy. She could feel the beams of the Pink Moon soak into her and steadily lift her energy. The feelings of detachment of last night had been banished from within her. She wondered whether this was what was caused her to feel a strong connection with the Moon yesterday and on many nights before that – was it due to the fact that she felt detached within herself and therefore needed the stability of the Moon to feel whole? In any case, tonight, during the Full Moon, she had no such feeling.

She continued to lean on Laith as she felt the moonbeams soak into her. She could feel Laith shuffling slightly. She knew that he was uncomfortable in this position for too long. She got up and brushed herself off slightly. Laith looked up at her. She walked behind him and pushed his back slightly. He understood what she meant by this gesture and leant forward. Esmeralda took his shield off his back as he manoeuvred his arms to help her. She placed it on the floor behind him and gently pulled him back, knowing that he would trust her to guide him. He shuffled into position so that his head was resting on his shield. A stray strand of his hair blew across his face and got caught in his beard. Esmeralda moved it for him – she knew that he would let her - before laying herself down next to him, and resting her head on his chest. She could feel his heart beating – a feeling that made her feel even more content. Being so close to him made his heartbeat seem so loud, and it made her aware of her own too.

The night was not particularly warm, but her inner warmth and the sense of the magic in the air around her made her glow. She could feel comfort radiating from Laith too as she realised that she had never felt more content than in this moment. She gazed up at the stars, twinkling peacefully in the dark sky. The longer she looked, the more they seemed to sparkle. Their beauty was a reward, she felt, for one's desire to see it. As she remained motionless on Laith, the faint stars began to brighten and the even fainter ones revealed themselves. A wave of comfort enveloped her. She was always awestruck by just how many stars were visible to those who took the time to look properly. The night sky had never looked so beautiful. She dared not avert her gaze from the sky – she wanted to see how many stars would reveal their beauty to her. She became lost in the history of the stars - the night sky was unchanged from twenty years ago to the night. Her ancestors would have been looking at the exact same blanket of stars that she was looking at. The land that they were on had been changed beyond recognition but the cosmos remained constant, and this was something that nobody could take away from her.

She wanted to get lost further in the stars. She felt a connection. Her mind told her that it was a connection to her ancestors who pored over the same beautiful celestial tapestry, but deep inside her she knew it was a connection the stars themselves. The longer she gazed upon them, the more she felt as though she was part of them and not part of the Earth. She began to wonder if there was anybody on that fateful night twenty years ago who had been feeling as serene as she was right now. A pang of guilt jolted her stomach as she thought about the serenity that would have been ripped away from them, whilst she lay here twenty years later feeling the happiest that she had ever felt, on a night where she should surely feel a sense of mourning.

Esmeralda moved her head slightly – not out of a necessity of comfort, but out of a necessity to feel that Laith was still there with her. As she did, she felt Laith's heart start beating faster. She must have broken him out of whatever thoughts he was having. She wondered what they were. As she became aware of Laith's rising heart rate, her own heart started beating faster too. Thoughts that she had been striving to avoid fought and forced themselves into the forefront of her mind. What if, she felt herself begin to think, her feeling of loss disappearing tonight on the night of the Full Moon was nothing to do with the Moon being full? Her heart began to beat faster still. But the feelings of loss and longing disappearing must be partly due to the Moon being full, she argued with herself. Although that would not explain why such feelings would generally intensify on the nights of other full Moons – being honest with herself, she knew that the more beautiful the Moon looked, the more intense became her feelings of longing for something that she was unable to identify. But it could be due to tonight's Full Moon being particularly special, she told herself. After all, this was the anniversary of the Full Moon that caused her loss and so surely it was bringing back the aura of those people that she had lost. That must be what was making her feel more content today, she pleaded with herself. With this conclusion, she felt the intensity of her heartbeat subside.

She focused her attention back on the night sky. Some of the stars had gone back into hiding. She took a deep breath that seemed to disturb Laith once and for all from his own thoughts. He looked down at her and smiled as she looked over at him. Her heart began to beat faster again as she quickly looked back up at the stars. They were beautiful. The same stars that were there every single night were shining with a beauty much more intense than with which they had ever shone before.

Fuck.

Chapter 13 ~ Esmeralda

"Are you worried about tomorrow?".

The sound of her grandfather's voice coming from the hallway jolted Esmeralda violently from her thoughts as she was sat at the kitchen table. She had gone straight to her room when she and her grandfather had come back from the square. She was not in the mood to talk to anybody tonight. However, once she had got into her room, her thoughts began racing. She could not take her mind off laying in the field with Laith. If she was being honest to herself, she had be acutely aware of her own feelings for a very long time. However, the far more concrete knowledge of the impossibility of the situation gave her the resource required to suppress her real feelings and pass them off as anything other than what they actually were. This was an impossible situation. Firstly, she was technically engaged. Furthermore, they were from two different tribes. Even if her grandfather would allow it, which he would not, Laith's father certainly would be against it. She had known this all her life, and it was probably this knowledge that had given her the ability to ensure her feelings did not develop into anything more. Or so she told herself until tonight.

She had been unable to relax in her room and so, once she was happy that her grandfather had gone to bed, she went back out into the kitchen to prepare herself some warm milk. She had been sat at the table for around fifteen minutes with an empty mug in front of her when her grandfather must have seen the light, prompting him to come out and ask the question. Esmeralda gave a very brief murmur of agreement, afraid that anything more would betray her thoughts.

"I could tell something was off with you tonight", her grandfather told her, knowingly. "I thought you would be happy to be going with Laith", he said as he walked over.

Esmeralda was sure that her grandfather would have heard her heart beating in response to these words. She felt hot. If her heart didn't betray her, surely her face would have. She didn't want to say anything. Her voice would surely give her away. She gave another murmur in response. This time non-committal. Her grandfather looked over at her and she realised that her feigned speechlessness was not helping her cause. She cleared her throat so that her voice did not break when she spoke. She offered a meek "I'm glad we are all going together, but I am just a bit nervous". 'Perfect', she thought. She didn't single Laith out; she went with her grandfather's suspicions; she was wonderfully vague. Going with her grandfather's suspicions, she thought, was the best thing that she could do – everybody likes to be right, so he would have no reason now to question her further.

By now, her grandad was already at the stove with his favourite pan in his hand, posied to make tea. With his back to Esmeralda, she felt safe to look up and watch as he silently glided around the kitchen collecting his various ingredients as though by instinct. Something about his aura changed when he was doing things like this. He was in his element. At times, especially recently, she had moments where she started to realise that he was, in fact, an old man. However, in his element now, it was as though he had been transformed back to his youth. Esmeralda thought she noticed a slight stutter in her grandfather's movements as he was selecting which beams he would use, and she was sure she heard a slight chuckle as he added some to the mixture. She wondered what was so funny. Even though she had not had any tea yet, the knowledge that she was about to brought her comfort. She felt her heart relax and her mind too calmed down. She knew that her grandfather always had the right concoction for every moment.

She sat in silence as her grandad continued to work. He

turned around and picked up the empty mug that was sat in front of her, and looked inside it before turning it upside down as if to inspect it. He glanced at her and chuckled again. His small smile lifted Esmeralda's spirits even more. A few moments later, he returned the mug with steaming hot tea inside it.

"Thanks", she said, as she held it tight with both hands and pulled it towards her chest.

"Wait", said her grandad. He dropped a chunk of panela inside it. "Wait for it to dissolve and then stir it", he said, putting a spoon beside her. He then did the exact same thing to his own mug. Esmeralda wondered why he didn't just put it in the pan as he normally did.

"I'm going to take mine to my room", he said. "Turn the lights off when you go to bed".

"Okay, Grandad", Esmeralda replied.

"Goodnight", he said, as he walked off towards his room.

Again, Esmeralda was sat alone in the kitchen. However, she now felt calmer. The warmth and the smell from her cup had settled her slightly, but she could still not get her thoughts off the day's earlier events. Her heart was filled with happiness during every moment that she spent with him, especially when the two of them were alone together. She loved helping him in his father's field, making deliveries with him to other fields – everything. Watching how he was when he thought he was alone, watching him change around his sister and then around his father, and feeling how he changed when the two of them were alone together – all of these things were magical. She knew him better than anybody else. She knew the real him, and had done for a very long time. She loved watching him play with the twins and see how they lifted him, but, most of all, she loved knowing that she was the one who lifted him more than anything. This was something that she knew for a fact. And she had known all of this for a very long time. Tonight, laying with him and looking up at the stars – that's when she really knew. That was when she knew beyond a shadow of a doubt what her true feelings were for him. She remained fixated on this moment for a while. She wanted to savour it and bring back the exact same feelings of happiness that she had laying there with him. She tried to recall every single moment and every single detail - the moment that her dull pain and vague emptiness disappeared. She suddenly felt a bit sick again, remembering that they would not have the future together that she wanted. She sipped her tea, which had become cool enough to drink, before remembering that she needed to stir it. This was a horrible situation for her to be in. She could not do anything about her feelings – now that she had finally admitted to herself what they were, it had become far too late. She had fallen as deep as the stars. Well, she would have to try – she didn't have a choice. She was conflicted. She wished that she didn't feel this way, but she was so glad that she did. She felt sick with herself for having the most wonderful feeling ever. She sipped her tea. It was a cruel irony that she would normally speak to Laith about anything and she could rely on him to always make her feel better. Always. Now she did not even have that. Her heart dropped again thinking about it. One moment it would be high and light, thinking about being with Laith. The very next, it would plunge, when she thought about the reality. The reality made her sick. There was no way that she could confide in her grandad about this, and she was not close enough to Sarama. Even so, Sarama was Laith's sister. There was no way that she could tell her. She wanted nothing in the world more than for Laith to know how she felt, and she dreaded the thought of him finding out. What would he do if he knew? Would it ruin what they had? But what if he felt the same? She would give anything for him to feel the same. Her heart rose at this thought – imagine if he did feel the same. It would be the most wonderful thing in the world if he did feel the same. If he did, surely they could tackle any obstacles in their way. Any obstacles apart from the ones that were actually in their way, she realised. Hypothetical obstacles are a whole lot easier to tackle than real ones, she thought to herself. And, in any case, he did not feel the same about her. It suddenly brought her crashing back down to reality again.

She finished her tea and walked slowly towards her bedroom, turning off the kitchen light on the way. She was dejected. Sick. She got into her bed and immediately her thoughts went back to laying down with Laith in the field. Her pillow was Laith's chest and she was looking up at the stars with him. Together they were looking deep into the beautiful abyss – the past and the future intertwined. She could feel them now, the stars - their gaze penetrating the roof and falling upon her. Her heart was connected to them, particularly after this evening. She knew that she was special to the stars – they understood her. The stars knew exactly how she felt. She closed her eyes to allow herself to connect with them even more. With this, she became overwhelmed with emotion. Her eyes began to feel warm as she felt tears welling up beneath her eyelids. They started to roll down her cheek. She did not wipe them or try to stem their flow. She wanted them to come. Esmeralda eventually went to sleep heartbroken - the happiest that she had ever been.

Chapter 14 - Sarama

Sarama woke up the next morning with a feeling that she supposed fell somewhere between excitement and apprehension. She hadn't fallen asleep immediately when she had got into bed the night before. In fact, she had been tossing and turning for quite a while thinking about today. When she did fall asleep, however, she slept quite soundly. She knew that today was a big day, but today it was big for a very different reason than yesterday. She went over her dad's plan again in her head, as she had done what must have been a thousand times already whilst lying in bed the night before. It seemed so simple. Evidently, her dad had been thinking about it for a very long time – he had thought of all of the practicalities. She wondered whether it had always been in the back of his mind, especially during the last few times the community had had to move fields. It struck her now, not at the time, as odd that her dad would be the one to suggest not dismantling and moving all of the dwellings whilst they were moving farther and farther south. He was never one to take shortcuts or make any task easier for himself. On the contrary, she was certain that, on occasion, her dad would intentionally make things more difficult for himself just for the sake of it. She thought back to just yesterday as an example, when her father insisted on shuffling around bundles of wheat for a reason surely completely undiscernable to any other human. He always had a rigid idea on what the proper way to do things was and, to Sarama, suggesting that the community does not completely dismantle the old settlements now seemed as though maybe he had always had a hidden reason. At the time, he had insisted that it was a needless effort – it would tire out the people and the horses unnecessarily at a time where people needed to conserve energy as much as possible. He had preached that, with the community getting smaller, being more tight-knit was more important than ever. Large cabins were incongruent to this ideal and so, he had said, it would be sensible to leave a few standing and make everybody's slightly smaller. There would be plenty of material from the ones that they do dismantle. He had always been an excellent speaker and, of course, the community did not question his decree on the matter. It wasn't just due to his speaking, Sarama knew, that the community did not question her father – he was well respected due to the fact that he genuinely always looked out for everybody. He always seemed to do the right thing by everybody, even if it meant that he himself had to sacrifice a little bit of himself. If he had any faults, leadership certainly was not one of them.

Sarama got herself out of bed and headed for the bathroom. She could not hear her brother or her dad and wondered if they were still asleep. It was not likely that her brother was, and almost impossible that her dad was. She splashed water on her face in the bathroom. The colder-than-expected feeling startled her into waking up fully. Annoyingly, she got a bit more than she'd intended to on a loose strand of hair. She knew that it would annoy her later if she did not dry it properly now but she decided that a mild annoyance later was preferable to a slight inconvenience now. It could stay wet. She got herself ready and headed towards the kitchen. Her brother was sat at the table with his back to her. She braced herself for his comments about how she was so lazy, or how he and their dad had been working hard while she was sleeping. Thankfully, none were forthcoming today.

"Have you eaten?", she asked him.

"Yeah, I just had a bit of toast", he replied. His response seemed slightly odd to her. There was no sarcastic comment or any desire to start an argument. And there was something about his tone that seemed a little bit too polite. She decided to test the water.

"Do you want some tea? I'm gonna make some", she asked him knowing full well that he had some sort of phobia against drinking tea. He claimed that he didn't like it. She could never understand this - one of them must have been adopted.

He let out a small chuckle and smiled at her. "No, I'm alright, thanks", he said, before turning away and adding "Idiot" just loud enough for her to hear.

This tone and response was much better. He seemed fine, she thought. "I don't understand why you don't have it. It's delicious". This was one of her go-to criticisms of her brother, when she fancied a bit of an argument but didn't really have much that she could argue about.

"It's disgusting. I don't know why you bloody have it all the time'.

"It's delicious. I'm gonna put extra beams in it today. Lovely and beamy, it'll be."

With her brother's 'tut' that followed, Sarama was quite satisfied that she had managed to start the day with a nice, short argument, and that everything was fine in the world. With that formality out of the way, she could now start to have a more serious conversation.

"Are you nervous about today?", she asked him

"No, not really. Actually, maybe a bit. I dunno. Are you?"

"Not really. Dad has it all planned out. He's obviously been thinking about it for ages. You heard his plan yesterday. It seems pretty watertight".

"Yeah". His response seemed slightly apprehensive to Sarama.

"You don't think so?"

"No, it does seem good. He knows what he's doing. Well, I mean, he doesn't actually have any more information about the compound and stuff than anybody else, though, does he?".

This made Sarama think. This never actually came across her the thousand times that she went over the plan last night. But what her brother had just said was true. The way that her dad spoken so confidently last night left no room for doubt in her mind about whether or not he knew what to do. However, now that her brother had mentioned it, it did seem as though at least part of it was based on some speculation. He really was an excellent speaker.

"Oh yeah, that's true", she concurred. "He doesn't actually know about the compound, does he?"

"No. But what he was saying last night will be true. It all made sense, what he was saying. He hasn't seen it recently, but how else would they have it? Why would they change it from how it was before?"

"Yeah, he will be right", Sarama agreed.

"Anyway," said Laith "it doesn't really matter, does it?"

"True", Sarama laughed "we are going to do it anyway".

"Exactly".

"Where is Dad, anyway?", Sarama asked her brother.

"He's gone to get a horse"

"Ooh, yeah. Which one?"

"I'm not sure. He didn't say. He has packed up all the food, though – rice, chickpeas, beans and stuff. At least somebody is organised. Unlike you, who just sleeps all day and lets everybody else do all of the work".

Sarama had never been so happy to hear her brother criticise her sleeping habits. Obviously he had been over the plan in his head last night, just as she had, but, unlike her, he had managed to find a flaw. Speaking about it with her had obviously made him feel better, even though he was the one who argued that it was not really a flaw. He must have just needed to say it out loud. That was why he seemed a bit off earlier, but Sarama was glad that he was happier with it now.

"Oh, bugger", Sarama shouted, realising that her tea had boiled over.

"Not beaming any more, are you?"

"Shut up."

Now that Sarama was well and truly satisfied that her brother's worries had been alleviated, she could clean up the mess she had inadvertently made and then pour her tea in a comfortable silence, and also in a mug, while her brother remained sitting at the table. She stood for a while, behind him, sipping her tea slowly, neither of them saying a word. She eventually decided to sit down next to him.

"Delicious", she declared, looking over at him whilst taking her next sip. Her brother looked over at her. She felt his eyes roll despite the fact that they did not physically do so. She directed an exaggerated a smile towards him in

retaliation.   She heard a noise coming from outside –
clearly her father had returned with a horse.

"Ooh, I wonder which one he had brought", she said out
loud, though not particularly addressed towards her brother.
She decided that she would go outside to check.   She
picked up her mug of tea with both hands and clutched it
towards her chest as she walked – she enjoyed the warmth
and, possibly, the radiating beams.   Uncle Cahya would say
it was the beams.

Her dad looked over to her as she stepped outside.

"Hi, Sarama", he said, as the crispness of the air
smacked her in the face.   She pulled her tea closer towards
her.

"Hi, Dad", she said cheerfully.   "Ooh, you've brought
Acira", she noted, looking over at the horse.   She could tell
by the particular shade of brown, the small white circle
between the horse's eyes and the very thin white line
running down her face that this was Acira.   Her black mane
was incredibly neat, and her coat was pristine.   It was a
mark of respect to ensure that all the animals were
incredibly well looked after.   Acira, as all the animals were,
was a fundamental part of the community.   The animals did
their part just like all other members of the community and
were treated with no less respect than any other person.
Some people, her father included, made it a point that one
should never eat until they had fed their animal.   Sarama
walked over to pat and greet Acira.

"Hi Acira", she smiled.   "I thought you would bring Acira",
she said to her dad whilst still gently patting the horse.   As
her own words reached her ears, it occurred to her that she
did not actually get any further than wonder which horse
her father had gone to collect.   However, she concluded
that, had she given it any further thought, she would have
guessed Acira, and so what she had just said could be
considered to be the truth.

"We will need to load her up and get going soon", her dad
told her.   "Where's Laith?"

"He's inside", Sarama replied.

"Okay, well, we will need to start heading out soon.   Your

uncle will be waiting for us by now. Have you nearly finished your tea?". This last part sounded to Sarama as though it was leaning more towards being a demand than a question, however softly her dad had intended to say it. She gave what she deemed as the only correct response to the quasi-question and made to quickly finish her tea. She gave Acira one more quick pat and followed her dad inside.

"You ready, Laith?", she heard her dad ask.

"Yeah", replied her brother. She sensed no emotion in his voice at all.

Her dad walked over to pick up some of the bags of food that he had prepared earlier, and Laith dutifully followed.

"We better get these loaded onto the saddles", her dad said. She watched as they both walked outside, and went to wash her mug of tea and the pan that she had left earlier. Her dad walked back in, followed by her brother.

"Right", he said, "have you two got everything you need? Clothes? Everything?"

"Yeah", said Sarama. She saw Laith nod whilst standing unhelpfully behind their dad. Idiot.

Sarama and her brother went to their respective rooms to collect what they had packed the night before. Sarama put her shield on her back, followed by her quiver of arrows and her bow. She walked back into the living room where she and her dad waited a few moments for Laith to appear out of his bedroom with his own sword, shield and pouch. Now that the three of them were armed and ready, they stepped out of the house. Sarama stepped out of the way so that her dad could close the door behind them.

"We'll be back in a few days", he said.

Sarama's dad untied Acira and the four of them walked the short distance to Uncle Cahya's house in silence as Sarama took in the beauty of the morning dew glistening in the newly empty fields. Even though this happened every year, it still seemed to come as a surprise to her how different everything felt the day after the Pink Moon. It suddenly dawned on her, however, that this would be the last time that the harvest would be a scarce one. She wondered whether this feeling would therefore be intensified next year. She tried to imagine how the fields would look the day of next year's harvest – saturated and bursting with crops as had been described to her in the past. She tried to cast her mind back to her earliest memories in the fields, where she would be engulfed by wheat, corn and whichever other crops the community would grow. A wave of joy mixed with fear swept over her. She tried to concentrate on the joy.

The four of them arrived at Uncle Cahya's cabin, where Sarama's dad handed her the rope with which he was leading Acira. He started towards the front door, but it was opened just a fraction from the inside before he got there. Sarama's dad hesitated to see how this situation would pan out, and then the door opened further. Sarama saw Uncle Cahya at the door with a small black sack, which he was holding by its drawstring. He stepped outside, and smiled at Sarama's dad, who greeted him in return. Uncle Cahya continued towards Sarama and Laith.

"Hi, you two", he said, cheerfully. "Are you ready?"

"Born ready", Sarama smiled.

Uncle Cahya chuckled. "Good", he said, before turning towards Acira. "Hello, Acira", he said as he patted her and shuffled around some of the food she was holding to add his small sack to her load. "I'll just go and get my bag. And my granddaughter", he said to Sarama and Laith. Sarama watched as he disappeared back into his house, leaving the door wide open behind him and emerging moments later with a rucksack on his back and Esmy by his side. Sarama was not the least bit surprised when Esmy, of course, headed straight to Laith and smiled. She then greeted Sarama, her dad, and Acira. The slight red colour and ever-so-subtle puffiness of Esmy's eyes gave away that she had not slept much, if at all, last night. Just as Sarama and her brother had, Esmy must have spent a large proportion of the night thinking about today. Sarama thought about striking up a conversation about this, and how she and her brother had been over the plan this morning too. However, she thought better of it and decided to allow Esmy and Laith to continue to enjoy each other's company undisturbed. The two of them always seemed so comfortable together, even when in complete silence like at the moment. All three of them were probably too tired to talk just yet, Sarama thought. This was something that was clearly not reciprocated by the two men in charge. They seemed to be in a happy conversation about something - probably about the fact that they were soon to have a solution to the problems that had plagued them since the massacre, Sarama pondered. Well, one of the problems, anyway. It certainly was something to be cheerful about.

"Right, come on, let's go", Sarama's dad announced. Sarama started walking towards him and Uncle Cahya. Laith and Esmy followed behind. Sarama's dad held out his hand towards Sarama to gesture that he would hold Acira.
"No, it's okay", Sarama said, as she patted her with her free hand "I'll hold her. She likes me better."
"Okay ", laughed her dad.

The six of them started to walk north. They walked past their own bare field again, where the dew was easing up. This somehow made it look ever more bare – there was an emphasis on its emptiness. The other fields in current use were south of theirs, so it was not long before they were out of their current settlement. Sarama followed her dad and uncle, with Acira in hand. She looked back and noticed that Laith and Esmy had dropped behind a little bit. They were not so far as to separate themselves from the rest of the group, but they certainly were making no concerted effort to keep up either. Sarama looked at their settlement now with a different perspective, getting smaller as she walked away. It had always been small, but this was the first time she had actually realised it. Leaving the comfort of her settlement awoke something inside her that made her realise the gravity of the task that they were undertaking. She had no distraction from her own thoughts now. She felt exposed. She could hear nothing but the gentle footsteps of Acira on the soft ground, and the light wind blowing past her, very occasionally picking up to whistle in her ears. It wasn't particularly cold, but something made her want to tighten her cloak around her slightly more. She turned to Acira, strolling alongside her blissfully and stroked her nose to comfort the two of them.

The sky began to get bluer and the day began to get warmer. It was not very long at all before they reached the first set of barren fields that they would encounter today. These were the ones that they had tended to when they first moved into their current settlement. They would always try to make the most of the land by moving fields more than they would move their dwellings. There would normally be three sets of fields per settlement – one slightly north of the dwellings, one in the middle, and one slightly south. When these all became barren, they would move their settlement farther south and begin again. They were currently tending to the second set of fields in their current settlement, but did not have much farther south they could travel. These fields now looked so lifeless as Sarama looked across them. She could remember when these were the ones that were tended to - there would be scores of people making the most of the land. There would always be noise and life around - a stark contrast to now. The field lay bare and forgotten. It seemed like a lifetime ago. How quickly it had become forgotten. Would their current field suffer the same fate? Would it soon be resigned to becoming a forgotten footnote of the past? Her dad's plan was watertight, she thought. But, as her brother pointed out, it was only watertight based on things that he could not possibly know. There was plenty of opportunity for things to go wrong.

"Are you lot okay?", Sarama's dad projected loudly as he turned around.
"Yeah, I'm okay", said Sarama quite softly. Her dad was not far enough ahead of her to warrant an unnecessary expenditure of her energy by raising her voice. She turned around to see Laith and Esmy's reaction. Laith raised his

hand as if to gesture that they, too, were fine.

"Do you want to carry on for a bit or shall we rest here for a while?", her dad asked her.

"I don't mind"

"Let's stay here for a few minutes then – we can give Acira a bit of a rest too. Does anybody need some water? The river is not too far from here".

"No, I don't really fancy any yet", Sarama replied.

"You might as well just leave that rope", her dad said. "She'll be fine – she's not going to go anywhere".

Sarama let Acira's rope drop to the floor, and she dutifully stood by.

"I'll go and get her a bit of water", said her dad as he collected a bucket from Acira's side. He put a hand up to shield his eyes from the sun as he began to walk towards the river. Laith and Esmy eventually caught up and lowered themselves to the floor.

"Bit slow, aren't ya?", Sarama asked her brother.

"Well I've got as far as you, haven't I?", he replied.

"Well maybe we'd all have got a bit further if you didn't dawdle so much"

"Oh, shut up", he said, and laughed. He was definitely a lot more responsive than he was this morning. The journey seemed to have had the opposite effect on her brother than it did on her.

Chapter 15 - Esmeralda

Esmeralda was sat at the side of one of the many fields that had, in the last twenty years, fallen into disuse. Laith was sat to her left, joking with his sister. He seemed happy. He had seemed happy to her all day – clearly unburdened from the worries that had been weighing her down the night before. Although, to be honest, she herself was also unburdened from the worries that had been weighing her down the night before. It was not that she was trying to ignore them - her worries had genuinely disappeared now that she was around Laith. She had woken up in the morning feeling exhausted. She didn't remember waking up in the night, but she couldn't have slept very well, given that she woke up feeling as tired as if she hadn't slept at all. Her head had been pounding when she woke up this morning, and she wanted nothing more than to fall back into a deep sleep and forget about everything. But she couldn't. She was dreading seeing Laith after her realisation. What if she gave something away? How could she act normal around him now? But, at the same time, her heart longed to see him, just as it always did and just as she knew it always would. The difference was that, now, she was being honest to herself about it. That was one burden that had been lifted from her but, with the one that had replaced it, she did wonder whether, maybe, she would have been happy continuing to live in denial.

However, that was this morning. And this morning was a long time ago, provided that time was measured in feelings and not hours. The moment she had laid eyes on Laith this morning, everything that had been worrying her disappeared into the ether. She was her old self again – nothing had changed. She was not trying to ignore her worries – if anything, she had been trying to do the opposite. She had spent the morning trying to force herself to think about the fact that they had no future together – trying to get back to how they were before. This was something that she knew to be true, no matter how much she wished it wasn't. But being with Laith in the moment genuinely made all of those worries disappear. She felt so complete when she was with him that nothing could bring her down – not even the knowledge that she could not have him forever.

She watched on silently as Laith and his sister continued to argue about who was the laziest. They were currently debating whether holding a rope to lead a horse should be regarded as equally exhausting as carrying said horse above ones head. Esmeralda couldn't help but be impressed by the rigour with which Sarama asserted that the two should be regarded as one and the same.

"Either way gives you the same result, doesn't it? It's not my fault that I'm clever enough to find more efficient ways of getting the same result", she argued. "If anything, that makes me a genius". Laith turned to Esmeralda.

"Can you tell her she's an idiot?", he asked. "Oh actually, don't bother", he added, quickly. "You'll just side with her and then the two of you will bloody gang up on me".

Esmeralda took this to be an invitation.

"Well, she did get the job done, didn't she?"

"I hate both of you", stated Laith, before giving Esmeralda's arm a playful shove that made her heart beat ever so slightly faster.

"Oh, Dad's on his way back from the river", said Sarama. Esmeralda felt her heartbeat rise ever so slightly again, but this time it was accompanied by a different feeling – one of a slight unease. She knew how her uncle felt about how close she was with his son. What would he think now, if he knew the reality? She looked over at Laith and, like magic, she suddenly felt calm again. Her uncle had no way of knowing the reality – she was being paranoid. As far as everybody was concerned, everything was exactly the same as it had always been. Being with Laith made her feel as though she was part of this particular 'everybody' for the moment.

Esmeralda's uncle placed the bucket of water in front of Acira and gently patted her back. He pulled out a little bit of hay from one of her pouches and placed it in front of her to nibble. Acira seemed to be the only one who felt like eating or drinking at the moment.

"We should probably start walking up the river soon", said Uncle Kabili in a tone of voice that alluded towards it merely being an idea to be considered. Esmeralda knew, however, despite her uncle's tone of voice, things that he said were rarely only suggestions. "We don't have to do it right now", he continued, "but there are bits of grass growing close to the banks that Acira can have, and we need to start following it north anyway soon".

Laith stood up.
"We aren't going right now", Uncle Kabili told him.
"No, I know", he replied. "I just wanted to get up anyway". Esmeralda knew that he was never comfortable sitting on the ground for too long. Laith brushed himself off. Esmeralda tapped his hand to let him know that she, too, would like to get up. He offered her his hand. It was these little, consistent gestures that made her feel the way she did about him. She took his hand to hoist herself up and, as his hand gripped hers, happiness radiated from her heart. It was amazing how something so small and simple could make her feel so happy. Her insides were glowing just for that short moment.

Esmeralda brushed herself off too and looked over at her grandfather, who was smiling at her. She reciprocated. He had been sitting alone, cross-legged, since they had stopped there, facing towards the bare fields. Esmeralda thought that he seemed happy. He must have been thinking about the good memories that they had tending to these fields. It was not too long ago, and the crops would never have been in great abundance here as they were in the past, but Esmeralda knew that her grandfather always had a knack for looking for the best in every situation. She had no doubt in her mind that he would currently be thinking about the joy he received helping the community in these fields, or collecting beams here by himself.

Esmeralda noticed that Acira had finished the hay that had been placed in front of her, and it seemed as though she had finished drinking too. The group hovered around for a bit longer. It felt as though everybody was ready to go, but were just awaiting an instruction from Uncle Kabili. It was Esmeralda's grandfather, however, who got up. This seemed to be the indication that Uncle Kabili was waiting for, and the group got ready to move on. Uncle Kabili spilled the remaining water from Acira's bucket into the field and secured the empty bucket to Acira's side. He picked up her rope and began to lead her.

"I'll hold her, Dad", Sarama told him, reaching for the rope. Uncle Kabili handed her the rope and went to join Esmeralda's grandfather at the front.

"Aren't you gonna lift her?", Laith asked his sister.

"No need – I've already explained this to you", she replied.

Sarama walked ahead while Laith turned back towards Esmeralda. He offered her his hand once more and, this time, her heart fluttered when his fingers interlocked with hers. He pulled her forwards, as though he was trying to tell her to hurry up, but she was certain that he kept her hand a fraction of a second longer than he really needed to once she had joined his side. He let go of her hand and they both paused for a moment before following the group along the vacant fields, her heart still beating hard.

"This one was your dad's one, wasn't it?", she asked him, gesturing her head towards the field on their left. This was a rhetorical question. It wasn't very long ago that they would make the short trip from their current settlement to this field. What she actually meant was 'Do you remember when we used to come here together? Did you used to feel how I now know I felt when we were together in this field?'

"Yeah", replied Laith. It sounded slightly elongated to Esmeralda, as though he was distracted. As though he was reminiscing. "This was the field you lost your bracelet in, wasn't it?", he continued. His tone of voice seemed to have gotten more jovial.

"Yeah, it was", laughed Esmeralda. It was a light-hearted memory now. "At the time, I was so worried", she reminded him. "I thought I'd never find it". She shook her left wrist in his direction, as a reminder that they did find it. It was a bracelet that her grandfather had given her, which had previously belonged to her mother. It was a simple, copper bracelet, with a small, teal stone in the middle. There was no clasp to the bracelet – just a small gap that allowed it to flex slightly – sometimes, evidently, slightly too much.

"Yeah, you were so worried, I remember", Laith said.

"You calmed me down". He always had this effect on her.

"Yeah, well, I knew it would be there somewhere. And we obviously weren't gonna just leave it. Not something that means so much to you".

She smiled at the ground.

Esmeralda looked ahead to the front of the group where her grandfather seemed to be deep in conversation with her uncle. They had passed the vacant fields and were now making their way past some land on which, as far as she was aware, nothing had ever grown.

"We might as well head towards the river", Uncle Kabili announced. "It will be quicker, and it'll be nice for Acira too".

He started to veer to his right, towards the river. The rest of the group followed. Esmeralda could hear the running water of the river get louder as she walked towards it.

"I like the sound of the river. I find it relaxing", Sarama said, turning around to Esmeralda and Laith.

"I think the sound of you shutting up is more relaxing", replied Laith.

Sarama laughed. Esmeralda was surprised that this was her reaction – she definitely expected a more cutting retort. Maybe the sound of the river did have a calming effect on Sarama. Esmeralda never understood it herself – she did know that a lot of people found relaxation in the sound of running water but, for her, it was only the sound of silence emanating from the stars that had that effect. That or being with Laith.

Small patches of grass were growing along the banks of the river, but the ground itself was quite firm. Acira stopped every now and again to when she saw a particular patch of grass that tickled her fancy, which meant that Esmeralda and Laith caught up to Sarama and Acira quite quickly. The four at the back of the group continued to walk in a comfortable silence – the only sounds coming from the gently running river and the even gentler clip-clop of Acira's hooves. Sarama would call out to her father to stop every time Acira did so that they did not get too far ahead. Esmeralda saw that her grandfather was, perhaps, more grateful for these breaks than the rest of the group. The next time Acira stopped, Esmeralda touched the back of Laith's hand with her own to indicate that she was going to catch up to her grandfather. He responded silently by gently squeezing her fingers as she was walking away. Esmeralda left Laith with his sister and Acira to see how her grandfather was doing. As she walked towards him, he smiled at her and initiated the conversation.

"Having fun?", he asked her. "Not too tired, are you?"

"I was going to ask you the same thing", she replied.

"Me? Tired?", he responded, laughing. "You lot are the lazy ones", he said, waving his had to indicate he was referring to the younger members of the group. "Me and your uncle are always up working hard while you lot are still sleeping. This is nothing to us". He looked towards Uncle Kabili to back up his claim.

"These kids don't know", agreed Uncle Kabili, with a chuckle.

"A little bit of walking and you lot act like it's the end of the world", Esmeralda's grandfather continued. "We used to run up and down here every day to get to the fields faster. Well, not this exact place, but we used to run up and down to get from the huts to the fields, and from one field to the next."

"And carry the tools", interjected Uncle Kabili.

"And carry the tools", agreed Esmeralda's grandfather,

nodding. He laughed. "And then carry them back. And all of this was just a warm up before your uncle's training." Uncle Kabili nodded, and patted his sword in agreement. "Don't worry about us. You lot worry about yourselves", said Esmeralda's grandad.

"Okay, Grandad", Esmeralda laughed. He seemed to be in his element. He did always get on very well with Uncle Kabili. Maybe he was still a lot younger and fitter than she was giving him credit for.

"Is she ready?", Uncle Kabili shouted towards Sarama

"Yeah, nearly, Dad", Sarama shouted back, as Laith went to pour the unwanted water from Acira's bucket back into the river.

Esmeralda's grandad took the first step to continue the journey without hesitation, as if he had a point to prove. Esmeralda let her grandad and uncle go ahead so that she could wait for Laith and the others to catch up. It wasn't long before she was joined by Laith, Sarama and Acira, and the four of them followed the path set by the two elders of the group.

Esmeralda noticed the day get warmer and was grateful when Laith veered off towards the river to dip his canteen in there. He passed it over to Esmeralda who took a few sips before passing it back to Laith.

"No, I'm okay, thanks", said Sarama sarcastically to her brother.

"I was getting you some too - stop bloody moaning", responded Laith, waving the second canteen in his hand in her direction. "I was just gonna fill this one up again too".

"Oh. Thanks", Sarama said, smiling sweetly.

"It's okay", said Laith, trying to sound as grumpy as possible, and failing.

"Are there some old fields over there?", Laith asked Esmeralda, gesturing somewhere over to their left.

"Yeah, I think they will be around here somewhere", said Esmeralda. She knew that they would be passing in the vicinity of some of the third set of fields from their previous settlement. At the time, she and Laith were old enough to remember them, but too young to remember exactly where they would be in relation to the river. Acira stopped to graze on any patches of grass that she wanted to every now and again, and Laith consistently grazed on dried and roasted corn kernels from one of Acira's pouches. Every so often, Esmeralda would tap his arm to indicate that she wanted some too. Sarama would help herself to some from Acira's pouch too.

"This is nice, isn't it?", Laith said to Esmeralda. "I'm glad you came", he continued, rather than waiting for a response. Esmeralda's heart jumped slightly.

"Obviously, I was going to come", she said. She thought about telling him that she knew he would mess up the mission without her. The truth was she couldn't even imagine the prospect of being left alone at home while he went away for a few days. In the end, she decided to say neither of these things, and hoped that her silence said enough. Then, worried that her silence might have said too much, or maybe not enough, she gave him a quick push in the arm.

"We are getting quite close now", Esmeralda's grandfather turned around to tell them. "We can start heading away from the river soon, so have any more water now if you want any. Does Acira want any more?"

"I'll give her some, Uncle", Sarama replied, moving to detach the bucket from Acira's side.

"You don't need that", Esmeralda's grandfather told her. "Just lead her close to the river. The banks are fine here, and she will have it straight from there". Sarama obliged, and the group waited there for a while. Esmeralda took in the beauty of her surroundings – the natural beauty of the river shaping the rocks lying in its bed. The rocks seemed constant. They wouldn't notice the minute changes being made to them over time by the water flowing around them. She began to wonder what it was that shaped her as the river shaped the rocks. What would the rock look like if it was sat in a different part of the river. What would she be like if she had been raised in different circumstances? She looked down at her bracelet and then back up again. The land surrounding the river was now bare. She tried to imagine how the land would look if things were growing in abundance, everywhere and without discrimination. Would it be more beautiful? Or would it just be different? To her mind, the scene that she was looking out upon right now was beautiful. She found it difficult to imagine it being any different – it was all she had ever really known. She looked over towards Laith, whose hair had began to blow across his face. He was doing nothing about it. She had an urge to move it for him, but decided against it. Eventually, when Acira decided that she had had enough water, he did so himself. Esmeralda told herself that she could now stop being bothered by it, but deep down she knew that that's not what was bothering her.

The group walked diagonally away from the river – it was evident that the two men at the front knew the area very well. Even Esmeralda herself had some vague sense of familiarity. She supposed that she must have been in this particular area once or twice on the way from the fields to the river. It seemed as though some fatigue was setting in, as the group were now walking in silence – including, tellingly, Esmeralda's grandad and Uncle Kabili. Up until now, had been in animated conversation throughout the day. The rushing of the river slowly got quieter.

"There are some of the fields", said Esmeralda's grandfather to the group, gesturing off into the distance. Esmeralda could not easily distinguish them from the rest of the land. She supposed that this was due to a combination of them being too far away and them probably being quite indistinguishable from the rest of the dying land. As they continued to walk closer, Esmeralda was able to distinguish the bare field from the rest of the land. For some reason, a slightly eerie feeling crept over her that did not occur when they were at the last set of fields. Maybe it was because these ones were used much longer ago. She ever-so-slightly diverted her path so that she would bump into Laith. He responded by gently touching the ends of her fingers as they now walked parallel to the fields.

"I think this one here was your Uncle Reyhan's", Esmeralda's grandfather told the group. "Wasn't it?", he added to Uncle Kabili

"Yeah, I think it was", Uncle Kabili replied.

Esmeralda's feelings of unease had disappeared. Maybe putting a name to the field grounded her somehow. She knew that Uncle Reyhan was waiting for them back at their current settlement. This was just the field that he used to tend to, alongside the fields that the rest of the community tended to.

"Laith", called Uncle Kabili. Laith looked up, and Uncle Kabili gestured for him to go towards him. Laith quickly touched Esmeralda's fingers again and then went to join his father. Esmeralda saw that he was pointing something out to Laith off in the distance, but she could not make out what he was saying – nor was she trying to. She was distracted now by feelings of what she supposed were nostalgia, but it didn't seem quite right to describe it as such. There was nothing warm about it, like the sensation one would normally associate with nostalgia. This was a cold and haunting version of nostalgia and it began to intensify as she noticed what the group was heading towards. The old settlement started to come into view, but it was a shell of what it had once been. There were loud bare patches where cabins had once been. Their emptiness had a different quality - a greater intensity - to the emptiness of the rest of the land. It seemed to take more away from Esmeralda. The feeling of incompleteness that she sometimes felt inside resonated with the emptiness of the settlement, and those feelings amplified. She felt uneasy. Glancing over at the rest of the settlement, the desolation resounded everywhere. It consumed the settlement and echoed noisily inside Esmeralda. Entire cabins had been dismantled to transport to the new settlements. Some of the dwellings had been left half-standing – not all of the materials were needed, as she knew. The half-standing cabins retained imprints of the families that had lived there before, exacerbating the feeling of eeriness niggling within Esmeralda.

Esmeralda heard Acira's footsteps slowing down. They gradually came to a stop as Sarama and Acira joined the three at the front. Esmeralda stopped too, just behind Acira. She wanted to go and join Laith, but felt uncomfortable doing so at the moment – Laith was still with his father, and she didn't want to seem too attached. She knew that Uncle Kabili was inwardly wary of the two of them. He never, ever intended to make Esmeralda feel uncomfortable – Esmeralda knew this. If anything, sometimes it seemed as though he would make more of an effort with Esmeralda than with most people. But Uncle Kabili was not the kind of person whose presence naturally made people feel at ease, and Esmeralda definitely felt this. Despite how he acted outwardly, Esmeralda could feel his inner feelings. No matter how hard one tries, their aura cannot be easily masked.

Esmeralda waited by Acira, stroking her back and waiting for her feelings of unease to subside. There were only two cabins that were still fully standing. Either this was incredibly fortunate, or it was good forward planning. One of them, she thought she remembered, belonged to the twins' parents. She occasionally used to walk there with Laith when they would spend time with the twins' older brother. She supposed that this was the one that Laith would be staying in, with Uncle Kabili and Sarama.

"Let's take all this stuff off Acira", her grandfather said to her, as he began to detach some of the bags from Acira's side. Uncle Kabili began to do the same on Acira's other side. He passed some of the bags to Sarama, who was standing by, and then to Laith who came and joined them.

"Here", said Uncle Kabili, passing a bag to Laith, "this is yours, isn't it?"

"Yeah, Sarama's", Laith replied, taking the bag. "That one's mine", he added, taking the next one.

"Okay, good", Uncle Kabili continued, seemingly unbothered by the actual owner of each bag. "Do you two want to put these inside, and I'll get the rest?' he asked, gesturing towards one of the cabins.

"Yeah", said Laith. His tone sounded apathetic.

"Esmeralda?", her grandfather called out. She was jerked out of her thoughts.

"Yeah, sorry, Grandad", she responded, walking around Acira to where he was and took some bags off him.

"Do you want to put them inside there?", he asked, pointing towards the other cabin.

"Yeah, okay, Grandad", she replied, smiling. She was hesitant about going inside alone, and so decided to wait until her grandad had finished and would accompany her.

Esmeralda's grandfather took the last of the bags off Acira, removed her saddle, and left her rope on the floor.

"We can let her wander around for a while, if she wants to", he told Esmeralda. "She won't want to go very far".

The pair of them walked towards the cabin that would be their home for the night, bags in hand. Esmeralda's grandad turned the brass doorknob of the wooden door and pushed it open gently. The dull creak told Esmeralda that it had not been opened in quite some time. Esmeralda let her grandad cross the threshold first and she followed quickly afterwards, leaving the door open. They stepped straight into the dark and dingy living room, attached to what would have been the kitchen. The layout was very similar to the cabin in which she currently lived – well, she supposed there was no reason for it not to be. The main difference was that this cabin lay bare. It smelt and felt disused. A tiny shiver ran through Esmeralda's body. The cabin was ever so slightly cold by virtue of the season and it was lacking in warmth by virtue of its abandonment. The daylight hesitantly filtered in through the dusty windows, but all this did was highlight the emptiness of the cabin as it bounced off the overwhelming volume of the nothingness inside. Esmeralda's grandfather went to open the nearest window. This allowed slightly more light in, as it was no longer competing with the darkened windows. The faint light illuminated the dust in the air that began to dance the moment her grandfather unsettled it. Esmeralda remained motionless near the door as her grandfather silently opened another window. He reached into one of his pouches and pulled out a small, glass flask, which he uncorked and placed on the floor in the centre of the living room. Esmeralda could see a faint energy inside it that she knew would be brighter to her grandfather. She wasn't sure exactly what was in there, but she had a rough idea. What she was certain of, however, was that her grandfather always knew what he was doing. The faint energy began to flow from the bottle and disperse itself around the room.

"We will need some water for later, to cook with", he told her. This broke Esmeralda out of her daze. She looked over at him but did not respond, verbally or otherwise. He chuckled. "There is a metal bucket by Acira", he continued. "You could take that. Take Laith with you to help. I will sort things out here. It won't need two of us to sort this place out, and I'm old and tired – I don't feel like a trip down to the river".

"Old and tired?", Esmeralda asked him. "About an hour or two ago, you were ready to run up and down the river, weren't you?"

"Well, I've aged since then, haven't I?", her grandfather responded. "You understand about the passage of time, do you not?"

"Yeah, I'm sure that those two hours made all the difference", said Esmeralda. She was laughing with her grandad as she made the comment, but it felt more out of obligation than desire. "I'll go and get the water. I fancy a walk", she continued. This was out of desire, not obligation. She had not felt comfortable since they had reached the settlement, and she did not feel comfortable now. She wanted to get away, especially with Laith, even if it was just for a few minutes. Maybe this would help her settle, she thought.

"Do you want me to close the door, Grandad?", Esmeralda called, as she stepped outside.

"No, no… Leave it open. We can bring a little bit of energy inside".

Esmeralda left the door open and went to find Acira, who

had not wandered far. She had chosen to go and stand in one of the fields. There were some tufts of grass growing sporadically that Acira could graze on, but it seemed as though she didn't want to. Esmeralda walked away from both cabins and towards Acira. As she walked away, she saw that Laith's cabin door was closed. She wondered how he was finding his. Would he be feeling slightly unsettled, as she was? He must be, she thought. The experience as a whole would, at the very best, be slightly unsettling for anybody. Esmeralda stood near Acira, stroking her. Acira seemed unperturbed. 'Charming', thought Esmeralda. She could probably quite easily collect a bucket of water from the river by herself, she thought. It wasn't particularly far, and the bucket wouldn't be unbearably heavy for her but, still, she would rather wait for Laith. She felt uncomfortable knocking on the door of his cabin to call for him, but she knew that he would be coming out soon anyway. He must be. She chose to wait. She had nothing else to do, anyway.

Esmeralda could hear nothing but the occasional eerie whistling of the wind. When the wind carried the sound of a slight creak of a door to her ears, her heart instinctively wished that it was Laith. Her brain caught up and she turned to face the two cabins. Her heart was lifted when she saw that it was Laith emerging, alone, from the cabin on the left. Perfect. She looked down at the ground but then back up again nearly immediately to see that Laith was walking towards her. He joined her by Acira. Her heart felt another pang as she made eye-contact with him, but it quickly settled, such was the comfort that he brought her.

"Dad was on about getting some water from the river", he told her. "He said that he was gonna go, but I told him that I would. I fancied the walk". He paused, clearly waiting for a response from her.

"Yeah, Grandad told me to go and get some too", she replied.

"Oh, good", he said. "I was going to ask you if you wanted to come". He paused again.

"Yeah", Esmeralda smiled, her spirits lifted.

"Do you know where the bucket is?", he asked.

"You walked past it just now", Esmeralda laughed, rolling her eyes. "You're the least observant person I've ever met". This time, her laugh was not out of obligation.

"Oh. Well, I wasn't really looking for it at the time", Laith defended himself.

"Let's go", Esmeralda told him, pushing him with both arms in the right direction.

Esmeralda walked with Laith back towards the cabins. As they passed the bucket, she gave it a little tap with her foot.

"See?", she asked him. "It's right here".

"Oh, yeah", he replied. "I think there's a bigger one inside, but we don't really need that, do we? Let's take this one".

The two of them veered towards the right, past the cabins and towards the river. As Esmeralda was walking away with Laith, the feeling of isolation brought on by the old settlement began to escape her. She began to feel more cheerful again, and soon found it hard to imagine that she had ever felt any differently. It was a bit silly, she told herself, that she had been filled with negative thoughts and emotions simply due to the place that she was in. She was still the same person as she always was regardless of her location. Nevertheless, she was quite grateful that her unnerving feelings had subsided.

"How's your cabin?", she asked Laith.

"Like a palace", he replied, joking. "Well, I dunno. It was just a bit weird when we first went in – probably because it's so different. I know that it used to be Ayan's, but I can't really remember it. But, yeah, it's not that bad. Just a cabin, I suppose. It's not too bad at all, actually. I don't mind it".

Laith's unsure answer told Esmeralda that he had been having the same type of feelings that she was having on arrival – vaguely negative and not grounded in any logic. There was nothing overtly bad about the place. In fact, thinking about it, everything there taken individually was perfectly fine – quite nice, if anything. But there was something about the sum of the parts that was unsettling. She was happier now she knew that Laith felt it too – she was not alone and she was not being silly. Being away from the place now, she was happy, anyway. She'd get used to it.

The pair reached the river. Laith moved forwards with the bucket but Esmeralda pulled at his arm. He turned around to face her, his hair blowing over his face again.

"Let me do it", she said to him. He smiled and handed her the bucket without saying a word. She smiled back, her smile possibly a bit wider than one might expect from somebody whose treat was nothing more than collecting some water in a bucket. But she was happy. Her smile reflected her intrinsic happiness, not her happiness at the less-than-exciting prospect of collecting some water. She edged closer to the river with the bucket. She reached behind her for Laith's hand, and held the tips of his fingers gently, pulling him forward with her. He obliged and walked towards the banks with her.

"Okay, I'm gonna get the water", she told him. "Don't let me fall in".

He let out a little chuckle. "How would you fall in?", he asked her. "You've crouched down before in your life without falling over, haven't you?".

It made Esmeralda happy when he spoke in this tone – she knew that he only did it when he was relaxed and happy. She also knew that this was mainly when the two of them were alone together, which made her glow.

"Just don't let me fall in, okay? It's different when there's a river. More pressure. Different circumstances. Higher stakes". This time, he laughed.

"I'm gonna push you in", he told her. Nevertheless, he crouched down behind her and held her hand firmly as she reached down to put the bucket into the river. Her heart jumped as she felt his hand squeeze hers even more tightly as she leaned forwards. She didn't need him there for such a simple task. She needed him there regardless.

"I think you've got enough", he told her, as he stood back up without loosening his grip on her hand. She loved how his hand felt in hers – it felt at home. He pulled her arm upwards, helping her to stand too. She stood up and did a small, unnecessary, jump at the end to indicate that she was, now, fully stood. She did this when she was in a good mood, which she was at the moment. She had the bucket of water in her right hand, and still had Laith's hand in her left. She put the bucket down only to free her right hand.

"Does this water seem good?", she asked Laith, dipping her hand into the bucket and splashing some of it on his face. She laughed. He held her hand even tighter, and pulled her with some force towards him. He wrapped his arm around her midriff to hold her away from the bucket as he tried to get closer to it, surely to enact his revenge. He quickly let go of her hand, whilst still holding her, so that he could splash some water back on her. She squealed.

"No, stop it", she protested, mildly, whilst reaching for the water in the bucket herself. He let go of her so that she was able to get some water to splash him once again.

"Okay, stop now", she said, as he went to do the same. He splashed her anyway, ignoring her half-hearted request. She grabbed both of his wrists with her hands, laughing. "Okay okay okay, definitely stop", she said, still smiling. It was beyond belief that less than half an hour ago she was feeling in the slightest bit down. Happiness filled every part of her body – the kind that she couldn't imagine ever not being there. Once she felt his arms relax, she let go and then quickly cupped her hands to splash him once more with the water from the bucket. She laughed and then screamed as he came for her. He grabbed her midriff tightly from behind and marched her towards the river.

"That's it", he said. "I'm gonna throw you in".

"No, no, no", she screamed, laughing, as he began to sway her from side to side. She kicked her legs in apparent protest, but really to facilitate him lifting her off the ground slightly. The wind was gently blowing her hair over her face.

"No, I'm gonna", he said. She didn't think that it was possible to be as happy as she was now, especially after the realisation that she had that night under the stars. She genuinely felt as though things were perfectly normal between them, as they had always been. This was as happy as she had ever been, and she didn't want anything to ever change.

He loosened her grip on her slightly, allowing her to spin around and face him. She put both arms up on his chest and looked him in the eyes.

"Okay, sorry, sorry, sorry", she said laughing. "But you splashed me too, so you have to say sorry too". She tried to keep a straight face whilst saying this last part, but her smile will have given her away.

"Hmm...", he said. "Well, you did start it. So... no. I'm not sorry. You deserved it". He was still smiling. Esmeralda felt his grip loosen even more, but his hands were still resting on her waist. She kept her hands on his chest, where they belonged, and her eyes fixated on his. She did not want to break this gaze but knew that she would have to. Their faces were close. She knew what she wanted, but she knew that she could never have it.

"Okay, fine", she said. "Well, I'm not sorry either, because you deserved it too".

"What?", he asked her, feigning horror. "What did I do?"

"I dunno, you just deserved it, okay?".

She felt his hands relax slightly and so she, somewhat reluctantly, removed her hands from his chest and walked back towards the bucket.

"I'll take care of this", she told him. "I don't trust you".

"Give it to me", he told her.

"No."

"Okay, fine. Suit yourself".

She handed him the bucket anyway. "Fine. Here", she said, trying to sound angry. "But you're not allowed to splash me". She tried to sound as stern as possible but was acutely aware that she wouldn't have minded if he did.

Esmeralda walked back to the settlement with Laith. She stayed close to his right hand side so that she was safely away from the bucket on his left. These special little moments made her happier than anything else ever could. She was always happy when she was around him. Occasionally, on the walk back, she intentionally bumped into him just so that he would look at her and she could smile at him. He always smiled back, clearly glad for these little interruptions from whatever he was thinking about. Every time he smiled at her, she saw it in his eyes. This was not just a reflex or a smile out of obligation. His eyes told her that it was real.

Heading back towards the cabins, she did not feel the same apprehension that she felt the first time that they approached. Even on arrival, she felt no emptiness or isolation or any of the other vague negative feelings she had when they had first arrived. The settlement itself was, of course, just the same as it was a few hours ago. The only difference was that now there was a roaring fire that had been lit close to the cabins. It seemed to saturate the entire area and change the mood of the whole place. The fire had displaced the icy emptiness from the air, and replaced it with happy warmth. Her grandad always knew what he was doing.

Esmeralda and Laith walked towards the fire, where Uncle Kabili and Sarama were sat on a log, facing them. Her grandad had his back to them, sitting cross-legged on the floor and looking out over the vacant fields where Acira had previously been standing. Acira was now standing close-by, grazing on some small tufts of grass nearer to the fire.

"Cold?", Esmeralda heard Laith ask his father.

"No, not really", he replied. "But we needed to get it ready for the food anyway so we just lit it now", he added. "Have you got the water?", he asked, glancing towards the bucket in Laith's left hand. Laith responded by raising the bucket slightly.

"Oh, okay. Good. We can get started on that in a while. Didn't you take the big bucket?", he asked, before quickly adding "Well, no, there was no need, I suppose".

Laith put the bucket of water on the floor and walked around the fire towards the log where Uncle Kabili and his sister were sitting.

"It would be nice if we could all sit down", Laith told his sister. She tutted at him and made space on the log.

"Can never just let people be comfortable, can you?", she asked him.

Laith sat close to his sister on the log. Close enough so that there was space for Esmeralda to sit next to him too. Normally, she would have chosen to sit on the floor. She preferred sitting on the floor, like her grandad, though she knew that this was something that Laith would never choose. However, she was feeling particularly close to Laith today and wanted to join him on the log. She sat close to him. Once she sat down, she noticed that Laith shuffled across slightly away from his sister and towards her. Her heart did the tiniest of flutters.

The group sat around the fire in silence. The tiredness was possibly setting in, Esmeralda supposed. She didn't mind. She enjoyed meditating on the crackling of the fire, whilst it radiated its warmth deep inside her bones. It brought her peace. She was relaxed. Peering through the dancing flames, she could see her grandad still sat cross-legged and closed-eyed. She glanced to her right, where Laith was sat, also staring at the fire. She wondered what he was thinking. Her mind flashed back to when she was with Laith by the river, her hands on his chest whilst she was staring deep into his eyes. His eyes had been smiling at her. She wriggled slightly at the thought of his hands on her waist, but then suddenly became aware of her surroundings, which jolted her out of her thoughts.

Uncle Kabili stood up. "I'll get a start on dinner", he said, heading towards his cabin.

"Yeah, I'll help you", said Sarama.

"No, it's okay. There's nothing really to do", he replied. "I'm just gonna start boiling the rice and chickpeas – that's all there is really – then it can just cook slowly".

Esmeralda was very fond of Sarama, and so was a little bit ashamed of herself for being glad when Sarama got up and followed Uncle Kabili anyway. It may have been out of fear of Laith following the two of them, or due to the fact that she was slightly more comfortable now that his family had left, but she allowed her head to drop to the side and rest on Laith's shoulder. She smiled when she felt him move his own head towards hers in response. She was no longer at an old, lonely settlement.

Esmeralda had not noticed that her grandfather had opened his eyes until he uncrossed his legs and arose as gracefully as ever.

"Happier?", he asked Esmeralda.

Esmeralda smiled in response. Her grandad had obviously been able to tell that she was unsettled earlier, even though she had not told him and had, in fact, tried to hide all indication of the matter.

"Good", he said. "Laith, I've got something for you, too, actually – when you're ready".

"Oh", said Laith, sounding intrigued. "Yeah, I'm just sitting now".

"It's nothing too exciting – don't get your hopes up", Esmeralda's grandad told Laith. Esmeralda was intrigued too, and so she got up and pushed Laith towards the cabin.

"Come on, Grandad", Esmeralda called as she was pushing Laith, "I want to see what it is too".

This time, Esmeralda was happy to step over the threshold of the cabin first. She stepped to the side, giving room for Laith and her grandad to follow her in. The feeling on the inside of the cabin was a stark contrast to what it had been on first arrival. There was no dust riding the air. Even though there was no more sunlight coming in than before – in fact, if anything, there was less, given that the day was now thinking about ending – the cabin somehow seemed lighter than before. There was still nothing in the room but, significantly, it was also devoid of emptiness.

Esmeralda's grandad walked to the middle of the room

and picked up the glass jar that he had put there earlier. He held it up to his eye and then corked it before putting it in his pouch on the side of the room. As he did so, he drew out another glass bottle that Esmeralda knew, to Laith, would look empty. He held this one a little bit lower down and looked at it for a few seconds before handing it to Laith.

"Here. Open this and put it in the cabin next door" he said, without further explanation. Laith took it.

"Okay, thanks", he said. Esmeralda knew that Laith had no understanding of why her grandad gave him the bottle, or why he should open it and place it next door. She also knew that Laith was not the type of person who would question anything that her grandad told him to do. It was testament to his character, Esmeralda considered, that Laith had enough respect for her grandfather to simply thank him and prepare to do as he asked. She also found it quite funny that her grandad would just give Laith an instruction and either expect him to understand, or not care if he didn't.

"Aren't you even gonna tell him what it's for?", she asked her grandad, laughing.

"He knows", her grandad replied. "He helps me collect them sometimes".

"What's it for, Laith?", she asked him, gently nudging him as she did so.

"I do know", he told her. "It's beams, isn't it?", he asked her grandad. "To make the room warmer?". Esmeralda noticed his sounded less certain on this last sentence but, to be honest, she wasn't too sure herself.

"Yeah, warmer in a way", her grandad confirmed. "It will give the room more of a living energy", he told him. "Because people haven't been here in a while, it is just a way of giving it a quick boost. It should make you dream a bit better too".

"Told you I knew", Laith said to Esmeralda, trying to look as pleased with himself as possible.

"You didn't know properly", she reminded him.

"Yeah but it's what I meant – I just didn't know the exact words".

Esmeralda could feel her grandad smiling just out of her

periphery.

"Just open it whenever you go", he told Laith.

"I'll go and do it now, before I forget", Laith said. "Do you want me to close the door or leave it open", he asked, as he stepped outside.

"No, leave it open", Esmeralda's grandad told him. "We will let some of the fire inside, too – fill the house properly'.

Esmeralda watched Laith walk towards the other cabin. She quickly realised that there was nothing for her to actually do inside the cabin, and there was nowhere particularly comfortable to sit.

"I'm going to go and sit by the fire, Grandad", she said. He smiled knowingly and nodded at her.

Esmeralda walked outside and towards the fire. Now alone, she chose to sit cross-legged facing the field, close to where her grandad was sat previously. She noticed that there was a glass bottle on the floor, corked. Her grandad must have left it there earlier. She held it to her eye to confirm that it was empty before pocketing it, making a mental note that she would give it to her grandad later. She looked up at Acira, who had stopped grazing and was now just wandering around the empty fields. Esmeralda closed her eyes so that she could concentrate on the crackling of the flames and let their energy wash over her and seep inside her. Her bones were already warm, but warming them up a tiny bit more would certainly do her no harm. She heard a door creak. Her heart instinctively, as always, hoped that it was Laith, but she did not move nor did she open her eyes. She was disappointed when, from the footsteps, she could tell that it was not.

"This should be enough for all of us", she heard Uncle Kabili say, presumably to Sarama. "Where's that pail, Laith?", he said a bit louder.

"It'll be by the fire", Esmeralda heard Laith call from farther away, his voice as gentle as the fire. She heard his footsteps emerge from the cabin. "There it is".

Esmeralda opened her eyes as the three approached her. Sarama smiled at her, and she smiled back.

"Here, Laith – pour some of that water in here. Just enough to cover it and then a tiny bit more". Uncle Kabili had a smaller container in his hand, presumably containing rice and chickpeas. He watched purposefully as Laith poured some water into it. Uncle Kabili then swilled the water around the container and looked at it intently. "Yeah, that'll do", he said, before placing it on the fire. "We can leave it now for a while. It'll be ready by the time we are hungry. You might as well fill up your flasks from the water that's left. It'll probably be more than enough for tonight. Esmy?", he called. She looked up. "There's lots in there for you and your grandad whenever you want to fill up". His tone was purposefully sweet.

"Okay, thanks, Uncle", she replied.

Esmeralda tried to not make it too obvious that she was watching as Laith took a seat on the log opposite her with his sister. Uncle Kabili ventured off towards Acira, and then Esmeralda closed her eyes again. She could feel the fire saturating the air and she was at peace.

When Esmeralda opened her eyes again, she could see that the day was beginning to get darker. The Moon was visible in the still-blue sky, which, unlike her, was incomplete. She enjoyed the feeling of twilight more than she enjoyed the daytime, especially at the moment. The sun was making way for the stars to have their say, and it was the stars that she enjoyed most of all. She could feel them building up. Uncle Kabili came back to the fire to inspect the food.

"This should be ready soon", he said. "I hope you're all hungry". She hadn't considered it up until now, but Esmeralda was quite hungry.

"I'll go and call Grandad", she said. Another thing that she hadn't considered up until now was what her grandad had been doing all this time. It was unlike him to be away from the magic of the fire, especially after he prepared it with whatever he did from the glass bottle. Before she had time to get up, Laith had got up from the log and was standing by her, offering her his hand. It was these little

125

things that Laith consistently did without thinking that made it impossible for Esmeralda to feel anything for him other than what she did. She looked Laith deep in the eyes as she took his hand and pulled herself up. She could see that he had no idea what she was thinking or how she felt. He looked completely devoid of all thought, as she pulled herself up and brushed herself off.

"No little jump?", he asked her.

"What little jump?", she replied. She knew what he meant. He laughed and did not say anything further.

Esmeralda walked into the cabin and called for her grandad. She could not see him in the front room, and supposed he would have been in one of the bedrooms at the back. The cabin was a bit darker now, with the natural light outside dimming. Her grandfather had not lit any candles and, of course, there was no generator here for electricity. She heard her grandfather's footsteps before he emerged from one of the bedrooms.

"I was just filling your room", he told her. "You will need it later".

"Oh, yeah, this was by the fire", she said, remembering the glass bottle that she pocketed earlier. She rummaged for it in her pocket and then handed it over to her grandfather. "It's empty".

"Oh, thanks", he said, taking it off her. "I left that there earlier".

"Yeah, I assumed", she said, laughing. "Anyway, the food is nearly done – shall we go and eat?"

"Yeah, come on", he told her, and the two of them left the cabin and headed towards the fire. Uncle Kabili was pouring some of the food into a bucket and swilling it around, evidently for Acira. Esmeralda sat on the ground with her grandfather and then turned to see Laith emerging from the other cabin with some plates.

"Shall I start putting it in?", he asked Uncle Kabili

"Yeah, you can do", Uncle Kabili replied. "This'll be cool enough for Acira soon – it'll cool down in the metal bucket quite quickly", he said, swilling it around some more. "And I need to put a bit more water in it for her, anyway".

Uncle Kabili finished preparing Acira's food and put it down near the fire, before leading her towards it. Acira started eating as Laith put the food in for the rest of the group. He handed the first plate to Esmeralda's grandfather before giving the food, in turn, to Esmeralda, Uncle Kabili, and Sarama. He then put his own in and left the container near to the fire, replacing the lid. Esmeralda's hunger became more apparent to her. She could see the steam coming off the plates of rice and chickpeas so took a spoonful and carefully blew it. Her mouth was already watering, but she didn't want to burn it.

Everybody ate in silence. This might have been because of hunger, or fatigue, or, maybe, she considered, nerves were now beginning to set in. It wasn't long before she and the others had finished. The comfort of the sun had left them, and now everybody was under the watchful eyes of the stars and the Moon, which had become the centerpiece of the sky. Maybe everybody's mind had turned to the task in hand. Esmeralda was trying to make herself consider the same but, truth be told, she was relaxed. She remembered the glass bottle she had found earlier. Her grandad always knew what he was doing.

Uncle Kabili picked up the remaining food and put a little bit on everybody's plates, which drew some faint protests, as a formality, from everybody apart from Laith. He put none on his own plate, Esmeralda noticed, and, instead, poured a bit of water over it and left it by the fire. Uncle Kabili took the plates, one by one, as everybody finished, and did the same to those plates as he did to his own.
"I'll do it, Uncle – don't worry about it", Esmeralda said, as he gestured to take hers.
"It's no problem", he replied to her. "Just doing it quickly now, and then we can do it properly by the river tomorrow. Oh, actually, I should do some corn in here now too, so we can have it tomorrow", he told the group. "You all should go to bed – we will be starting early tomorrow." He gestured with a bit more insistence for Esmeralda's plate,

and she felt slightly awkward as she handed it over to him.

"Thanks", she said, making only brief eye contact and smiling awkwardly. Uncle Kabili smiled back. The smile seemed genuine. She had never really felt that Uncle Kabili was particularly fond of her, but maybe she was wrong about this. He wasn't the type of person who was easy to read. He was always kind to her, so maybe she was being unfair in thinking what she did – it was possibly just as a result of his general demeanor, not of who he was as a person or how he actually felt. But she just had an inkling.

Sarama was the first to get up.

"I *am* quite tired", she told the group as she did so. "I'm going to try and sleep now – I'll see you all in the morning".

"Goodnight", said Esmeralda, as did her grandfather and Uncle Kabili. Laith lifted his arm in acknowledgement as Sarama headed towards the cabin on the left.

"You should probably go to bed as well, Laith". Esmeralda's heart dropped slightly when she heard Uncle Kabili says those words, which was silly, she thought. She knew that they were going to bed eventually, and she knew that they would be seeing each other in the morning. But did he really have to leave right now? She thought back to the past – to all the other times that they would say goodbye. It never felt as intense as it did now. Maybe it was because all of those times she had never admitted to herself how she really felt. No – it must be the fact that they were in a new and unfamiliar place. This was just making her more susceptible to negative feelings and emotions. She tried to pull herself together by thinking these logical thoughts. The stars were in the sky too – they always brought her some solace.

"Yeah, I am gonna", Laith replied to his father. "Goodnight, Uncle", he said, looking over at Esmeralda's grandfather. "Goodnight", he said again, this time to Esmeralda. He smiled as he did so. Did he maintain eye-contact with her a fraction longer than he needed to? He certainly looked away with more intent than was natural when he finally did so. He was always a bit more awkward when they were not alone together, Esmeralda considered, but was this more than usual? They had been so comfortable when they were alone walking to the stream and back – nothing could ever feel more perfect and natural than how they were just a few hours ago. She reiterated to herself in her mind that she was fully aware of how Laith would become more awkward when they were not alone, but she couldn't help but question whether he was even more so tonight. If he was, was it because she had given something away earlier? He did look away with more vigour than was necessary – was he trying to tell her something with this action? Her heart dropped at this thought – she hoped that this was not the case. Or was his awkwardness simply because he, like herself, was changed slightly by the unfamiliarity of the surroundings. Her grandad had done a good job of changing the energy of this old settlement, but of course it was not perfect, so it was reasonable that it was affecting Laith in the same way that it would affect her and everybody else. This seemed overwhelmingly more likely, especially taken in the context of the fact that Laith was always awkward when they were not alone anyway. Now that she had thought about it, a part of her heart that she tried her utmost not to focus on was possibly hoping that Laith *had* picked up on something earlier. She did not know why she would possibly want this – it would be disastrous. But then at least he would know. But did she want him to know? No – it would be a disaster. Definitely. She suppressed this feeling and got up too. She hated being so confused.

"Yeah, I'm gonna go to bed too", she said. "Goodnight, everyone".

She smiled at Laith before they both turned to walk towards their respective cabins – his on the left and hers on the right.

Esmeralda felt a creeping chill as she walked away from the fire, not due to the fading of its heat but due to the increasing intensity of the coldness of the cabin. She stepped inside and realised how uncomfortable she felt. What had happened to the energy that was present there earlier? It has disappeared. This was horrible. She didn't want to linger in the living room for longer than necessary. Feeling slightly overwhelmed, she headed straight into the room where she knew that she would be sleeping for the night. She took a deep breath to try and calm herself as she looked upon the sparse room. She tried to tell herself that she was longing for her own room but she knew that this was not really the case. The bare room merely compounded what she was feeling in her heart. There was no bed, but her grandad had already laid out the soft blankets that she would be sleeping on. This made her feel slightly better – she could hide away between the blankets and be protected from the outside world. There was no pump and therefore no running water in the old settlement, so Esmeralda took her flask and her toothbrush to quickly brush her teeth outside. As she went outside, she saw that her grandfather and uncle seemed to be having a hushed conversation about something. She was glad that they were preoccupied with whatever they were talking about, because she was not in the mood to be seen. Her eyes unconsciously flicked towards Laith's cabin as she was brushing her teeth. She caught herself and quickly looked away again. There was nobody there, anyway. She rinsed her mouth with the water from her flask and spat it on the ground, turning her back towards the fire and trying to be as silent as possible. She still hoped that she was not seen, for no particular reason, but she did not turn around to check. She rushed back inside the cabin and to the room where she would be sleeping. She changed her clothes as quickly as possible so that she could head for the protection of her blankets. She pulled them right over her head, wanting to hide away from nothing in particular. She felt slightly safer in here – slightly less exposed. Now that she was safe and cocooned, she let down her guard and allowed her feelings to come rushing back to her. She couldn't hide from them much longer, no matter how tightly she pulled the blankets around her. Had Laith picked up on anything? He probably hadn't. When she thought that he had, she wished for nothing more than for him not to know anything, so that they could just be normal. She loved and cherished her relationship with him and would hate to have to sacrifice it. When she consoled herself that he had not noticed anything, a small part of her wished that he had. Imagine if he felt the same. If he felt the same, she would do anything to make sure they were together forever. But there was nothing that she could do. The brief flicker of the thought that he might feel the same made her feel, just as last night, that they could tackle all of the obstacles in their way. But, just as last night, she realised that they could not. The circles in her mind began to spiral. He did not feel the same. She would give anything for him to feel the same. Anything. But he didn't. And she didn't want him to, because it would never work out for them with their strict culture. It would be even more cruel if he did feel the same. It would be cruel on both of them – she did not want him to feel the way that she was feeling, and him feeling the same way would make it worse for both of them. They would be so close, but there is no way that it could work out for them. But, if he did, she could and she would do anything to make it work. She tried to connect with the stars, as she always did when she was in need of comfort, but, in this unfamiliar place and in her worked up state, she even found this difficult. She tried to calm herself down, and she did so the only way that she could – she imagined that Laith was lying beside her. How could the Universe be so cruel to her? The thing that calmed her was the thing that caused her anxiety. As she felt herself calm down, her heart breaking and soothing at the same time, she started to imagine that the blankets on which she was resting her head was Laith's chest. They were lying under the stars. She could feel the warmth of the fire that they were lying next to – its wonderful energy penetrating both of their hearts. The stars beamed down on them both and she felt connected to them once again. Their gaze could not penetrate the blanket she was hiding underneath – they could not see what she didn't want them to see – but their energy could. Their energy could connect with her and bring her the smallest bit of solace. She lay alone, hiding under her blanket, wondering if Laith was doing the same. Was he comfortable? Was he able to sleep? He was a few feet away, in the cabin on the left. But, in the cabin on the left, he was so much further away than the stars currently flooding her heart. For the second time in two nights, Esmeralda cried herself to sleep, a complete slave to the cruel fate of the Universe.

Chapter 16 - Laith

Laith awoke with a blissful feeling of absolutely nothing as the sunbeams from the morning sun burst in amidst the cracks and the dirt on the small window in the room in which he was sleeping. However, after the most fleeting of moments, his brain succumbed to its unfortunate habit of becoming engaged and this wonderful feeling disappeared. He felt as though he had not dreamt last night, and he was grateful for this. Had he dreamt, his dreams would probably not have been amongst the nicest he'd ever had. He had fallen asleep quite quickly last night and, although he felt as though he had slept incredibly deeply, he was still tired. Only now that he had slept did Laith realise just how unimaginably exhausted he was. The amount of walking and equipment-carrying they had all done yesterday seemed like a good justification for a person to be tired, but this was a different type of exhaustion. His body felt fine. It was his head that was tired. He was mentally drained. He never imagined just how strong an effect this could have on his body. His eyelids were trying to force themselves shut. He had never known just how incredibly draining it was to be upset. As soon as his thoughts came flooding back to him, his head felt heavy, his heart felt heavy and he had an overwhelming feeling that he needed his brain to shut down and force him back into a blissful sleep.

He closed his eyes again – not of his own free will, but out of necessity. He couldn't have kept them open any longer if he had tried. Thankfully, he had no desire to try - he needed a few more moments to compose himself and try, in some way, to expel the heaviness from his head and from his heart. Once he was able, he opened his eyes. His gaze was drawn towards the years of accumulated dirt on the window that, although his father had done his best to clean on arrival, inevitably ended being partly engrained even deeper within the glass. He was caught in a conflicting position of wanting to hurry up and get this mission done, and not wanting to do anything at all. He wanted to go home despite knowing that there was nothing at home that would help him. In any case, there was no comfort to be found lying on the floor, and so he got himself up. He wondered how well Esmy had slept last night, and he also wondered about everybody else. He took his canteen and headed outside to brush his teeth. He noticed that the door of the room in which his sister had spent the night was still closed – she must still be asleep. He walked through the living room and saw that his father's blankets had already been rolled up and packed away. As always, his father was up first to lead the way.

Laith stepped outside and looked instinctively over to the cabin on his left. It looked as though it was still sleeping, surrounded by dew in the soft, morning light. He then looked towards the fire where he saw his father cooking something that he supposed would be porridge. Laith did not think his father had seen or heard him come out – he had his back towards him – and neither did Laith call out to greet him. He finished brushing his teeth and then went quietly back inside.

Laith went back into his bedroom and changed his clothes. In the mood that he was in, had he been home, he would have liked to have sat alone for a while in his bedroom. However, given the bare nature of his current habitat – he had nowhere to sit apart from the floor - he picked up his sword and shield and headed outside. This time he opened the front door with a little bit more intention. His father heard him and turned around. Without outwardly acknowledging him, Laith's father turned back around to tend to the breakfast on the fire. Laith was not offended by this – this is what they were both like. Laith headed towards his father and sat down on the log opposite him.

"Alright", Laith mumbled as a greeting. Laith was very rarely enthusiastic at the best of times, and certainly not this early in the morning when he was feeling how he was feeling.

"Alright", his father said back. He said it slightly more cheerfully than he usually would. Laith wondered if this was genuine or a forced attempt to either lighten the mood given the situation, or compensate for not greeting him earlier.

"You woke up really early", Laith stated to his father in a tone that he hoped suggested that he would not be unwelcoming to an expansion into a conversation, if his father so pleased, but not so far as to be a question or a demand for an explanation.

"Yeah – I just slept out here last night, by the fire. Thought it would be nicer outside".

Laith supposed that it would have. He did not say anything until he felt his thoughts start to trail off to where he did not want them to, at which point he attempted to snap himself out of it by replying "Yeah, it does sound nice. I saw all your stuff all packed up. I wondered why it was so neat".

"Yeah, I didn't use it in the end. I had the fire to keep me warm".

Laith imagined that this would have been nice, but he was conscious that the two of them had possibly already passed their quota of using 'yeah' as a response. He decided that he would nod in agreement instead, whilst mumbling a sound that he hoped conveyed agreement.

Laith sat for a moment before standing up. "I'm gonna go down to the stream and wash", he declared. "Do we need any water?"

"No, I already got some earlier for the porridge, and there's plenty left over there too", replied his father, gesturing vaguely behind him. "You just go and sort yourself out".

"Yeah, ok. See you in a bit, then".

"Yeah".

Laith was glad of his need to go to stream - he quite fancied being alone at the moment. Well, out of the choice of sitting with his father or being alone, he wanted to be alone. He didn't have anything against his father, but he was not relaxed with him like he was with Esmy, for example. He would feel a lot more comfortable once he was alone, he thought, and so he headed past the cabins and towards the river feeling quite optimistic that this would lift his spirits.

Even having only taken a few steps out of the vicinity of the settlement in which they were staying, he already felt as though maybe he had made a mistake with this journey. The walk already seemed a lot longer than it did yesterday, and his spirits were dampened, if anything. Maybe he should have just used the water his father had collected to wash, and stayed by the fire. Well, it was too late now, anyway – he was already on his way. Maybe he would begin to feel a bit better as he got closer to the stream, as he did yesterday.

As he continued his journey towards the stream, long and arduous in comparison to yesterday's, he realised that his straw-clutching of being alone lifting his spirits was not a prophecy that was to be fulfilled. His mind threatened to slip back into thinking what he was thinking when he found out his father had slept outside by the fire. The real reason for today's journey not lifting him in the same way that yesterday's was slowly creeping its way to the forefront of his mind despite his best attempts to suppress it. Laith tried to concentrate on the grass, focusing his thoughts on how Acira would love to graze on it. 'She would be in her element here', Laith told himself, knowing full well that she would not actually care in the slightest. But a distraction is a distraction.

Laith's mind overpowered his attempted suppression and forced itself to where it had been trying to go all along. Laith wondered what Esmy was doing – if she had woken up yet. Was the sunlight streaming into her room in the same dusty way that it had streamed into his? Had it awoken her as it had him, penetrating his eyelids in an accusatory manner, or was she able to sleep through it?

These insignificant questions suddenly meant the world to him. He wanted her to be awake. He didn't want to go back to the settlement and then be sat alone with his father again – he wanted to spend his time with her. All of it. They had always been close, and he had always wanted to spend time with her anyway. They had been inseparable for as long as he could remember. But he felt different now. He had felt different over the last few days, once he allowed himself to realise how he actually felt. He knew that he and Esmy could never be together and married – she was from a different tribe, and her tribe did things differently. Her marriage had been set a long time ago, when they were both children and long before he ever considered it to be unfair. He considered whether he should internally reprimand himself for this use of the term 'unfair'. Was it unfair, or was it a difference between their culture that he would have to accept? Well, there was nothing stopping it from being both. And it was quite clearly both. It was unfair that she should have to marry somebody she did not choose, and it was something that he would have to accept. It was unfair on her, and it was unfair on him. But was it actually unfair on her? He had no actual reason to suppose that it was anything other than what she wanted. Just because he himself did not like the idea, it did not mean that she didn't. Apart from the fact that he knew her, and he knew that she would not like the idea deep down any more than he did. She might act as though she didn't mind, but surely this was just to appease her grandfather. Surely she would eventually speak to her grandfather about her unhappiness at this idea, and he would, of course, understand. Uncle Cahya was the most caring man that Laith knew – of course he would understand. But then Laith reminded himself again that he had no reason to believe that she had any qualms about the situation as it was. Except for the fact that he knew her very well, and he knew that she would. Of course she would. He knew her. Or was he now just projecting his own feelings onto her? Was this another straw-clutching prophecy that was to remain unfulfilled? His head began to feel heavy again. This was draining. One thing that he was certain of was that, when he found out that his father was sleeping alone by the fire, he would have happily given him the room in which he was sleeping if it meant that he could sleep with Esmy basking in the warm glow of the slowly burning fire under the watchful gaze of the stars – the same stars that were watching over the two of them lying in the field two nights ago when he first admitted to himself that he was in love.

Chapter 17 - Sarama

Sarama had been lying awake on the floor of her temporary room for a few minutes watching the dust particles in the air dance in the spotlight of the light from the small window. She was not particularly fascinated by them – she just really couldn't be bothered to get up. Everybody else would be up and ready by now, and she knew to expect some light-hearted jibes from her brother and Uncle Cahya about her being so lazy. If she stayed for another few minutes, she considered, she could quite truthfully respond that she had been awake for a long time but just in her room. She decided to get up anyway. She had already been awake for long enough to have that response, she decided - not that it really mattered, and she did need to get ready so that they could continue their journey.

Sarama forced herself up and went to locate her toothbrush and canteen before heading outside. She walked out of her room and saw that the door to her brother's room was open – as expected. Through the living room, she saw that her dad's sleeping equipment had all been rolled up and packed away. Again, this was no surprise to her. She stepped outside and looked towards the fire, where her dad was sat with Uncle Cahya and Esmy. She wondered where her brother was. It was unlike him not to be in the vicinity of Esmy. Sarama's dad turned around to face her when he saw Uncle Cahya and Esmy look up towards the cabin. Her movement was in their peripheral vision.

"Hi, Sarama", her dad shouted towards her. Sarama waved in response, her toothbrush already in her mouth. Uncle Cahya and Esmy waved back.

Sarama finished brushing her teeth and went back inside to get ready. She changed her clothes, picked up her shield along with her bow and arrows, and headed outside. She chose to sit by her dad, with her back to the cabins. Acira was already eating, as were the rest of the group. Her dad put his porridge down and collected a bowl and a spoon for Sarama, into which he used a ladle to pour a bit of porridge.

"I had to make it with water, obviously", he told her, clearly absolving himself from any blame for the taste as he handed it to her.

"Thanks", she replied, making a mental note that she would compliment it in a moment or two, after it had cooled down enough for her to have her first spoonful.

The rest of the group seemed to be nearly finished with their own breakfast.

"We should make it past the garden today", Sarama's dad said to the group. Even though there had been a number of places referred to as 'the garden', she knew the place her dad meant when he said it without further clarification, and she knew its significance – it was the place her mother was killed. That's where they would be going today. She expected to feel some emotion on hearing that they would reach the garden, but the only thing she felt was confusion due to the fact that she did not feel anything at all. She told herself that she should have some kind of emotional reaction. She felt bad for not doing so, but there was nothing she could do. She, possibly out of guilt, tried to focus on the negative in order to muster up a feeling of sadness. When she concentrated, she managed it. This would have to do for now – surely the garden would later bring her the sadness she owed.

"Following the river north will be the quickest route for this part, I think", her dad continued. Sarama knew that the 'I think' at the end of his statement was merely decorative. She knew that he knew full well that nobody would have a differing opinion – this is what they would be doing today. As expected, there was no disagreement, although there was no outward agreement either. Esmy and her grandad were both unmoved. Sarama's dad did, after all, make a statement that needed no acknowledgement.

Sarama noticed Esmy look up at something behind her. Given Esmy's unwitting smile, Sarama knew before turning around to confirm it that Laith must be back. As he was walking towards the group, he raised his hand to greet everybody there.

"Alright", he said, as he got closer. "Good afternoon", he said to Sarama, despite it surely being not much past eight o'clock in the morning. She was waiting for this, and so already had a cutting retort prepared.

"Shut up", she told him. He laughed as he walked past her and their dad to sit next to Esmy on the log opposite.

"Have some food, Laith", their dad told him, "then we can start going soon".

"Yeah, I'll get some", replied Laith as he reached for a spare bowl and spoon.

"You might as well finish it off", their dad told him, "unless anybody else wants any more?"

Nobody responded. Sarama suddenly remembered that she had made a mental note to compliment the porridge earlier.

"It's really nice", she said. "Thanks, Dad".

"That's okay", he said to her, smiling. His tone lightened.

Uncle Cahya and Sarama's dad put their bowls down almost simultaneously.

"We will need to wash these up, I suppose, and then we can start packing up". Sarama noticed that he took a glance over in her bowl to see how much she had left.

"I'll wash them after I've finished, Uncle", Esmy said. "I can take the big pot too".

"No, that's okay, we can sort it", Sarama's father replied.

"No, honestly, I wanted to go down to the stream anyway and wash myself a bit so it's no trouble".

"Okay, well, we'll see".

Sarama took a quick glance over towards Esmy to gauge her reaction. She was smiling slightly, seemingly forced, and then looked down towards the ground.

Sarama was nearly finished with her porridge. Laith was

rushing. Esmy seemed to be dawdling.

"There's no need to rush it, Laith", their dad told him. "Just enjoy it – we aren't in a rush".

"Oh, okay", Sarama's brother replied, and then continued eating at the same pace.

"I beat you", Sarama told him, putting her last spoonful of porridge into her mouth and smiling at him.

"It wasn't a race", he told her

"Not a close one", she replied.

Laith and Esmy were the last to finish, almost simultaneously, but neither put their bowls down. Sarama noticed that Esmy looked over into Laith's bowl to make sure it was empty before standing up. She picked up the empty pot and put her own bowl into it, and then took Uncle Cahya's and Laith's. She gestured to Sarama to take hers, and Sarama happily handed it to her.

"Thanks", she said, with a smile.

Esmy then took Sarama's dad's bowl, after he gave it up reluctantly. Sarama's dad wasn't the type who was very comfortable with other people doing things for him.

"You can leave these, there, Esmy", he told her. "I will take them later".

"No, honestly, Uncle, it's okay. I want to go anyway".

"Okay", Sarama's dad conceded, before adding, "Sarama, do you want to go with her to help her?". Her dad liked to ask rhetorical questions. However, unlike everybody else in the world, she could usually get away with actually giving an answer.

"Laith wants to", she replied. Normally, this was a reply that she would give to anything that she didn't want to do herself, regardless of the truth behind it. Today, as a happy coincidence, it did seem that Laith actually did want to go. He had already stood up and taken the pot off Esmy. That was lucky. It looked to Sarama as though her dad was thinking about a reply but, in the end, he didn't say anything. Sarama took this as her cue to relax. Well, her brother was going to go anyway, and he was probably happy to. And, as an added bonus for him, this would give him the opportunity to call her lazy, or saying something like 'no, don't worry – I'll do everything as usual. You stay sitting down'. Bracing herself for the insult, she was unsure whether she was relieved or disappointed when none came. Her brother just walked past her with Esmy reasonably content

'See you all in a bit, then", he said.

Sarama wasn't sure how to reply to that, and so she stayed silent.

Sarama's dad had already stood up and made his way around to the other side of the fire. He stood up, Sarama realised, when he was reluctantly giving Esmy his bowl. Maybe he saw this as a compromise, Sarama thought – he did not like the idea of other people doing things for him but, if he was to ever allow them to, he certainly did not want to be sitting down while they did so. Sarama noticed that he still had his eye on Esmy and Laith as they were walking away – it was probably eating him up inside that he had allowed somebody to do something for him, no matter how trivial. Sarama would not have been overly surprised if he had a change of heart and ran after them to wash his own bowl.

"Those two are getting quite close, aren't they?", Sarama's dad said to her.

"Yeah. Well, they always have been. You know they always have been", she replied, somewhat surprised at his question.

"Yeah they have", her dad agreed, with Sarama still unsure as to what brought this on now.

"She's going to be getting married soon, I suppose, isn't she?", he said. It seemed to Sarama that this was more directed at Uncle Cahya, so she did not say anything. However, it seemed as though Uncle Cahya must have thought that it was directed at her, and so he did not say anything either. Or maybe he thought it was another one of Sarama's dad's rhetorical questions. As far as Sarama knew, Esmy would be getting married in the next few years and this was common knowledge. Maybe her dad was just trying to make conversation. If so, it didn't work.

"Maybe it's about time we found somebody for Laith too", he continued, unperturbed by the lack of engagement.

"Maybe you should ask Laith", Sarama laughed.

"No, I know - I'm just saying".

It dawned on Sarama *why* her father might have been 'just saying'. She thought about whether she should reiterate to him that her brother and Esmy were just friends, but she decided that this might add fuel to the fire. Acknowledging what her dad was saying by defending her brother would necessarily mean that there was something to acknowledge, which there wasn't. She decided to stay silent. In fact, she decided to go one step further than that.

"I'm gonna go start packing my stuff up", she told him, before noticing that Acira had finished her breakfast and so decided to head over to her instead.

"Hi, Acira", said Sarama gently, stroking Acira's nose. Was there any truth to what her dad was hinting towards, she wondered? No, she didn't think there was. If there was, surely she would have picked up on it. Her dad was just paranoid because the stakes were a lot higher for him, for some reason, than for her. He seemed to care a lot more about tradition than she or anybody else did. He always had a rigid idea of what the right thing to do was, even if it made very little difference to anybody else. She thought back to the day of the harvest, where he rearranged her sheaves of wheat for no discernable reason. This was typical of him. He would have a fixed idea of the right way to do things, and heaven forbid anybody question this. That was the only reason he would be thinking there might be anything more between Laith and Esmy – it was just out of worry that somebody might break a tradition. But there was nothing to worry about at all, anyway. Her dad was definitely just paranoid.

Having reached this satisfactory conclusion, Sarama thought it was time to stop stroking Acira and go and pack her things up instead. She didn't want to be the last one ready. Well, to be honest, she didn't really care. But she had nothing else to do now that Laith and Esmy had gone to the stream, and her dad and uncle seemed to be in conversation about something that, even without knowing what it was, she was quite certain that she didn't care about. She patted Acira goodbye and took a slightly wider than necessary berth around the two elders, to rule out the prospect of her getting dragged into a boring conversation. She stepped back into her cabin – it seemed colder now that she had been out under the morning sun. She rolled up and tied up all of her bedding and put it next to her dad's by the door. She made sure that she took her time doing this. She needed something to keep her occupied. As Laith and Esmy were still not back, and she still had no desire to involve herself in boring conversation with her dad and Uncle Cahya, she headed into Laith's room to tidy up his bedding too. She was quite happy to see that he had not already done it himself – doing it for him would mean that she could hold it against him later. Perfect. He was the lazy one, out of the two of them, now that she thought about it. She took even longer doing his than she did her own. She didn't want to leave room for any jibes about her not doing a proper job when she was rubbing it in her brother's face just how lazy he was for leaving the work to her, and also she didn't want to finish too soon before he came back or she would have nothing to do.

Once Sarama had finished tidying her brother's bedding, she put it with her own and her dad's and went to stand outside. She didn't venture too far from the cabin, as her dad and Uncle Cahya were still in conversation about something boring. They looked like they were having fun, but only because Sarama knew them. Both men, particularly her dad, had a sombre air about their general personalities, and this would fool any other onlooker into thinking that the conversation that they were having now was serious. Sarama knew the truth – these two men were never more comfortable than when they were together. She could tell from their body language, not necessarily their facial expressions, that they were having fun about something. She didn't really care what, but she was happy that they were. It made her feel at ease about the rest of the mission, without prior realisation that this was not already the case.

Sarama heard a noise coming from her left. She turned to see that it was Laith and Esmy making their way back from the stream. She was glad to see them. They looked happy together, as always. She started wondering again about what her dad had alluded towards earlier, but quickly dismissed it. She had allowed his paranoia to get into her own head. Not that she would have a problem with it, of course. Well, she had never really given it much thought, because there was nothing to think about. But she didn't see why she would have a problem with her brother being happy. Anyway, she thought, it was irrelevant.

"Oi", Sarama called towards her brother. The two elders must have also heard this. Out of the corner of her eye, Sarama saw them look towards her but then towards her brother on realisation that she was calling towards him.

"What?", Laith called back. Not wanting to project her voice again, Sarama just beckoned him towards her with her arm. Their shouting had obviously interrupted the conversation between their dad and Uncle Cahya, as both men had now stood up and looked ready to start packing up.

"What?", Laith asked Sarama, when he reached her. He seemed intrigued, Sarama thought, which was a shame given the answer that he was about to receive.

"Nothing", said Sarama. "I was just bored".

"Oh. Well, I'm here now. Shall we start packing up?". Sarama had never been more delighted to hear these words than she was right now. She considered berating his apathy right now, for not having tidied up his blankets the second he had woken up and instead leaving it to her to do along with her own, but she decided against it. She wanted to drag it out and savour the moment. They hadn't had a good argument in nearly a day – it wasn't right.

"Yeah, okay", she replied, with all the coolness she could muster.

"I'd better go and do mine too, actually", said Esmy, and she left Sarama and her brother to head towards the other cabin.

Sarama waited for Laith to step into the cabin first, and then followed afterwards. Her dastardly plan, concocted a mere thirty seconds ago, was to allow Laith to go into his room, see that everything had been tidied up, and then berate him whilst he was in a state of utter bewilderment. Perfect, she thought.

"Is this our stuff here?", Laith asked, pointing to all of the bedding at the door that Sarama had placed there earlier and forgotten about. "Dad must have done it already", he continued, not waiting for a response to his original question. Sarama hadn't thought about this obvious flaw in her plan.

"No, Dad didn't bloody do it. I did it. By myself. While you were off gallivanting around to the stream and back, leaving everything to me, as per bloody usual". Sarama had to take the opportunity now – a change to her original plan, but effective nonetheless. After all, what plan ever worked perfectly? Especially one that took under a minutes planning. She was nothing if not adaptable, and she would make the most of this situation.

"Oh", said Laith. "Thanks".

Sarama's heart dropped. She knew that her brother had been a bit off yesterday, but she thought that they had sorted it when they went through their dad's plan together. He was apprehensive about it at the time, but then his spirits had definitely lifted when they had been through the plan together that morning at their kitchen table. There was absolutely no way her brother would respond with a simple 'thanks' in normal situations. There was clearly something wrong. He had just been to the stream to clean pots and bowls – he even still had them in his hand – it couldn't possibly be any easier for him to rub how much work he had actually done in her face, and defend himself from her slightly exaggerated accusations. There must be a reason he chose not to. Sarama's plan had just failed. Was this a foreshadowing of the events that would occur in a few days time? Is this what Laith was worried about? No, don't be silly – there weren't too many parallels to be drawn between a plan she had devised in thirty seconds in order to orchestrate an argument with her brother, and a plan that her dad had clearly been thinking about for years in order to orchestrate an intricate heist and save the future of their community. They were both plans - the similarities stopped there. But any plan can fail, if not thought through thoroughly. Her dad had thought things through thoroughly, though. Her dad thought about *everything* in such excruciating detail all the bloody time that it was impossible that he could have missed anything at all, let alone anything as simple as leaving blankets by the door. And her brother had thought about it too, and didn't seem to find a problem. Except that he had – he did make the point that the plan was based on some assumptions that they could possibly not know for sure. But they had been through this the morning before and realised that the assumptions were pretty solid. But then why was her brother behaving strangely now? There must be something that he realised but he didn't want to tell her. What was he hiding from her and why?

"It's okay", Sarama replied, worried slightly about the mission but worried more about her brother.

Chapter 18 - Laith

His sister's tone indicated to Laith that he had upset her. Inadvertently. He had been acting differently – he knew this – and she had picked up on it. She didn't smile at him when she replied, like she normally did. He hoped that she didn't think it was anything to do with her. His mind quickly raced back to anything that could have happened between them to make her think that he was upset with her. He couldn't think of anything – that was a relief. Surely, then, she knew that it was nothing she had done. He had been acting differently, though. He had allowed things to get him down after that night under the stars. When he was with Esmy, things seemed as normal and as natural as they ever were. When they were apart, however, he felt the distance unlike he ever had in the past.

"Well, it bloody better well be okay", Laith said. "I had to go all the way to the stream, dragging everybody's dirty dishes, washed every single one and then had to trek all the way back. You, on the other hand, woke up when the sun is basically about to set, sat on your arse stuffing your stupid face, thrusted your dirty bowl demandingly upon me, and now expect a medal for rolling up a bloody blanket – a thirty second job". He hoped this didn't sound too forced. He did have to force it at the start but, once he had started, his words flowed as naturally as ever. He saw a small smile on his sister's face. He was relieved.

"*Esmy* took my bowl, not you", she replied. "And 'thrusted' isn't a word – it's 'thrust'. And I didn't do that, anyway. Esmy politely took it off me. And she was probably the one who did all the washing. You probably just stood around doing bugger all, as usual". Laith's heart jumped slightly on hearing Esmy's name. Did his sister suspect anything? Surely not.

"'Thrusted' is a word. It's the past tense of 'thrust' I

wanted to make it clear that I meant you did it, and I wasn't asking you to do it. It's important to be clear. That's the point of language. Otherwise we might as well just point and grunt. And anyway, 'probably this, probably that'. Were you there? No. For your information, we both cleaned them as much as each other. It takes two people to do it properly. You'd know that, if you ever did anything".

"It only takes two people to do it properly if you're one of those people. Otherwise people can do it perfectly well by themselves. People who aren't stupid like you".

Now that they had gotten fully into their argument, everything felt normal to Laith again. This is what he longed for. He had been upset, realising how he felt about Esmy and knowing that he could do nothing about it, and it was affecting him when he was alone. With Esmy, earlier, he had been perfectly happy. It genuinely felt as though nothing had changed. He was just as comfortable with her as he ever was. Even though he was hiding this from her, it didn't feel like he was hiding anything. Their relationship was unchanged, particularly as far as Esmy was concerned. When Esmy left, he felt it. It forced him to realise that he missed her presence. Knowing that he would eventually lose her to her marriage made him feel the loss every time she walked away. How silly. He would not lose her – they would still be friends, as they were now. Maybe they wouldn't be able to spend all their time together, as they currently did, but their relationship was a special one and nobody could take that away from them. He wished that they could continue as they were forever. Or even end up together. *Together* together. But this wasn't an option. Esmy did not feel how he did. She was engaged, technically. They were from different tribes. His father would never allow it to happen. And, again, *Esmy did not feel how he did*. Arguing with his sister helped to console him – it helped him to focus on the fact that things would not have to change too much. He would still be friends with Esmy. Very very good friends. Things wouldn't have to change too much. As far as everybody else was concerned, everything was still the same. This was some consolation, he supposed.

"Okay well, next time, you bloody do it then", he told his sister. "Then we'll see how easy it is"
"Okay, I will".
"Hope you fall in the bloody river".
"Well I won't".
"You will if I push you".
"I'll move".
"Oh, shut up".
"You shut up".

"Are you two packed up?", Laith heard their father shout from outside. He looked outside to see him heading towards the cabin.
"Yeah we are, Dad", Sarama shouted back. Their father stepped inside the cabin. Laith stepped slightly to the side to give him more room.
"Okay, good", said their father, looking around the room. He seemed satisfied. "Shall we start loading up Acira, then?". Laith looked at the pot and bowls in his hands.
"Have you got the sack for these?", he asked his father. His father looked towards him, and Laith was sure he saw an element of confusion or surprise on his face for just a split-second before it disappeared.
"Yeah, just pass them to me, I'll do it", he replied. It felt to Laith as though he was forcing himself to sound cheerful. Laith handed over what he had and then went to pick up the bedding. He picked up his father's in his left hand, and then his and his sister's in his right hand. She had tied it up quite well, he thought to himself – it made it quite easy for him to hold both in the same hand. He was pleasantly surprised.
"Looks like you've done a good job of something, for once", he told her, lifting his right hand slightly to indicate to her what he was referring to.
"Obviously", she replied.

Laith stepped outside and then realised that Acira was not ready. She was off grazing on a patch of grass a few yards away from where the fire had been. Laith turned to put the blankets back down just inside the doorway, and went to ready Acira. He walked towards her and stroked her nose. He had always liked Acira, and he knew that she had always liked him too. She had been born when he was quite young – maybe around the age the twins were now, he couldn't really remember. He was glad that his father had brought Acira, though, instead of any of the other horses. Acira was the one who seemed to like him the most. For some reason, she was the one that he would always stroke and want to be around the most when he was younger. His sister was the same, he thought. There was something special about Acira. She was calmer than the rest. He tapped her side to show her that he wanted her to follow him closer to the cabins, which she dutifully did, and then he stroked her nose when they got there. He thought he should probably put her saddle on her, and her rope. As he was doing this, his father and sister emerged from the cabin.

"Oh, good, Laith. Nice one", his father said to him, on seeing that he was readying Acira. His father did sound more cheerful today than he normally did, or was it forced? This was the second time that Laith was surprised by his father's tone. He had nothing to be cheerful about, Laith considered. But then he had no reason to force it either. Maybe he was trying to lift everybody's spirits, knowing what was to come. The last thing that anybody needed now was for anybody to lose faith in what they were doing. His father was naturally always the leader, and he must have been taking it on himself to ensure that everybody's spirits were kept high.

Laith's father stepped towards him and Acira, sacks in hand, and started tying them onto the saddle. Laith stepped round to the front of Acira to give his father some space, and continued to stroke her nose. He realised how this was helping him to void his mind of thoughts. Unfortunately, this realisation brought with it the thoughts that he was hoping to void his mind of. He went back inside to pick up the blankets but first had a quick look around the other rooms to make sure that his sister and father had not missed anything. They hadn't. Nothing that he could see, anyway. His father must have already picked up Uncle Cahya's glass bottle that he had given him the day before, which was the main thing that Laith was looking for. He went back towards Acira and started passing his father the things he needed to tie on.

"Thanks", his father said, each time he took something off Laith.

Esmy and Uncle Cahya came outside. Uncle Cahya started tying some things onto Acira's other side. Esmy was passing things to Uncle Cahya, just as Laith was to his father. Laith wondered whether she was also doing it just to feel useful, as neither of them were actually making the job materially easier.

"Okay, are we all ready to go? Got everything?", Laith's father announced, standing up. "Okay, let's go then". Silence was agreement.

Uncle Cahya walked from the far side of Acira to join Laith's father, and the two men led the group. Laith's father turned to hand Acira's rope to Sarama, who hopped forwards to take it off him. Laith's felt his heartbeat rise slightly. He wanted to stay at the back with Esmy, as they were yesterday. He hoped that she would not move too far forward to join with the rest of the group. His heart smiled when she lagged back, too.

"Did you sleep okay last night?", Laith asked Esmy
"You already asked me that earlier", Esmy reminded him. "Why are you being weird? Did you sleep okay?". She looked directly into his eyes as she said this. Her eyes – the most beautiful eyes he had ever seen – portrayed her genuine concern when she asked him this. Laith remembered that he had asked her how she slept earlier, when they were on the way to the stream. He was being weird, and she had noticed. He hadn't quite settled yet, as he had earlier when they were alone and everything was

perfect.

"Yeah, I slept alright. I just forgot that I asked", he told her. The concern from her beautiful eyes turned into relief and happiness. She smiled at him without moving her mouth and he felt it in his heart. He felt just as comfortable as he always did when he was with her. Everything was perfect, as long as one was willing to overlook the fact that it most definitely was not.

The group headed diagonally towards the stream. They would be following it north. The farther Laith and Esmy lagged behind the rest, the more relaxed Laith began to feel. He couldn't describe how he felt when he was with her. It was as though, when she wasn't there, he could feel that she was missing. And it wasn't in a way that he was necessarily upset – it was more that something just wasn't quite right. As though something was off - it wasn't right for them to be apart. When they were together, however, it felt natural. He felt it inside him that this was how things should be. He wondered whether this was because of the fact they grew up together and did everything together since they were small. This must be part of it, he thought. But he knew inside him that it was more than that.

Laith looked down at Esmy's hand down by her side. She was wearing her bracelet on her left arm – the one that she had panicked about when she thought she had lost it all those years ago. It was beautiful. She made it beautiful. He wanted nothing more in this moment than to reach out and hold her hand. Would that be strange? Probably. They had held hands before, but only ever briefly. And it had normally been for a reason – he was helping her up, or guiding her, or something. He had never just held her hand simply because he wanted to, like he wanted to now. Her skin was lighter than his, and softer. He had never really paid much attention before to how smooth her skin was whenever he had felt it in the past. However, in retrospect, he was amazed each time at how soft it was. He wondered how his felt to her. Did she enjoy the feel of his touch the way he did hers? Probably not. His hands were rough. He had callouses from working in the fields and from training with his sword. She never seemed to mind them, though, when he had held her hand in the past. But she definitely would not want to hold his the way that he wanted to hold hers.

Laith looked ahead of him, trying to focus on something else. The stream was coming into view. He could hear it too. The two elders were already nearly at its banks, with Sarama not too far behind them. It looked to Laith as they were heading to stop at the stream rather than continue up it.

"Looks like we're stopping", said Esmy.

"Yeah, I was thinking that", replied Laith. "Probably just for Acira".

"We probably could have waited, you know, and washed those bowls now", Esmy laughed. "We were coming anyway, you idiot", she continued, and pushed his arm playfully. "I'm glad we didn't, though. I had more fun coming with you". Laith's heart jumped at this last line, and he was even happier that she smiled while she said it. It was a genuine smile. It was from her heart - he could feel it. She had the most beautiful smile he had ever seen, and it echoed his own sentiments exactly.

"Me too", he replied, smiling. He gave her a little playful shove back. This would do, in the absence of being able to hold her hand.

Laith and Esmy caught up to the rest of the group at the river. Acira was taking a drink from the stream.

"Do you want to fill up your canteens here?", Laith's father asked them. "There will be a few more places where there is easy access to the stream before we get to the garden too, but you can fill up here if you want too". These words brought Laith crashing back down to reality. He had not really thought about where they were going today. His mind was occupied with what it had been since that night under the stars. This might prove to be a very difficult day for everybody. He had struggled with remembering much about what happened on the night of the Pink Moon

Massacre. Every time he had strained himself to try and remember anything, he could only remember the same thing - a general air of panic and confusion, and his dad holding him and his sister as he jumped over the ten-foot wall. There was a large bonfire beforehand, but this was obvious anyway – this was what would happen at the gatherings every year. There was some kind of a toy that he vaguely remembered entertaining his sister with, an inexplicably grey sky and, probably, Esmy. And, of course, there was the faceless man and black-haired woman at the top of the wall that had haunted him ever since.

"Are you gonna fill yours up, Laith?", his father asked him.

"Oh, yeah, I might as well", he said, unhooking it from his side. He held a hand out towards Esmy to indicate to her that she should also pass him her flask. She smiled sweetly as she took her flask from her pouch and handed it to him. Her hand briefly brushed his as she was giving him the flask and it felt to Laith as though it was the first time their hands had ever touched. He was still surprised by just how soft her hands were. His heart jumped slightly. He couldn't believe how much had changed since that night under the stars.

Laith made his way closer to the banks of the stream, closely followed by Esmy. He gestured to his sister, as he passed her, to pass him her flask too. She took a sip from it and then shook her head at the same time as shaking the flask to indicate to him that it was full.

"Some of us filled it up twenty minutes ago while you were still faffing around being slow", she said, after gulping down her mouthful of water.

"You've been here for a minute", he reminded her, rolling his eyes.

As Laith bent down at the banks of the stream, he felt Esmy's hand rest gently on his shoulder. His heart jumped again, slightly, and he took ever-so-slightly longer than was maybe necessary to fill up the two flasks with water. As he swiveled round, ready to stand, Esmy's hand moved from his shoulder and reached for his, helping him up. She smiled at him as he got up, and he kept hold of her hand for longer than he needed to, squeezing her fingertips ever-so-slightly harder than usual to say thank you when the time came that he had no choice but to let go.

"Shall we go, then?", Laith's father announced to the group. For the second time in just a matter of moments, Laith came crashing back down to Earth.

The group arranged themselves in the formation that had become second nature to them. Laith instinctively allowed Sarama to pass him with Acira after she collected her from the banks as he lingered back with Esmy. He wondered what being at the garden would be like for everybody else. He was only very young when it happened and could not remember much – would it bring back more memories for him and help him to remember details that were currently just out of his grasp? He thought specifically about the faceless man and the black-haired woman. Even though he knew that these were just two of many, many people who were there on the day, something within him felt that there was something significant about them. Well, looking at it sensibly, maybe he didn't *feel* that there was anything significant – it was likely to just be hope manifesting itself as a gut feeling. He knew them to be insignificant – he had brought it up once with his father who did not remember a thing about them specifically. Laith had only been three years old – an age where he would have been a sponge to the surroundings, especially at such a huge event like the Pink Moon Massacre. His mind would have attributed significance to things and people that his father – an adult – would not have. His father was more concerned with getting Laith and his sister to safety – he did not have time to remember anything major about the hundreds of people that were trying to escape at the same time. Laith – a very young child at the time – would not have had the same filter. His mind would have taken in anything and everything it could, regardless of its significance. Even so, he did not know why it was so important to him to find out who these people, if they existed, were. He just had an inexplicable feeling that it would bring him the solace he so desired.

He wondered about the effect of revisiting the garden after so long on the other members of the group. The two elders would surely be affected the most. They would remember the horrific night in much more detail than anybody else. Laith could only imagine the horrors that being back there would bring them. Why would they even want to go back? As a mark of respect, he supposed. Maybe as a proper chance to say goodbye. His mother had died there, and his father had not had a proper chance to say goodbye. This was going to be a big day for him. Imagine visiting, for the first time, the site where your wife was killed by your side and you had not been able to do anything about it. Imagine the horror of being forced to leave your dead wife in order to protect your children. As he had told them in the past, his only priority was making sure that Laith and his sister were safe and, for that reason, they had to escape quickly. There was violence in the aftermath of the attack that lasted for days. People from their community were being dragged from their houses in the dead of night and killed under the instructions of the North. It wasn't even the North who were carrying out the horrendous acts – it was members of their own community that the North had managed to convince it was the right thing to do. To their own people. They had managed to corrupt them with notions of power. Divide and conquer. They had torn the community in two so that the easily corrupted could do their dirty work for them. When they were worried that the community might start banding together again, they had partitioned the land exactly where they knew it would cause the most disruption. People then focused their attention on crossing the newly-formed border to be with their loved ones. This understandably became everybody's main priority. The North took advantage of people's instinct towards self-preservation, and it allowed them to get away with the atrocity that they had caused – nobody cared about revenge or justice when they had to focus on their family's survival. A perfectly calculated distraction. These were things that Uncle Cahya had told Laith on occasions when he had asked him about why things were as they were. Laith found it easier to talk to Uncle Cahya about it than he did his own father. How must Uncle Cahya be feeling now? He knew everything that had happened. He had lived through it and was clearly intelligent enough to understand the horrific reasons for why it had happened. 'Control the flower, control the power', he had often told him, wryly. A lifetime of suffering - a whole community mourning their dead reduced to one simple maxim. The lives of thousands of people were just collateral damage in the North's greed for power. The sense of loss and longing that Laith had grown up with – the one that intensified the night before the harvest just a few nights ago – were of no significance to the people responsible. Power corrupted.

Sarama was only a baby when it happened – Laith knew that she would not remember a thing. She had told him as much on those occasions when she would ask him what he remembered. He wondered if being at the garden would trigger anything in her memory at all. How would she react? It would probably just be like a completely new place to Sarama. That would be eerie in itself, he considered. Sarama would know that she had been there, and she of course knew of the horrors that occurred there, but she would not be able to remember a thing. Esmy, on the other hand, was the same age as Laith. Exactly the same age. He always supposed that she would have the same type of broken memories that he had of the day. It was always during the night, when he was looking at the stars, that his mind would go back to the night of the Massacre. This was normally the time when his emotions would intensify and his feeling of loss would become apparent, just as a few nights ago when he had been looking at the stars and feeling there was something missing. It was never long before his thoughts turned to Esmy during these nights – although they were as close friends as could be possible, curiously they had never spoken about the night of the Massacre to each other in any more depth than acknowledging it had happened, if they'd even done that. Laith couldn't remember a specific example of talking about it at all with Esmy. He always thought this to be strange whilst he was alone and feeling a wistful longing for the past. He would always plan to speak about it with Esmy and see if she felt the same way. She must have similar feelings of confusion, he always considered, being the age where she would have been able to remember things in a manner that were frustratingly just out of reach. It was always a genuine, honest plan to speak to Esmy about it but, whenever the time came that he was with her, he never did. It wasn't out of nerves or not knowing how to approach the subject – this could never be the case with him and Esmy. He was always so comfortable with Esmy that he could talk about absolutely anything with her. Actually, the reason he did not ever bring it up with her was the exact opposite of nerves. He felt so comfortable when he was with her that all of his feelings of loss and longing that he might have had the night before completely disappeared. They were no longer there and therefore no longer a concern for him. They had never been there. It would have seemed silly to talk about feelings that did not exist. When he was with her, it was as though those feelings had never existed and would never exist again. This was, of course, until the next time he was alone and looking at the stars.

The group had been walking for quite a while. It suddenly dawned on Laith how hungry he had become. He knew that he didn't have any snacks in his pockets or pouch, but he checked just to make sure. Nope - nothing. They would be with Acira, probably. He tapped Esmy on the arm to alert her to the fact that he was going to walk a bit faster to catch up with Acira and Sarama. She jumped slightly. She must have been getting lost in her own thoughts too. But then she made eye-contact with him and smiled. Her face had been deadly serious before he had jolted her from her thoughts. Her smile warmed him from the inside.

"Are you hungry?", he asked her. "I'm gonna go and grab

some kernels off Acira. They will be in one of her saddlebags".

"I'm not that hungry, but okay", she replied sweetly, still smiling. The two of them caught up to Acira and Sarama.

"Hi, Acira", said Laith, stroking her nose. "I'm just gonna look in your bags because I'm hungry".

"You're always hungry, you fat git". Sarama took the liberty of replying on Acira's behalf.

"Are you hungry, Laith?", his dad turned around to ask. "Is everybody hungry? We could just stop to eat here, if everybody wants to. I've made some lunch already – we just need to heat it up, really".

This seemed like a genuine suggestion to Laith, not an instruction disguised as one. He looked around to try to gauge everybody's reaction, not accustomed to being handed this level of responsibility from his father. Nobody reacted apart from his sister who, incredibly unhelpfully, merely shrugged her shoulders.

"Umm, I don't mind", said Laith.

"Let's eat", interjected Uncle Cahya, to Laith's relief. "I'm hungry too, and we can go down to the banks quite easily for some water just a few yards down that way", he said, gesturing down the stream the way that they were walking. He clearly knew the area quite well, thought Laith.

"Okay, good. Shall we stop here, then?". This was more comfortable for Laith – this wasn't a suggestion.

"Okay", he replied, happy with this resolution, as the group slowly seemed to settle.

"Do you three want to go and get some water? Acira has a pan", said Laith's father, as he was taking some things out of Acira's bags. "We can start making the fire. I've got some bits already, and there's wood and stuff around here that we can use". Laith had been doing so much thinking earlier that he was glad at being directed. He was even more relieved when his father handed him a pan – he didn't even have to decide which size would be the most appropriate. "Take Acira too – she might want a drink".

"There's a really easy access just a few yards down that way", Uncle Cahya told them. "Do you want me to come and show you?"

"No, Grandad, it'll be fine", Esmy gently replied.

Laith went to stroke Acira's nose again as the four of them set off down the stream to find the easy access to the water.

"Here, lead her", Sarama said to Laith, handing him Acira's rope. Laith was happy to take it, but wondered in the back of his mind why Sarama asked him too. Normally she didn't give up Acira this readily. She must be getting tired, Laith concluded. She had been the one responsible for leading Acira today and yesterday. Laith took the rope and his sister stayed close by. He looked over his shoulder to make sure that Esmy was coming, waited a moment for her to catch up, and then continued. Uncle Cahya was right – it was only a few yards down. It came into view quite quickly, and Laith navigated his way down, Acira in tow.

Laith patted Acira on the side once they had got down to encourage her to drink some water. She hesitated for a second but then did so. Sarama had the pan in her hand and went slightly upstream of Acira. She crouched down at the banks of the river.

"I'm gonna push you in", Laith told her, remembering their earlier conversation. "See how you bloody like it".

"I'd be too quick for you – I'd just move and push you. You'd probably just fall in yourself, actually, you're so stupid".

Laith's spirits lifted slightly. Earlier, he had been getting lost in his thoughts about what it would be like later in the day, when they reached the garden. It was nice to have this distraction where things were back to normal.

"Pass me your canteen", he said to Esmy.

"No, it's okay – I'll do it. I want to wash my hands too", she replied. "Pass me yours".

"I want to wash my hands too", Laith replied. "And I want to push Sarama in".

"Want to. But can't. Too stupid", Sarama replied, looking up.

Esmy crouched down at the banks of the river as Sarama stood and moved out of the way to make room for Laith. Laith crouched next to Esmy as they both filled up their canteens and washed their hands.

"Laith". He heard Esmy call him and turned to look over his right shoulder to see why, as he felt water splash in his face. Esmy laughed. He loved the sound of her laugh more than anything. She was radiating happiness on a day that everybody would need it. Her happiness soaked inside him. But he still splashed her back.

"No", she shrieked. "Stop it. Not again". Laith noticed the half-hearted nature of her protests, and so continued, as did Esmy.

"Oi – you two bloody stop it", Sarama shouted from behind them. "We're gonna get late with all your faffing about". This was true, Laith thought. The two elders would probably expect them to be back by now. He stood up and offered his hand to Esmy. She held it. Her hand felt cold, because of the water, but still as soft as ever. He held it tighter, telling himself that this was to do her a favour by warming her hand up for her. She squeezed his tighter in return. This was probably for the same reason, he thought, though his heart was warmed more than his hand.

"Here, grab that water", Laith heard his sister demand of him whilst pointing at the pan that she had put on the ground earlier. "And give me Acira". Laith did as he was told. When he was this happy, even being bossed around by his little sister didn't matter to him.

The four of them made the short trip back to where they had earlier left. Laith was glad to see that the fire was already burning when they got back. He reluctantly let go of Esmy's hand before anybody noticed and then put the pan of water on the fire so that his father could use the hot water to heat their food. His father preferred doing it this way, depending on what they were eating – he said that it heated it properly rather than burning it. Acira's food was already being warmed.

"I hope everybody's hungry", Laith's father said, cheerfully, as he took Acira's food off the fire and made sure it was not too hot. He swirled it around in her bucket and then put it in front of her. He patted her as she began eating.   Laith had already decided that his father was putting on a cheerful persona today to distract himself and everybody else from what was to come. His tone of voice was definitely happier than it usually was, but it didn't seem natural to Laith.

"Yeah, I am", Sarama replied. She too had a lightness to her voice, but this was her usual tone of voice anyway.

"Yeah, me too – thanks", Laith added. He felt that he should partake in the small talk, but his voice did not convey the same cheery emotion as his father nor his sister. This was despite him actually feeling quite happy on the inside – he was around Esmy, after all.

Once the food was heated, Laith's father started putting it in bowls for everybody. Laith got up to take them off his father and start passing them around the group. Once Uncle Cahya, Sarama and Esmy had their food, Laith took his own and sat down next to Esmy. His father put in his own food last. Laith detected an air of awkwardness around the group. He looked up to see if anybody else might be feeling the same. He only succeeded in making eye-contact with his father who raised his eyebrows and smiled slightly in acknowledgement. There was definitely a hint of awkwardness at the very least.

"So, we will be at the square soon", said Laith's father to the group. Although the terms 'square' and 'garden' were used interchangeably, Laith knew that his father more often used the term 'garden'. His tone was still cheerful, but the word he used may have been indicative of his real feelings, thought Laith. "It will be nice to go and see it and pay our respects", his father continued. "Well, not nice. But it would be good". His tone now changed to one that Laith considered more accurately conveyed his feelings. It forced the gravity of the day to resonate within Laith. His warmth subsided. "It would be good for you all to see where everything happened – you were all too young to remember, but it would be good, I think". It seemed to Laith that it was very important to his father that they did go to the garden, but he did seem apprehensive about forcing them to do so. His father was never this hesitant about anything.

"What do you all think? Are you happy to go?", he asked. His father must have discussed this with Uncle Cahya earlier, as his uncle had no reaction at all to what his father was saying.

Laith had wanted to go to the garden. Well, up until now, he didn't even consider that he would have a choice. With it being a given that that was where they were going, Laith had built it up in his mind, especially today, that going there would reveal some hidden secrets of what happened on that fateful night twenty years ago. Even though he knew logically that nothing new would be revealed to him, he could not shake the nagging feeling that there was something there that was waiting to reveal itself. Now that he realised that he had the option to not go, he did wonder whether this would actually be better. Was it worth going back there? Did he actually have anything to gain from it, or would it just be another source of misery for him? He knew deep down that there was no secret and, even if there was, going to the site would not help him uncover it in the slightest. He very quickly came to the conclusion that he would still like to go. It wasn't just because he previously thought he didn't have a choice – he did actually want to go to the place where the atrocity occurred. He wanted to see it from a new perspective and, maybe, piece together some of the broken memories that he had. More importantly, he wanted to go and pay his respects to his mother who was not as lucky as he had been on that night. He owed her that much.

Laith knew that Sarama would feel the same way that he felt. They had spent time discussing it in the past, and he knew that she, like him, wanted to know as much as possible about the night. Going there would help them both to learn about it. He made eye-contact with his sister, and she non-verbally confirmed what he thought. Esmy, on the other hand, Laith had never discussed this with. He had nothing to suggest what her thoughts on this might be, other than gut feeling. His gut told him that she also wanted to go to the garden, but he did not know why. Was it just because it was what he wanted to do, so he hoped Esmy was the same? Or was his gut feeling genuinely correct?

"I want to go, Uncle", Esmy said, somewhat hesitantly. It broke what had been a quite lengthy silence in which the tension had been building. Laith noticed that she only looked up at his father nervously as she was saying it, and then looked back down at her bowl again quite quickly afterwards. Was there a hint of a smile from his father?

"I do, too, Dad", Laith added, a bit more confidently than Esmy had spoken. "I want to see it". He had thought about adding a reason, to let his father know that he was not just saying this out of emotional coercion, but he realised that he did not have one that he was willing to say out loud.

"Me too, Dad", added Sarama. The lightness had left her voice.

"Okay, good. That's what we will do then", said Laith's father. He seemed relieved. It was clearly very important to him, and so Laith was glad that there was no conflict or difference in opinion. It would be a hard day for his father too, and Laith had to make it as easy for him as he could.

The group finished eating in silence. There was a heaviness in the air. Once they all finished, Esmy started to collect everybody's utensils. Laith automatically got up to help her.

"Thanks", Laith heard Uncle Cahya say, but he wasn't really paying attention. It washed over him in his state of distraction – he was too busy still trying to piece together his broken memories, but the gaps still remained. He was not getting anywhere with this other than working himself up. He looked over at Esmy and noted that she seemed more relaxed than he felt. This was comforting. He didn't actually have any reason to be anything other than calm either, he supposed.

"Do you want to give them to me, Laith?", he heard his father ask. As usual, it seemed as though his father had already made up his mind as to what the answer was going to be.

"No, it's okay. I'll do them", Laith said, for decoration.

"No, I can do them", his father insisted. "Well, we can go to the stream together. Is Acira done too?", he said, looking over at her. "It looks like she is. Sarama, will you grab that off her and then we can all go down to the stream?". It was obvious to Laith that his father wanted to speak to him and his sister alone – he could tell by the forced relaxation in his tone of voice. He always sounded this unnatural whenever he had some news that he was going to announce. Sarama went and picked up the bucket near Acira. Laith kept hold of the pile of dishes and the three of them began the short trip to the stream.

Once they were a few yards from the fire, Laith's father gestured for Sarama to hand the bucket over to him.

"No, it's okay, I'll hold it – it's not heavy", she replied. Some lightness was returning to her voice.

"Laith, do you want to pass me those bowls?", his father asked him.

"No, it's okay, I've got them".

"Give me a few of them," he said.

"No, don't worry – they are all balanced. We are basically there now anyway". Laith knew that his father didn't like to be more relaxed than anybody else in the group. He had such a strong work ethic that even watching people carry things made him feel that he should be helping. He was the same at the harvest, and he had been like that all his life. He needed to be helpful to be happy, which is why Laith had to reassure him of his capability of carrying a few bowls. They all carried on to the stream in silence, with Laith's father leading the way. He got to the bank first and crouched down, insisting with a gesture that Sarama pass him the bucket. She duly obliged.

"Here, Laith, put those down here", his father told him, patting the ground next to him. "I'll do them after". Laith knew that he had no choice but to do as he was told, so he also obliged and then stood next to his sister, both of them looking at their father. It felt as though they were both waiting for something, but they didn't know what.

"Are you two going to be okay going to the square today?", his father asked them. Laith noticed that, as he said this, he made sure that he was still focusing all of his attention on washing the bucket. He clearly wanted to make sure, but he was too nervous to look at them whilst asking them.

"Yeah, it will be good", Laith replied. He still didn't have a solid reason he was willing to share, but he knew that he did want to, and so he just repeated his father's vague reason from earlier.

"Yeah", Sarama agreed.

"Good", their father continued. "It will be good", he confirmed. He seemed more relaxed now, from his tone of voice, but he still avoided eye-contact. He put the bucket down, picked up the first bowl and continued. "I don't know what memories you will have of the day. Probably not very many. I know Laith can remember a little bit but even you can't remember anything properly. You were both too young. It might be a bit sad for you both. It's sad for me too. It will be sad, seeing the place where your mother... You know. But it's sad for all of us". The sadness that Laith felt was mainly for seeing how much this was affecting his father. His father continued to wash the bowls, avoiding eye-contact, placing the bowls one by one on the floor and then moving onto the next one. "The important thing to remember is... Well, it was just so unfortunate what happened on that day. That whole event – the gathering, the riots afterwards... I wish that we were all here together now, but sometimes life just doesn't work out like that. The important thing to remember is that you two are my priority. And your mum..." He trailed off. It seemed as though he needed a chance to compose his thoughts. And himself. "You two might feel some, I don't know, confusion or something when you get there. Things might seem different. That's what they say about memories. But the important thing to remember is that your mum loved you both". Laith realised that this was it – this was the main thing that his father had been trying to tell them. Laith's heart dropped when he heard the words. It dropped because of the reminder that both he and his sister grew up without their mother. There was always that slight feeling of emptiness inside of him. He was able to mask it sometimes, particularly around Esmy, but it always came back. His heart dropped at the reminder that it was there, and the niggling feeling of emptiness became more apparent to him. He knew that he had his father, his aunt and the whole community, especially his Uncle Cahya. But it's just not the same. His heart dropped also because he could feel how difficult it was for his father to say this to them. He couldn't even imagine what his father must be feeling right now. He must be in so much pain himself – he had lost his wife and was left to raise his children on his own. Laith wanted to look over at Sarama, but he could not bring himself to do so. Was she feeling the same way that he was feeling? She must be. This was exactly the same for her as it was for him, but he found it impossible to look up from the ground and at his sister for any kind of communication at all. "It's sad that we can't all be here together now, but that's the way it is", his father continued. "Sometimes we can't have what we want because of circumstances beyond our control. It's just the way things have to be sometimes. And it's not any one person's fault. You might start feeling angry when you are there, but it doesn't do any good to hold onto anger. It was the whole regime that was responsible, no single individual, and it was something that was beyond our control. But we are together – us three – and you will both always have me, so make sure you remember that. Here, do one of you want to grab those bowls?". He stood up and picked up the bucket. Sarama moved forwards to pass the bowls.

"Here, give me some", Laith said to her, mindlessly. He didn't really know what he was feeling. Numb, he supposed. He had been given no information at all that he didn't already know but, still, it was too much to take in. His father had tried to be philosophical in what he had told them, but he didn't really have much to say that could help. He could only try his best to make them feel better. Thinking about it in the way that his father had just described it – philosophically – must be the way that his father had coped all of these years. He clearly had not wanted to hold onto hate for any one person and it must have helped him to assign guilt to the regime as a whole. The regime had now gone and, with it, so had his father's anger. Maybe his father's words had helped. The circumstances were out of their control. There was nothing that anybody could have done. There was nothing that anybody could do now apart from be grateful for what they were left with. Sarama handed him some bowls and they both walked back to the fire, led by their father. He had still not looked at them, and Laith understood why.

They got back to the fire to see that Uncle Cahya and Esmy had already readied Acira to leave. Her saddle was back on, and all that was needed was for their father to attach the bucket and put the dishes in one of her saddlebags, which he and Sarama passed to him to allow him to do. Laith was glad once it was done, as it allowed him to go and stand by Esmy. As soon as he saw her, his spirits had lifted slightly. He knew that he just needed to stand near her to start making himself feel better. As always, being in Esmy's company helped to fill the slight feeling of emptiness that had recently been exacerbated by his father's talk. It worked this time too. It was unbelievable how much she meant to him.

Laith noticed that his father made his way towards Uncle Cahya with a little bit more intent than usual. His father was clearly affected by what had just happened by the stream. Maybe he needed his friend just as Laith needed Esmy. Laith grabbed Esmy's hand and pulled her towards his sister. He wanted to be near his sister too. Or, more accurately, he didn't want his sister to be without him. He caught up to his sister and Acira, but did not let go of Esmy's hand. It felt natural. He looked into her eyes and she smiled at him – it felt natural to her too, he could tell.

They were both comfortable.

The two elders set off and led the way, as they had been doing. The rest of the group held back.

"Do you want me to hold Acira?", Laith asked his sister. He was surprised at the politeness in his own tone of voice.

"No, she likes me better", his sister replied. She must have intended this to be more aggressive than her tone of voice conveyed. Both of them were not back to normal with each other just yet, but Laith knew that they would be soon.

Laith did not feel in the slight bit anxious or apprehensive any more about reaching the garden. He knew that his father would be, and suspected that his sister might still be, but he was not in the least bit worried about it now. He didn't even have anything to be worried about, thinking about it. He didn't know why he felt as he did earlier – he already knew everything that his father had told him. He must have just been feeling upset seeing his father like that. He wondered how Esmy was feeling. She had more reason than he did to feel sadness on returning to the scene of the massacre. He had lost his mother, but still had his sister and father. She had lost both parents as well as both of her older siblings. They never talked about it but, if he felt an emptiness due to the loss of his mother, he could only imagine what she must be feeling. Did she feel the same longing that he did when she was alone at night? He knew that she too enjoyed the company of the stars. He wondered now if it was for the same reason. Did they bring her some comfort and solace as they did him? Did she feel their magic or did she just enjoy their beauty? He still had her hand in his. He squeezed it a bit tighter and looked over at her. She looked back and smiled. It looked genuine. Well, it felt genuine. He always felt it when she smiled. The emptiness inside him always disappeared when he was with her. For a fleeting instant, before quickly suppressing it, he dreamt how wonderful it would be if he had the same effect on her.

The two elders at the front started to veer away from the

stream. This must mean that they were getting close to the garden, Laith thought. The stream got quieter and the sound of Acira's hooves became more apparent. Soon, the sound of the running water faded completely and all that was left was the dull thud of footsteps. Laith expected to feel the same eerie feeling that he had felt yesterday on approaching the old settlement but, for some reason, he did not. Maybe it was because he had already experienced it once, and that helped him become desensitised to it. Actually, maybe it was because of the fact that this was actually home that they were approaching – it was their original settlement. Was the lack of any negative feeling inside him now due to the fact that he was returning home? His real home. It had not been his home for very long – only three years. They had been in their current settlement for longer than that, and it had the added advantage of him remembering it. But their ancestors had been in this first settlement for a very long time. In that sense, it was home. Maybe that was the reason for Laith feeling a lot more comfortable on approach than he had felt yesterday – this place had the energy of his family. It contained the spirit of his ancestors. It held onto the spirit of his mother.

Some cabins began to come into view. This was not like the settlement where they had stayed the night before, which was bare but for two cabins - this one looked to have nearly as many cabins as their current settlement. And the cabins were larger. They also, somehow, looked more sturdy. They had an air of permanence. Although the number of cabins was about the same, the area of the whole settlement was a lot larger. The cabins seemed to be spaced out a lot more and so this settlement felt more vacant than yesterday's. This caught Laith by surprise – it was not what he had expected at all. Their whole community, at its current size, could easily come and live here. Just as he finished having this thought, the reason for this settlement being as it was hit him and he felt sick. It became apparent to him that the cabins were not evenly spaced. It was not a matter of design. The spaces were due to the cabins that had been taken down and transported to the new settlements. Not all of them were needed when they moved – they had only taken enough to house the number of people who were leaving the settlement. The lucky ones. The aura of vacancy that Laith felt around the settlement was not in spite of there being a number of cabins there - it was because of them. The empty space was not responsible for the feeling of vacancy – it was the cabins that exuded it. These were the cabins of the families who did not leave. Entire families felled - their homes left standing and spectres of their energy in the air amidst the spaces left by those who were lucky enough to be able to leave. Laith was grateful he had Esmy by his side – he didn't know how he'd be feeling if she wasn't next to him. He squeezed her hand and wondered if she felt the same.

"The square is in the middle. It's not too far". The sound of his father's words made Laith feel a bit nervous. It wouldn't be long before he came face to face with the place that he had wondered about his whole life. The wind either blew with a little bit more intent or Laith had simply become more sensitive to it. He felt a silence around him despite the wind whistling loudly in his ears. He tightly squeezed Esmy's hand as he walked even closer to his sister.

"Okay?", he asked Sarama, quietly.

"Yeah", she replied, earnestly. She did not sound as nervous as Laith felt. He looked Esmy in the eyes to gauge how she was feeling and, as he did, he realised that he was not so nervous. His sister was fine and so was Esmy. There was nothing for him to be nervous about.

"Laith. Sarama", Laith heard his father call. He had separated himself slightly from the rest of the group. Laith felt Esmy squeeze his hand and then let go, squeezing his fingertips as she did. She knew that his father wanted to speak to them alone. Sarama dropped Acira's rope as she and Laith walked slowly towards their father. Laith was apprehensive, and his pace demonstrated this to his sister who reciprocated in her own footsteps. Their father didn't seem to mind. He had his back to them, looking in the direction where Laith suspected the garden was.

"We aren't far", he said quietly, when they got to him. "I thought it would be good if we all walked in together". There was silence but for the wind that had definitely picked up now. Laith's hair started to blow across his face with some loose strands getting caught in his beard. He turned slightly to his right so that the wind would blow his hair in the right direction - the act of lifting his hands up to move his hair would have taken a lot more energy than he was able to happily expend at the moment. One cabin, standing alone, caught his eye. There was a lot of space around it. A number of families in that particular area must have been lucky enough to survive the massacre, but not this one. The unlucky ones. Laith wasn't sure whether it was the wind continuing to blow that made him stay facing that way or if something about that cabin was drawing him in. He realised that he knew nothing about most of the families that did not make it. The number of people that died was in the thousands, his father had told him. Nearly two thousand people murdered in the Massacre and in the violence that ensued. Nearly two thousand people whose homes were still left standing. But - this cabin that he was looking at – its inhabitants must have all been murdered. They would have left that exact cabin as a family on what was supposed to be a day of celebration, expecting to return that night with their hearts filled with joy and their stomachs filled with corn and raas. Laith felt cold. The emptiness that he had felt earlier had returned. His father must have noticed him staring at the cabin for such a long time.

"Not everybody was lucky like us", he said with a solemn air.

"Yeah", Laith replied. He hoped that his tone conveyed that he already understood the standing cabins and that his father did not need to elaborate further. It was obviously very difficult for his father too. There was surely only one person about whom he must be thinking.

Laith's father started walking in what must have been in the direction of the garden. He was walking as hesitantly as Laith had been earlier. Laith and his sister followed closely behind, not saying a word. He turned to look behind himself briefly. Esmy was with her grandfather. He wondered what she was feeling. Her family's cabin would be here somewhere. He wondered whether her grandfather was telling her about it, and whether she would want to see it. Laith felt guilty. He had survived such a horrific event that nearly two thousand people had not. He knew a little bit about his mother, but he knew nothing about the other people whose lives had been taken away from them in the cruelest of circumstances. They continued to walk past empty space and vacant cabins. These cabins had once been filled with life, Laith thought. And now they felt cold. He knew nothing about the people who had lived in there. He had no idea what their lives were like before they had been stolen from them, and he had not even given them a second thought until now. He had survived while their memories were being lost - their spectres slowly fading.

As they walked past a vacant cabin, Laith felt himself being drawn towards it. He wanted to have a quick glance inside the window as he passed, just to see how these people had lived. He might learn something about them – any little thing that could tell him about the poor people who had lost their lives when he hadn't.

"Laith!", he heard his father say sharply. He must have seen or heard him veer slightly from the path. Laith's heartbeat raised and he looked at his father. His father had never used such a sharp tone before, but it felt to Laith as though he had. He felt as though he was a child being reprimanded for something he was unsure of. "Laith", his father said again, but this time in a much calmer tone of voice, "that's not the way we do things". Laith immediately understood. His heart sank at his own actions. How could he have acted in a way that was so disrespectful to those who had their lives taken away when he was just a toddler? He wouldn't dream of going and peeping through a stranger's window in normal circumstances, and now he was about to invade their privacy simply because they had died – as though their death meant they no longer had a right to privacy from his prying eyes. He was embarrassed that the thought had even crossed his mind that this was an acceptable thing to do. He should have had more respect.

"Yeah", he said quietly to his father. "Sorry. I...". He trailed off. He didn't have an explanation to give. He knew that he should have known better himself. He shouldn't have had to be told something so obvious.

He walked back to his father and sister sheepishly, still embarrassed by his actions. He just wasn't thinking – that's the only thing that he could tell himself. He didn't think of himself as a disrespectful person. He had just momentarily stopped thinking. He would never intentionally do something that was so disrespectful.

"It's just over here now", his father said to them. "Let's go and pay our respects".

The path bent to the left and, looking around another vacant cabin, a walled off area came into view. This must be the garden. Laith looked back to where they had come from and saw that Esmy and her grandfather were not following. Maybe they wanted to go by themselves. Laith's heartbeat started to rise again – this was the place that had haunted him for so long, but he did not recognise it at all from the outside. It was entirely walled off from the side he was looking at but for one small gap the size of a doorway to the right. This must be the entrance. Laith and Sarama walked closer to the entrance, side by side, led by their father. As they got closer to the wall, Laith noticed that the bricks looked like they were beginning to crumble. He didn't know too much about how well bricks aged, but it looked older than he expected. The garden must have been built a long time before the Massacre too, he supposed. It must have been host to so many joyous times – many happy harvests as well as families going there on a day to day basis to enjoy it. And then it was host to one dark day. The very last time that it had been used - the day that's memories would become synonymous with the garden.

Their father stopped at the doorway-sized gap and briefly looked back at Sarama. He entered first, followed by Sarama. Laith walked in behind them. They were in a small alleyway that was not wide enough for two adults to stand comfortably side-by-side. Laith felt a chill. It was definitely colder in the alleyway. The hairs on his arms stood on end. Families would have ambled through this alleyway, excited for the celebration that was waiting for them at the other end, not knowing the fate that was awaiting them also. He imagined that he would have probably been walking this exact path just over twenty years ago to the day. He would have been so small that he would probably have been able to walk at the side of one his parents. He wished it was his mother. Would he have been holding his mothers hand, standing at her side the last time he was here? Or would he have been too excited and have wanted to bounce around the alleyway completely independently, as children often did? Something inside Laith had him hoping that he was holding his mother's hand the last time he walked through here. His heart dropped at the thought that maybe he hadn't. What if his mother had asked him to hold her hand to keep him safe but he, in his childish excitement, had refused? This would have been one of the last opportunities he had to spend with his mother. What if he had not made the most of it? No matter how hard he tried, he could not remember this entrance at all. He could not remember if he had come in holding his mother's hand, his father's hand, or just bouncing around independently. He imagined the twins walking through this same alleyway – they were now about the age that he would have been then. How would they be acting as they came through? Would they hold their mother's hand? He had a memory of another alleyway – the one through which they escaped – but that was much larger than this. And that was the one where his father was holding him and running after his mother had already been killed. As he walked through the alley, he had a thought of touching the brick. The coldness he felt, though, made him not want to. He didn't need it shooting inside him.

They reached the end of the small alleyway and their father paused again.

"This is it", he told them.

They turned to the left and looked out. Laith felt nothing. He shouldn't be feeling nothing. The view from the alleyway made the garden look quite small. Laith stepped out properly, following his father and Sarama and turned to his right so that he could get a proper view of the whole of the garden. The coldness of the alleyway was still inside him. The garden was a lot smaller than he remembered or expected. His first thought was that it was tiny. How could nearly two thousand people have died here? It didn't look as though two thousand people would have fit. It must have been very busy. When the massacre began, there must have been nowhere to run. There was hardly any space as it was. His heartbeat rose again as he imagined the panic that the first arrows must have brought. People trying to escape, but they were walled in. There was nowhere to escape to unless, like his father, they had somehow managed to scale a ten-foot wall. There must have been so much confusion, panic and fear as the arrows came raining in. Poison-tipped – his father had told him. People watching their loved ones die right in front of them and able to do nothing about it. Laith could not get over how small the space was. He remembered his thoughts on the settlement when they first arrived here – the community then would have been a lot larger than it is now. The gatherings then must have been huge compared to the ones they have now. Even now they were quite lively. Back then, they would have included all of the people who were murdered as well as people who were now settled in the Northlands. Shooting at thousands of people in this small space – it would have been impossible to fire an arrow that did not find a target. A target. A person. On top of that, people panicking and rushing to escape must have crushed each other. He was lucky that his dad had been able to pick him and his sister up and somehow scale the wall. Surely they would have been crushed in the stampede otherwise. The cowards who did it knew that there were so many people in such a confined space and, even worse, they picked such an important day to do it on. They had no regard for the significance of the day – all they cared about is that those who were usually armed would have come unarmed to the Pink Moon Harvest. Defenceless, innocent people in a confined space unable to escape were slaughtered in a mad grab for power by the North and their sycophant supporters. How quickly must the mood have changed after that first arrow was fired? How long before people realised what was happening? When did their joy turn to fear? This small space must have always been bursting with joy and life, and now it contained the vacancy of sadness and loss. Laith felt sick, but at least he felt something

Laith looked at his sister. She would not be able to remember a thing. His father, on the other hand, would be able to remember everything. How must he be feeling at this moment? What a sickening position to be in, to be able to remember in vivid detail everything that had happened on the day. How would he have felt standing where he was currently standing when an arrow had hit Laith and Sarama's mother, and he was unable to do a single thing about it other than to leave her body to be crushed in order to save his two children. Laith's heart dropped even further. He was responsible - his father had had to leave his mother in order to save him. He hoped that his mother's body was treated with more respect until it was safe for the families to come back and gather their dead. What a horrible scenario it was to be looking for any crumb of comfort that he could. Laith didn't dare look over at his father.

Laith wanted to know how they had managed to escape on the day. He wanted to learn as much as he could about the day – he thought that it might bring him some peace. He still was apprehensive about disturbing his father's thoughts, but he did want to have a look around the garden to try and take in as much as he could about the Massacre. He wondered if it was the right thing to do. He wasn't sure if enough time had passed that he was allowed to move away. He tentatively shuffled from where he was standing, taking two small steps towards the centre of the square. His father looked up at him.

"You two can have a look around, if you want", he said. "It would be good for you both to try and get an understanding of what happened on the day. Let's all take a walk around." Laith's father started walking around the garden. Laith and Sarama followed behind him. Laith could see some broken arrows and arrowheads still on the ground. They had not all been cleared up properly. He tried to use these as a memory aide but to no avail. He tried to put himself in the position of a person at the Massacre who was aware of what was happening – forcing himself to imagine these arrows flying overhead and raining down on the crowd, knowing that one hitting you would mean the end. It seemed so surreal that he could barely picture anything in more resolution than feelings of fear and sadness.

"Dad?", Laith asked tentatively. His father looked at him. "Do you remember how we escaped?" His father nodded.

"I'll show you", he said quietly. Laith was relieved that his father's tone did not suggest that he was angry or upset that Laith had asked. If anything, Laith thought that his father seemed glad for the question. This made sense, he considered – after all, his father had taken them there to pay their respects and to learn about their history. "I picked you two up after...after we had to escape", his father continued. Laith knew why his father had hesitated. It wasn't hard to infer what he was going to say but couldn't bring himself to do so. "We were about here, I think, when I picked you up", he said pointing to a spot somewhere towards the left of the garden. Laith expected to feel a chill down his spine or a drop in his heart when he looked towards where his father was pointing but, in all honesty, he felt nothing but numb. He tried to imagine the day, because he could barely remember a thing. He owed it to his mother to feel something more than what he was currently feeling, but it was all too surreal. It felt to Laith as though he was just listening to a story – something surreal that could not possibly have happened. It certainly couldn't have happened to him. "I knew that all of the exits would be blocked. People were standing at them and firing from them. They had poisoned the arrows – there was no getting up from them. I knew that we would not be able to go through there without you two getting shot. You two were my priority." He emphasised this last bit and made sure that he looked at them both as he said it. Laith felt something in his throat and nodded ever so slightly to show his dad that he understood. "By now, everybody had already realised what were happening. Some people were rushing towards the exits because they were panicking and just didn't think. I had already figured out that that wasn't a very wise thing to do, so I carried both of you to the wall at the back". Laith's father looked towards the wall he was referring to. This must have been the one that had been in Laith's memories. He looked towards it too, hoping for a revelation, but nothing came to him. The wall was nothing like he remembered. Laith's father led both Laith and Sarama to the back of the garden. "This was where we escaped from", Laith's father said quietly. Laith could not believe how small the wall was. From the memory he had of being on top of it, he had estimated it to be about ten foot high. He remembered his father jumping down from it and it had seemed as though they were falling for an eternity. In reality, the wall was not even as tall as Laith. Standing next to it, he could see over it and at the wall that formed the other side of the alleyway through which they had escaped. Standing on his tip-toes, he could peer over the wall and at the ground on the other side. It was not as large a drop as he remembered. It all seemed so different now that he was here as an adult. Being a small child, he supposed, everything had seemed much bigger.

The wall was in a similar state to the one that formed the alleyway through which they had entered. This time, Laith did put out his hand to feel it. He ran his fingertips gently down the rough brick hoping that this would somehow connect him with the past and make clearer any memories that he had, or trigger any emotion. He owed it to his mother to feel something other than numb. He had escaped from here and she had not. He reminded himself that he had made it over this exact wall in this exact spot while she lay dead on the ground. He tried desperately to trigger some emotion. Again, nothing.

"Dad?", he asked. He was surprised at the confidence in his own voice. He expected it to break, but it was clear. His father looked up at him. "I do remember this wall. I thought it was much bigger. When I was small, it seemed much bigger".

"Yeah", his father replied. "Well, you were small. It would probably have seemed bigger, I suppose".

"Yeah", Laith replied. He realised that, even though the wall was not ten foot high, it still would have been impossible to climb whilst holding two children. "How did you manage to climb it?", he asked, whilst still feeling the wall, hoping that it would reveal some hidden secret. "While holding me and Sarama", he added. He retrospectively hoped that his tone sounded impressed rather than accusatory – he had asked quite absent-mindedly. His father looked blank for a moment.

"I don't really remember", he said. "I might have put you on the wall first while I climbed with Sarama. Maybe I trusted that you were old enough to sit for just a few seconds. I can't really remember – I was just acting on instinct, trying to protect you both". Laith thought back to the faceless man and the black haired woman. Had they helped? Is that why they were in Laith's memory?

"Did other people help?", Laith asked.

"Yeah", his father confirmed. "We were all helping each other. That would have been it. Somebody offered to help hold you two while I climbed up, and then I could take you and get down the other side. We were all helping each other, even though there was so much panic". Laith realised that even his dad's memory was not perfect from the day. How could he expect it to be? It was twenty years ago amidst unprecedented levels of fear and panic. His dad had probably not have even been thinking about half the things that he was doing. As he had made it clear to him and his sister before, his main priority was to keep them safe. He had been acting on instinct rather than conscious thought – it was no wonder that his memory was also hazy. Laith wondered if his dad came here hoping to jog his own memory. Is that why it was so important to him that they come? Although there was no real need for it – it wouldn't help anybody – it might help to give him some closure on the events. Maybe that was what his dad had meant when he talked about paying their respects. Laith wondered if he could trigger his dad's memory himself by sharing his own very broken memories of the day. He could remember only the black haired woman and the faceless man, but he kept having a strong feeling about their significance that he could not quash.

"One of the people that helped...did she have black hair?", Laith asked, tentatively. He was slightly more hesitant with this question than he had been earlier. His father looked at him. It was a look that pierced Laith. The moment he saw it, he knew that his question had been a misguided one.

"Laith, most people have black hair so, yes, she probably did". Laith wasn't sure if his father sounded angry or upset. Well, he sounded angry, but Laith knew his father well enough to know that this was probably because he was upset. He had upset his dad with a pointless and insensitive question when he was already clearly going through such an ordeal. And for what? Nobody was to gain anything from such a stupid question, and Laith knew that he should have known better. His father did not have the benefit of having forgotten the horrors of the day as Laith had. Just because Laith felt okay asking it, he should have known that his father would not have felt okay hearing it. It was the second time today that he had acted insensitively, as if the day was not difficult enough for everybody already. Laith knew that now was the time to put all of these thoughts to bed. He had been to the garden in the hope of some magnificent piece of information suddenly revealing itself to him. As the day progressed, this hope had foolishly turned into expectation – for some reason, he began to expect that revisiting the scene where such an atrocity took place would suddenly make everything better. He had thought that, simply by being there, everything would fall into place and all the feelings of confusion and the vague emptiness he had felt his whole life would magically disappear. In his stupid desperation for this to happen, he had lost all rational thought and ended up embarrassing himself on two separate occasions today and, more importantly, upsetting his dad, without whom he would not have been here.

Laith stood quietly. He realised that he did not get any of the answers that he had hoped for today but, thinking about it, how could he really have expected to? He thought that the visit would trigger more memories and emotions and so, in this sense, the trip to the garden had been quite underwhelming. He decided that now was the time to leave those thoughts behind him and concentrate on the actual reason why they had made this whole journey. They needed to get the red flower to save their community. He knew that he was standing on hallowed turf despite the fact he did not feel as connected to it as he had hoped. It was now his duty to make sure that the people responsible for all of those deaths were not responsible for any more.

Chapter 19 - Sarama

Sarama was concerned for her brother. Today had seemed to affect him more than it had affected her. He was a bit older when it happened and this was probably the reason, she supposed - it might be bringing back some memories for him that she was too young to form. Maybe that was the reason that his mood had been up and down all day. Even though he had not told her anything about his moods, nor had he really done anything to indicate them to anybody, she knew her brother well. She could tell by his body language. Earlier today he had been happy and relaxed. Now he was the complete opposite. Nobody else would be able to pick up on the subtle changes in his body language, but she could. She wanted to do something to help, but she didn't know what she could do. Feeling down at the moment, given where they were, was to be expected, she supposed. But her brother's mood seemed even lower than she expected it to be here. She wondered whether maybe this was because she was judging him by her own standards and so reminded herself that he had memories that she did not. Notwithstanding this, Sarama was surprised that she, herself, was actually quite unaffected. Again, she considered that she was too young when it had happened to remember anything. This must be the reason.

"We can go out through here", her dad said, pointing to an exit at the end of the wall that he had jumped over twenty years ago. Sarama was closest and so she led the way. As they got to the exit, she expected her dad to say something about the people firing arrows from there on the day of the massacre, but he said nothing. His silence, however, said a lot. She stepped aside to let her dad through the exit first, partly as a mark of respect, but mainly because she wanted to drop behind to be with her brother.

Sarama and her brother followed their dad through the alleyway that he had carried them through twenty years ago. This one seemed wider than the one through which they had entered, though not by much. It didn't feel as cold, either. She wanted to make eye-contact with her brother, or at least have some form of non-verbal communication but, when she would look over at him, he kept his eyes firmly on the ground. Their dad had spoken to him quite harshly. This was probably a factor. It wasn't the kind of thing that she expected her brother to normally be bothered by, but she could see how it would exacerbate negative feelings that he was probably already having.

They reached the end of the alleyway and were back out in the open. The sun was beginning to get lower in the sky now. The shadows of the remaining cabins were noticeably longer than the ones on the other side of the garden had been. This side of the settlement looked very similar to the other, with large gaps between the cabins. Sarama was also able to confirm something that she thought she had seen on the way to the garden, but had been too far away to be certain - she thought she had seen the burnt remains of wood where she expected cabins would have stood. She was previously too far away to be sure that this was what it was, but now she was close enough to another one to see. She knew that riots had succeeded the massacre, but she didn't know much about their extent. She could now see that, as well as families being murdered while they were defenceless and at a celebration, the people responsible had also torched some of their homes. She felt sick at the thought. When did this happen? Were the families in their homes when they were being set alight? She wondered if it had happened at night, whilst families were asleep. Imagine the horror of witnessing innocent people being killed – the chances being that a lot of them were members of your own family – then thinking you had managed to escape only to find your home being set alight by a cowardly mob. She couldn't comprehend the level of fear people would have felt during the massacre and the riots – despite the fact that she had lived through it, it was unlike anything she could even come close to relating to. She wondered if her brother had noticed the charred remains of some of the cabins. She hoped not.

"Shall we wait here for your Uncle Cahya?", Sarama's dad asked.

"Okay", Sarama replied, trying to sound cheerful enough so that she did not increase the negativity already in the air, but not too cheerful that she did seemed disrespectful. Her brother, as she expected, did not respond.

"They wanted to do their own thing", her dad explained. "And I thought it would be nice for us to do our own thing here, too", he added.

"Yeah", Sarama replied. This time she decided to sound more solemn. She hoped that this was the end of the conversation for now. Although she was not as affected by the trip as her brother clearly was, she was far from being in the mood for a conversation, and she knew that her brother would not contribute so it would all be on her. He would not contribute even on a good day. Sarama got her wish, as the three of them stood silently, waiting.

Sarama noticed her brother was taking a look around. She was worried that he might notice the burnt-down cabin, as she had, so was relieved when he seemed to focus on a fence a few yards away from where they were standing. It was a very simple fence – a few posts connected by two horizontal beams. Sarama's brother walked towards it and sat on the lower beam. She hoped that he was seeking a seat and not solitude. In any case, she didn't count when it came to her brother seeking solitude – she knew that he didn't ever mind her being around him, and so she decided that she would go and join him. She reached the fence and realised that sitting on the lower beam was a poor decision on his part. He had to lean forward to avoid the upper beam, and the upper beam was not so high that he couldn't have jut sat on that. He wasn't going to move now, though. Sarama sat down next to him, having to pay for his poor decision-making with her own slight discomfort.

"Hi", she said. She could be more cheerful now than she

was earlier, as her dad was out of earshot.

"Hi", Laith replied. His voice was lacking any kind of tone or intonation, as usual.

"Alright?", Sarama asked.

"Yeah". His lack of tone would have been the same whether he was telling the truth or lying. In this instance, Sarama knew he was lying. She knew her brother. She also knew that he wasn't in the mood to talk – that would not help him at all. His mood would lift itself later, as it always did. He probably just needed the distraction of continuing with their journey. She chose to just sit silently by him, despite his stupid choice of sitting on the lower beam when the top one was perfectly accessible. Solidarity.

Sarama saw her dad look up at them and she looked back. Once he knew that she had seen him, he walked off around the perimeter of the square. He gave no reason why, and Sarama didn't ask. She continued to sit silently with her brother. The wind had settled leaving an eerie calm. Sarama was unsettled. She only managed to last a few moments before deciding to break the silence.

"Is your arse hurting, sitting on this beam?", she asked her brother.

"No, not really", he replied. There was no 'my ears are hurting', as she expected him to say.

"My bloody ears are hurting listening to you ramble on, though", he added, after a pause.

"One bloody question is hardly rambling on", she told him.

"It's enough", he said. He paused again, before adding "What did you think about the garden? Did you remember anything?"

"No, I couldn't remember it at all. How about you?"

"I couldn't really remember much. The bits I could remember seemed so different, though. Just the wall, really. And the size. I thought it was a lot bigger".

"I wonder what Esmy thinks", Sarama said. "They are probably in there now. I wonder where they went".

Her brother's silence told Sarama that he was probably thinking the same thing.

"I wonder where Dad went, too", Sarama added. Her brother looked up, looking for him. He clearly hadn't even realised that he had left.

"I dunno", he said - helpful as always.

Their questions were answered when their dad appeared around the perimeter of the square and headed towards them with Acira - he had gone to collect her.

"They are just in there now", Sarama's dad told them both, when he and Acira stopped by them. Laith stood up and started patting Acira on the nose. Sarama *knew* that his arse was hurting – he just didn't want to admit that she was right, so he was looking for an opportunity to get up and pretend it was for another reason. Typical.

"We will head to your granddad's place when they are ready", Sarama's dad told them. Sarama knew that her dad was referring to their mother's dad, not his own. His own had passed away long before the Massacre took place. Sarama, however, was surprised to hear that her grandparents' cabin was still standing. She knew that they had not died in the attacks, but they had died a year or two afterwards – she was still too young to remember them but, knowing that they had survived, she expected that their cabin would have been taken down in order to move to the new settlement with the rest of them. She thought better of it than to ask her dad why it was still standing, and then quickly came to the realisation that not all cabins would have been moved anyway, even for the people who did survive. Families who were previously living apart would have moved in together. It was probably the case that her grandparents had moved in with them when they had moved settlements. Maybe her brother was old enough to remember. She made a mental note to ask him later, when their dad was not in earshot. Now wasn't the time to ask such questions, she thought.

Uncle Cahya and Esmy appeared from the alleyway exiting the garden. Sarama could not judge the expressions on their faces yet – they were too far away for her to see properly. She noticed, however, her brother keeping a close eye on them. She suspected he wasn't much concerned with Uncle Cahya.

The pair reached the rest of the group.

"Alright, Laith?", Uncle Cahya asked. "Alright, Sarama?"

"Yeah", Laith replied. "You?" This time his tone suggested that he was actually telling the truth. It was certainly lighter than when Sarama has asked him. 'Charming', she thought. Although, to be fair to him, he had had time to settle since seeing the square. He would have had a chance to process it by now.

"Hi, Uncle. Hi, Esmy. Yeah, I'm okay. How are you both?", Sarama said.

"Good, good", Uncle Cahya replied, somewhat vacantly. Sarama wasn't sure whether he was saying that they were good, or if he was showing that he was pleased that Sarama and Laith were fine. It didn't matter. Esmy smiled as Sarama's brother took his natural position by her side.

"Shall we go, then?", Sarama's dad asked. He paused to give everybody a chance to compose themselves and then led the way. Sarama took hold of Acira's rope and followed her dad and Uncle Cahya, as her brother and Esmy dawdled behind as per bloody usual.

"It's a little bit further", her dad told them. "It's just a bit further out from the main part of the settlement – it was one of the bigger ones on the outskirts". Sarama didn't mind – she quite enjoyed walking. She enjoyed it more than she had enjoyed spending the night at the last settlement – at least, when walking, she had something to do.

As she followed her dad and Uncle Cahya, she looked around the settlement. This was the place she was born, she realised. She didn't remember it in the slightest. She tried to get an idea how many cabins had been taken down and was also looking out for any more that she could see had been burnt down. Even the thought of finding any more made her feel a bit sick, but she wanted to try and gauge the extent of the atrocities committed. She hoped that reality would not be as bad as her imagination. She looked around as they walked but, if she was honest with herself, she was not looking particularly hard. She didn't want to find any. It would be easier on her to not find any more evidence of the extent of the horrors so she could console herself with the fact that they weren't as bad as she imagined. Deep down, she knew that they were probably worse.

As they got farther from the centre of the settlement, she noticed the number density of the cabins decreasing. This did not seem to be because more had been taken down, although this might have been a factor. It seemed intentional - they were built further apart to begin with. They must be reaching their grandparents' house soon, which was good, Sarama thought, because the sun was beginning to go down. Her dad and uncle turned off the main path onto a smaller path to the right, and she followed with Acira. She had the urge to pat Acira but she didn't know why. They passed two more cabins – these cabins seemed to have a lot of land between them, but nothing to suggest that there were any that had been taken down between them. The bottoms of the cabins were brick, but the top halves were wood. Sarama's dad and uncle finally stopped outside the third cabin. It looked no different from the others in the vicinity but Sarama knew that this had been her grandparents' cabin. It was larger than the ones closer to the square, and certainly much larger than the one that they currently lived in. Sarama joined her dad and uncle outside, and Laith and Esmy eventually caught up.

"This is it", her dad said. "Shall we get Acira sorted? Here, I'll take her around the back", he told Sarama. "But let's get all this stuff off her first". Sarama's dad began to take things off Acira's saddle, and Laith stepped forward to help carry them. Sarama went to take some things too, and both she and her brother left them by the front door of the cabin. She did not feel comfortable opening it and clearly neither did her brother. It seemed presumptuous, for some reason. Or disrespectful. Even though it was their grandparents' cabin, it felt as though it belonged to strangers towards whom opening the door would be a violation.

Their dad took Acira's saddle off and went to take her around the back of the cabin, taking her bucket with them. It was getting darker, but there was still a little bit of daylight left. Sarama waited at the front of the cabin with her brother and Esmy. Uncle Cahya had gone with her dad. She saw that her brother was looking intently at the cabin.

"Do you remember it?", she asked him. She realised that he probably came here quite a few times. Well, she probably would have too, but she would have been a baby and couldn't remember it at all.

"No, I don't think so", her brother told her. "I don't think I remember it. The brick bit kind of looks familiar but I'm not sure".

The front door opened from the inside. Sarama jumped. Her dad was standing at the threshold and chuckled slightly.

"Did I scare you?", he asked.

"No. I just wasn't expecting it", she replied.

"Here, help me grab some of this stuff". He picked up a few bags from the front step and carried them inside. Sarama and her brother did the same as they stepped inside leaving only one small bag for Esmy, who picked it up. It was dark inside. There was very little light coming in through the windows. Even though it was hard to see, it was quite clear to Sarama that this place had not been lived in for quite a while.

"I hope the generator still works", Sarama's dad said. "I'll go and see". As he went towards the back of the cabin, Sarama noticed Uncle Cahya pull something out of his pouch. It was a small glass bottle, which he uncorked. He left it on a table at the side of the room and then pulled out another glass bottle exactly the same. He headed towards the back of the cabin where Sarama assumed he would be doing the same.

Sarama heard a sound coming from the back of the cabin

followed by a faint buzzing and the light above her head filckering on.

"Oh, good", she heard her Uncle Cahya say from the back. Her dad came back and flicked a switch to illuminate the rest of the room. It was a lot bigger in the light, and bigger than Sarama expected it to be from the outside. She had never been in a room as big as this one. Well, apart from probably this one. The light illuminated the layer of dust that coated everything in the room.

"We will probably need to give this a bit of a clean", Sarama's dad said, running his finger along one of the surfaces and inspecting it. "Where are those cloths that we used last time? We should get that stove going too", he added, pointing to a small stove to Sarama's right. "Laith, do you want to help me grab some wood from around the back? There was some around there".

Sarama's brother went with their dad around the back of the house. Sarama went to search the bags for the cloths to make a start on the cleaning.

"Pass me one too, please", she heard Esmy say. It was nice that Esmy offered to help her, Sarama thought. Normally she would want to do whatever Laith was doing. Maybe the thought of collecting wood didn't appeal to her.

"There will be one there for me too", Uncle Cahya added.

"No, don't worry, Uncle – we will be able to get this done", Sarama replied. There was no way that she expected her uncle should help her. "Bloody Laith can help us afterwards, the lazy sod", she kindly reassured him.

"Grandad, you can be in charge of the tea once Uncle Kabili gets the stove going", Esmy added

"It's going to have to be without milk", Uncle Cahya warned Esmy.

"Yeah, but it will still have beams. And panela. And it's better than no tea", Esmy said.

"It is better than no tea", Uncle Cahya agreed, smiling. Sarama watched as he located the pan and then went out to the back of the house, presumably to collect some water.

Sarama's dad and brother came back with some wood

from around the back, followed shortly by Uncle Cahya and his pan.

"Just put that down there by the stove, Laith. Yeah, that's good", said her dad as he made a start on lighting the stove.

"Oi", Sarama shouted to her brother. "Catch this, you lazy git". She threw a cloth at him, which he did catch, and the three of them got underway with the dusting while the two elders tended to the stove. Sarama made a start on some chairs and stools whilst Laith and Esmy made their way to the kitchen area. She quite liked the furniture that was left behind. It made her feel as though she was getting to know her grandparents. The chairs and stools were both made with wooden frames woven with cotton that had been dyed green and white. The colours had faded, but Sarama enjoyed the rustic quality of the furniture. It struck her as something that a typical grandparent would have in their home.

As the three were cleaning, Sarama's dad came in with a bucket of water that he had snuck out to fetch. "You can use this for now", he said. "I'm just going to sort the pumps and stuff out now so the taps should work soon".

"Okay, thanks, Dad", Sarama replied. She went to rinse off her cloth in the bucket, as did Laith and Esmy. Sarama was happy to see that her brother's mood had picked up a bit now. She knew it would – he just needed to get away from the square and distract himself. Sarama decided to join her brother and Esmy in cleaning the kitchen, where she could hopefully start an argument to make sure that her brother had cheered up.

As Laith and Esmy continued with the counters and table top, Sarama made a start on the cupboards. She opened the cupboard above the sink and saw that it contained a set of china plates, cups and saucers. The white china had intricate blue patterns on it. They were very pretty, she thought, and, again, they seemed to her to be typical of something that a grandparent would own. Even if she did not know that this had been her grandparents' cabin, she was quite confident that she would have guessed that somebody's grandparents had lived here.

"Look at these cups", she said to her brother, holding one up. "Look how pretty they are". She handed it to her brother and watched as he inspected it.

"I don't really like it", he said to her. "They're a bit...scary". Sarama was delighted with his response. She knew that the cups were pretty – anybody in their right mind could see that. The only possible reason that her brother would have disagreed is because he wanted to start an argument, which was a good sign – he must be in a better mood. He couldn't agree with her that they were pretty but then, just before stating overtly that they were ugly, he must have remembered that they belonged to their grandparents and so he couldn't really criticise them – it would have been disrespectful. He paused to search for the first vaguely negative sounding word in his head that wasn't too disrespectful to their grandparents' tastes. Luckily for Sarama, he had chosen something stupid and so this was yet another argument that she would win.

"How can a cup be scary, you idiot?", she asked him.

"Well, I dunno. Not scary. But just... I don't know", her brother backtracked.

"They are pretty. They're pretty and you're stupid.", she told him. After she said it, she immediately wished that she'd called him 'pretty stupid' – that would have been funnier, but it was too late now. It didn't matter, she thought – she managed to get her point across.

"Well people are allowed to like different things. I dunno, just shut up", he replied. Good - he was definitely in a better mood than he was earlier.

Sarama's dad walked back in from the back of the house as Laith walked towards the back of the large room to begin cleaning there.

"The taps should work now", her dad announced and then looked expectantly at Sarama. She took the hint and tried the kitchen one. After a bit of spluttering, water began to flow smoothly from the tap.

"Yeah, it works", Sarama told her dad.

"Okay, good – just let it run for a few seconds", he told her. "Have you got another cloth? Or just give me that one if you haven't". 'Typical', Sarama thought. Her dad was never going to relax while other people were doing something – he never had and he never would.

"We are pretty much done now anyway", Sarama said. This was perfect timing, she thought, as the smell of her uncle's tea began to waft towards her. She had been looking forward to this. She quite enjoyed the tea that she could make herself, but nobody in the world could make it quite like her uncle – she was certain of that. "It smells like Uncle has nearly finished the tea, too", she told her dad.

"Yeah, nearly done", Uncle Cahya confirmed.

"Ooh, Dad – look at these cups I found. Look how pretty they are – we can use them", Sarama suggested. Her dad looked up at what she was holding.

"No", he said quite sharply. Sarama was shocked. This was the same tone that he had spoken to her brother earlier, and Sarama realised that it was probably for a similar reason. "No, no", her dad repeated, but this time his voice was a lot calmer – he was almost chuckling as he said it. "We don't need to use them – we have our own cups. Those have been there for quite a while, it's probably better to just use our own". Maybe her dad was just on edge – tomorrow was going to be a big day, after all.

"It's ready now", Uncle Cahya announced to the room. "Esmeralda, will you get cups for everybody?" Sarama headed to the area of the stove and perched herself on a small green and white stool that she had earlier wiped down. Esmy returned with four cups as everybody but Laith joined the group around the stove.

"Laith, are you going to have some too?", Uncle Cahya.

"No, thanks, Uncle", Laith called from the back of the room. Sarama knew that this would be his answer, as did everybody else – it was the reason that Esmy had only brought four cups. Laith refused to even entertain the idea of drinking tea. He was too stubborn to even try it. The idiot didn't even know what he was missing.

The excitement built up inside Sarama as she watched her uncle pour the tea for everybody. He passed her the first cup – he knew that she loved it.

"Thank you", she said, as she blew across the top of it too cool it slightly. It would be too hot to drink yet, and she knew she should really wait anyway until everybody was given their respective cup. She clutched it close to her chest as her uncle gave a cup to her dad, then to Esmy and eventually poured one for himself. Sarama looked up to see if everybody was ready, and therefore could have her first sip. She noticed her dad looking intently over at Laith who, in turn, seemed to be engrossed in something at the back of the room.

"Laith", her dad called "leave that and come and sit with us even if you don't want to have tea". This was nice of her dad, Sarama thought. He must have been trying to make up for the way that he had spoken to them both earlier – it was out of character for him, but there was nothing to really make up for, Sarama thought. It was perfectly reasonable for somebody to be a bit tense or on edge. Her dad had clearly planned for this for a very long time and, on top of that, it must be such an emotional time for him. Being in this cabin now must be bringing back memories of their mother – it was her parents' cabin after all. He must have shared some wonderful times with her here. It must be difficult for him. He needed both of his children around him.

Laith came over to join the rest of the group. Esmy shuffled over as he came to make room for him on the stool she was sitting on, and he sat down.

"What were you looking at?", Sarama asked him.

"There were some toys there, at the back, just on the shelf", Laith replied, quietly. Sarama understood why his tone was like this – he must be thinking the same thing that she was thinking. Did these toys belong to them when they were younger? They must have done. At the time, Sarama and her brother were the only two grandchildren. She wondered if Laith could remember the toys, but she was nervous to ask in front of her dad. It was a perfectly reasonable question, but her dad was going through a lot today and she didn't know whether or not this would set him off. She decided that she would rather not find out, and so kept quiet.

"They would have belonged to you two". Her dad must have picked up on the awkward silence and he confirmed her suspicions. He seemed a bit awkward himself, saying it. His voice was louder than usual and he was trying to sound too relaxed about it. Sarama was right not to have asked. "You two had so many toys when you were younger", he said, chuckling. Sarama was unsure whether he was trying to be cheerful to mask the sadness of his memories or to try and make up for the sharp way in which he had spoken to them both, but his chuckle was definitely forced. Sarama didn't know which reason would be worse – she hated the idea of her dad being burdened with all of the sad memories, but she also hated the idea of him thinking that he had anything to make up for. The worst thing of all for Sarama was that she did not know what to do to make him feel better. She forced out a chuckle with a very vague "yeah".

"I'll get started on dinner soon, actually", her dad said. "I'll go and fire up the bigger stove in the kitchen. Might as well do it now, I suppose". This was just to the left of the room as they had entered. The layout of this cabin was similar to their own, but just a lot bigger. As Sarama's dad and uncle got up and went to the kitchen, Sarama decided to take the opportunity to go and have a look at the toys herself. She left Laith and Esmy by the small stove in the sitting area, and she headed towards the back of the cabin.

There were only two toys on the shelf – it looked to Sarama as though they had been displayed there intentionally. Her heart sank and she felt a pang of guilt for not knowing her grandparents. The toys wouldn't actually have been on display. What was more likely was that these were her and her brother's favourite toys, and so their grandparents had them ready for when they used to come around, on the shelf that was easily accessible. When they had left during the riots, the toys would have been left behind there. If they were their favourite toys, maybe she would remember them. She took a close look at them and it was clear which was hers and which belonged to her brother. There was a little wooden worm that was clearly designed for a baby. She picked it up to inspect it further. It had colourful little balls carved within it that were free to rotate – red, yellow and green. She knew that, if she shook it, the balls would rattle, but she looked over at her father and decided that she did not want to draw too much attention to herself. She imagined though that, as a baby, this would have been something that she would have been entertained with. She wondered if her grandparents or her mother would entertain her with the colourful balls and sounds that the toy would make. She felt guilty that she could not remember a thing about it. The other toy looked as though it was made for a slightly older child – this would have been her brother's. Again, it was carved out of wood but this one was slightly more intricate, and it had been painted. It was a toy bicycle being ridden by a monkey. Sarama rolled the wheel and saw that it was able to rotate. As it did, the monkey's legs moved too, giving the impression that the monkey was pedaling the bicycle as it was rolled across a table – something that would no doubt amuse a simple mind such as her brother's.

Sarama looked again over at her dad. He was busy making the food with Uncle Cahya, deep in conversation about something. She saw that Laith and Esmy also seemed to be enjoying each other's company on the opposite side of the room. Sarama was curious to see if Laith remembered the toys and so she took them both over to him. She sat near him and saw that he noticed the toys that were in her hand. He looked up at her but didn't say anything. Sarama knew that he was anticipating a question, and so she obliged.

"Do you remember these?', she said in a mumble just above a whisper. She didn't want her dad to hear, just in case, but neither did she want him to think that she was deliberately hiding anything from him. And there was no need to actually whisper, she considered, as she was not really doing anything wrong. Laith put out his hand and Sarama passed him the toy that she knew to be his. He looked at it intently, as he was looking at it earlier. It seemed as though he was trying to remember something. He gestured to Sarama that he wanted to see the other toy again too. She passed it to him. He rolled the colourful balls with his fingertips.

"I think you had this at the garden", he told her. "We must have come here afterwards, unless I'm remembering wrong. I can't really remember it properly".

"Do you remember the monkey?", Sarama asked. Laith looked at it again and rotated the wheels.

"It looks kind of familiar, but...I don't know", he said hesitantly. "I can't really remember things properly".

Laith seemed lost in his own thoughts. Sarama knew that her brother was probably having similar feelings to her now. Being in her grandparents' cabin made her wish that she could remember them. She was sitting on their stool, next to their stove, and enjoying the protection of their house, but she could not repay them by even with the simple act of remembering them. She had hoped that the toys would be at least something – if she could remember playing with them, that was at least a small memory of her grandparents, but she could not even do that for them. She was glad that tomorrow was the big day. They would get what they needed and could go back home where she belonged.

Chapter 20 - Esmeralda

There was something about this cabin that made Esmeralda feel, on the whole, more comfortable here than she had at the cabin last night. She tried to convince herself that it was because the luxuries of electricity and water were available, but she knew it was really because she was sitting next to a warm fire next to Laith. Her grandfather had prepared the fire, so Esmeralda was confident that it would have exactly the right energy that they all needed. It must be a bit more difficult for Laith, though, she thought. And Sarama. It was their grandparents' cabin and Laith had seemed preoccupied ever since he had found the toys that used to belong to them – even more so since Sarama had asked him about them. Esmeralda felt useless knowing that she could not do anything for Laith. She was quite happy when Sarama took the toys back off Laith and went back to put them on the shelf. Maybe this would help Laith concentrate on the positive energy coming from the fire.

Esmeralda shuffled intentionally closer to Laith and rested her head on his shoulder. This always made her feel happy, and she hoped it made him feel the same. She couldn't see how he reacted, but she felt him get happier. She wanted to hold his hand, but did he want her to? How would he react? Her heart had been full earlier in the day when they had held hands. It felt so natural. Had his heart been as content as hers had and, if so, would he want her to hold it now? She wanted to bring him the comfort that he deserved, but he did not have the same feelings as she did when they were together like this. On top of this, they were now around his family and her grandfather. He was always different when he was around them - he was never as relaxed. She wanted to hold his hand, but she thought better of it. It wouldn't help him, she decided. She stayed next to him with her head resting on his shoulder, hoping that the energy from the fire would warm his heart where she could not.

"Do you all want to start putting your food in?", Esmeralda heard Uncle Kabili say from behind her. She lifted her head off Laith's shoulder and turned around to face the kitchen. Laith belatedly turned around too.

"Yeah, coming", came Sarama's voice from the far side of the room. Uncle Kabili took some food outside, presumably for Acira, as Esmeralda gave Laith a gentle push to tell him to get up. He obliged and the two of them followed Sarama into the kitchen.

"Just sit down at the table, I'll put the food in", said Esmeralda's grandfather.

"No, it's okay, Uncle – you sit down and we will do it", said Laith.

"You can help with the plates, actually, if you really want to", said Esmeralda's grandfather, pointing to a cupboard. "Do you want to get those down and wash them so we can use them? We might as well eat off proper plates today". Esmeralda watched as Laith pulled some white, china plates with an intricate blue pattern down from the top shelf of the cupboard and began to wash them.

"Put them on here to dry them", her grandfather told her, pointing to an area on the large stove. Esmeralda obliged.

Esmeralda was slightly startled when she heard Uncle Kabili come in through the front door, having left through the back. He must have walked around the outside of the house for some reason – maybe he was just taking in the surroundings before it got too dark. It was beginning to get quite dark, Esmeralda thought. She was pleased – she was looking forward to the stars taking over. Uncle Kabili came over to the kitchen and saw what Laith and Esmeralda were doing.

"Here", he said to Esmeralda, "I'll put those out on the table for you". He took the plates from the stove and made to shake off any remaining water before placing them on the table.

"Sarama, do you want to get knives and forks?", he said to her. Did Esmeralda notice a slight hesitation before Sarama obliged? Her voice didn't seem to carry the same lightness as it normally did when she replied "Yeah, okay" but then, when she actually started to help, her body language conveyed her usual warm nature and so Esmeralda was confident that she must have imagined it.

Uncle Kabili insisted that everybody sit down as he put in food for Esmeralda's grandfather first, followed by Esmeralda, Sarama, Laith, then himself last.
"Thank you", said Esmeralda. Uncle Kabili smiled at her in return as everybody else remained silent. Laith still must be distracted by these surroundings.

The group ate in silence. This was becoming a habit. Tomorrow was going to be a big day. Esmeralda wondered if everybody was nervous about it. She was actually quite calm, herself, not that she had any reason to be. Maybe it was due to the energy of the stars, but she had a feeling that everything was going to be fine. She normally attributed quite a lot of weight to her feelings, and a lot of her feelings to the stars, so this was enough for her.

Esmeralda looked over to her left where Laith was eating. He was nearly finished, as was she. It was getting quite late, and everybody had had quite a big day. Tomorrow was a big day too - she had to remind herself because her feelings told her it wasn't. Maybe everybody would be going straight to bed after dinner. She hoped not, though. She wanted to stay up and spend some time with the stars. She hoped that Laith would too. She tried not to think about it too hard. She was worried that, should she think too loudly, somebody would hear. But she wanted to go outside tonight and be under the stars with Laith. She wanted to recreate that same feeling that she had two nights ago when she realised that she was in love. This time, however, she wanted to savour it and embrace it as it washed over her rather than try to suppress it and hide from it as she had before. She wanted to feel it in her soul and for it to resonate in her heart. She wanted Laith to feel it too. She wanted him to feel it more than she wanted anything in the world, even though she knew that they could not possibly have a future together. Why did she want to be so cruel to him? Why did she want him to feel as intense a feeling as she felt knowing that it would not last? Was the joy worth the pain? Was the feeling that she had for him now so wonderful that it would be worth the inevitable pain in the future? For her, it was. The feeling of loving somebody this much was worth everything in the world to her, even though she knew that it could not last. Esmeralda looked up sharply. She was afraid that her thoughts had become too loud. Her heartbeat rose as she looked around the table wondering if anybody had picked up on what she was thinking, but then slowly subsided once she realised that she was being silly – how could they have? She looked again at Laith, who was now just finishing his last morsel of food. She quickly finished hers too and then joined Laith in collecting everybody's dishes.

"Just leave them in the sink, Esmy – I'll wash them", said her uncle.

"No, it's okay, Uncle", she replied. "I'll do it". Uncle Kabili's silence suggested that he was not going to argue any further, which was surprising.

Esmeralda washed the dishes as Laith hovered around, presumably thinking of a way that he could be useful. He didn't know it himself, but he was being useful just by being there. Uncle Kabili wiped the table clean and then told Sarama that he was going to set up their bedrooms.

"I'll sleep out here", he said. "Sarama and Laith – are you okay to share a room tonight? Then your uncle and Esmy can have one each".

""Yeah, that's fine with me", Sarama said, happily.

"Yeah, I'm happy", said Laith.

"Kabili, it's fine", interjected Esmeralda's grandfather. "Esmeralda and I can share a room and then you can have a bed too – you need to be well rested for tomorrow".

"No, I'll be fine", Uncle Kabili replied. Esmeralda expected this to go on for quite a while – neither would want to give in. She finished the dishes and asked Laith if he wanted to join her outside. It seemed like an eternity before Laith replied even though he responded almost immediately.

"Yeah, I do". He smiled at her with his eyes as he replied. Esmeralda's heart jumped.

"Sarama, we are going outside. Do you want to come?", Esmeralda asked her. She told herself that she asked Sarama because she enjoyed her company too and because she thought Sarama would enjoy theirs. If she was being honest with herself, a part of her only asked Sarama to come so as not to arise suspicion within Laith or anybody else about her true feelings. But only a small part. She did want to spend time with Sarama too, she convinced herself. And she knew that Laith enjoyed spending time with his sister. He would have probably asked her if she hadn't.

Esmeralda patted Sarama on the back of her arm to indicate that she should lead the way. As soon as she did it, she had second thoughts. Was it weird? She didn't normally do that to Sarama. Did Sarama notice that it was weird? Probably. Or did their trip bring them closer together so that they were now comfortable enough around each other that it seemed natural and not forced? Well, it was too late now. And she was overthinking things. She needed to relax. Esmeralda walked behind Sarama and consciously ahead of Laith. But not too far ahead, because that would be weird too. She followed Sarama out of the back door and was immediately astounded with how large the back garden was. She saw that the cabins on the outskirts did have a lot of space, but she never expected it to be this much. The artificial light of the bulb above the back door faintly illuminated Acira, who was grazing on some grass in the distance.

"I'm gonna go say hi to Acira", Sarama told them.

"Okay", replied Esmeralda, trying to sound happy in a friendly sort of way, but overall apathetic. She watched as Sarama went towards Acira and started stroking her.

"Her and Acira really get on, don't they?", Esmeralda said

to Laith.

"She likes me better", joked Laith.

"Well, you are her brother", said Esmeralda, deadpan. Laith looked confused for a moment.

"No, I mean… You know what I meant", he said, realising Esmeralda was joking. "Acira likes me better", he explained, needlessly. He was relaxed.

"Well, I thought you might mean that, but then I thought that that's so obviously wrong that you couldn't possibly think it, and so you must have meant Sarama. Because that one is close enough for it to be up for discussion".

Laith tutted. "Even when she's not here, you two gang up on me".

"Don't worry", said Esmeralda pushing Laith's arm playfully with her forehead, "I like you better". She looked at him and smiled. The moment he looked back into her eyes, her heart rate rose. Laith's face carried no expression. Esmeralda couldn't read what he was thinking. What was he thinking? Her heart would not subside as she waited for his reaction. It was only a split-second later, but it felt like an eternity to Esmeralda, that Laith smiled - first with his lips, slightly, but then tellingly with his eyes.

"I like you better, too", he said. Her rapid heart beat turned into a flutter as he turned on the ball of his foot and shuffled slightly to face her. He rested his hands on her hips. She put her hands on his arms, thinking back to when they were alone together at the river this morning. It had been perfect – they had been so comfortable together. Were they having fun now? She looked deep into his eyes. She was trying to gauge what he was thinking but she couldn't. She wondered what would happen next. She knew what she wanted to happen next, but she also knew that it was impossible. Neither of them moved. Her heartbeat began to rise again and the two of them just stood still. She noticed that Laith clenched his jaw for a second, and then unclenched it again.

"Shall we go and sit down?", he asked her. "We can look at the stars. I love looking at the stars with you".

"Yeah", Esmeralda smiled. This was what she had been hoping for when she was sat inside even if it was less than what she was hoping for a moment ago. She loved looking at the stars with Laith too, and this was exactly what she needed, if not exactly what she wanted, right now. "I love looking at them with you too".

Esmeralda allowed Laith to lead her to a nice looking patch of grass a few yards from the back of the cabin. Their footsteps must have disturbed Sarama, who looked up from patting Acira.

"I'm getting bored. And tired. I'm gonna go to bed", she said. "Goodnight".

"Goodnight", replied Esmeralda as Laith waved. She felt a bit guilty for being happy about this.

"Do you want me to turn the light off?", she asked, as she reached the back door.

"I don't mind", said Laith. Typical of him to not have an opinion, Esmeralda thought, smiling on the inside.

"Yes, please", she said. Esmeralda loved the magic of the moonlight and the stars. She wanted their energy to saturate the air without being diluted by the artificial light from the bulb. Sarama obliged and turned off the light before going inside.

Laith took off his shield and placed it on the ground. He sat near it looking as though he was preparing to rest his head on it. He looked up at Esmeralda and immediately she felt her heart jump. She knew what she wanted and hoped Laith wanted the same thing. Laith reached out for her hand and held it tight, guiding her to the ground next to him. His grip was strong. Stronger than usual. He lay down and rested his head on his shield, just as Esmeralda had guided him two nights ago when she admitted to herself that she was in love. This time, he guided her down so that her head was resting on his chest. They had the stars gazing down on them and their magic was saturating the air. This was perfect.

Esmeralda looked towards the Moon. The Moon was waning, but the affinity that she always felt with it was even stronger tonight. It was the strongest it had ever been. A part of her soul was up there amongst the Moon and the stars in the sky and their magic was penetrating deep inside her. She lay on the ground with Laith, gazing up at the magnificent sky. The Moon was brighter than it had ever been. There had never been this many stars in the sky before and they were all twinkling gently to the sounds of their own energies. The beautiful silence that saturated the atmosphere penetrated her. The magic of the stars filled her soul. This moment was forever.

She felt Laith's heartbeat rise but she did not dare move. The sound of his heart beating in her ear made her own heart rate increase. Thank God he couldn't hear hers. She focused her mind on the Moon that always made her feel at ease. It was beautiful. Her heart began to slow down and she felt around her side for Laith's hand. She found it and held it tight – her fingers interlocking with his. She felt his thumb rub hers up and down but she could hear that his heart would not subside. She could not calm him down how she normally could. Keeping his hand held tightly in hers, she lifted her head slowly off his chest. She turned around to look him in the eyes. He looked back into hers and her heart fluttered. The magic of the stars was glistening in his eyes. In this moment, with her soul full and her eyes looking into his, she felt more connected to him than she ever had before. She saw him clench his jaw for a second before unclenching it again.

"I love you", he told her. Esmeralda's heart exploded with the magic of a million stars.

"I love you, too".

Esmeralda kept hold of Laith's hand and rested her head back where it belonged. She lay on top of him, grateful for the Moon and the stars, and listened to her heart gently beat inside his chest.

Chapter 21 – Kabili

Kabili awoke to the faint sound of birds chirping outside. He still felt quite tired, but he knew that the sun had begun to rise. The early morning light was bouncing off the long-forgotten furniture in the bedroom in which he had slept last night. It was time to get up. He was surprised at how easily he had fallen asleep last night – he had had difficulty sleeping the night before and expected more of the same last night. He had too much going around in his mind that had been troubling him, and a lot of it was due to what was going to happen later today. He was the person responsible for this – the planning was all on him. Him and Cahya. How could he expect to breach a compound, steal a flower and subsequently escape with just three people? Reclaim, not steal – but the sentiment remained the same. Cahya and his granddaughter would not be going in – they would not be of any help in there. In fact, there was no real reason why Cahya's granddaughter should have come at all. It would have been better if she had stayed at home. Better for her – she would have been safer there. It would just be him and his children that went inside the compound. He needed Cahya nearby to prepare any potions or remedies in case things went wrong – to knock out the guards or to help him or his children should something go wrong. Maybe it was a bit too dangerous for his children. Was it irresponsible of him to put his children in harm's way? He was an accomplished swordsman and archer. He didn't really need his children to go either – he could easily go in there by himself. But, he reminded himself, he didn't know exactly what he would face in there. It should be easy enough. But it might not. And his children also had to fulfill their responsibilities.

This was one of the things that had been going around in his head for the last few days. Maybe it was due to the stress and the overthinking tiring him out, or it might have been the two-day long journey, or it might even have been the fact that he had a mattress last night, but he had fallen asleep the moment that his head hit the pillow and he had not woken up once all night. It wasn't the only thing that he had been worried about – he had been worried about how his children would react at the square, but he knew that they needed to go. They needed to have an understanding of the regime that they were fighting against. He had also been worried about the memories that he might have invoked in Laith and Sarama by coming back here. He had previously thought that they would both have been too young to have any memories here but realised yesterday evening that this might not have been the case, by which time it was too late. He thought that it was probably okay, though. It didn't seem so bad now that he had been to sleep. They seemed happy enough.

Kabili got out of bed and got dressed. He opened his bedroom door and peered down the corridor into the living room. Nobody was in there. The other two bedroom doors were closed, suggesting that he was the first one up. He knew he would be up before his two children, but Cahya was normally quite an early riser too. Kabili decided that, after he got himself ready, he would get started on breakfast to have it ready and waiting for everybody when they woke up. He went into the bathroom and turned on the tap. It spluttered a bit and spat some water at him before it started running smoothly. The cold water on his hands and face startled him awake and the morning chill flowing throughout the cabin suddenly became apparent to him. It would disappear with the heat from the stove while he was making breakfast, anyway. It would be nice and warm for everybody else by the time they got up. Kabili finished in the bathroom and headed back to his bedroom. He should probably pack his things now so that they could leave as soon as they got back from the compound. This thought worried him again – if the mission failed, it was all on him. But he had a duty to try. He was the head of the community and it was his responsibility to save them. It was all on him.

Kabili rolled up the blankets that he had laid out on the mattress the night before and tied them up. He picked up his shield and placed it on his back and then buckled his sword in its sheath around his waist. Today was a big day.

As Kabili headed to the kitchen, he noticed that the back door was ajar. It must be Cahya, he thought – nobody else would be up this early. He should head outside to check, just in case. The children were outside last night – maybe they forgot to close it as they came back in. He had been asleep by then, so he didn't hear them all come in. Kabili walked to the door and pushed it open. As he stepped outside, the crisp air hit his face. It felt different. Today would be the dawn of a new era, he reminded himself. The dawn of a new era, and it would be thanks to him. He needed to keep that in mind today. He looked to his left, out into the open, and saw Acira peacefully grazing on some grass. He didn't immediately see anybody outside and wondered why the door had been ajar. He then looked to the side and saw the reason - Cahya was sitting cross-legged facing the rising sun. Kabili noticed that Cahya had a couple of his glass bottles by him – his friend must be feeling the significance of today, too. Cahya looked towards Kabili and lifted his hand in greeting. Kabili nodded to return the gesture. He left his friend to his rituals and went inside to make a start on breakfast.

Kabili headed back inside and lit the stove. He would start making the porridge, with water again of course. It would have been better if he could make it with milk so that everybody could enjoy it more. Even though he knew that should be the least of his worries today, it did not stop him from wishing he had some. He started cooking it when Cahya came in through the back door.

"Good morning", said Cahya

"Alright, Cahya. How's it going?"

"Good, good. You're making the porridge? I'll get started on the tea".

"Here – you can come and do it over here", suggested Cahya, indicating a space by him on the stove.

"No, it's okay – I'll do it on the little one so we don't get in each other's way", said Cahya. Kabili watched as Cahya lit the smaller stove across the room from him, in case he needed any help. He did not, and so Kabili continued at his own task. It wasn't long before the smell of Cahya's tea drifted across the room towards Kabili. As soon as its warm and rich smell hit his nostrils, he knew that he was ready for the day ahead.

Kabili went outside to give Acira her oats. She walked towards him when she saw the bucket in his hand, and he put it on the ground for her to eat. The day was definitely getting a lot brighter now – the sky was a light blue and the air retained its crispness. Kabili headed back inside and put in some porridge for his friend and himself. He placed it on the table, waiting for Cahya. At nearly the same time, his friend joined him with two cups of tea. Perfect timing. Kabili noticed that Cahya had used the metal cups that they had brought with them on their journey as opposed to the china cups in the cupboard. He wondered if he had overreacted yesterday, but quickly dismissed the thought. It didn't matter now. It was no good dwelling on the past. He had enough to worry about today.

"I wonder when those lazy lot will get up", said Cahya, laughing.

'I'm sure they'll get up when they smell that the food is ready", Kabili laughed back. He felt a lot more positive about the mission now. He had planned everything methodically and today was the day that it would all come to fruition. Today was the day that he would save the future of the community.

As the two men were enjoying their breakfast, Kabili heard a door open.

"The tea smells nice, Grandad", came Esmy's voice from down the corridor. "I'm gonna get ready and then come – make sure you save me some". Kabili heard the bathroom door close and then Cahya looked over at him and chuckled.

"That didn't take long, did it?", he said with a smile. Kabili chuckled back.

"Now we just need to wait for my two to get up". He suspected that it would be Laith up next – he was normally up earlier than Sarama and Kabili suspected that the sound of Esmy's voice would have given Laith a little bit more incentive to get up. They had always been close and were perhaps getting a little bit too close for Kabili's liking. It is excellent to have friends across different tribes – he was currently sitting with his very best friend even though the two of them were from different cultures. He was not prejudiced in any way but, sometimes, some traditions needed to be adhered to. When choosing a partner, it was important to stick to your own tribe. Kabili was beginning to get a little bit more concerned that Laith was heading somewhere that he should not be, and it would end in disappointment.

Esmy finished getting ready and came to join the two men at the table.

"Morning, Grandad. Morning, Uncle", she said cheerfully. She went over to the stove and poured herself a cup of tea.

"There's some porridge in there for you too, Esmy", Kabili called to her.

"Thank you, Uncle", she replied, as she went across to put some in for herself. Kabili noted how cheerful Esmy was despite the day. She was a lovely girl. She was always cheerful like this. He had nothing against her at all, personally. In fact, he was actually very fond of her. If things were different, he would actively encourage a partnership between her and Laith, probably, but traditions were there for a reason. It was important to respect them.

Kabili heard another door open and footsteps go across to the bathroom. The fact that he had walked across in silence was a tell-tale sign that it was his son and not his daughter. Kabili instinctively looked up at Esmy, who he noticed was arching her neck to see down the corridor.

She caught his eye then quickly looked away. Kabili didn't want her to feel embarrassed, but maybe she did. There was no need for her to be – he was happy they were friends, as long as it stayed that way.

"Do you want some more porridge, Esmy?", he asked her, trying to indicate with his tone that she should be relaxed around him.

"No, thank you, Uncle", she replied. "This is plenty".

"Okay, well tell me if you want more, because I have made lots. There's more than enough. Eat until you're full", he said, smiling. She returned a smile. Good.

Laith came and joined everybody in the kitchen.

"Hi, everyone", he said. He put some porridge in for himself, poured himself a glass of water, and sat next to Esmy at the table. Kabili noticed that even Laith seemed in a good mood today, which he didn't expect to be the case. Kabili didn't understand his son, sometimes. Laith's moods were definitely quite variable – he would sometimes be quiet and down for no apparent reason, and then the next day be relatively cheerful. Today, when Laith actually had a reason to be concerned or worried, he was happy. Kabili knew that if anybody was going to be down about the mission, it would definitely be Laith. The fact that he was happy showed Kabili that his son must have a lot of faith in his plan and the mission. He knew it himself, anyway - it was a solid plan and today would be a good day.

Sarama was the last to join everybody, quite soon after Laith.

"Ooh, tea?", she said, on approach. "Thanks, Uncle".

"We knew that the smell of all this would wake you lot up", Kabili told his daughter, chuckling slightly. "There's porridge there too, for you to have. You might as well finish that lot off and then we can start heading out soon".

"Thanks, Dad", Sarama replied, pouring herself some tea and then getting some porridge.

Kabili considered making a comment about everybody being ready for the mission, but he decided not to just yet.

He had already decided that there was no need for Esmy to go with them at all, but he felt that it would be best coming from Cahya rather than from him. It was to protect her, and she would more likely see it that way if it came from her own grandfather. He didn't want her to get the wrong idea. In the back of his mind, Kabili was acutely aware of the secondary benefit of making sure that Laith and Esmy spent some time apart – they had been spending too much time together and it wasn't healthy for either of them. By Esmy staying home, he was protecting her in two ways, as was his responsibility. Kabili noticed that Cahya had finished his porridge, as had he.

"Shall we finish our tea outside, Cahya?", he asked him. "Leave these kids to wake up properly".

Cahya laughed and agreed. "Let's go and enjoy the outdoors", he said, getting up from the kitchen table.

"Leave those bowls there. I'll do them afterwards", Kabili told his children as he also got up. Cahya led the way to the back door and stepped outside. Kabili followed and closed the back door behind him. Cahya looked at him, expectantly. His friend clearly knew that he had wanted to speak to him in private, but Kabili wasn't sure where to start.

"I was thinking that maybe none of you need to come with me across the border – it might be a bit too dangerous. It's not far now and I could probably just go myself, especially now when I just need to see what it's like in the daytime. And then I could even go back myself at night too, probably". Kabili considered that there might be every opportunity for him to do it alone.

"You can't, really. We need to go together and see it so we all know exactly what we are doing when we are going back at night. We need to finalise the plan together".

"Well, maybe I could just go with Sarama and Laith. We should be able to handle it ourselves, and you can give us the potions and serums that we'll need before we go".

"You know that I need to be there to judge it properly". Cahya was firm. "It's too dangerous to rely on just telling you which ones you might need. That's the reason that I came with you. If I was worried, I would have just stayed at the settlement." Kabili knew that this was true – he did need Cahya there even though he did not want him there risking himself. However he tried to dress it up or whatever alternatives he could suggest, he knew that, ultimately, he needed Cahya. It was telling that Cahya didn't refer the settlement as 'home'. It was just as important to him.

"Yeah – it is true. I just didn't want you risking yourself if you didn't have to"

"We are all risking ourselves, but we need to work together. We are all needed"

"Maybe you should ask your granddaughter to stay here, though. Unless you need her help? But you don't, really, do you? Maybe it would be better to keep her out of harm's way".

"Yeah, that is true. It was never really the plan for her to come in the first place, but she wanted to – you know what kids are like. I suppose that there's no need for her to come with us to the compound. It would be an unnecessary risk." Kabili was glad that Cahya was seeing things his way. He was only trying to protect Esmy, and he was sure that Cahya would be grateful to him for that.

"My two have been training for this – you've seen Sarama with her archery and Laith with his sword – this is their duty. But it's too unsafe for your granddaughter". Kabili thought that he would reiterate to Cahya that he had made the right decision. "I care about your granddaughter like she was one of my own – I want to protect her just like you do, and so her staying here is the best thing to do".

"Yeah, it is", Cahya agreed. Good.

"Do you want to tell her, and I will get Sarama and Laith ready?", Kabili asked. "She will probably be relieved that she doesn't have to come". Kabili laughed to try and lighten the mood.

"Yeah, they will be done by now", replied Cahya, not reciprocating the laughter.

The two men headed back inside.

"Do you two want to get your shields and weapons? Are you nearly ready?", he said to his children across the room.

"Yeah, we've finished", said Sarama as Laith stood up

and gathered the bowls.

"Leave those – we can do those afterwards", Kabili told Laith. He waited for his two children to head towards the back of the house, where he was standing and also where their bedroom was. He followed them into their bedroom and he closed the door behind him while they strapped on their shields and weapons. It was okay that they were going around the house without them, but they should never leave the house unarmed – this was their tradition, ensuring that they were always prepared.

"We will be stepping into the Northlands today", he reminded them. "I've never been since it became the Northlands, but it's not very far from here at all. I've seen the compound before, but we still need to go in the light so we can all see it and we will know exactly what we are doing." They knew all of this, but he needed to make sure. "I wanted to go myself to check it out but your uncle said that we should all go. And he is right. But we aren't going to do anything silly". He paused here to look at both of his children in turn and make sure that they understood the importance of sticking to his plan. His daughter nodded but Laith, frustratingly, remained expressionless as always. "Laith?", said Kabili. He needed to make sure that Laith understood and gave his acknowledgment – he couldn't have anybody risking the mission by not following his plan.

"Yeah, I wasn't gonna", said Laith.

"Okay, good", Kabili continued. "I don't think it will be much different to how it used to be, but we need to be absolutely certain. The future of the community depends on it". He hoped that the emphasis on this last line instilled in his children just how important it was that they do exactly as he said. Surely it had.

He opened the bedroom door and stepped out into the living room. His children followed him out, armed and ready as they should be. Cahya was waiting at the kitchen table with his pouch ready, filled with his ointments and elixirs. As a group, they had absolutely everything they needed – weapons, potions, trowels, and a bolt cutter. This was going to be an exact dry run to make sure that nothing could go wrong when they returned tonight – every last bit of equipment and every last bit of weight needed to be accounted for.   They were even going to dig up some plants from the outside to make sure that they would be able to transport them back safely. Two plants. Because they would be taking two flowers, to be safe. Kabili was nervous. Very nervous. But there was no way on Earth that he was going to show this in front of his children. In their eyes, he was the strong leader that they would need to be in the future. He couldn't unsettle them by showing any sign of weakness at all – he was the one who had to lead by example. Kabili walked towards the front door and opened it. He stepped outside and to the side so that his children and Cahya could follow.   Once they were all outside, he closed the door behind them and made his way to the front of the group.

"Let's go".

Chapter 22 - Esmeralda

Esmeralda was left sitting at the kitchen table alone. Last night had been more perfect than she could possible imagine. Everything that she had ever wanted, despite only admitting it to herself a few days ago, was given to her yesterday. The last few days had been a whirlwind. She went from trying to suppress her feelings to admitting them to herself but wanting to hide them from Laith to revealing them to Laith but being worried about their future. On some level, she had always wanted Laith to know how she felt, but she had been scared. It seemed like such a long time ago now when she could not have imagined loving anybody as much as she loved Laith and would have given anything to have him feel the same way. Now he did, and she could not believe how lucky she was that the Universe had responded to her wishes. When she had loved him in secret, she did not think it possible to love anybody any more than she loved him. Her heart was full. The moment he told her how he felt, however, her heart exploded - she felt even more love than she could have ever conceived of as being possible. Her heart had expanded at the sound of his words and had filled with more love than could surely exist. There was nothing more perfect than that moment - being with the love of her life under the magic of the stars and looking up into the forever.

She got up from the kitchen table, deciding that she would do the washing up left over from the breakfast. She had nothing to do but wait for Laith and the rest of the group to return. Her grandad had already told her that she should not go. She hated the idea of letting Laith go without her, but she knew that she had better not protest too strongly. In terms of the mission and only the mission, she could see why her staying behind was the best thing to do. She didn't really have anything to add to the ability of the group and, if anything, she supposed that she would be a hindrance.

She gathered the rest of the washing up from the kitchen table and took it over to the sink. She began to wash it and let her thoughts take over. She had to stop for a moment and make sure that she was not dreaming. She had always suspected, on some level, that Laith must feel the same way about her. It was impossible for two people to be as perfect for each other as they were but not both feel it. She felt complete when she was with Laith and now, knowing that he felt the same, she was happier than she ever thought she could be. It was the kind of happiness that one could only dream of. It was the kind of happiness that filled her entire soul. It lifted her and placed her within the stars. Why had she ever tried to suppress her feelings? As soon as she asked herself this question, the horrible answer came flooding back to her. Nothing could possibly bring her down from the cloud that she was on apart from this one thought, and it did an excellent job of manifesting itself deep in the pit of her stomach whenever her love felt too strong. Now she had something different to suppress. She wanted the love to wash over and engulf her whilst she suppressed the bleak reality of the future. She loved Laith more than she loved anybody, and Laith felt the same way about her. This was all that mattered. Apart from it wasn't. It clearly wasn't all that mattered, and she hated it. She didn't want to think about it, but the horrible feeling in the pit of her stomach grew. It overcame the magic radiating from her core and began to force its way up into her throat. She knew that she was expected to marry somebody from her own tribe. And not just some vague idea of a theoretical somebody, but an actual physical somebody who existed right now and was waiting for her back at home. She had met him a couple of times, and he was nice. She might even go so far as saying he was very nice, based on the limited interactions that she had had with him. But he wasn't Laith. He was nowhere near Laith. And she was made for Laith. And he was made for her. They were perfect for each other. Perfect. She loved Laith more than she thought it was possible to love anybody. She had a connection with him that nobody else in the Universe had ever felt with anybody else – a connection surely forged within the stars themselves. When two people love each other as much as they do – when they have the connection that she had with Laith – they owe it to the Universe to be together no matter what. She was sure that Darma was perfectly nice, but it would not be fair on anybody for her to be with him after experiencing what she had with Laith. All the love that she had in her heart was for Laith – she would be living a lie with Darma. Her heart grew when she was with Laith. It was impossible, but it physically grew. And her soul grew with it. And she felt more magic within it than could possibly exist. But she was sure that her grandad would not let it happen. And, forget about her grandad – her uncle would be dead against it. She knew that he didn't like her anyway, and he was even stricter than her grandad when it came to traditions. There was no way that she could possibly have a future with Laith.

But she was made for Laith, and Laith was made for her. The Universe brought them together, and surely the Universe would find a way. She regretted that it was the daytime because she longed for the Moon and the stars. Instead, she sat back down at the table and closed her eyes, picturing last night and refilling her body with the energy that the dark feeling in her stomach had stolen from her. She loved Laith, and Laith loved her. Nothing else mattered. Please, let nothing else matter.

Chapter 23 - Kabili

The compound came into view – surrounded by a wire fence and flanked by thick bushes. Kabili had not seen it in over twenty years. It looked exactly as he remembered, if not slightly smaller and slightly less threatening. He had not been sure what to expect when he crossed over the border. He knew roughly where the boundary line was – the line over which some defectors crossed to cosy up to the people responsible for the massacre of their own community, but he was unsure on what to expect when he got there. He had heard some rumours of a wall being built to mark the boundary but had never seen it for himself. When he reached the boundary, all that was there was the pathetic remnants of a feeble attempt at masonry. There were huge gaps where it had been left unfinished and shoddy workmanship ensured that, even though only twenty years had passed, parts of the wall had already fallen down and other parts were crumbling. He had been nervous when they had left the cabin, and he expected to feel some fear or apprehension when crossing the boundary but, when he did so, he felt nothing. If anything, seeing the utter shambles of a boundary gave him a boost in confidence and strengthened his resolve. The same cowards who attacked an unarmed community and were responsible for tearing his family apart were not even capable of such a simple job of building a wall. Twenty years and it had already become derelict. No honour and no pride.

He expected a resurgence of nerves when he saw the compound but, as soon as he clapped eyes on it, he felt nothing but disdain. If anything, seeing the compound in real life made him feel calmer than before. It did not have the same sense of foreboding as it did in his imagination. Twenty years of thinking about something tends to build it up in your imagination. The compound was controlled by the same cowards who were responsible for the crumbling wall – the same cowards who are only capable of attacking people when they are unarmed and celebrating. He remembered how, once upon a time, everybody had access to the red flower. Everybody lived together in perfect harmony until the Far North had come to leech off their prosperity and milk their community. This compound was a representation of that. And they had told the people that it was for their own good. And the people believed them. And some of them turned against their own community for it. He would never forgive them. But, no, he was not here for revenge, he reminded himself. He was here only to ensure the survival of his own community. The people who had defected, they could cosy up to the Far North for as long as they wanted. As soon as Kabili got what he wanted, he would be leaving. He had no interest in harming anybody – only in protecting his own people.

Kabili positioned himself safely in some bushes at the side of the very thin dirt path that led to the compound from the south. The path had become narrower since partition, with plants beginning to grow over it since the access from the south fell into disuse. Kabili instructed his children and Cahya to take cover in the bushes too. He knew that the main settlement was farther north from here – they had partitioned the land to ensure that the compound was on the side of the Northlands – this was their main aim. If they had been able to take more land, they would have. It was only due to heroism from members of his own community that his children's grandparents' area had not formed part of the Northlands. Thanks to their heroics, the compound was not as far from the boundary as the Far North and their sycophants would have liked it to be. But the Far North kept the compound, which was all they wanted in the first place.

Kabili ensured that he was in a position where he could see how the compound was being guarded. There were no guards at the south fence but, in the past, there had been guards stationed at the north fence – the only entrance. There had also been guards who would patrol the whole perimeter, but he had not seen them yet today. As was the case twenty years ago, there was a simple chain link fence around the perimeter of the compound, with barbed wire on the top. He could not see the red flower from his current position – small one storey wooden shacks had intentionally been placed between the south fence and the area in which the flower was grown to decrease their visibility. The North must have felt that seeing the flower would lead to a temptation to take back control – the revolution they feared. The east and west fences both had thick, high bushes growing close to the fence – these fences were nearly impossible to access, although he had sometimes been able to see the red flower in the compound in the past by looking through the bushes at certain angles. The north fence was the one that they needed to stay away from. This was the only entrance and so would be heavily guarded. They would do their best to stay away from it now whilst they were gathering information, and when they came back tonight to actually reclaim a flower.

Kabili expected that he would have seen a guard on patrol by now coming around the south fence, but nobody had come. They must have had relaxed the security even further since the pre-partition days. This did make sense to Kabili – it was something that he had predicted and his logic had been proven to be correct. They were able to relax the security now that the only people left in their community fell into one of three groups: the beneficiaries of the regime; their sycophants; and cowards. They were either liars, being duped by the lies fed to them about how this was for their own benefit, or they were too cowardly to do anything about it. Either way, there was no need for as strong a security presence as in the past when the unrest was growing. The unrest that led to the massacre.

Kabili knew that the aim for this part of the mission was to actually get a sight on the red flower. He needed to make sure that he could see exactly where it was – make sure that it was still growing in the same area as it had twenty years ago – and then come back at night time to take it. Making two trips wasn't ideal, but they couldn't break in during daylight and they wouldn't be able to get good visuals at night. He certainly wasn't going to break in without a solid plan in place. As Cahya had said, it was important that everybody knew exactly where it was and knew exactly what their roles would be later tonight, especially given that they would be coming back under the cover of darkness. The best view that he would be able to get would either be through the bushes on the east fence or, preferably, between the shacks along the south fence. No guards were patrolling, so now was a good a time as any to confirm that they were not at all far from what they had come for. He needed to see the flower.

"I'm going to step out now", he said quietly to the rest of the group. "I'm going to make sure that the flower is where I think it is. Laith and Sarama, you need to make sure that you are on guard all of the time, as you always should be anyway". This time they both nodded in acknowledgment. Good – Laith was learning.

Kabili stepped out into the open from the safety of the bush. He felt exposed now that he was in the open. He had brought his sword with him. Maybe he should have brought his bow and arrow today instead. He was accomplished with both but always had favoured the sword. Maybe he should have thought about what the mission would require as opposed to what his favourite weapon was. He had justified it previously because Sarama was the archer for the mission, and they might need more close combat fighters just in case. He was better with the sword than his son so he thought that he should bring that but, now, maybe the approach required him to have a bow and arrow. He edged slowly towards to south fence of the compound, occasionally looking back towards the area where his children and friend were waiting for him. He made sure that he continued to look around as he was walking – he needed to make sure that he was well aware of his surroundings. He was always prepared.

He made it to the fence, but was directly behind the shacks. He had no way of seeing the flower from where he was – he had to try and look for a gap between the shacks or, failing that, between the bushes. He laid a hand on the fence, trying to gauge how easy it would be to cut, and how much he would need to cut in order to bend it enough that they could fit through. It didn't seem like it should be too difficult – pathetic security. He started to head west first – there might be a gap between the shacks there to save him from going around the side of the perimeter. He walked slowly and carefully, trying not to be too noisy or draw too much attention to himself. There were no windows around the back of the shacks, but there was every chance that people might be inside to hear him. He was walking slowly towards the end of the shack when he heard something behind him. He turned around to see a guard turn the corner from the east fence. He looked young – around the same age as his son but, he was proud to say, not as physically threatening. What did he expect from the son of a coward? He had short dark hair and was clean-shaven. Kabili noticed that he had a sword by his side, but doubted whether he even knew which way up to hold it, let alone how to swing it. What was of the utmost importance at the moment was that this young guard did not shout for help, which is what he surely should be doing – these people clearly were not very clever either. Kabili was too far away to knock the guard out. If he spoke to him, his voice would surely alert anybody inside the compound that there were intruders here. The last thing that he needed was more attention. On seeing Kabili, the young guard froze. He looked confused. He had obviously never experienced anything like this, and was not sure what to do. How long before he realised that he should shout for help? Kabili could charge at him, but this would surely scare him into alerting everybody else by the time Kabili was able to get to him and knock him out. Kabili had to come up with a plan, and quickly. From Kabili's right, faster than he had time to decide what to do, came an arrow that stuck into the young guard's thigh. He, thankfully, didn't shout in pain – he only let out a feeble grunt, probably in surprise more than anything. He seemed drowsy. Immediately, Kabili knew that Sarama would have coated the arrowhead in the sleeping potion of Cahya's, and he knew exactly what he had to do. He had just enough time to make it over to the young guard and lower him slowly and silently onto the ground to prevent him collapsing with a great thud himself. It worked perfectly. As soon as he lowered the guard onto the ground, he heard another sound come from behind him. He turned around to see him son rushing towards him. Kabili put his hand up gesturing for his son to stop – he was making too much noise and was going to get them caught. Now was not the time to get hot-headed. Laith stopped for a split-second, but then continued forwards slowly nevertheless.

"We need to move him out of the way quickly before anybody else sees", Laith whispered. Kabili knew that this was true, but wanted to make sure that Laith did not risk himself being noticed either.

"Yeah, but I would have been okay to move him myself, Laith – you could have stayed hidden"

"We need to do it quickly, now".

Kabili wasn't convinced that Laith coming out was the right thing to do – he was sure that he could have moved the guard himself in good time but, now that Laith was out, there was no sense in arguing about it.

"Let's lift him so it makes less sound", Kabili told his son. "Get his legs". Kabili thought he had better take responsibility for the heavier top half of the body. Laith did as he was told, and the two of them carried the guard towards the area of the bush in which they were hiding. Cahya and Sarama were still in there, Sarama poised with another arrow just in case. Seeing his daughter filled Kabili with pride in her actions. He remembered why he had chosen to bring the sword himself – he was in a team with his two children, and he had his daughter's excellent marksmanship to cover him. It was a good decision that he had made. His daughter was ready as soon as he stepped out, which was exactly how he had brought her up. His children should always be ready. Cahya was there to provide the sleeping potion to coat the arrowhead with, and his daughter had clearly got this ready just as he had told her that she needed to be on guard.

"How long before he wakes up?", Kabili asked Cahya in a whisper.

"It's hard to say", Cahya replied in a low but soft voice. "It went straight into his bloodstream and it's hard to judge how much went in. It acts faster, but it also wears off faster. It's easier to judge when they drink it". Kabili thought that Cahya seemed a bit tense when he said this, but hoped he was just imagining it.

"Can we give him some more in his mouth now to try and make sure some more kicks in when this one wears off? Drinking it is slower, so it should give us a bit more time". Kabili wanted to make sure that the guard was out for as long as possible – he knew that the plan had to change because of what just happened. They would have to go in now – they didn't have a choice. Security was relatively lax at the moment. As soon as they notice that a guard is missing, it will alert them to step up their security efforts – it would be impossible to get in. There was no way that they would be able to come back tonight and expect there to be no security.

"No." The normally soft-spoken Cahya was very firm. "You know better than anybody what will happen if he has too much, and it is too much of a risk. I don't know how much is safe to give him, and we didn't come here to kill anybody". Kabili knew that there was no way Cahya would let anybody else go near his potions, and Cahya was right anyway. Cahya was in charge of the potions – that was why he came – and he had made the right decision. Cahya was the one with the expertise. This boy, even though he was working to help the Northlands, was not trying to harm anybody himself. He did not know that guarding the flower was wrong. He had been brought up amidst all of the propaganda that many people, as adults, had fallen for when the Far North sectioned off the flower in the first place. Cahya thought it was too risky too give him any more sleeping potion, and therefore it was.

"We haven't come here to kill anybody", Kabili confirmed to the group. "We just want to get the flower and go. But the plan is going to have to change now. We are going to have to think on our feet".

Kabili knew that leadership was his strength. Leadership, planning and logic. He had made an initial plan, but he was already ready for this to be adapted if it needed to be. Now it needed to be. He had initially wanted Cahya to go inside with them – he knew that his friend had a good eye for energy. Cahya would be able to see which flower was the best to take. Now, Kabili would need his friend to stay with the guard to make sure that he did not wake up and alert anybody. On the other hand, there was no way that they were going to remain undetected. They no longer had the cover of darkness. They would have to go into the compound in broad daylight - they would definitely be seen. It might be safer that Cahya did go inside with them – at least that way they would be able to protect him. No. Him staying hidden was the best way to protect him. He would just be another target if they took him inside. He was not able to defend himself like the three of them were – protecting Cahya on the inside would surely make the job more difficult. Time was still of the essence – Kabili needed to make his decision quickly. The three of them, without Cahya, would cut the south fence and get inside, get the flower, and get out. They wouldn't have time to get two flowers now – they were definitely going to be seen.

"Right – we need to act quickly", Kabili told the group. "Sarama – cover all of your arrowheads with the sleeping potion".

"We already have, Dad"

"Okay, good. Make sure you don't accidentally cut yourself or get any into your own bloodstream. Laith, give me the bolt cutters. We have to go inside now". Laith did as he was told. "We don't have time to have a look at the layout before we go in now but you two need to remember that we are outside the south fence now. There will be guards stationed at the north fence without a doubt – the one directly opposite this one. We need to break in through the back and then, Sarama, as soon they are in range, you need to get them in the thigh before they can raise the alarm. Well, we will see anyway. Cahya – will you stay here and make sure that this boy doesn't wake up? Stay hidden".

"Yeah, don't worry"

"We won't know which flower is the best but…"

"Whichever one you get will be better than nothing. We all know how well they grow anyway – just get one and it will be fine".

"We should probably put a bit of that on our swords too", Kabili said. He was referring to the sleeping potion, and he knew that Cahya would know what he meant. "How much shall we put on?"

"Put a few drops on now – you never want more than a few at a time if it's going to go into a cut". Cahya pulled a vial out of his pouch. It contained a deep blue liquid. Kabili found it difficult to distinguish between the many different potions and elixirs that Cahya made over his lifetime – some strong, some weak, and all for different purposes – but the deep blue of this particular potion was one that was instantly recognisable to Kabili. Even he could sense its power. Cahya carefully poured two drops onto Kabili's sword, and then did the same to Laith's. He corked the vial and then handed it to Laith.

"In case you need to add more, but be careful". Kabili watched as Laith took the vial off Cahya. He thought about taking it off Laith and taking responsibility for it himself – it could be dangerous – but he decided to trust Laith with it, as his friend had.

"We need to go. We don't know how much time we have", Kabili said. He was beginning to feel nervous but he knew that he could not let this show. Thankfully, as soon as he stepped out of the bush, all of his nerves disappeared and he was focused solely on the task in hand. Some called this 'being in the zone'. He knew it to be his responsibility as a warrior.

Kabili led the way to the south fence, bolt cutters in hand. Laith followed behind him, hand on his sword and his shield already out. His daughter was behind the both of them, poised with her bow and arrow, constantly surveying the area. He had brought his children up well, but it was not yet time for him to well up with pride. He placed the mouth of the bolt cutters on the first link that he needed to cut and squeezed the handles together slowly and carefully. Time was of the essence, but now would be the worst time to get caught. He couldn't risk being heard here. He was relieved that it broke easily. He estimated that he would need to cut about ten links before they were able to bend the fence enough to fit through. He cut the next link, then looked up and around to see if anybody was yet alerted to their presence.

"Dad, don't worry – just cut it – me and Sarama are guarding", Laith told him. There was a sense of urgency in his voice. Kabili had to remind himself again that now was not the time to well up with pride at how well his children were supporting him. He carried on cutting the fence. After he made the tenth cut, he put the bolt cutters down and tried to bend the fence as much as he could. The gap was not big enough to get through. Time was of the essence. He cut another link – the eleventh. The twelfth. He pulled the fence again, but it would not bend enough. Laith joined in, but they could still not get it wide enough. The harder they pulled, the more noise they began to make.

"Stop", he told Laith. How long before anybody realised the young guard had not come back? That was something to take into account too. Laith pulled out his sword and put it between the links in the fence. He levered it against the post and managed to bend the fence enough that they would be able to fit through.

"Good, Laith", Kabili said, feeling prouder by the minute. His children used logic. Laith had brains as well as brawn – exactly as he had instilled in him.

Kabili told his daughter to go through the hole first, as Laith held it open. Kabili went through afterwards and then held the sword steady as Laith came through. Laith took his sword back off Kabili. The three of them were inside the compound.

They were shielded from the flower by the shacks at the moment. They did not know what was on the other side or who was inside. Had anybody heard them come through? The closest gap between the shacks was towards the west fence, and this also provided them with more cover from the north gate, based on what Kabili remembered. There was a building on that side that should obscure them from the view of the guards at the north gate once they get around the shacks. Kabili didn't know where any other guards might be, but there would definitely be some at the north gate so this had to be his priority. He wished he could have left his children outside, but he needed them in here.

"Be ready", he whispered to them.

Kabili led his children around the side of the shack. The three of them were able to stand in the narrow gap between the first shack and its neighbour. Kabili was right – there was a building that shielded them from the view of the guards at the north gate. From his current position, Kabili could see nothing but the shacks he was standing in between, the side wall of the building directly in front of him and, if he peered out from between the shacks, the bushes through the outside of the east fence. He knew that he would need to step out and go to the front face of the building to get to the flowers. How many guards would there be? There would definitely be at least two guarding the front entrance. There should have been at least four guarding the perimeter, if they were doing a proper job. In the past, there were days when there were only two. Today, only one had come by. Was there another that would come by? Surely he would have come by now if there was. But the guards at the front will realise soon that something is amiss. Would it have been better to wait and maybe split them up if one of them came looking for the missing boy? No. This was the right thing to do – he needed to stop second-guessing himself. This was not like him at all. If they split up, surely they would alert more people. And there was no guarantee that they would split up anyway. What he was doing at the moment was the right thing. Surely there would be at least five or six guards in the main building and then more in the shacks. This would be a test. They were outnumbered, without a doubt, but three warriors could defeat three thousand cowards. Victory was in sight.

Kabili stepped out from the shacks and stood against the side of the building. Facing his children, he beckoned them forward - Laith first, and then Sarama. Both had their weapons ready, and Laith had his shield ready to deflect anything coming their way. Good. They were a good team. Kabili edged closer to the front face of the building. He realised that he would now be in the view of anybody in the shacks but, as he looked through the windows at the best angle he could, they appeared to be empty. He peered around the side of the building and breathed a sigh of relief as he laid eyes on the flower. They were growing in abundance – plenty around for everybody, but he knew that not everybody in the Northlands would be getting their fair share. Well, everybody in the Southlands would be, soon enough. As long as nothing went wrong now. There was still plenty of time for things to go wrong.

Kabili beckoned his two children forward.
"That's the flower", he said, pointing to them. He saw that both of his children looked somewhat confused, and it suddenly occurred to him that they had never actually seen one before. Kabili had never realised before, but the name 'flower' was a bit misleading – it was unlike any other flower. Having known it all his life, he had never considered that it was not actually a flower. It was a red plant with a small circular base. It had thick and fleshy leaves growing directly from the base, wide at the bottom but getting gradually thinner and growing into points. These leaves, when tall enough, would bend and grow back towards the ground, which is how they were able to

233

reproduce. They grew very easily, which was one of the ways that the Far North had managed to convince the easily-manipulated that they were dangerous and needed to be controlled.

Kabili leaned back so that the three could take cover from behind the wall again. They could not be seen in this position from anywhere around the perimeter but, if a guard was to come to the south fence, surely he would see the hole and the bolt cutters that they left there. Kabili peered around the building again, this time in the direction of the north gate. He was right – there were two guards stationed there. They were, however, in range of Sarama's arrows. He was an accomplished archer himself – he should take responsibility for this.

"Sarama, give me your bow and arrow. I'll take down the two guards at the gate. I can do it from here".

His daughter looked at him and paused. Out of the corner of his eye, Kabili saw that Laith was also looking at him.

"No", said Sarama. "We don't have time for that. By the time you shoot them, others might see. Then you won't have time to get the flower because we will get charged down. You need to head towards the flower now. I will cover you from here. As soon as they look your way, I will shoot them. And I won't miss".

Kabili was proud of his daughter. He had given her the option to back down, and she had not taken it. She had shown him what she was made of. This was the right thing to do, and she was willing to step up and take responsibility. She spoke with such confidence that Kabili could not doubt her abilities. He knew that she was the best archer around, and she now given him proof that she had the confidence needed to be able to cope under pressure. This was exactly what he needed.

Kabili put his sword back in its sheath and pulled out a trowel instead. What a sight he must look, he thought – the most feared warrior in the Southlands was now wielding gardening equipment. But this was about doing what was needed, not peacocking. He had to rely on his children now to keep him safe as he stepped out into the open. A true leader did exactly what was needed of him and relied on his team to do the same. He didn't know which flower would be the best one, so he just headed for the nearest one, about twenty paces away. He had taken fifteen of those paces when he saw one of the guards turn round and shout. This was it.

Straight away, an arrow went flying past his shoulder and into the thigh of the guard. His daughter was never going to miss the first shot. The second guard shouted as he progressed towards Kabili. How much progress would he make in the time it took Sarama to reload? His answer came quickly – not very much at all. Quicker than he could have hoped for and probably even quicker than he could have done so himself, Kabili heard a second arrow come shooting past him and struck the second guard in the leg. Both guards stumbled to the ground, knocked out. His daughter was the best archer he knew, but Kabili had no time to stop and admire her handiwork. How many other guards had their shouts alerted? Kabili knelt down by the flower and started digging. He quickly looked behind him as he dug – his children were both poised and ready. He had to act quickly and carefully.

Kabili heard guards coming out of the shack closest to the east fence. He looked up to see that there were only two. He had not been able to see them from the difficult angle previously, but this was as good as he could have hoped for – he knew that his daughter would be able to knock them both out in the time it would take them to get to him. The two guards took out their swords, but Kabili concentrated on the task in hand. He needed to have faith in his daughter whilst he made sure that he kept this flower alive as he was taking it out of the ground. He had to make sure that he took out enough of the roots and the soil so it stayed alive during transport, and he needed to concentrate. He would do his job and his daughter would do hers. He heard his daughter fire an arrow at the first guard. He looked up to see the second guard pull his shield in front of him. Sensibly, from the guard's perspective, he pulled it in front of his chest. For all he knew, Sarama was trying to kill him. This worked well for Sarama, who then had a clear shot of his leg, which is what she was aiming for. How long before people in the building realised? With the ease that the guards were falling to the ground, they would have every reason to believe that the arrows were poison-tipped. But that was for cowards. Kabili did not want to take any lives. He never took any lives unless it was absolutely necessary. Thankfully, so far, none of the guards had been particularly clever. They had been easy to pick off one-by-one. How many would come from the building? This would be harder. He needed to focus on getting this flower out cleanly and quickly.

The deafening sound of a piercing siren rang loudly in Kabili's ears. Somebody in the building must have set it off. Everybody in the building would be coming out, and it was loud enough to alert anybody in the vicinity too – not necessarily only those on the relatively small compound. Five guards came out of the building at once. Sarama would not have time to pick them off one by one – they were too close. This was where him and Laith were needed. All of the guards had swords – clearly none were skilled enough for archery. Sarama managed to take two of them down as another two came running out of the building. Laith rushed towards the group of five. Time was running out and Laith was trying to buy just that little bit more.

Finally. Kabili managed to get the flower. He pulled it out and put it in his pouch. Kabili rushed towards the group of five guards to join his son, and watched as Laith struck one of them on the head with his shield, knocking him out.

"Use your sword, Laith", he shouted at his son, while he managed to easily block a guards strike with his shield, and then strike by slashing him on the side. The potion on his sword ensured that the guard stumbled and fell to the ground, but Kabili was unsure if this would work again now.

Maybe Laith was right to use his shield where he could. He looked up and saw that the remaining three guards were all advancing towards his son. Kabili knew that he had a chance of maybe helping his son by taking one of them out and so he ran towards him.

"Dad, move!", came a shout from behind him. His daughter had a shot at one of the men, but he knew that he was blocking her way. He had a split-second to decide whether to trust his daughter or to continue on his path so that he could help Laith himself, blocking his daughter's shot. Even if his daughter took one of the men out, which she could, this would leave Laith fighting two by himself. The way that they were advancing towards him, with one on either side of him, this would be impossible. He had to continue on his path and help his son. He could take this guard out and still have enough time to reach his son and help with a second. This was the kind of experience that his daughter did not yet have – she was looking only at what was happening right now, and could not look two moves into the future as he could. Kabili ignored his daughter's call and slashed at the guard. The guard was hurt, but didn't seem at all drowsy. No potion had entered his bloodstream. The guard turned to face Kabili and swung his own sword at him. Kabili blocked the shot with his shield easily and looked up towards his son. There were two guards now on Laith – he wouldn't stand a chance against two. His son was an excellent fighter, but he had one guard coming at his left hand side, and another at his right. As Kabili went to strike the guard he was holding off, he heard the whoosh of an arrow. It flew into the leg of the guard that he was fighting. His daughter, in the heat of the moment, had chosen the wrong guard to fire at. If she chose one of Laith's, she would have given him a chance. Kabili now had no time to reach his son, and Sarama would not have enough time to reload.

Kabili looked up as the two guards took aim at Laith. He watched as Laith used his shield to block the shot of one guard whilst, somehow, sidestepping the other one. He took the opportunity of the first guard stumbling from his

237

blocked strike to position himself perfectly. The strength of his block combined with his footwork meant that, even though it was still two against one, he manipulated their positions so that they were both in a line with him at the front. He used one as a shield from the other – they could no longer both attack him at once. All of the training that Kabili had made Laith do had just saved his life. He couldn't have been more proud as he watched Laith hit the guard closest to him with his shield, making him stumble backwards. He then managed to cut him on the leg. The sleeping potion on his sword must still have been in tact, as the guard seemed to stumble and fall. Laith charged at the remaining guard with his shield, blocking his attempted strike at the same time. An arrow came flying into the guard's calf. Laith had bought Sarama enough time to reload. The guard fell to the ground as two more arrows came flying in their direction. They missed everything. Kabili realised that there were archers in the building. He didn't know how many, or how many more people might come out. With the thundering siren still blaring, Kabili didn't know how much time they had, but he knew it would not be very much. They needed to escape.

He made sure that he had the flower and beckoned Laith towards the cover of the side of the building. They both ran towards there, where Sarama was waiting.

"Thanks", Laith said to her. Sarama didn't reply. Kabili felt her silence. Was she angry with him? He had done the right thing, but maybe she didn't see it that way in her inexperience. Maybe her silence was just due to the shock of what had just happened. Now was not the time, anyway. They needed to escape. With the flower safe, the three of them went in between the shacks and back to the broken fence. They managed to squeeze through it. How long before the archers came after them? Would they come after them now, or would they wait for back-up? They must have seen from the windows that he and his children were not a force to be reckoned with. They didn't fire their own arrows when he and Laith were in close proximity with the guards – they must have realised that Sarama was more skilled. It wouldn't make sense for them to come now if there were not a lot of them. Maybe this would buy them a bit of time to escape. Whether their back-up came quickly or not, Kabili knew that they all had to escape as soon as possible. He pushed back the broken fence as he crawled through first, the roaring siren urging him on. He then got his sword to open it and give enough space for his children to come through, glancing at the area between the shacks all the while prepared for guards to come bursting through. He picked up the bolt cutters and put his sword back in his sheath and headed to where they left Cahya.

"Got it. Come on, quick, let's go", Kabili told his friend.

"Excellent – well done", Cahya said, looking at the pouch. Kabili angled it so that his friend could see it.

"Yeah, it's good", Cahya confirmed. Kabili was relieved. He wasn't sure how much of a chance they would stand going back in there now, now that the blaring siren had called for reinforcements.

"How's he been?", Kabili asked Cahya, pointing to the boy.

"He hasn't stirred – I've not had to give him any more at all"

"Okay, good. Come on, let's go", said Kabili, as he led the way. His children followed behind him. He turned to see Cahya leave some more vials on the ground near the bush where they had left the sleeping boy. The vials looked empty to Kabili but Cahya always said that he could see things inside them.

The four of them walked away from the compound, with the siren still ringing loudly in the air. Kabili felt a mix of pride and relief. He was proud of himself and his children – they had done the near impossible, and they had had to do it in broad daylight. They now, against all odds, had the flower in their possession. This would save their community. But there was a small nagging feeling – they still had to get away. Surely it wouldn't be long before the Far North and those running the compound for them realised that the breach must have come from the

Southlands. Nobody in their own community would be able to pull it off, so that only left Kabili's. Would they now come after them to try to destroy the flower, or would they be happy to allow Kabili's community to have a flower as long as they could control their own? They might be fearful that the Southlands would now destroy the control that they had of the flower amongst their own community. In reality, Kabili had no interest in destroying the Far North's monopoly over their own community – he had responsibilities towards his own. The defectors had made their bed and now had to lie in it. But the Far North might not see it that way. They might be fearful that this could be the beginning of the end of the control that they had enjoyed for so long. A cataclysmic event that would be the beginning of an uprising. As Kabili learnt twenty years ago, fear made people do unpleasant things.

Chapter 24 - Laith

Laith's heart was still pumping. Looking back, he couldn't quite believe what had just happened. If somebody had told him that that was what he was going to need to do, he would have expected to feel some fear or at least be a bit hesitant. In fact, he had felt none. He wasn't sure what he felt at the time. He did not remember feeling particularly confident. Maybe he just felt nothing, if that was possible. He knew that it needed to be done, and so he did it without thought or feeling. It was a difficult fight, but he always backed the three of them to come out on top. It was how he had been brought up – he should have the confidence alone to beat one thousand men. And, charging at the guards, he knew that his sister would have his back. Maybe that was why it was so easy for him to do so without any worry. But maybe there was another reason too. Since last night, Laith had felt as though he was on top of the world and nothing could bring him down. Since the love of his life had told him that she loves him back, he felt invincible. If that was possible, anything was.

The group fled the compound, led by Laith's father. Laith stayed at the rear with his sister to ensure that they could protect their Uncle Cahya from any attacks that came from the rear – they were not out of the woods yet. With the siren still blaring, Laith knew that being tailed by guards was a very real possibility. Neither Laith nor his sister had overtly spoken about remaining at the back – they had just done it on instinct. Their father was leading and protecting from the front, and Uncle Cahya would not be able to protect himself the way that they could. They also needed to make sure that they did not flee to fast for him. He was incredibly fit for a man of his age so sometimes it was hard to remember that he was not as fit and healthy as Laith and Sarama, or even their father.

As they turned the corner, their father slowed down. He must have felt that they were a bit safer now. It didn't look like anybody was coming. Surely, if they were going to come, they would have come by now. Laith's father turned around to face the rest of the group

"We all did brilliantly in there. We worked together as a team and did exactly what we needed to. Well done, you two".

Laith wasn't accustomed to hearing such compliments from his father – he only ever said things that he actually meant. Laith knew that his father must have been proud of the way that they acted inside. Laith never particularly considered himself to be the type of person who needed recognition but, coming from his dad, it actually meant a lot to him. He felt a sense of pride that he had never felt before.

"Thanks, Dad", he said. His sister, curiously, remained quiet. Their roles had reversed – normally it was Laith who stood quietly. Well, Laith considered, the reason he normally didn't speak was because his sister did it for him. Now maybe she was enjoying the same luxury. Or maybe she was shaken up about what had happened inside. Just because Laith had managed to cope well, it didn't mean that his sister felt the same way. The adrenaline began to wear off as Laith started to worry about his sister. He looked over at her to try and see what she was feeling, but he could not read her facial expression. All he knew was that it was not as soft as usual. She was still concentrating on her surroundings, so maybe now wasn't the best time to interrupt her. But he still had better make sure she was okay.

"You okay?", he said to her, quietly.

"Yeah". Her tone was not as soft as it normally was, but he wasn't sure if this was because she was scared, upset, or concentrating. Laith realised that he got precisely as much information from this exchange as he had by simply looking at her face. But at least he had given the information that he was there for her. He decided that he would see how she was when they got back to the cabin.

Laith was excited to see Esmy again. She would surely be surprised when she found out what had happened. He was excited to tell her. Laith knew that getting the red flower was the best thing that could happen for the community. He should be delighted about this but, really, it paled in comparison to the fact that he had Esmy and that she had him. He had never had the feeling of loving anybody this much. He had never had the feeling that he belonged to somebody like he belonged to her. They were made for each other and they had both finally admitted it.

They were approaching the boundary wall – crumbling and decrepit. Laith's father found one of the many gaps to walk through, and the rest of the group followed. As soon as Laith stepped foot across the boundary, he somehow felt safer and more relaxed. It was silly, thinking about it – a boundary that had not even existed when he was born, marked by a half-hearted attempt at building a wall that provided only slightly more security than a damp paper towel was enough to make him feel safe – like he was now somehow more home than he had been twenty seconds ago. It's funny the power that false boundaries have if one adheres to them. It's funny how much can change if one ignores them.

They were not too far from the cabins now. Laith saw his sister put her bow back on her back. His father too put his sword away. They were in the clear. Laith put his sword back in its sheath and began to process what they had just done. He looked over at his sister, who turned to face him and smiled. Her expression was soft again – she was back to normal. She must have felt scared trespassing in the Northlands. There was something unnerving about it, Laith conceded – the feeling that they did not belong had been forged out of the weakest of boundaries. It wouldn't be long now that they were back home.

Laith could make out his grandparents' cabin. They were not far. Esmy would be waiting for him inside. Laith looked at Uncle Cahya – Esmy's grandfather. How would he feel if he knew? Laith had always had a good relationship with Uncle Cahya. A very good relationship. He knew that his uncle was as fond of him as he was of his uncle, but would this be enough to get his blessing? He certainly would not get his own father's blessing – this was completely out of the question. His father was very traditional. Laith knew that his father had very set ways of deciding what was right and what was wrong. Traditions were things that were always right. Having a partner from a different tribe, regardless of how perfect they were, was always wrong. Laith would have liked to have his father's blessing, but he knew that this was something that was impossible. Well, this was just something that his father was going to have to deal with. He loved Esmy and Esmy loved him. They were perfect for each other and such perfection certainly trumped tradition. On the other hand, and perhaps curiously, Laith felt less comfortable with having such an attitude towards his uncle's opinion. It mattered more to him that Uncle Cahya gave his blessing. Maybe this was because he didn't want Esmy to upset her family, or maybe it was because, in a way, he felt closer to Uncle Cahya than he did to his own father. Either way, Laith knew that he and Esmy had things to discuss. The main thing, though, was that he and Esmy would be together forever – this he knew. It was a fact. It was impossible for two people to be as perfect for each other as they were and not end up together. Now it was just a matter of 'how', and not 'if'.

Laith's father reached the front door of the cabin first and pushed it open. Laith followed his father and his uncle through the threshold. The first thing he did was look to his left, where he had left Esmy. She was still there, sat at the kitchen table, looking as beautiful as ever. Laith couldn't believe that she loved him back. It seemed as though their arrival had jolted her out of her thoughts, and Laith could tell that she sensed something had not gone to plan at the compound. She looked at Laith expectantly, flicked her eyes over to her grandfather, and then straight back at Laith waiting for an explanation.

"We had to go in now", Laith told her. "Dad's got the

flower".

"What? Why? How?" she asked, clearly surprised.

"We need to go now", Laith's father interrupted. "You two," he said to Laith and Sarama, "make sure that you have packed everything you need, but hurry up. We need to try and get back to our settlement by tomorrow. If they come after us, we need to make sure we have back-up and that we are ready for them"

"Yeah, okay, I'm pretty much ready anyway", Laith told his father. "I'll tell you on the way", he told Esmy, quickly. Despite the air of panic and fear his father seemed intent on creating, Laith was content ruminating. He felt the biggest smile deep in his heart just by talking to Esmy. Just by thinking about her. The world could be falling down around him but, as long as he had Esmy, nothing else mattered.

"Okay, good. I'm gonna start loading Acira. Can you all come and give me a hand with your stuff then, when you're ready?".

Laith headed to the room in which he and his sister had slept to pick up their belongings. His sense of urgency was driven not by his father but by to wanting to be back by Esmy's side. He had thought that their relationship was perfect before – their friendship – but now that he had more, he couldn't believe that he had ever done without it. How had it taken him so long to admit to himself how perfect they were for each other? Well, it didn't matter now, because they had both realised and now all he wanted was to be by her side. Laith picked up his bag and his blankets and took them outside. Esmy was already there with her grandad, and Laith could not help but smile. His sister followed quite soon with some more belongings. His father had already attached Acira's saddle. She was drinking contently out of her bucket while Laith's father was loading things onto her right side, and Uncle Cahya on her left. It was quite funny, Laith thought, how Acira had no idea what she had just helped them to do. She had supported them in completing something that, in hindsight, was really quite dangerous. And here she was, drinking her water, with no idea how valuable her strength had been to them.

"Here, Dad, I'm gonna leave this here, okay?", Laith said, as he put down everything that he had brought from inside. "I'm gonna go check inside to make sure that we have everything".

"Okay, good. Make sure that you check we haven't left any food behind". Laith knew that, now they had the flower, growing food would no longer be as difficult as it had been. However, he knew why his father made a point of checking for the food – regardless of how much they had in the past or will have in the future, it was a mark of disrespect to waste any. They had had to do without having as much as they might have liked for so long, and it would have got worse in the future but for their intervention. They had been brought up to always appreciate what they had. His father was making the point that this should never change.

Laith stepped back inside his grandparents' cabin. He checked the kitchen counter and the cupboards first. They were bare, apart from the cutlery and china that had been there before. Laith had known that his father would have already taken care of the food. He glanced around the living room and could not see that anything had been left behind. He went back into the room in which he had slept – empty. His father's room was also empty. He quickly opened the back door and saw that the light was already off, and he could hear that the generator was off anyway. He had a quick peek in the room that his uncle and Esmy had slept in. He wasn't sure if they would have wanted him to, but nor did he think it nice to ignore their room whilst checking everywhere else, so he split the difference by looking inside, but not concentrating too hard. A good compromise. He knew inside him that there was a reason that he volunteered to come back inside here, and why he was taking his time checking that everything was in order. There was a part of him that didn't want to lose the connection that he had with the cabin – it was his link to his grandparents and his mother. She had grown up here, and he imagined all of the fun times he must have had here with her when he was a baby. Surely they would have come to visit often, when times were better. Being inside alone, he felt tinged with a hint of sadness. He knew, though, that his father would have finished loading Acira by now and would be getting impatient. They did have to leave and try to get home as soon as possible. Laith looked over at the shelf where he had left his wooden monkey and his sister's worm. It wasn't really stealing, considering the toys technically do belong to him and his sister, he thought. It would be a nice connection to have – something that he could look at to remember his mother. But was it disrespectful to take them from the place where they belonged? Would it be better to leave them in the past? He didn't want to leave his mother and grandparents in the past – don't be ridiculous. He wanted to remember them. Looking at the toys made him feel sad, but he thought that maybe he needed them to feel some kind of connection with his mother – the one that he had been missing all his life. His sister would surely appreciate it too. They had spoken about it in the past – about how they don't really remember their mother and found it hard to feel much. Maybe this was what they needed. But what would his father think?

"Laith, hurry up", he heard his father shout from outside.

Laith picked up the toys hurriedly and placed them in his pouch. He took one last look around the cabin, knowing that he would probably never see it again, and whispered a quiet goodbye to his mother as he stepped out of the front door and closed it behind him.

Chapter 25 - Kabili

"Come on", Kabili said to his son. "We need to go". He thought that he had already explained the importance of leaving quickly, but obviously his son had better ideas as he ambled to join the rest of them. Kabili watched him as he went to stand by Esmy's side. He knew the reason, but this would have to take a back seat for now.

"We need to try and get to where we stayed last night by tonight", he told everybody. "Then, from there, we can go home in the morning. That's the best that we can really do". Kabili knew that the situation wasn't ideal, but it was the best that he could do. He was responsible for leading the team and he had to act in everybody's best interests. Given the time of day it was now, they would not be able to make it all the way home safely, particularly with Cahya. It would be nearly impossible for him and his two children to do the whole journey in one day, even with how fit they were. For Cahya, it would be impossible without a doubt. They would bypass the square and the settlement – it was quicker to follow the river south from here. Kabili looked back on what he had achieved so far – more than anybody could reasonably expect, given the circumstances. But, if he didn't finish the job now, it would all have been in vain. Nobody remembers efforts.

"We need to follow the river', he told everybody. He knew that his judgement was trusted, and today he had proven why. As he led the group towards the river, he thought about the day's successes so far. Firstly, thinking on his feet and adapting the plan was an excellent thing to do. He was the one who had been seen, he remembered with a pang in his stomach, and therefore he was the reason that they had to adapt the plan. But being seen was always going to be a risk. He had done everything that he could have with the information available – he had waited a sensible amount of time hidden in the bushes to see if any guards were coming. He had only stepped out once everybody was satisfied that the coast was clear, so it was just bad luck that he was the one who had been seen. He shouldn't be too hard on himself for this. And, in any case, once it had happened, he made sure that he thought on his feet and still came out on top. Actually, he thought, maybe it did work out for the best that he was seen. If he had not been seen, they would have come back at night. There might have been just as many guards at night and, if they had been seen then, they would have lost the advantage of Sarama. She was only able to perform as well as she did because she had the daylight to guide her. Maybe the guards could have used the cover of night more effectively. After all, they knew the compound like the back of their hand. It was Kabili and his children who needed the light, so maybe it was a good thing that he had been seen. Looking at Sarama's archery compared to the guards firing from the window, it was a good thing that they had had to go in the daytime. Sarama didn't miss a single shot. All those training sessions really had paid off, he thought. Maybe now was the time to allow himself to well up with a little bit of pride.

Kabili looked back towards his daughter who, as usual, had Acira's rope. They were close to the riverbanks now, but it didn't look like Acira really wanted any water. She had just had some. Behind Sarama and Acira, Kabili saw Laith and Esmy. They were holding hands. This was going to turn into a problem – he knew it. But he reminded himself that now was not the time.

Kabili knew that he should really be concentrating on what needs to happen now, in the immediate future. Laith and Esmy could wait, and there was no real need to keep on reviewing what happened earlier. That could wait too. What he needed to do right now was to make sure that he kept the flower safe and alive until they could get home and plant it. He looked in his side pouch and just stared at the

flower for a moment.   He could not believe he had it.
Twenty years.   For twenty years, his community had been
slowly dying because they did not have the flower that he
was looking at now.   Today, he had saved them.   Was
there any way that he could get it home today?   Not with
Cahya. Even without Cahya it would be difficult. With him,
it was out of the question. Or maybe he could leave Cahya
and the rest of the group at the old settlement, and then he
could continue alone through the night. This would be very
difficult but, if anybody could do it, he could. No, he thought
– that was too much of a risk. He shouldn't be going alone
– he could easily be ambushed. As much as he wanted to
believe that he could do it by himself, he could not risk
losing the flower by trying to be the hero. The reason why
they succeeded is because they worked well as a team.
His children had backed him up inside the compound and,
even though he would like to think he could do everything
by himself, he probably had to accept that he could not.
This time tomorrow, however, his community would rejoice.

Chapter 26 - Laith

Laith was walking along the riverbank enjoying the sound of the water gently trickling along. Despite the rocks in its way and the long journey it would have to take, the water would inevitably, certainly and without question, find the sea that it belonged to. The water in the river and the water in the sea were one and the same, and it was only a matter of time before they found each other.

The sun was getting lower in the sky, but the shadows that it was creating were not yet long enough to tickle the happily trickling water. A gentle breeze was blowing Laith's hair – it was the perfect accompaniment to the temperate weather. Birds were singing sweetly in the distance and Laith was holding the hand of the girl he had been in love with his whole life – the girl that was more lovely than the day itself. He squeezed her hand just a little bit tighter, making sure that it was real. He could finally do this knowing that she wanted it too. She looked up at him and he looked deep into her eyes. He felt his happiness resonate in hers. Every moment, his heart expanded and he could not explain it. Esmy was the perfect girl. She completed him.

Esmy had just finished quizzing Laith about the day's events. It was only once Esmy had begun questioning him that Laith realised that he did not remember much about what had actually happened – his mind had obviously been elsewhere. And it would probably be of no surprise to Esmy to find out where. Despite this, Laith wanted to give Esmy every last detail that he could remember. She had not been allowed to go, but Laith wanted her to feel that she was there with them. She had been there with him. Since she told him that she loved him, she was never going to leave his heart no matter how much physical distance was between them. She had, in an instant, become a part of him.

"So it sounds like it's a good job that Sarama was there then", Esmy told Laith.

"What?" Sarama had turned around at the mention of her name and was curious to know the context in which it was used. Her voice was toneless.

"Laith was telling me about your heroics at the compound", Esmy told Sarama, smiling. "It's a good job you were there".

"Oh", said Sarama. "Yeah, I suppose so, actually". Laith thought that her response was quite flat, all things considered. It sounded like Sarama might still need a little bit of time to process what had happened.

Laith felt Esmy squeeze his hand. It was tighter than usual, and Laith immediately knew what she was thinking. He hadn't really thought about it himself until now but, if Sarama wasn't covering him with her arrows, the outcome would probably have been a lot different. He didn't feel it at the time but he realised now, in retrospect, that he probably should have been scared. Now, though, he was out and safe and, with Esmy's hand in his, there was no prospect of any negative emotion at all. He was bursting with joy. He squeezed her hand back – they were together and that's all that mattered.

Laith saw his father turn around and look at them again, and he felt Esmy's grip loosen ever so slightly. Again, he knew exactly what she was thinking just by the squeeze of her hand. Maybe it was time that they spoke about it. He intentionally slowed down slightly until his sister was out of earshot so that he and Esmy could speak freely.

"Do you think we will end up together?", Laith asked Esmy. "I mean – do you think we will be together for the rest of our lives?". She hesitated. Her hesitation pierced his heart like a dagger. They both knew what they hoped the answer would be, but Esmy's hesitation forced Laith to confront the reality that he did not want to.

"I don't know", she replied. "I hope so. I really, really hope so. But..." She looked up towards her grandfather and Laith's father. Laith always knew that this was an obstacle. Esmy was engaged and they were from two different tribes. Neither his father nor Esmy's grandfather would be happy with their relationship. "Do you?", she asked him.

Laith thought about all of the things that were standing in their way – and there were a lot of them, and he answered in the only way that he could – honestly.

"Yeah", he said. He was certain. He knew beyond a shadow of a doubt that they would end up together. He felt Esmy's heart lift when she heard his affirmation.

"But how can you say that? How do you know?", she asked with a hint of pleading in her voice. Laith wanted to be with Esmy more than anything in the world. He didn't think it was possible for anybody to feel as much love as he did for Esmy, but he heard in her voice and he felt radiating from deep within her core that, somehow, impossibly, she loved him as much as he loved her. And this was how he knew they would end up together. The water always found its way to the sea. The water in the river and the water in the sea were one and the same – nothing could keep them apart.

"Because I love you. I can't even put into words how much I love you. The feeling is too strong".

"You don't need to put it into words, because I feel it too".

Laith's heart was already filled with love. It was bursting. It was impossible for it to fill any more but, nevertheless, on hearing these words from Esmy, it happened. A lot of impossible things had been happening. Esmy loving him back was impossible. Esmy being able to feel as much love for him as he did for her was impossible. His heart having the capacity to hold any more love than it had five minutes ago was impossible. But all of these impossible things had happened. It was impossible that both his father and Esmy's grandfather would allow the two of them to be together, but Laith knew that it would happen. The river always finds the sea.

"We will definitely end up together. If you feel a fraction

of what I feel, we will definitely end up together. There is no way that two people can love each other this much and not end up together", he told her. He knew it to be true.

"I want to be with you", she told him. "I only want to be with you. I love you".

"I love you, too".

Laith saw Esmy look up again at the two elders. They both knew that this was the last obstacle in their way. Her grandfather would need to allow her not only to break off her engagement, but then to marry somebody from a different tribe. As far as Laith was concerned, this was the only thing left to overcome. He knew his own father would never be convinced, but he loved Esmy too much to care. He could never ask Esmy, however, to betray the feelings of her grandfather. He was the only family that she had left and she needed him more than she knew. Laith did not know how her grandfather would come around to their way of thinking. What could he say to him? How could he convince him? Maybe once he saw how much they loved each other, he would come around. He was a reasonable man, and Laith knew that he cared for both of them. Surely he would come around. The water in the river shapes the rocks as it flows effortlessly around them, never faltering in its conviction.

Chapter 27 - Esmeralda

Esmeralda would be lying if she said that Laith's unerring confidence had not given her a boost. Last night was the most wonderful thing that she could have hoped for. Ever since she admitted her feelings to herself after that first magical night under the stars, she had wished for nothing more than for Laith to feel the same way. She told herself that, if Laith felt the same way, she would do anything to be with him forever. It was easier to think that when it was purely hypothetical. She confided in the Moon and the stars and they had responded last night. They had given her everything that she wanted. The stars burst last night when she was lying under them with Laith and he told her that he loved her. Last night, she had not slept under her blankets. She had been up there in the sky, her soul woven within the fabric of the Universe and her beating heart intertwined with the pulsating stars – the feeling that had been missing her whole life. When she had awoken, though, she was forced to confront reality. On seeing her uncle and her grandad, she had to face the inevitable truth that she did not even want to formulate coherently in her mind – the obstacles that both she and Laith knew to be true, and the ones that led to the conclusion that she could not bear to think about.

The rest of the group had gone in the morning to cross the border to, at the time, formulate a plan. She had been left alone at the kitchen table drowning in her own thoughts. It was horrible. Laith had had the distraction of the mission and of the people around him. Esmeralda had nothing but her thoughts. She had spent the whole morning doing nothing but replaying the same two things in her head. When she thought about how much she loved Laith and how lucky she was that he loved her back, her heart filled with more joy than all the stars in the sky could bring.

When she thought about the reality, her heart dropped. It did this all morning. Being alone and focused on her thoughts, however, did give Esmeralda the opportunity to ascertain the two things that she was absolutely certain of: that she and Laith would be together forever; and that their time together would inevitably have to come to an end.

Hearing Laith's confidence now lifted Esmeralda. He had not said anything practical. He had no suggestions or offered any logical reasoning as to how they would end up together. But he knew that they would. He was certain. He knew it in his heart, and his heart was Esmeralda's. It gave her hope.

"My grandad won't be happy", she offered. She wanted to highlight the things that she had been feeling bad about earlier so that Laith could make her feel better about every single one of them.

"No, he won't. But he will come around", Laith replied. He sounded confident.

"But how do you know?"

"He will. I just know".

"Your dad won't".

"No, he probably won't. Well not by choice. But he doesn't have a choice".

"I don't want your dad to be angry at me – he already hates me".

"He doesn't hate you. And he won't be angry at you. He might me angry at me, to start with. But then once he sees how perfect we are together, and how happy we are together, he will have to come around. He won't have a choice, anyway. I'm not going to let you go now. I wouldn't be able to handle it. There is no way that I could live without you now".

Esmeralda didn't want to let Laith go either. Laith's conviction made her more resolute that this would work out. But unlike Laith, for whom blind optimism sufficed, Esmeralda needed a plan. She needed something concrete that would show her that this would work out. She

256

had been drowning in her thoughts all day whilst Laith was out experiencing what happens when everything luckily falls into place. Or was it fate? She hoped it was fate. Either way, her heart couldn't take waiting to see what would happen. It had been up and down all day. She needed to make sure.

"What would Sarama think?", she said quietly to Laith. His sister was already out of earshot, but she didn't want to risk her ears perking up at the sound of her own name.

"Sarama would one-hundred-percent be on our side. One hundred percent". Laith was certain. He knew his sister well. Once Laith answered, Esmeralda knew that she should really have predicted this herself. All the emotions from earlier had clouded her thinking. She got on with Sarama, and she knew how important Laith and Sarama were to one another. Sarama would always put her brother's happiness first. Always. And her being on their side would definitely help when it came to Laith's father. Esmeralda always got the impression that Uncle Kabili found it more difficult to say no to Sarama than he did to Laith.

"That's good. Sarama will support us. Maybe you should speak to her first, before your dad. Then she could help you speak to your dad?". Even the suggestion made Esmeralda nervous. Her thoughts were manifesting into reality. What if it didn't work? She didn't want to think about it. This was becoming too real too quickly. She wanted to be back amongst the stars.

"Yeah I will speak to her first. She will be happy, though. I know", replied Laith. "Oh", he said, grabbing the outside of his pouch. "I've actually got something for her, too". He said this quietly and Esmeralda noticed that his eyes seemed to flicker upwards towards his father as opposed to his sister. She wondered what it was. She watched as he put his hand in his pouch and fumbled around a little bit. She could see that there was something large in there, but it looked as though Laith was feeling around it. His hand emerged and he was holding a little wooden toy worm – the one that had belonged to his sister when she was younger.

257

She had not even thought that that is what it would be but, on seeing it, she thought it was a lovely idea. Typical of Laith.

"That's really sweet", she said, squeezing his hand a little tighter. She wanted to show him all the love she had in her heart for him. "She will love that – it will be a nice memory for her of the past". She had nearly said 'of your mum', but she didn't want to upset Laith. She was quick enough to change it fluidly mid-sentence. Esmeralda then realised what the larger bulge must be.

"Is that your monkey?", she asked, pointing to the bulge in his pouch with her eyes.

"The wooden one, yeah", Laith said, smiling. Idiot. Esmeralda smiled back. She was happy that Laith had picked it up. It was a memory for him of his mother and grandparents – one that he deserved to have. She regretted not having any of her own.

Laith put Sarama's toy worm back into his pouch.

"I'll give her that later", he said. "Oh", he continued, sounding a little bit surprised as he pulled something else out of his pouch. "This is your grandad's. I forgot to give it him back". Laith handed Esmeralda a vial of blue liquid. She could faintly see the golden-black energy emanating from the flask, slightly distorting the aura around it. But she knew that, to Laith, it would just look like blue liquid. She immediately knew what it was, having been educated by her grandad about all of the different potions and energies growing up. She was a bit surprised that Laith had the vial. Her grandad was very protective of his potions. He didn't trust anybody with them. 'It's too dangerous', he would always tell Esmeralda. That was why he placed a heavy emphasis on educating her in their proper use – dosage based on factors such as age, body weight, gender and energy. It was too hard for others to make an accurate judgement, he had always told her, as they couldn't feel what he could and what he was developing within her. He was a very kind and gentle man who always looked for the best in everybody, but this was something he was always very strict with. He did not trust anybody with his potions.

And that was why Esmeralda was shocked that Laith had the vial. And she was even more shocked that her grandad had not yet taken it back off him.

"He gave that to you?", she asked him, failing to hide her surprise.

"Yeah", said Laith nonchalantly. He had no idea of the significance of this. Esmeralda's grandad must hold Laith in very high esteem if he trusted him with something as precious as his potions. Esmeralda's heart had never been so happy whilst thinking about reality. There was hope - very real hope - that her grandad would be happy for Esmeralda to spend the rest of her life with Laith.

Chapter 28 - Sarama

Sarama had been replaying the day's events in her head. She had been so close to losing her brother and it was only down to pure luck that she had not. Well, she was lucky that he managed to handle the two guards without her, but he shouldn't have had to. It could have been a lot different. She kept replaying the moment when she thought that she had lost him, but he somehow managed to manoeuvre the guards into a position from which he could win. She knew in her mind that he was a good fighter, but she never dreamed that he would have been able to do something like that. It was as though he had something guiding him, the way that he had done it so fluidly and seemingly without thinking. He definitely had something special pushing him at the time. But this only made her feel worse – she should have been the one covering him. She was the one who was supposed to make sure that the guards didn't get close enough in the first place. She was the best archer around and so it was her responsibility. The fact that she had come so close to losing her brother made her want to identify what it was that she had done wrong. She was looking to blame herself for something. She needed to reprimand herself – it would make her feel better. She tried to tell herself that she did not load her arrows quick enough, but she knew that was not true. She had been so fluid in her movements – no hesitation or fumbling at all. She had even been quicker than when she trained in a no pressure environment. She was actually quite proud of how well she had done in that aspect, which somehow made her feel worse. She knew that her decision-making was perfect too. She tried to reprimand herself by telling herself that she had gone for the wrong guards in the wrong order, but again she knew that this was not true at all. From her position, she did exactly the right thing. She didn't have the ability to curve arrows – she could only go for guards in sight. Then maybe her positioning had been wrong. Again, she knew this to be untrue. She had been in the perfect position to take out the guards without being too vulnerable herself. So how could she have come so close to losing her brother when she did everything right? If it happened once, it could happen again. She needed to have done something wrong – something that she could improve on to make sure that this never happened again. But she couldn't think of anything. She had done everything perfectly and, still, she could have lost her brother. She even, clutching at straws, tried to blame Laith in her mind. He had run at the guards – how stupid of him. But she knew that he had also done the right thing. He had to ensure that the guards didn't get close to his father – the sole purpose of the mission was to get the flower. No matter how hard Sarama racked her brains, neither she nor her brother had done anything wrong. They had not made a single mistake. Yet she was so close to losing him. It was scary that they could both do everything that they were supposed to and she could still have lost him. She just had to concentrate on the fact that they had managed to escape with their lives in tact and, as a bonus, with the flower that they went to get.

Sarama looked up and noticed that she was at a part of the river that she recognised from yesterday. The group had taken a short cut on the way back. They needed to escape fast and there was no reason to go through the settlement or past the garden. But now they had reached a part of the river that they had already walked along. It was slightly comforting to Sarama to be somewhere that she recognised, and she tried to focus on this as opposed to what had happened in the morning. Laith and Esmy had dropped off quite far behind her. She too had intentionally dropped off quite far behind her father and uncle at the front. She wanted to be alone with just Acira at the moment. She didn't fancy any human interaction.

Sarama noticed that her father and uncle had stopped. She did not really want to catch up to them, but it looked like they were planning on waiting there for her. She did not want to confront anything else in her mind about what had happened inside the compound – she just needed to concentrate on being grateful that her brother had not had to pay with his life. Sarama slowed down in the hope that the elders would continue, but it became apparent that they were in fact waiting. She stopped and turned around to face Laith and Esmy. She would wait for them to catch up and then they could walk together. She noticed that Laith smiled at her when he saw her turn around – this wasn't like him. He must have sensed that something was wrong with her. Normally, smiling came naturally to Sarama, but she couldn't bring herself to force one out in response to Laith. This must be how he felt when he was in one of his silent moods – she could finally relate, and all it took was for her brother to nearly die.

"Hi", he said to her, when he caught up. Again, this was not like him. He, more often than not, considered his mere presence greeting enough.

"Hi", she replied. She forced out a smile, but it was surely not enough to fool her brother.

"What's wrong?", he asked her. Obviously.

"Nothing. Don't worry".

"You still upset about what happened earlier? Don't worry – we've got it and we are out and safe". He smiled at her and, for the first time in his life, it seemed natural. He meant the smile. This was nearly shocking enough to snap Sarama out of her own negativity. Nearly. "Oh I've got a surprise for you, by the way", he continued. This helped too.

"Ooh, what is it?", she asked

"Surprise", he reiterated. He clearly didn't want to give anything away just yet.

"Do you know?", Sarama asked Esmy. She smiled and said nothing. "What is it?"

"A surprise", Esmy confirmed, nodding seriously.

"You two are so annoying", Sarama told them. They were. But at least they got her out of her bad mood, for now.

The four of them caught up to the two elders. Sarama felt

her mood dropping again. She did not want to relive the morning again. 'I wonder what Laith got me?' she forced herself to think.

"Is everybody ready to eat?", Sarama's father said. "We should probably cook here – we don't really want to be lighting a fire when it gets dark and we are at our settlement. That would be asking for trouble". Sarama was glad that his question was rhetorical so that the responsibility of answering, as always, did not fall upon her. She didn't want to risk her tone of voice betraying her true emotions. Unfortunately for her, her father looked at her first when he posed the statement – he was used to her being the spokesperson of, previously, herself and Laith and, now, everybody in the group. "Well, it doesn't look like anybody is coming anyway. If they were, they would have come by now. But it's better just to be safe", he continued. Sarama realised that he had misread her facial expression as fear, but she was fine with this. She just hoped that he didn't try to speak to her to try to allay her fears – she was not in the mood to speak about it.

Sarama distanced herself slightly from the rest of the group as the two elders set up the fire and began preparing the food. She left Laith and Esmy alone – they seemed happy in each other's company – and she walked downriver in the pretence that the bank had easier access there for Acira to drink from the river. Normally, her father would have told her that it was quicker or easier to do it a different way, but today Sarama was glad that he left her to the space she wanted. Acira stopped drinking long before Sarama was ready to rejoin the group, but she seemed happy to let Sarama stroke her until she really had to go back to the group and eat.

Sarama's father put Acira's food in her bucket first and offered it to her. Once Acira began to eat happily, Sarama's father, with the aid of Laith, put food in for everybody and handed it around.

"We should probably eat quite quickly so that we can leave. We will get back to the old settlement just when it is getting dark. We can rest and then we should try and leave quite early". Again, he looked at Sarama first seemingly for confirmation. Sarama nodded in acknowledgement and he looked away. She just needed to sleep, she thought. Her mood was one of those things that would be better in the morning.

She noticed that Laith had taken his food over to a particularly comfortable looking rock that he could sit on whilst eating. Esmy sat on the floor next to him. Significantly, Sarama realised, the rock that Laith had claimed as his own seemed to be big enough for a brother and sister to sit on together. She knew that Esmy liked to sit on the floor, although this was something that she never understood. Sarama took her food and went to join Laith and Esmy.

"Move", she told Laith. She was grateful for the fact that Laith never expected her to be polite with him at the best of times, and so she didn't have to force it now when she was not in the mood. Laith shuffled over as he was told, and Sarama joined him.

"I will never understand how you two think sitting on a cold, hard rock is more comfortable than sitting on the lovely, welcoming ground", Esmy said to them both, smiling.

"Less bending", Laith offered.

"Yeah – less bending. Good one", Sarama confirmed. Esmy laughed.

"Anyway, we better hurry up and eat so that we can go. And so that I can give you your present when we get to the old settlement", Laith said to Sarama. "You better like it".

"Well it better not be rubbish then", Sarama told him, despite knowing that she would definitely like it whatever it was. It was a cliché, but it really was the thought that counted with this one. Knowing that Laith thought of her was enough to lift her mood slightly.

Sarama finished eating at the same time as Laith and Esmy, and took their plates off them.

"Wow, what's wrong with you?", Laith asked her

sarcastically.

"Shut up – I always do everything for you", she told him.

She took the plates to the river and washed them quickly. She put them in one of Acira's bags as her father went to the river to wash her bucket as well as his and Uncle Cahya's plates. Uncle Cahya put out the fire and the group was soon ready to leave.

There was definitely more of a chill in the air as Sarama followed the two elders to the old settlement, maintaining a safe distance with Acira so as to avoid being spoken to. As usual, Laith and Esmy had dropped off too. The sun was beginning to set and Sarama began to realise how exhausted she was. She was looking forward to going to sleep. Tomorrow couldn't come quickly enough.

The old settlement came into view. It was funny how this had a slightly homely feel now to Sarama despite only spending one night here. She was glad to see it, if only for the fact that she would soon be able to sit in her room, away from everybody but Laith. She wondered what it was, actually, that Laith got her. She would find out soon – that was something else to be happy about.

The elders stopped in between the two cabins just as it was beginning to get dark.

"We timed that perfectly, didn't we?", Sarama's father announced, as she arrived with Acira. "We just need to get inside quickly now, really", he said. "Try to sleep early so that we can leave early in the morning. The sooner we get home, the better". Sarama silently began to unload Acira, ready to take some of the things inside the cabin. It felt more like hers, now. As she was about to make her way towards the cabin, Laith and Esmy finally caught up to the group. Sarama noticed that they were holding hands, as they sometimes did, but let go as her father looked up.

"Laith, come on, hurry up", he said to Laith. Sarama noticed that his tone of voice seemed slightly angry, not that he had any reason to be. Laith, however, remained unperturbed, not that he had any reason to be. "We need to get inside quickly and go to sleep early today. We don't want to get caught, and we need to get home as soon as possible so we need to hurry up". It was clear that he was trying to pacify himself but Sarama could not understand why. Laith had done everything right at the compound.

Sarama watched as both Laith and Esmy walked towards Acira and began to offload things from her. Esmy whispered something to Laith that Sarama could not hear. Laith responded by shaking his head – he clearly disagreed with whatever Esmy had to say. He grabbed her hand and then let go as he picked up some bags and joined Sarama. Sarama waited for her brother to catch up to her and then they walked into the cabin together. They both headed for the room in which they had slept in previously, and Sarama closed the door behind them.

"What's Dad so grumpy about?", she asked Laith. Laith let out an ironic chuckle. Did he know something that Sarama didn't?

"Do you know?", she asked him.

"I've got an idea", Laith responded, with a wry smile. Sarama waited for him to elaborate, but he did not do so. She raised her eyebrows to prompt him.

"Well? Care to share?", she asked, and then pursed her lips. He still seemed reluctant, as thought he was nervous. He was never nervous around her.

"Well…", Laith started, "…and I don't know this for sure…but I've just got a feeling that maybe he thinks that there is something going on between me and Esmy".

"Oh for crying out loud, why would he think that? You two have always been close", Sarama said. She waited for a response from her brother but, again, none was forthcoming. She looked at him and saw that he was looking directly at her, waiting. Sarama was confused, but only for a split-second, before it dawned on her.

"Oh? Oh, really?", she asked. This time it was his turn to purse his lips, as he nodded at her slightly without breaking eye-contact.

"I bloody knew it", she said, in a somewhat aggressive

266

whisper. She wanted to convey her level of bloody-knowingness, but wasn't stupid enough to say it loud enough to attract the attention of her father who could easily be in earshot. She realised that this response of hers may have been a knee-jerk reaction to actually being caught by surprise. She genuinely had no idea, but she couldn't admit this to her brother. Growing up, Laith and Esmy had always been close. Although the way that they behaved would have indicated a possible romantic relationship between any other two people, it didn't seem that way when it came to her brother and Esmy. Other people might consider them to be weirdly close for two people not in a romantic relationship, but Sarama had never seen it that way. They were just suited perfectly for one another. Sarama had known how close they were, so this should count as knowing that there was more going on between them, she told herself. She therefore had no moral obligation to retract her comment and tell Laith that, actually, she didn't bloody know it. On some level she knew. In a way.

Laith still remained silent. Now it seemed as though he was waiting for her to elaborate. What did he want to know? Oh – probably her thoughts about it. That's why he was nervous. Oh no – Sarama's excitement subsided and she realised what the blindingly obvious issue was that Laith was clearly nervous about – the tribe thing. Esmy's tribe and their own tribe did not marry one another. Ever. No wonder their father was in a bit of a mood.

"You know I'm one-hundred-percent backing you, yeah?", Sarama told her brother. She saw that he smiled.

"Yeah, I knew you would. I told Esmy you would be"

"Does Esmy know?", Sarama asked, surprised, before immediately realising it was a stupid question. "Oh, yeah, obviously she does", she laughed. She could blame her shock and joy for not thinking straight. Well, she was in a much better mood now than she had been earlier.

"How are you gonna tell Dad?", she asked him.

"I dunno", he said. The way he said it – it was clearly weighing on him.

"Well I'm backing you anyway", she told him. Her brother and Esmy were perfect for each other, and she would do anything she could to help her brother. She knew that she would have to help Laith argue the case with their dad, and she was more than willing to do so. "I'll help you speak to Dad, if you want". She hoped he didn't want, but suspected he would.

"Thanks", he said. He was smiling – a weight had clearly been lifted from his chest. "I've got something for you", he added. Sarama had forgotten about this mysterious present.

"Oh, a bribe?", she teased.

"I bloody knew you would say that – that's why I'm giving it to you afterwards". She didn't retract her comment – her brother would have known she was only joking. He still had his pouch around him and reached into it. Sarama was excited to see what he had. He pulled out a little wooden toy worm. She immediately recognised it. She hadn't realised how much it meant to her until her brother gave it to her now. She began to well up – it was a link to their past and, more importantly, to their mother. She took it off him and looked at it intently.

"Thank you", she said quietly, overcome with emotion. This was the first time she had ever been polite to him and did not wish for it to become a habit. Once was okay, though. She stared at it, trying to absorb all of its detail. By absorbing its detail, surely she could connect to the past. The light shade of the wood. The patterns in the grain. The colours that the balls were painted. The happy expression of the worm. Nothing. She couldn't remember a thing. It meant the world to her, nevertheless. She noticed that her brother still had something in his pouch.

"Your monkey?", she asked, nodding her head towards his pouch. He nodded as he slowly pulled it out. "You don't remember anything about it?", she asked him.

"I know that you had yours at the garden", he said. "Well, I'm pretty sure that I can remember playing with it with you. But I think I had mine before. I think I can remember, but I'm not sure if this is true – I think I can remember playing with this with Mum". Suddenly Sarama knew why the toys were important enough for Laith to pick up. If his was, in fact, an older toy, he would have played with it with their mum. It was definitely a connection back to her. Maybe hers, too, was older. Maybe her toy, too, contained the memories of a number of special moments shared with her mum. She hoped it did. If his was older, surely hers was too.

Both Sarama and Laith sat on the floor, leaning back on the wall and fully engrossed in their toys. What a sight they must be, she thought – two grown adults in their twenties probably more engrossed in children's toys now than they had been when they were children.

"Thank you", she said to her brother. Twice was fine.

Chapter 29 - Cahya

Cahya was waiting patiently in the living room. He knew that tonight was the night. It had been slowly building up for a long time and had accelerated rapidly over the last few days. Tonight was definitely the night.

On arrival at the cabin, Cahya had opened a jar of beams and watched as it had dissipated throughout the room. He probably could have gotten away with not using any tonight – the space still retained some of the energy from the beams that he had used a few days ago, or was it yesterday? It seemed so long ago. So much had happened. Either way, it still retained some of that energy as well as their own living energy from when they were there. It would still be nice to supplement it though, he thought, and make his granddaughter as comfortable as possible, and so he had selected an appropriate jar to open on arrival. They didn't need to be as intense as last time - it wouldn't be long before the room was saturated. He had a few beams that he had collected last spring which were perfect for the occasion. He had been meditating on the golden energy as it poured in all directions from the open jar, seemingly tangible but neither liquid nor gas. He took a moment to focus on his gratitude that he was able to experience this in a manner in which other people could not. He was truly blessed. The energy had slowly been flowing out of the jar and dissipating so that it became one with the room. Its visual intensity diminished, but Cahya could feel it where it mattered.

His granddaughter had not yet joined him, but he was expecting her arrival imminently. It was a shame that they could not light a fire – he was sure that she would have appreciated some tea, as would he. Although Acira was a giveaway that they were here for anybody who came close, they didn't particularly want to send a beacon to their location that could be seen from afar. Esmeralda would have to manage without tea tonight, unfortunately. She was taking longer than he expected to join her, but he didn't want to pressure her. She would come in her own time, and he knew that he needed to wait for her to be sure. He had been patient thus far – there was no need to start rushing now.

Cahya heard the door of the bedroom his granddaughter was in open. He heard her tentative footsteps approach and then watched out the corner of his eye as she sat down on the floor to his right, cross-legged. She sat in silence, but he knew that she would be able to feel the energy that he had prepared for her. She just needed time for it to soak into her, and Cahya was more than prepared to wait. Truth be told, he also needed the energy, but for a different reason. The mission so far had exhausted him, not that he was willing to admit it to anybody apart from himself. The energy in the room recharged him as well as it could for now, but he knew that he would need to be up at sunrise tomorrow to meditate outside and really feel himself again.

"Are you tired, Grandad?", Esmeralda asked him. She sounded nervous. She clearly needed the innocuous question to test her voice and prepare it for what was coming.

"No", he replied, as apathetically as he could muster. He needed her to know that he had all the time in the world for her. He was not going to rush her. "It's you lot who are the lazy ones, not me", he laughed. A standard comment like that would surely make his granddaughter feel more at ease. She remained silent, however. Maybe he should give her a small and subtle prompt. "Well, mainly you are the lazy one. Laith is normally up and helping me collect beams while you stay asleep".

"Once, he's done that, Grandad. One time. Probably", Esmeralda laughed. Cahya did not want to look at her to make her feel uncomfortable, but he could see clearly from the corner of his eye that her energy began to glow.

"A lot more than once", Cahya laughed. This time he looked at her, and he could feel that she was much more relaxed.

"Maybe twice", she conceded. Cahya laughed. "Laith really likes you, you know?", she said to him. Cahya noticed that his granddaughter's voice was beginning to falter a bit. She was surely building up to it now, trying to butter him up like that, and he didn't want her to lose her confidence. Cahya turned his neck so that his granddaughter could see that he was smiling. If this wasn't an indication that he would not be an obstacle, nothing was. Maybe he should make sure, though.

"I know he does. He's a very nice boy", Cahya replied.

"The thing is, Grandad, is that I really like him too. We really like each other". Esmeralda stopped talking to give Cahya a chance to air his thoughts, but he was not going to interrupt her now. "We like each other a lot". Another pause. Cahya smiled to convey to his granddaughter that it was safe to continue. "And…we really want to be together". The floodgates were now open – his granddaughter began to speak very quickly. The poor thing had been so nervous. "And we know that we really shouldn't because he is from a different tribe, and we know that tradition is important and that you and Uncle Kabili wouldn't be happy about it but we really can't help it – we really really like each other a lot, Grandad, and we really want to be together". She stopped and stared at him. Cahya could see how scared she was, anticipating his reaction. Clearly his smile had not done enough.

"Well, it's about time you realised", he said to her.

"What?", she asked him. He felt that she was more relaxed, and she even let a small, slightly confused, slightly nervous smile appear on her face.

"It's about time that you two realised how you felt about each other", Cahya clarified. "Don't you think I can see how your energy changes when you are around him, and how his changes when he is around you?".

"So, you knew?"

"I knew a long, long time before you did. I was waiting for you two to figure it out".

"Grandad", she said, her relief manifesting as laughter, "I can't believe you knew all this time". Her laughter subsided, and she became slightly more serious. "And you're okay with it?", she asked. She clearly needed the confirmation that she could relax. "You're not upset that he's from a different tribe?".

"I'm not delighted about that part", he admitted. He had to be honest with her. "But I have had a long time to come to terms with it. A very long time. Your happiness is more important to me". His granddaughter's energy became more intense than he had ever seen it – even more than when she was around Laith. It warmed Cahya's heart to see his granddaughter so happy. Her whole life had been filled with loss and she had finally realised what she needed to feel complete.

"But what about Uncle Kabili?", she asked. "He is probably more traditional than you". His granddaughter needed confirmation that everything was going to be okay.

"We are both traditional", Cahya corrected her, possibly more firmly than he had initially intended. He certainly did not want to leave her with the impression that their rich heritage was something to be dismissed at the drop of a hat. Kabili was certainly no more traditional than he was – Cahya knew the importance of what he did and how generations of his tribe had lived, and it was important to him that his granddaughter knew it too. She needed to carry on the traditions after he was gone. But, as important as traditions were, nothing was more important than his granddaughter's happiness. Nothing. He would give his own life for his granddaughter's happiness and so he would certainly make this concession. He did know, however, that Kabili was going to offer more resistance – he had already been doing so - and he did not want to lie to his granddaughter. "But even though we are both traditional", he continued, "you and Laith will come first. Your uncle isn't very happy about it, that's true". His granddaughter had enough sense to have picked up on it. "But he will have to come around. And he will come around. We have been speaking about it, and he isn't happy at the moment, but you just need to give him time to come to terms with it like I have".

"So you weren't happy at first?"

"Well, I wouldn't say I was unhappy. I probably would have preferred it if you did fall in love with somebody from our tribe who knew our ways. But why do you think I have taken Laith out into the fields with me all those times? He is willing to learn our ways too, and respect them. He might not be as natural as me and you and others in our tribe, but he tries his best. He tries harder than some people born into our tribe, and that shows that he will be encouraging of your children to continue with our traditions too. Oh, but how many times was it that he has been out with me? Once? Twice? Surely not enough", he teased her.

"No, you're right, Grandad. I remember now, it was loads more times – at least a million, I think", she laughed, but then abruptly stopped. One last thing was troubling her.

"And I will speak to Darma's parent's too", he told her. "You don't need to worry. I know it is our tradition but your happiness is much more important. And it's not like you two have even really met". He had to reassure his granddaughter about this. And himself. He wasn't happy about this part. He was not comfortable breaking from tradition and he hoped he hadn't given the impression that he was flippant about it – he most certainly was not. But when the Universe provides you with something as special as what his granddaughter had with Laith, you have to listen.

"You should go to bed, Esmeralda", Cahya told her.

"Thank you, Grandad. Thank you so much. I've been so scared. I can't tell you how much this means to me. Grandad, he means so much to me". Her voice began to crack and Cahya felt tears building up in his eyes. He knew how much it meant to her. He knew even before she knew. He hugged his granddaughter and felt the joy radiating from her heart. This was the happiest she had ever been and her happiness flooded his own heart.

274

Chapter 30 - Esmeralda

Esmeralda had tears of joy in her eyes. She couldn't believe how quickly her grandad had accepted that she wanted to be with Laith. He had claimed that he had known for a long time. How could he have known? How could he have seen it coming when Esmeralda herself had not? However he had, Esmeralda was grateful for the fact. It had given him all the time in the world to process it.

She left her grandad before he had a chance to see that she had started crying. She didn't want to start him off too. She left him to his meditation and she went into the bedroom at the back. She hid herself away but now for a different reason. She could not believe her luck – not only had her grandad proved to be no obstacle at all, he also was going to help them. She would never in a million years have guessed that her grandad would facilitate her being with somebody from a different tribe. Surely Uncle Kabili would now come around. Esmeralda knew that Uncle Kabili was the man in the community that everybody respected the most. She also knew that her grandad was the man that Uncle Kabili respected the most. He was the perfect ally.

Esmeralda wondered if Laith had told Sarama yet. He must have done. It was such a long time ago that they had arrived and gone into their cabin. Esmeralda had taken a long time to build up the courage to speak to her grandad. Laith surely had not needed as much time to speak to Sarama. They could tell Uncle Kabili when they got back home – when her grandad could speak to him.

Esmeralda was listening out for her grandad to go to bed. She wanted to do one last thing, but she did not want to pass her grandad in the living room. She knew that she would not be able to control her emotions if she saw him – she would surely burst into tears and embarrass both of them. She was so happy at the moment that she could barely believe what was happening. She heard some shuffling coming from the living room – it sounded like her grandad was getting up. She heard him walk gently to the back of the cabin, to the bedroom opposite hers.

"Goodnight, Esmeralda", he called from outside her room.
"Goodnight, Grandad".
"I love you"
"I love you too, Grandad".

She listened as the door to his bedroom creaked open and then firmly shut. She waited a few moments to make sure that he had settled in for the night and then slowly opened her own bedroom door – she didn't want to disturb him. She crept slowly towards the front door and opened it as carefully as possible. She stepped outside and took a deep breath. She looked up at the stars and realised that, however close she felt to them in the past, she never felt closer to them than she did right now. They shone within her. The Moon no longer provoked hauntingly beautiful feelings of longing – it resided within her.

She looked across at the other cabin. Laith was in there and he must have already spoken to his sister. Esmeralda half wanted to go and share the good news with him – that she had spoken to her grandad and all of their worries had disappeared. Everything was going to work out, exactly like he had known all along. She felt a little flutter in her heart, as she often did when she thought about him – he had known all along. He had faith that the Universe would find a way, and it had. She couldn't wait to tell him about how supportive her grandad had been, and how fond he is of Laith. She wanted to tell him that her grandad had known all along and had been intentionally training Laith up – this was so funny. She could not believe her grandad had been doing this right under their noses. Both she and Laith were completely oblivious. She had so much to share with him, but she knew that it would have to wait until morning.

Uncle Kabili wouldn't be happy with her turning up at this time – she would wait for her grandad to speak to him. Esmeralda hoped that Laith would come out of his own accord so that she could speak to him, but she knew that he would not. He must be in bed by now, as instructed by Uncle Kabili. But it didn't matter, because he was also in her heart. She looked back up at the stars and meditated on every ounce of magic that was soaking into her. For the first time in her life, Esmeralda was complete.

Chapter 32 - Cahya

Cahya woke up before the sunrise. He knew that the group would be leaving early today – it was only a matter of time before Kabili would be waking his children up, making breakfast and getting ready to leave. Cahya wanted to make sure that he was up even earlier than this so that he could watch the sunrise and recharge himself. The Sun would be coming up very soon, but the energy at the moment seemed slightly different to his expectations at this time of day. It was not as crisp or pure – he couldn't quite put his finger on it. That would surely change, anyway, when the Sun did start to rise, which would be any moment now.

Cahya stretched out on the blankets on the floor and then slowly sat up. Getting up was becoming harder and harder – he was looking forward to tonight when he would be back in his own bed recovering from this mission. He knew that it was an important thing that they had done, but he was definitely glad that it was over and he would soon be able to go back to his more sedentary lifestyle. He slowly got to his feet and peered at the sky through the small window in his room. It was beginning to get lighter. He opened his bedroom door carefully so as not to make a din and looked at his granddaughter's door opposite him. It was still firmly shut, of course. She must have slept soundly last night. His heart glowed thinking about how she was finally happy after all these years. He was glad that she had finally realised what she was missing.

Cahya crept slowly towards the front door, careful not to wake his granddaughter. He opened the front door and looked out on the bare fields in front of him. They wouldn't have to be bare for much longer, he thought. He always tried to remain as humble as possible but, thinking about what they had managed to achieve for the community, a feeling that was definitely akin to pride started to rear inside him. He wasn't feeling egotistical – he knew that he had played a very small part in what the group had achieved – but as he pictured how different these fields could look soon with the magic of the red flower at their disposal, he felt proud that his community had managed to overcome such turbulent times. Twenty long and difficult years had finally come to an end. No longer would the community have to move on when fields quickly became barren. The droplets of dew that coated the bare ground would soon be sprinkled atop an abundance of crops, their magic glistening in the sunlight. Maybe, now that they had the resources, the community would grow larger and larger. By the time Esmeralda's children had grown up, the community could well have spread out to all of the old settlements that they themselves had been squeezing a living from for the last twenty years. In twenty years time, there was every chance that his great-grandchildren would be running around amongst tall stalks of wheat in the now-barren field that he was looking out upon. They would be able to experience the joy that he had had when he was a child – the joy that his own granddaughter had had stolen from her. He realised that it wasn't pride that he could feel inside – it was happiness. Pure, unbridled, happiness.

On the matter of unbridled, he realised that Acira was not wandering around in the fields in front as she normally was. She must have wandered around the back. Cahya looked up and around but could not see her. She would be around the back – she didn't ever wander very far. Cahya looked around with a bit more conviction and, before he could even process why, his heart instinctively dropped. In the distance, he could make out a man on horseback. He quickly looked left and right and saw that there must have been at least twenty men – and that was without looking behind him and in the areas blocked by the cabins. In all probability, they were surrounded. How had they been found? The men were fast approaching. They had come for the flower. Cahya knew that they were outnumbered.

Cahya ran to the adjacent cabin as fast as he could. How could they get out of this? Kabili, Laith and Sarama were the best warriors around but surely even they could not defeat twenty men alone. Cahya needed to help too – but he had no weapons. There were none spare and, even if there were, Cahya would not stand a chance. But he needed to help in some way. Or they needed a way to escape. But no – they were surrounded. What could they do? His mind was racing as he burst into Kabili's cabin.

"Kabili!", he shouted. "Laith! Sarama! Quick! They've come for the flower! Twenty men at least!".

Cahya's mind was still racing – how could they get out of this? He needed to help – the three of them would not be able to handle it by themselves. They had come for the flower, and there were more than twenty of them. There was no way that they would be able to defeat them and there was surely no escape.

"Kabili!", he shouted again. His friend came bursting through his bedroom door with venom in his eyes. Cahya had never seen such fearsome intensity. In this state, Cahya could see why Kabili was the most feared warrior in the community. There was a loathing in his eyes that Cahya had never seen before, and an energy of loathing so intense that it struck even Cahya. Kabili stood taller than Cahya ever remembered and looked as though he had packed on muscle overnight. Kabili must have known that his back was against the wall and it brought out all the spirit that he had inside. His aura was at least twenty years younger than his actual age. In this state, Kabili was a man to be feared. He had his shield in his left hand and his sword was already raised. If he was going to go down, he was going to go down fighting with every last ounce of strength and courage that he could muster.

Cahya knew that he had to help in any way that he could – there was no backing down now. There was every chance that his friend would be going down today. He would at least be severely injured. Cahya had ointments that he had taken to the compound in preparation for any injuries that might occur there. They had not been needed then, but they would certainly be needed now. Cahya was no warrior – he was a healer. And now he would be needed more than ever. He needed to be prepared just as Kabili was. He needed to be prepared to go down fighting.

With his mind on his bag of ointments, Cahya looked as Sarama came storming out of her bedroom with her bow and arrow. Her unfaltering conviction was something to be admired. She was certainly her father's daughter. She clearly had no intention of losing this battle. Kabili, who had certainly not brought his children up to be lacking in confidence, was already half out of the front door.

"Let's go!", he shouted behind him. His voice was powerful and confident. It was impossible not to be moved by it. This short, simple, war-cry instilled within Cahya confidence that he had no right to have. He should not be this confident when they were as outnumbered as they were but, with Kabili and his children on their side, this was surely a battle that they could win. One versus one thousand was a motto that Cahya knew his friend lived by. This was a battle that they surely would win.

Cahya followed Kabili out of the door and Sarama came bursting out after them. Cahya noticed a hint of fear in her eyes.

"Where's Laith?" she asked. "He's not in the room".

Kabili had already run out in front of the house and had spotted the men approaching. He positioned himself at the side to prepare himself but then turned around and suddenly sprinted off behind the house. Cahya suspected he knew what Kabili must have seen, but he didn't want to think about it. Sarama and Cahya followed in his footsteps. Standing in Kabili's previous position, Cahya's suspicions were confirmed. He spotted what Kabili had seen that had made him run with such conviction in that direction. Two men were already bearing down on Laith. Cahya could not see the physical object very clearly from the distance that he was at, but the energy emanating from it was clear. It was diminishing – it needed to get into the ground soon - but it was unmistakable nevertheless. In a pouch around his side, Laith had the red flower, and he was defending it with his life.

Questions came flooding through Cahya's mind. Why did Laith have the flower and what was he doing outside? He must have somehow seen the people come from afar and try to go and hide it somewhere near the river before they managed to steal it, but he had been caught. There were already two men on Laith with backup arriving soon. Cahya could do nothing but watch – Laith was too far away. Kabili was running with ferocity towards his son, but Cahya knew that he, too, was too far away. Laith needed to take these two men by himself.

The man on Laith's right swung his sword down towards Laith. Laith, who was excellent with his shield, blocked the strike with a swift upward motion of his shield.
"DAD! MOVE!", Cahya heard Sarama shout. Cahya had never heard Sarama sound so commanding. He did not think it was possible. In fact, the only person who he had ever heard speak with such unwavering authority was Sarama's father. Cahya looked over at Sarama who was poised with her bow and arrow. It was a difficult shot – impossible for anybody but Sarama – but her brother's attackers were in range of her arrows. Kabili would never make it in time, but Sarama's arrow might. Kabili must have realised this, or he was simply swayed by his daughter's conviction, because, for the first time in his life, he allowed somebody else to give him an instruction. Kabili, without hesitation, threw himself to the ground. This was the only thing that he could do to save his son. Cahya watched as Sarama fired her arrow. It was an impossible shot, but there was hope with Sarama. The arrow flew towards Laith and his two attackers. It somehow, miraculously, managed to find its target and pierced the side of the attacker on Laith's left. Cahya saw that Laith still had his shield raised from blocking the first strike. Laith

had blocked it with such force that he had forced his attacker to stumble backwards. Laith had blocked it with such force that he followed through with his own shield and it was still in the air when the wounded attacker saw his opportunity. He raised his own sword and pierced Laith in the chest. He pulled out his sword before he began to reel from his own arrow-wound. Cahya could do nothing but watch as Laith collapsed to the ground.

Cahya heard a door open to his right. His granddaughter must have heard the commotion and had come outside to investigate.

"Esmeralda!", Cahya shouted in her direction. "Get my ointments now!"

"What? What's happening?". She sounded scared and confused.

"Now! Quickly!". His granddaughter clearly sensed the urgency in his voice and turned back into the house to collect Cahya's bag. Kabili pushed himself up from the ground and ran towards his son whilst Esmeralda loaded another arrow. The unwounded enemy regained his balance. He had the chance to finish Laith off – he was defenceless. He moved towards Laith, lying wounded on the floor, and pulled the flower from his bag. He mounted his horse and left Laith lying on the ground. The wounded attacker managed to get onto his own horse and the two of them fled. Cahya saw that Sarama had her arrow aimed at the back of the man who had stabbed her brother. Kabili was too far in front of her to notice. Sarama hesitated and then lowered her arrow, allowing the two men to flee. She ran towards her brother. The other invaders on horseback seemed to turn around and leave too – they had got what they had come for.

Cahya ran towards Laith who was lying, bleeding, on the ground. Cahya just hoped that the sword had missed Laith's heart.

"Laith! Laith! Stay awake, Laith", Kabili was saying, kneeling down by Laith's left. As Cahya approached, Kabili got up and moved around to join his daughter on his son's right, giving Cahya room. Cahya was the best chance he had of saving his son, and Kabili knew it. He gave him space. Cahya looked at Laith's wound – it looked serious. Even more significantly, Cahya could sense that Laith's energy was diminishing.

"Laith", Cahya said. Laith looked towards him and looked searchingly into his eyes. Cahya could sense some confusion in Laith's eyes. He seemed to slightly furrow his eyebrows as he tried to look deep into Cahya's eyes. It was as though he didn't recognise him. Cahya's heart broke as he realised that Laith, a boy whom he had brought up as his own son, seemed to struggle to even recognise who he was. Cahya knew that there was no coming back.

Esmeralda came running towards them and saw that Laith was lying on the ground.

"Laith", she cried. She knelt down next to Cahya and put her hand on Laith's torso. For a brief second, Laith's energy brightened. Even in the state that he was in, where he couldn't recognise Cahya, his energy instinctively responded to being in the presence of who clearly was the love of his life. "Grandad – the ointments", she said, thrusting the bag towards him, but Cahya knew that it was too late. The living energy emanating from Laith began to fade. Laith's left hand twitched. He was reaching for Esmeralda's hand and she grabbed it and held it tight. She rested her left hand on Laith's chest and looked up towards Cahya, her eyes filled with tears.

"Grandad...", she pleaded. "The ointments... Grandad...". Cahya shook his head. It was too late. "Grandad..." She begged him. Cahya's heart broke for his granddaughter, but this paled in comparison to what she must be feeling. He felt helpless. Through the tears in his own eyes, he could do nothing but look at his granddaughter as tears streamed down her cheeks. She turned back towards Laith and looked into his eyes. He looked back into hers. Anybody could see the love that they had for each other. Sarama and Kabili remained motionless, sacrificing their last moments with their brother and son so that Esmeralda could have hers.

Cahya could do nothing but look on as his granddaughter and the boy who meant more to her than anything in the world held hands, knowing that this was the end. Tears streamed down Esmeralda's face and Cahya felt Laith's living energy diminish. Laith closed his eyes as his living energy faded into nothing, his hand firmly in Esmeralda's until the very end.

From Laith's body arose something ethereal - not liquid nor gas, not tangible but very real. It somehow managed to be purple and silver at the same time, and it shone with such vivid intensity that Cahya could hardly believe that nobody else reacted. It hovered above Laith's body and seemed to linger for a few moments around Esmeralda before floating upwards towards the sky. As this strange, ethereal cloud got higher up, it began to spread out – its intensity diluted as it spread throughout the Universe, rejoining the Ocean from which it initially came.

Chapter 33 - Kabili

Kabili was left standing, useless, by the side of his only son who had just lost his life in front of his very eyes. He watched his only son sacrifice his life for the sake of a mission that he had arranged. A mission that, he just realised, bore no fruit. His son had died in vain – the red flower that he was defending snatched from his dying body by members of the very community who, twenty years earlier, had forced his wife's death. He had arranged this mission. He had brought his son along. Now his son was dead. Kabili would have to go back to his community and explain to them that his only son had died for the sake of a failed mission. He had not been able to get the flower for them, and their community would soon, too, be finished.

Kabili couldn't move. He couldn't think. He could not accept what had just happened. Why had Laith even been out there by himself? He could have avoided this fate if he had just told his father that they were under attack instead of going out by himself. As soon as Kabili finished this thought, he felt sick. He couldn't blame his son for his own death. His son had died a hero. He sacrificed his life because he believed in doing the right thing for the community. His son had done the right thing in the circumstances, but it had not worked – and he had paid the ultimate price.

His daughter was in shock. She had not moved. She had always been very close with her brother – this was going to be impossible for her to deal with. Kabili wanted to say something to her, but he didn't know what to say. Even if he did, he doubted very much that he would be able to speak at the moment.

Kabili watched his daughter kneel down by her brother's

side and hold his hand. He could hear her struggling to breathe – trying to stem the flow of her tears now that they had started to come.

"Esmy…", she said, her voice breaking. Esmy's gaze remained fixed firmly on Laith. Kabili had known how fond his son and Esmy were of each other – this would be hard for Esmy too. It would be hard for everybody.

Kabili had no idea what to do. He needed to let his daughter and everybody say goodbye to Laith, but he did not want to leave his son's body lying on the ground for too long. He hated not being able to do anything. He had just lost his only son, and there was absolutely nothing he could do about it. Kabili decided that he would give his daughter time to say goodbye to her brother. He walked back alone to the cabin in search of a blanket to wrap his son's body. He noticed the chill of the morning as he walked back to the cabin, his mind still racing. There was no way of bringing his son back. What could he do? What could he have done differently? He had dived out of the way and allowed his daughter to fire her arrow at Laith's killer. Why did he do this? He and his daughter both knew that the arrow would not kill the man immediately. All it did was anger him and make him more determined to exact his revenge. If Kabili had ignored his daughter's instructions, maybe he could have gotten there to help his son. Kabili was supposed to be in charge. Instead of fighting by his son's side, he was lying on the floor watching his son get killed. He should have taken charge. Instead, he would be remembered for being the man who lay in the dirt while his son was murdered in front of his eyes. No. This wasn't true. Even if he had carried on running, he would not have made it in time. Whether the arrow hit its target or not, Laith's killer had a clear shot at him. Why didn't Laith defend himself better, like he had at the compound? He was capable of it then – couldn't he have done it just once more?

Kabili's stomach sank as he realised that his last exchange with his son had not been a pleasant one. The last time he had spoken to his son, he had spoken to him in an angry tone. And now he was dead. Had his son died angry at him? Kabili could not bring himself to think that this could be true. Surely his son knew how much he loved him. All his life, he had protected him and brought him up to be the best man that he could be. Kabili loved his children more than anything in the world – surely his son would have known this as he lay on the floor dying. Surely he wouldn't have held their last exchange against him – he couldn't have. Laith would have surely known that, even though his tone might have been angry, he was just trying to protect him and everybody else, as he always did. Everything that Kabili had ever done was for the good of his family. Surely his son knew that he meant well. The sinking feeling in Kabili's stomach subsided, but not by much. Surely his son knew that he was just trying to protect him, but maybe he could have spoken in a nicer tone. Now, it was too late to take it back.

Kabili reached the cabin and located Laith's brown blanket. He could not bring himself to accept what he would be using it for. He picked it up, draped it over his shoulder, and began the long walk back to his son. Acira walked towards Kabili. She must have sensed that something was wrong. Her rope was still attached from last night – Sarama must have forgotten to take it off – and so Kabili held it whilst she walked alongside him. He didn't even need to hold it – Acira did not stray from his side as he walked back towards his son.

Kabili stood by his son's body as his daughter embraced Esmy. Tears were flowing down both of their cheeks. Kabili knew that Laith meant a lot to both of them. He knew how much he meant to Esmy. He knelt down by his son's side and placed the blanket on his son's far side. This is where he should have been as his son died – by his side. He should have been with his son as he died. Instead, he had stepped aside to allow Cahya to save him. What good were all of Cahya's potions if he couldn't do anything with them? He sacrificed his last moments with his son for nothing. He shouldn't be thinking this – he knew that Cahya would have tried his best. And Laith meant a lot to Cahya too, as did Cahya to Laith. Kabili's stomach dropped again as he thought this. He cradled his son's head and then lay it down gently as he stood up. He put his hands underneath Laith's shoulders and looked up towards Sarama. His daughter knew to go and lift Laith's legs. Together, they lifted Laith onto the blanket and lay him down gently. Kabili whispered goodbye to his son and wrapped the blanket delicately around him. He gently lifted him and carried him back to the cabin. He wanted nobody to help him. He was his father. In the absence of protecting him as he should have in life, the only thing left that he could do for his son was to care for him in death.

Chapter 34 - Esmeralda

Esmeralda sat alone in the bedroom in which she had spent the previous night feeling as happy as she had ever been – a stark contrast to how she was feeling now. The dark, dingy walls imprisoned her spirit. She was isolated and she wanted to be. For one magical night, everything had been perfect. She had found the thing that had been missing from her life. She had found the thing that had made her complete and she had known that it was forever. Until it had been cruelly torn away from her. Her own heart had been pierced by that sword, and she was left with Laith's. She had his heart, but she no longer had him.

She heard a faint knock on her door but she had no soul to respond. The door opened slowly and her grandad stepped in. Saying nothing, he walked towards her and offered her his hand. She took it and pulled herself up. A sharp pain pierced her heart as she remembered how Laith used to do the same. He would never do it again. Her grandad pulled her towards him and wrapped his arms around her in a tight embrace. She could feel his warmth but it could not penetrate her in the way that Laith's did. She would be cold forever. She put her head on his shoulder and began to sob. She felt her grandad squeeze her tighter but nothing was going to take this pain away. She had lost a part of herself and nothing could ever bring it back.

Esmeralda cried on her grandad's shoulder for what seemed an eternity before pulling away. She felt no better despite her grandad's best intentions, and she never would. She dried the tears from her eyes. Crying had not helped. Nothing would help. She suddenly became aware of the cold, unfamiliarity of her strange surroundings. She needed to go home but she didn't want to return to the place where she had so many memories of Laith. She needed to go and collapse on her own bed, but she couldn't bear the thought of returning to the area where she had spent so much time with him knowing that he would not be there. She needed to go home but she would not be able to exist there without him. It wouldn't be home without him.

She hadn't said goodbye to him. She had held his hand as he was dying but she could not bring herself to say goodbye. She could not bring herself to say the words that meant that she would never see him again. She never took the last chance she had to tell him once again that she loved him. He had told her with his eyes as he was dying that he loved her. She could feel it in her heart. But what if he hadn't felt that she was saying the very same thing to him with hers? What if he had died without knowing that she loved him more than she loved the Moon and the stars? What if he had died without knowing that he had become a part of her and would be a part of her forever? She had had the chance to say all of these things but could not bring herself to do so. She could not bring herself to accept that that was to be the last time she would ever be with the person who completed her.

Tears silently began to stream from Esmeralda's eyes again. She couldn't stop them and she didn't want to. She didn't even wipe them aside – she let them drip down onto the floor as she made her way out of the room – another part of herself left behind in this place where she had already left behind the most important part of herself.

Esmeralda knew that they would have to start making their way home soon. She noticed that her grandad had already packed everything up. She wasn't sure how long she had been sat in her room for. Her grandad came out of the bedroom after her and put his arm around her as she stood looking at the empty cabin. Why did they have to come here? Why could they not have just stayed at home? If they had stayed at home, she would still have Laith. Their community had been coping fine without the flower.

Now she had lost her best friend and the love of her life. She had lost a part of herself. She had lost everything.

Esmeralda walked outside the cabin and saw that Acira was there ready and waiting. Her saddlebags were full and she stood perfectly still, dutifully waiting to be led. Esmeralda looked out over the barren fields as she stood by the faded remnants of the fire that had been blazing with such beauty when they had arrived.

Esmeralda heard somebody come out of the other cabin, but she did not care who it was. She looked down at the ground so that she did not have to face anybody. Her tears fell onto the cold, hard ground as Sarama came and stood next to her.

"He loved you so much", Sarama told her, her own voice breaking. Esmeralda could not respond. She felt another surge of emotion rip through her heart. It tore in two. She knew that he loved her. She knew that what they had was real and it was forever. But now he had left her alone.

Esmeralda heard more footsteps approach from the other cabin. This time she turned around and looked up. Uncle Kabili was carrying Laith in his arms. Esmeralda quickly turned back around and back down at the ground. She could not bear to look. She couldn't believe that he was gone.

Esmeralda heard Uncle Kabili walk towards Acira. She turned to watch, her vision obscured through tear-filled eyes, her uncle gently put Laith on Acira's back. Acira remained perfectly still while he did so. Once Uncle Kabili seemed happy that Laith was secure, he turned to the rest of the group. Nobody said a word, but it was clear that it was time to leave.

Uncle Kabili led Acira in the direction of the stream. Sarama followed, and Esmeralda saw that her uncle handed Sarama Acira's rope. He was going to let her have the honour of leading her brother back home. Esmeralda felt her grandad rub her arm. She looked at him and he looked back at her before following behind Acira. Esmeralda followed too. They walked in silence towards the river. Esmeralda could see Laith's hair blowing in the wind as he lay on Acira's back. He looked so peaceful. She was in turmoil. He could have been sleeping.

They reached the river and began to follow it south. Two days ago, she had been here alone with Laith. He had threatened to throw her in as revenge for splashing him. She would have given anything at all to go back. It was now just a beautifully devastating memory.

The group continued to follow the river south to their settlement in complete silence. Esmeralda did not want to stop. Thankfully it didn't look like anybody else wanted to, either. The sun was high in the sky by now but it brought no energy with it. Esmeralda was numb to everything around her and was simply replaying the same thoughts in her head. Why did they have to come to try this mission? It was always going to fail. How did they think that they would get away with it? It had been doomed from the start. She had lost the only thing that she cared about. They didn't even need to come. They would have been happy. They would have spent the rest of their lives together. She didn't know how she could possibly cope without him. She looked at Laith again – at peace on Acira – they had grown up together. He was a part of her. Impossibly, he had come to mean even more to her over the last few days. She didn't think it was possible, but it had happened. And now he was gone.

The sun was getting lower in the sky and the surroundings started to become more familiar. For a split-second, Esmeralda believed that Laith would be here waiting for her – back in their settlement, standing in the fields in which the had spent so much time together. Tears welled up in her eyes again when she came to the realisation that this was not true. She was going to have to spend the rest of her life here without Laith. Every single place in this settlement was a reminder of him. They went absolutely everywhere together. She would not be able to go anywhere without Laith's ghost accompanying her, but neither did she want to. She never wanted to forget the love of her life. She would carry this pain forever if it meant that Laith stayed with her in her heart, where he belonged.

Laith's old field came into view - the one where they had spent the most time together. Esmeralda could see the small shelter with the simple tin roof that Laith had reminded her on many an occasion that he had built. She always reminded him playfully that it was Uncle Kabili who did most of the work. They used to sit near it at night, looking at the stars. Looking off into the forever.

As they approached, Esmeralda saw Tammi and Tamsyn playing in the field. They would have been expecting them back today – something that Esmeralda had completely forgotten about. The twins saw the group approaching and, as soon as they did, stopped their game and started running excitedly towards them. Tamsyn dropped his wooden sword whilst running, paused, and turned around to pick it up before running to catch up with his sister. Before Esmeralda realised what was about to happen, she saw her grandad pick up his own pace and rush to get to the twins before they reached the group. Esmeralda watched him crouch down as the twins hugged him, one on either side.

"Uncle Cahya", Tamsyn squealed in delight. "You're finally back".

"Mum said that you would all probably be coming back today", Tammi informed him. "We've been waiting for you". Esmeralda was too far away to hear her grandad's response as he said something quietly to the twins.

"Where's Laith?", Tamsyn demanded, excitedly. "I've been practicing and I want to show him". By now, Esmeralda had got close enough to hear her grandad's low voice.

"Come on, we need to find your mum and dad first", he told them. Esmeralda had a lump in her throat. How would they possibly break it to the twins that Laith would not be coming back?

"Esmy!", Tamsyn said excitedly. "Look what I've learnt. I want to show Laith". He twirled his wooden sword around and looked at Esmeralda expectantly. It was impossible for Esmeralda's heart to break any more than it had this morning when Laith left her, but it did just now. Tamsyn looked at her. Surely he could see the tears in her eyes and her stony expression that she could do nothing to hide. He began to worry.

"Esmy? Esmy, where's Laith?, he begged, looking frantically around the group. She could not speak.

"Come on, we need to find your mum and dad first", her grandad told the twins, standing up and holding their hands. Tamsyn started pulling in the direction of Acira but Esmeralda's grandad would not let go of his hand.

"Is that Laith?", he asked, his voice faltering. "Is he sleeping?". Esmeralda could hear it in his voice that he knew something was wrong. "Esmy? Is Laith sleeping?" he pleaded. Her heart was crushed.

The twins' parents by now must have seen that they had arrived. They came walking towards them. Tamsyn saw them coming and he ran straight to his mother. Esmeralda watched as he grabbed onto her leg and started to cry. She initially looked down at him, confused, before looking up at Esmeralda's grandad. She then looked at Esmeralda and realised that something bad had happened.

"What's happened?" she asked, concerned. She looked towards Acira and must have realised herself. Esmeralda could not bring herself to say anything, nor could she bring herself to listen. Without saying a word, she walked as fast as she could away from everybody and towards her own cabin. She didn't slow her pace until she had reached it. She wanted to run away from everything. She swung open the front door and immediately went to her bedroom. She closed the door firmly behind her and collapsed on her bed. She needed to be alone. Overcome with emotion, she could not think. She could not comprehend what had happened today. She could not bring herself to accept that she would never see Laith again. Her head felt heavy. Her brain was overwhelmed. She could not cope. She passed out on her bed with tears running down her face.

Esmeralda woke to the sound of her grandad gently knocking at her door.

"Esmeralda?", he called, softly. "Esmeralda, I've brought you some food". He opened the door slowly. "You need to eat something". She didn't even have a blissful second when she woke up of not remembering. She felt just as bad now as she had when she had passed out on her bed. She did not want to eat – she felt sick. She shook her head slowly. "Well at least have some tea", her grandad said. "I've made...well, it'll help". Her grandad clearly took her lack of protest as acceptance. He handed her the tea, and she took it off him. "I'll leave you alone", he said. "But I'm just going to be out there if you need me". Esmeralda nodded. She wanted to be alone right now.

Her grandad left and she took a sip of tea. Nothing was going to make her feel better. She had lost a part of herself. She saw from the window that night had fallen. The stars were out. She went to her bedroom window and looked up at them. All her life, their beauty brought her a slight melancholic longing. For a few days, they had meant so much more. For a few magical days, since she fell in love underneath them, they had brought her all the magic that her soul could take. They filled her very being with the most wonderful energy that one could not even possibly begin to comprehend.   Now, their very same beauty brought nothing but devastation. The same stars in the same sky had a completely different meaning. Maybe they had never brought anything different to her. She always felt as though she was a part of them. Maybe the energy that they brought simply resonated with the energy that was already inside her. Now that her heart had been taken from her, the stars' energy would echo with the emptiness inside her. She could not look at them any longer. She wanted to hide from them. Hide under her blankets where they could not find her – where their potent magic could not penetrate her and amplify the pain that she had inside her.

Esmeralda lay on her bed and pulled her blankets over her. She rolled over and felt something dig into her hip. She put her hand in her pouch and pulled out a vial. It was filled with blue liquid and, when she looked closely, she could see its golden-black aura emanating from it. Laith had given it to her to give to her grandad. She looked closely and turned it slowly and deliberately in her fingers. She couldn't believe how lucky she was that she had forgotten to give it back to her grandad. It wasn't luck – it was fate. It was written in the stars. The vial was nearly full. They had only used a few drops – most of it was still here. She uncorked it and held it thankfully to her lips. She paused, thinking of the stars. It was enough. It was more than enough. She tipped her head back and felt the wonderful cool liquid flow down her throat, lighter than water but heavier than air. Even before it had reached the bottom of her throat, she felt the magical cold spread quickly throughout her body. Ice formed in her veins and shot across her skin. The beautiful, numbing, cold reached every part of her body. It encased her broken heart in a magical, wintry bliss and she collapsed backwards onto her bed. And nothing hurt anymore.

Prologue

Long after the final star exploded, all of the matter in the Universe could do nothing but float further and further apart in the dark and cold abyss. Had the Universe contained only matter, this would have been the end of the story. Everything would float further and further apart as the Universe got colder and colder before reaching an inevitable heat death. Thankfully, this was not the case.

Instead, a force woven within the fabric of the Universe caused its expansion to slow down. Predictions made in the past had suggested that this could be possible, provided that there was a significant presence of dark matter or dark energy hidden somewhere within the depths of the Universe. Both reasons can be considered to be somewhat correct, I suppose. But what these predictions failed to take into account was, not only was it possible, it was inevitable. The expansion of the Universe slowed down, as did time itself. Time stopped. Everything in the Universe remained static for both a split-second and for eternity before slowly starting to gravitiate towards each other in the most literal sense of the word. Time began to reverse. There were sudden flashes of light as pieces of matter began to combine. What had been dead for aeons was suddenly bursting back into life. Just as when the first star was born, beacons of joy were sent out to all corners of the Universe so that every last part of it knew that something special was happening. As the previously lifeless fragments of the Universe got closer and closer, they got faster and faster. More and more fragments combined, giving out bursts of light and heat, illuminating everything in their vicinity.

All matter and all energy hurtled towards the vacant centre of the Universe where, billions of years ago, the very first star had lived and died. The entire Universe was collapsing on itself from all directions. The fabric that had spent an entire age expanding was now shrinking. Everything was accelerating ferociously towards the centre. As the Universe contracted, the speed of everything within it became terrifyingly high. It contracted faster and became hotter and hotter. Everything that had previously been torn apart was being thrown violently back together.

Had you been watching carefully, you might have noticed something quite peculiar. Floating towards the centre was a single cloud - a cloud that somehow managed to be a combination of purple and silver and green. Amidst all the violence, this cloud happily floated towards the centre of the Universe. If you were to assign some level of consciousness to it, you might think it was blissfully unaware of all the chaos surrounding it. This, of course, was impossible - it simply didn't care. It paused, seemingly to allow the rest of the Universe to collapse around it. The entire Universe became compressed into a small point of infinitely hot energy in an infinitely small space with infinite density. The Ocean was compressed into a drop. The mysterious cloud took a moment by itself, and then rejoined the Ocean once it was ready.

And lived happily ever after.

Printed in Great Britain
by Amazon

66183847R00177